Narrelle M. Harris

Ravenfall

Clan
Destine
Press

First published by Clan Destine Press in 2017

PO Box 121, Bittern

Victoria 3918 Australia

National Library of Australia Cataloguing-In-Publication data:

Harris, Narrelle M

Ravenfall

ISBN: 978-0-9954394-6-7 (paperback)
ISBN: 978-0-9954394-7-4 (eBook)

Cover Design © Willsin RoweDesign & Typesetting: Clan Destine Press
Design & Typesetting: Clan Destine Press

Clan Destine Press

www.clandestinepress.com.au

Part One

THE VAMPIRE

Chapter One

'THOSE BASTARDS ARE STILL WATCHING ME, DR SHARPE.'

The heavy-set man's gaze darted about the surgery, momentarily alighting on the doctor's face and then away again. 'The pigeons at Boleyn Ground. My neighbour's bleeding cats. A mongrel outside the offie on Queen's Road followed me all the way into West Ham Station last week, right onto the platform. And last night a wolf followed me home.'

James Sharpe made a note in Mr Bernetti's file but didn't bother to point out London didn't have wolves. Mr Bernetti imagined he was watched by a lot of things, from the ducks in Regent's Park to tiny people hiding in post boxes. He claimed that zombie mice were living in the walls of his Barking Road flat, when he wasn't suspecting the council workers of casting spells on the traffic. Poor sod.

So many people claimed to see monsters, but most people were utterly self-delusional, or, like Mr Bernetti, labouring under a messed up brain chemistry that wouldn't leave them be.

'We'll look at that prescription of yours, then see if it helps.' A faint rolling of the r's, a mild flattening of the vowels, betrayed a residual Scots accent, the remnants of James Sharpe's Edinburgh childhood.

'Please,' Mr Bernetti's palms pressed to his bald head as though to keep it from splitting. 'I can't sleep. Fucking cats watching me all night. And that wolf downstairs, rooting around the bins and setting off all the car alarms. Big red eyes and howling at the moon.'

The moon *had* been full last night, and would be again tonight. Something for James to check out, then. He knew Mr Bernetti's address and it wouldn't hurt to go for a walk and take a sniff around. The poor beggar might be delusional, but from time to time, even the delusional were not mistaken.

After all, James Sharpe hadn't come back eighteen months ago from the war in Afghanistan, undead and with an inconvenient craving for human blood, just to believe that *all* monsters were imaginary.

James referred Mr Bernetti to the psych clinic in Upton, renewed his anti-psychotics in the interim, and sent him on his way.

The nurse ushered in the next patient. The boy was skinny and unkempt, not at all unusual for the people who came to this clinic. The Lester Avenue Community Clinic in Plaistow had a waiting room full of people surviving on the poverty line; and many who were barely surviving at all. This boy was one of the many who had no real address. "In the alcove under the railway bridge" was hardly something the Royal Mail would recognise anyway.

James gestured towards the chair.

'How can I help you,' he glanced at the paperwork the nurse had handed him, 'Peter?'

'Don' call me that,' said the boy irritably.

'All right. Can I call you something else?'

The boy peered at him. 'Folks call me Blue.'

James made a note. 'All right, Blue. How can I help you today?'

'I need me blood done.'

James's fingers tightened imperceptibly around the biro he held. His teeth itched but remained retracted, and he heard his grandfather's voice in his head. *Shouldnae be hungry. Fuck yer dain, Jamie?* Damn. Mr Bernetti's full moon wolf story had him twitchy.

With deliberate calm, he asked, 'You need a blood test?'

'Yeah. Make sure it's clean an' that.'

'Do you think you have an infection?' James's fingers relaxed. *Gud lad,* said his grandfather's voice, that angel on his shoulder.

Cheers, Granda.

'Nah, I reckon I'm good. I ain't done any needles since last test, an' I ain't even give a blow job wivout a condom neither since then, an' I don't never do fucking, so iss prob'ly fine.'

'I don't like to order blood tests without a good reason, Blue. If you're confident, and your last test was clear, you don't have to.'

'But I want to. Iss like a promise I made, see? He said iss all right, but if he's gonna take care of me, like he said, I thought this would be proper.'

'Who's taking care of you?' James laid the pen down so it was clear he wasn't going to make notes, but Blue shrugged awkwardly and said nothing.

In the silence, James inhaled. Held his breath. He could smell a confusing bundle of scents, most of them unpleasant: body odour, unwashed feet, stale beer, halitosis. The boy had made some attempt to bathe with rainwater in the last week. James couldn't detect anything more sinister, and while he wasn't happy with the implications, Peter – or rather, Blue – was recently eighteen and legally capable of making his own decisions, even terrible ones.

'Do you feel safe with this man?' said James.

Blue stared at him with large eyes, astonished that anyone would care. 'He's all right.'

'You know you don't have to–'

'Better'n most,' Blue said, regarding James through narrowed eyes, 'An' better'n the street, y'know?'

James knew, in a roundabout way. He'd walked the streets a lot in the months he'd been back in London after his medical discharge from the army. Night after long night, week after lonely week, month after interminable month, he'd walked away his unsleeping nights. He'd seen things that might have shocked him, if he hadn't already spent years in Afghanistan, seeing many things that were so much worse.

Doing things that were so much worse.

James shut down that unhelpful train of thought. 'I can order a test if you want to be sure.'

'Yeah. I do.'

'I'll give you a general exam as well.'

Blue shrugged again, but nodded too, so James gave Blue a physical and took two vials of blood. Apart from being undernourished, the boy seemed in good shape.

'Come next week for the result,' James said, 'I'm here Wednesdays and Thursdays. But I don't think you've anything to worry about.' The blood smelled healthy, but James couldn't exactly say that.

Blue scurried out of the surgery. James waited until the door shut before he took up the second vial of blood. He only needed one sample for the test, but he always extracted blood himself instead of sending the patient to the nurses, and he always took an extra vial. Not strictly ethical, but so much better than the alternative.

James unstoppered the vial, held it to his lips and tipped it back. The blood flowed over his tongue and down his throat, but was absorbed long before it ever got to his stomach. He licked at the glass to capture every drop. No sense in wasting any.

Blue was fine. James could taste the vitality in the sample. Low on sugars, overactive thyroid too, but no diseases, no infections. Provided his new guardian didn't turn out to be a violent bastard, Blue would be fine.

James binned the empty vial in the hazardous wastes unit. He'd had his shot of blood now. He ought to be right for the rest of the day. No more supernatural jitters.

Last night, a wolf followed me home.

Ah, bugger. James wondered if he should go walking again tonight to search for that alleged wolf. It would get him away from the suspicious eye of his lodger, Baxter, at least.

The alternative was to stay at home, holed up in his room so as not to disturb the irritatingly necessary Baxter, and read all night. Or stare at the walls. Or clean his gun. Again. He'd done that every day after his return, as well. Disassemble the gun. Clean it. Reassemble it. Load it. Hold it.

But part of the curse was that James Sharpe had a fierce will to survive. That quality was what had made the transformation possible, he'd been informed by the sick bastard who'd *made* him. Without that implacable determination to survive, the process of dying and being reborn as this... this... *thing* would have foundered at the dying part.

'You're a long time deid,' his grandfather used to say.

You don't know the half of it, Granda.

James hadn't chosen this, but he had fought for it all the same. That will to survive had left him, every day, putting his service pistol back into a box, back into the drawer, away. This transformation had taken almost everything from him, but that drive to continue – whatever it took.

Yet he clung to the remnants of himself. He couldn't be a human being any more, but he could try to make up for what had happened after he awoke, *changed*. He'd sworn he wouldn't succumb to that again. He'd keep the beast chained, and be as human as possible, with the voice of the best man he'd known as the whisper in his ear to help. He would practise medicine and find a way to make this thing he was, if not of use, then not a danger.

A little blood once a week from samples he took at the clinic, he found, was enough. Sometimes he supplemented it with animal blood from the butcher – chicken and pig were most easily obtained, and a cup of it every few days was sufficient.

James washed his hands. He poured a glass of water and swilled it round his mouth, swallowed it down to make sure he got every last bit of Blue's blood into his system. Human blood was better than animal blood, more satisfying to his physiology. Better still if it was given freely, he'd learned, but that was hardly likely. Granda was long dead, James didn't have friends, and his lodger didn't like him very much. At least this way, he got what he needed with minimal harm.

The nurse knocked to introduce another patient – a teenage girl with her crying infant. James could already scent the ear infection. Surreptitiously, he spat on his finger and smeared it over the ear thermometer. He'd prescribe antibiotics too, to be on the safe side, but as he inserted the instrument in the infant's ear, he knew the healing properties of his saliva – evolved to cover up evidence of sharp-toothed bites – was the one good thing about being a vampire.

Chapter Two

'IT'S NOT *JUST* A BEDSIT,' SAID THE YOUNG MAN, ALL FLASH SUIT AND POSH aftershave, to the gangly, windswept fellow at his side, 'More bedsit-and-a-half, a kitchenette to go with the bedroom, and a cupboard for some storage space, which you said you were after.'

Gabriel Dare peered at the outside of the plain block of flats. Ivy Gardens. Without any ivy, or indeed, any garden. Two storeys of scuffed red bricks, small windows and peeling paint, encompassed by a low brick wall. It didn't look much. The estate agent's website pictures of the room-and-a-half for rent were only a little better; the tiny space had been recently repainted, at least. The pantry at the parental home was larger, but then3303 – Gabriel didn't need much space, and he'd lived in places far less salubrious than his father's house for many years. Even a tiny room in this unadorned building was better than what he'd had some months. (A couch in a student flophouse; an alcove out of the rain some nights; three weeks under a bridge one year. Something with both a door *and* a roof was a positive luxury.)

Gabriel nodded absently as the estate agent rattled on about value for the pound and proximity to buses and the Tube, but he was taking in the setting. A narrow path led down the side of the block to an area containing a communal washing line, bins and a strip of lawn, according to the online photos. That would suit his needs if he had private callers, or needed to get out by means other than the front door.

'The neighbours are pretty quiet,' the estate agent was saying as a heavy-set man with a suitcase and a scowl pushed past them towards the street.

'Get fucked!'

Behind him, a pale man with brown hair glared at the other's retreating back. 'You owe for electricity and groceries, you bast–'

'I didn't eat the bloody biscuits!'

'Who else w–'

'And why shouldn't I, anyway? You'd never eat them. You don't *eat*. You hardly *sleep*. You're a fucking *nutter*. Spend another night in your spare room, I might wake up with a fork in my kidney while you sip on a bleeding Chianti.'

The pale man glowered but made no reply. He opted instead to concentrate on getting his fists to uncurl. He glared at the estate agent and Gabriel.

'What the fuck do you want?'

'Er... problem, Mr Sharpe?' asked the agent nervously.

'Christ no,' replied Sharpe with weary humour, 'What on earth makes you think that?'

'Er...'

Gabriel scrutinised this fellow, Sharpe. He'd seen him from a distance before, near the Lester Avenue clinic, a few handy streets away. He hadn't paid much attention. A distinct mistake: he was certainly worth a closer inspection. Average height, but with broad shoulders and a compact, solid musculature of the type Gabriel had always found appealing, being such a contrast to his own lanky physique. Strong arms (Gabriel liked arms a lot, and hands, and... *stop that now*) and sturdy legs braced on the footpath, as though ready for an imminent call to action, his dark jeans clinging in all the right places. Light brown hair in a neat militarily short cut, clean-shaven, and sapphire blue eyes of a peculiar intensity. Very pale from his upper arms to his elbows, though his hands, forearms and face bore the traces of a faded tan. From his stance and body type, Gabriel suspected that Mr Sharpe had a good arse on him. He tried not to think about that. He liked a good arse on a man, and he'd made himself a very sincere promise not to let such things sway his judgement any more.

'How much?' asked Gabriel brightly.

God, he hadn't even seen the arse in question and his mouth was getting ahead of his resolutions. Story of his life.

Both estate agent and Sharpe blinked at the *non sequitur*.

'For the vacated room?' Gabriel persisted with the cheerfulness, 'How much?'

'I–'

'And how much space?'

'Two bedrooms, kitchen, living room. One bathroom,' said Sharpe, curious but wary. 'On the top floor.'

'Any room for storage?'

Sharpe regarded Gabriel quizzically, but with the beginnings of a smile. 'The cupboard under the stairs to the attic. I don't have much in it. Shared space in the downstairs laundry. The unexpectedly unoccupied bedroom is the larger of the two, faces the back. It's basic, but it's furnished. Some linens, though you might want to bring your own. Baxter used to eat in bed, the grubby reprobate.'

Gabriel found the faint lilt of a Scots accent deeply appealing, however fine or not the man's arse turned out to be. 'You own the flat?'

'Me and the bank, though without a lodger it'll be the bank's by the end of the year. Want to see the room? Two hundred quid a week. You pay half the utilities, and for your own groceries.'

'Yes, please.' That was nearly a hundred quid less than the poky bedsit he was supposed to be seeing. Helene insisted he had to move from that nasty basement room in Bexley, so full of damp and mould it might as well be part of the Shuttle River, but the costs of moving were making him edgy. 'Cleaning roster and responsible for our own cooking?'

'Naturally. Aren't you worried I'm a nutjob cannibal that's going to eat your kidneys one bright morning when I've had it to the back teeth with my dead end office job?'

Gabriel had once met a man who might have been capable of such a thing. Sharpe was nothing like him. 'Nope. You're a doctor at the community health centre on Lester Avenue. I've seen you there, anyway. Ex-army, I heard.'

Sharpe grimaced, his fingers automatically going to the lines of a tattoo visible under the sleeve of his khaki T-shirt: red flowers and the tail end of a caduceus.

'Combat Medical Technician; infantry,' said Sharpe. When Gabriel showed surprise, he added, 'At the time, being at the pointy end seemed a better use of my medical degree.'

'A bit quieter around here, I'm guessing.'

'Most days. I'm only at the clinic part time. None of that means I'm not planning to eat your kidneys. According to Baxter.' He indicated the general direction of the recent ex-lodger.

'My reflexes are top drawer, so you're welcome to try,' said Gabriel, bouncing on his toes to demonstrate his agility, 'And anyway, aren't you worried I'm a drifter looking for lonely victims to seduce and then murder for their army pension?'

Sharpe laughed, surprised and genuinely amused, which delighted Gabriel. Most people were shocked at his gallows humour. And Sharpe had a fantastic laugh, uninhibited, making him appear younger.

'Well, as you say,' said Sharpe, 'I have quality reflexes and you're welcome to try. Baxter's already let you in on my worst habits. Still want to see?'

'Sure. Your habits sound no worse than mine.'

'You intrigue me, Mr…?'

'Gabriel Dare.' He said it with a hint of defiance. He was used to how people reacted to a glamorous-sounding name that in no way reflected his actual life.

'Really?'

'Yes, really.'

'Fine then, Mr Gabriel Dare. If you like the room, it's yours. I'm James Sharpe.'

Gabriel tried not to be too swayed by the way that soft accent rendered his name so pleasing to the ear. He turned to the scandalised and uncomfortable estate agent. 'Thanks for bringing me to see the bedsit. I'll sort out the rest from here.' He shook the man's hand and strode through the gate in the low wall towards his new flatmate.

Gabriel approved of the flat and the offered room. Spacious, with convenient shelves in which to store his art supplies, and enough clear floor to work by the window, if Helene couldn't find him studio space somewhere else.

The window overlooked the narrow back garden. A convenient trellis ran beside it, holding up an unhealthy ivy vine; evidence that perhaps there *had* once been a garden. Gabriel leaned out of the window to check the trellis's strength. It wasn't great, but he could fix it later. The door to the ground-level laundry was immediately below, and that could be useful too.

'I experiment sometimes with pigments and finishes,' said Gabriel, figuring a full confession now would save being tossed out later, which had happened before, 'But I'll do that in my room rather than the common areas. I'm a trained chemist, so it's unlikely I'll cause any real explosions.'

Sharpe raised an eyebrow. '*Real* explosions?'

Gabriel's mouth pursed because once more he'd run off at the mouth, being frank rather than politic, and he'd blown it. Damn.

But Dr Sharpe was grinning at him, as if the idea that he could get blown up in a pigment experiment was divertingly funny.

'I did say it was unlikely,' Gabriel said cautiously.

'You can use the kitchen table if you like, as long as you clean up the aftermath,' Sharpe said good-humouredly. 'Any other potential hazards to life and limb I should know about?'

'I may have guests at odd hours,' confessed Gabriel, 'I'll keep it to a minimum. I expect I'll see most of them in the garden.'

'Day or night?'

'It could be any time. Is that a problem?'

'Give me a bit of warning if you can.'

'If it's a problem—'

'No, no, it's not.' Sharpe pursed his lips. 'I like to know when new people are around. I'm… Look. I should be frank, if you're going to live here. I have post-traumatic stress disorder. It's okay, except when it's not. Hence the insomnia Baxter was talking about, and… other things. I can get a wee bit fractious if there are unexpected visitors at strange hours.'

Sharpe looked unhappy, and Gabriel found he didn't like Sharpe looking unhappy. The poor bastard seemed so withdrawn. He'd met men like that before, not all of them veterans. They all held themselves like Dr Sharpe, though. Wary and reserved and so *lonely*.

'I knew an army veteran once,' he offered suddenly, 'Used to get the heeby jeebies at the smell of oranges, and he couldn't ever tell me why. Nice guy, though. He watched out for people.'

A little furrow of confusion made a wrinkle between Sharpe's eyebrows.

'All I mean is – I'll be mindful and let you know when I have callers if I can, or as soon as they arrive. They can't always let me know in advance. If that'll help.'

'Cheers, yeah.' Sharpe, satisfied, changed the subject. 'Well, you know I'm a GP. What do you do for a crust? You mentioned pigments.'

'I'm an artist, but I work part-time at an art supplies factory for regular dosh. I'm a qualified chemist.'

'Hence the pigment experiments?'

'Hence, though mostly they're for fun. If they'll be a problem…'

'No, that's fine. Surprisingly, loud bangs aren't my issue. Just unexpected midnight visitors, and only sometimes then.' Sharpe shrugged. 'Your visitors – are they… buyers… or…?'

'I'm not a drug dealer, Dr Sharpe. Or a user. I make a living with pigment chemistry and my art. My work's at the Dupre Gallery on Sutton Street, if you want proof.'

'No, that's all good. Sorry. I shouldn't have asked.'

'That's fine. Not a stupid question, under the circumstances. You don't know me. I could be a coke fiend.'

'No, I could tell you're not a user.' Gabriel raised an inquiring eyebrow. 'I'm a doctor,' said Sharpe, 'I know what to watch for.'

Gabriel wasn't inclined to take that at face value but it wasn't, for the moment, important. 'My visitors seek my help on other matters.'

'Oh-ho, I was right. You *are* intriguing. Care to tell me what kind of help and on what kind of matters?'

'If I don't care to, is the deal off?'

Sharpe grinned. 'Hell, no. I won't try to solve your mysteries if you leave mine alone too.'

'Unlike the late Baxter?'

'I wouldn't call him *late*. He was still breathing, wasn't he?'

'And still had both kidneys, as far as I could tell.'

Sharpe grinned again. 'Aye, he did. Surgery's not my thing.' The grin faltered and Sharpe retreated to the kitchen to flick on the kettle by the sink. 'Tea?'

Gabriel watched the man's back, the sudden hunching of the shoulders and wariness of stance. Maybe working patime at a community clinic was a sore point. Not surprising, if he'd been invalided out of the army on the grounds of PTSD. Sharpe didn't show signs of permanent physical injury, like some of the people Gabriel knew from the streets. Trimboll, for instance, who limped badly and got sick at the smell of oranges and cried himself to sleep on hot nights, and had got himself stabbed one night protecting an old bloke from a pair of drunk arseholes.

'I thought I'd get my things,' was all he said, 'Move in today. That is, if we have a deal.'

'Oh. Right. Good. Well.' Sharpe turned back to him, a set of keys in his hand. He dropped them into Gabriel's outstretched palm. 'Welcome to Flat Four, Ivy Gardens, Mr Dare.'

'Call me Gabriel.'

'Call me James.'

And that was that.

Chapter Three

JAMES WATCHED GABRIEL DARE STRIDE DOWN THE ROAD IN SKINNY JEANS that accentuated the delicious length of his legs and a well-worn, black T-shirt sporting a rainbow flag. The man had radiated a faint aroma of shaving soap, tea and oil paints, which should not have smelled as good as it did.

James wondered how he had so suddenly lost one irritating flatmate and acquired a brand new, sexy as all hell substitute. *A braw lad*, Granda would have said. Tall and very lean (maybe a touch undernourished), hair dark and tousled, sharp cheekbones and a sensitive mouth; a graceful mover, with beautiful hands and green eyes that shone with quick intelligence. James had always liked his men tall, smart and a tad unpredictable.

Stop that now.

That was no longer possible. That was no longer his life.

And yet, he had a new lodger.

James vowed he could *appreciate* the lean work of art that was Gabriel Dare, but nothing else was ever going to happen. He'd keep those old impulses – nothing but dead echoes of a real life now – well under wraps. Wouldn't do to frighten away his fortuitous new lodger, and it wasn't as if anything could actually develop. James wasn't sure what was physically possible any more, and surely you needed a soul to love. So, no. No future in that. *Dinnae even think on it.* Gabriel Dare was going to be a lovely-to-look-at lodger, and nothing more, ever.

A nothing-but-a-lodger who was moving in to the spare room in a few hours' time.

James's mouth tilted in a small, pleased smile. He caught himself doing it and stopped. When he looked down the road, Gabriel had vanished from sight.

I'm allowed a friend, though. Aren't I? Maybe we could be that.

A friend. As though he hadn't already withdrawn from everyone he knew. Civilian or army friends, how could any of them hope to understand who and what he'd become? He barely understood himself any more.

All fash and blether, Granda would have called it. *Truth, Jamie, is you're nae the first soldier tae come back aff yer heid.*

Finally, annoyed with his own see-sawing thoughts, James spent the next few hours checking out Mr Bernetti's story about the red-eyed wolf near his Barking Road flat.

The plain brown brick flat was situated above a mobile phone shop and a used furniture store, both closed up with roller doors painted respectively yellow and grey. The parking area in front smelled of engine oil and foot traffic. The scent emanating from the pie and mash shop two buildings down, mingled unpleasantly with the oil, traffic fumes, and the stale beer and worse smells from the pub on the next corner, and the dampness in the wind blowing north across Leamouth and the Thames.

The reek of London. He'd grown used to it again, and found comfort in its familiarity, even if it was so much more intense than it had been when he'd had merely human senses.

Unfortunately, steeped in all those other homely smells was confirmation that Mr Bernetti wasn't entirely delusional. The footpath, three cars and the trunk of the plane tree by the road were pungent with werewolf – wild, predatory and unnatural.

James could detect no scent of blood though, human or otherwise. No killing had taken place here. Perhaps the wolf was simply passing through. James dismissed the idea of seeking out the assistance of another vampire. Selfish pricks, the lot of them, he'd so far found, mainly interested in prancing about pretending to be Byronesque princes in make-believe courts, based on way too much sensationalist fiction.

The only useful information he'd got about being a vampire had come from a human hanger-on who donated blood to his... *patron*. The kid had been extremely proud of the service he offered. When James expressed his horror that the boy could be a true victim one day, the kid was filled with scorn. 'Blood given willingly is a hundred times more potent than blood taken by force. Don't you know *anything*?'

And no, James didn't, because the arsehole who'd made him hadn't bothered to share any details at all, let alone important ones like "murder isn't necessary if you can find a willing donor".

James would have scoffed at the purely metaphysical rule, if not for the fact that he'd proven it at the clinic. His patients didn't know the blood samples he took for tests were used in part to feed him, but the samples were willingly given at least. When that wasn't enough, animal blood was sufficient to curb his thirst until his next shift at the clinic. He'd never again be reduced to that *thing* that had woken from death.

Vampires. James *loathed* them.

Not that there were many of them in London, as he'd discovered when he went seeking answers. Vampires, it seemed, were not plentiful and, James was assured, very difficult to make. Most people lacked the significant level of willpower it took to survive the transition from dead to undead. That knowledge gave him little comfort, though at least it meant that London wasn't as full of bloodsucking homicidal maniacs as he'd feared when he returned home.

James followed the trail of the werewolf west then south, down Plaistow road, but he lost the scent of it at the A13. Too much car pollution.

James wasn't sure whether to be concerned or relieved. It wasn't like he knew what he was supposed to do with a werewolf if he found one. He'd keep an eye out for trouble, though. He wasn't going to tolerate some monstrous thing threatening his community.

He returned home as the light was falling to find a van parked outside the flat. A woman was talking with Gabriel as he stood on the kerb with a rucksack, a small suitcase, an easel and half a dozen canvases propped up on the red brick fence. The woman was in her mid-40s, James guessed, impeccably dressed, her dark hair dyed with red streaks and twisted up in a chignon.

Gabriel lifted his chin in a minimalist greeting. 'James.'

James eyed the stuff on the kerb. 'Is this it?'

'I live simply,' said Gabriel.

'You live like a vagrant,' said the woman, with affectionate frustration. She held her hand out to James. 'You must be Dr Sharpe. I am Helene Dupre. Please let me assure you that Gabe isn't half as irresponsible as he sometimes appears.' Her accent retained a blush of French.

James shook her hand, noting the softness of her skin, her subtle floral perfume, the way her nails were trimmed and painted in the barest of colours, and that her grip was firm and confident. 'Oh, I don't mind if he's exactly as irresponsible as he appears. I promise I'm only about half as civilised as I look.'

She hooted with delight. 'Oh, I see what you mean, Gabe. No wonder you like him.' She turned an impish grin on James, ignoring Gabriel's pained expression. 'He said you had an *outré* sense of humour.'

James cocked an eyebrow at Gabriel, a smile ghosting his mouth, which pulled an answering one from his new lodger. 'No humour here, Ms Dupre. Mr Dare and I were in deadly earnest when we mutually agreed not to murder each other in our sleep.'

She waved her hand dismissively. 'Oh, please, it's Helene. And this is for you.' She produced a cheque from her purse. 'Though I can give it to you in cash tomorrow, if you prefer.' At James's puzzled frown, she expanded: 'Gabe's rent for the next month.'

James took the cheque but the puzzlement didn't vanish.

'It's my advance,' explained Gabriel, 'She'll take it out of my sales. Assuming there are any.'

'Of course there'll be sales,' Helene admonished him, 'your work is gaining its audience at last.'

'It's not why I do it.'

'I know, Gabe, but be a dear, shut up and enjoy the money while it's coming in.' Helene opened the side of the van. Gabriel picked up one of the canvases by the fence and placed it onto a shelf inside.

The van was set up to carry a number of canvases securely, each on an individual shelf with a length of Velcro to hold the canvas in its slot. James examined the next painting Gabriel lifted into the van.

At first glance, the painting was nothing but smudged shadows, sombrely coloured, moody and almost threatening. Even so, the patterns and colours were arresting – and then James saw the figure emerging from an oppressive atmosphere. The figure was indistinct. Her eyes – definitely *her* eyes – were old and full of pain; yet dignity, too. Here was a wisdom that came of knowing too much, too soon, and the defiance from having survived the experiences that had given her such knowledge. She had strength in her. Courage. The darkness hadn't beaten her yet.

'That's extraordinary,' James said when he found his voice, 'There's so much hope in it.'

Gabriel paused in the act of picking up the third canvas. 'Not *depressing*? Or *brutal*?'

'No,' said James, 'Why would you say that?'

Helene grinned at Gabriel. 'You're right. He's smart as well as funny.'

Gabriel looked pained again. James tried not to preen too obviously. *He thinks I'm smart and funny.*

'Don't you have somewhere to be, Helene? Somewhere far away from here?'

'Oh, no doubt,' she said breezily, 'But I can't imagine it would be as fun as this.'

Gabriel finished loading the last canvases into her van. 'I'm sure it is. Much more fun. Unless you'd rather witness the unparalleled entertainment of me unpacking my worldly goods.'

'Pfft,' Helene plucked her keys out of her handbag, 'As if that will take you more than three minutes.'

Gabriel lifted his rucksack onto his shoulders and reached for his suitcase, encountering James's fingers as he, too, went to pick it up. They both pulled away as though an electric current had zapped through them.

Helene spared them further observations, though not a delightedly smug smile. 'You're right,' she said, 'I have places to be, and you have worldly goods to unpack and the charming Dr Sharpe–'

'James,' said James.

'And the charming James no doubt has a list of house rules to give you, beyond "Rule one, flatmates will not attempt reciprocal homicide".'

'Rule two is about not drinking milk straight from the carton,' said James, 'So the list isn't all that interesting.'

'Oh, I don't know,' said Gabriel, grinning slyly at him, 'I'm looking forward to negotiating Rule Three about helping each other hide the bodies.'

'As long as you pay the rent on time,' said James faux-sternly, 'I'm open to negotiation.'

'I'll leave you two to flirt,' said Helene, getting into the van.

'I'm not!' James began to protest. The van pulled away.

He turned to Gabriel. 'I don't flirt. I don't do that. Relationships. I don't. And anyway, I'm straight.' Which was a *lie, lie, lie*. When he'd been alive, James had dated both men and women. Now he was… whatever he was.

Alone.

Gabriel, he finally noticed, was just as mortified. 'No. Of course not. I'm not… I mean. No. It's fine. Helene has a ridiculous sense of humour, pretty intrusive at times, and she…' He swallowed hard. 'Helene has known me since I was very young. She was my *au pair*, and she likes to tease,' he ended awkwardly.

Until now, Gabriel had mainly spoken with a wry humour. James found this new flustered version quite appealing too.

'Ah,' said James, smiling mock-ruefully. 'Perhaps hers is the first body we'll dispose of together, eh?'

'The second,' replied Gabriel in a like tone. 'I have a relative who tops my list.'

James had someone else entirely on the top of his, but since his was a real list, and if he ever got his hands on the bastard who'd turned him there'd be nothing but dust and no corpse to dispose of, he chose not to mention it. Instead, he reached for Gabriel's suitcase – once more, just as Gabriel did – and their hands met. This time, James left his fingers on the handle.

'I'll take it,' he said.

Gabriel resettled his rucksack over his shoulders and hefted the easel. 'All right,' he agreed. Then he followed James into the flat.

It had been a mistake, Gabriel thought, to walk behind James Sharpe upstairs into the flat, because the doctor did indeed have a lovely arse, and it was shown off very nicely in those formfitting dark jeans he wore. With James a few stairs ahead of him, too, the loveliness was at eye height. Also mouth height. Biteable height. Fortunately, Gabriel had excellent impulse control.

Stop, he told himself firmly. *He's not interested. He's made that perfectly clear, even if he was lying about being straight. No straight man ever looks at another man's mouth like that. It's clear he doesn't want an entanglement, and I'm **not** getting into another doomed relationship. It's irrelevant that he's smart and funny and has a killer smile and the voice of an angel and a biteable arse and beautiful arms and, god, those hands of his. I want to warm them up for him.*

James smiled at him when they reached the door, and Gabriel, with that superb impulse control, simply offered him a bland smile in return.

James pushed the door open, took the suitcase through and turned again, amusement glimmering in his blue eyes. 'Consider this a formal invitation to enter.' James's expression was fleetingly sad and then sardonic once more.

Gabriel stepped past James and walked to his new room. He flung the rucksack on the bed and propped the easel against the wall. He'd shop for bedding tomorrow. The sheets Baxter had left weren't too clean, but Gabriel had slept on worse, and less. Then he'd get his art supplies from Helene's place, and work out what else he needed.

James dropped Gabriel's suitcase by the wall and withdrew again. 'Tea?'

'Ta, yeah.'

'Right then. No milk, sorry.'

'I'll live.'

A melancholy smile greeted the comment. Soon after, they sat down to strong black tea. James sipped his slowly, as though every mouthful was elixir.

'You Scottish, then?' Gabriel asked.

'Technically. I lived in Edinburgh with my mother and Granda until I was 15. We came to London after Granda died. Mum got a job at the London office of her insurance company. I lost most of the accent at school. How about yours?'

'My what?'

'Your accent. Though it's not an accent as such, but the way you talk shifts about. Ah. Sore point?'

Gabriel poked moodily at his black tea with a spoon, even though the sugar was well dissolved. He put the spoon on the saucer with a clink. 'Not everyone notices,' he said.

'It's only sometimes. I've got a good ear.'

'I'm out of practice, I suppose. I tried to get shot of the posh accent when I was at university.' And after, when it could get him beaten up by people wondering why a posh kid was sleeping rough. Gabriel tried to be wry about it. 'What gave me away?'

'You mentioned Helene was your *au pair*. You have some grand turns of phrase, as well.'

'And here was me thinking I was doing proper Estuary English, an' all.'

'Tell you what,' said James, all seriousness, 'I won't tell anyone you're secretly posh if you don't tell anyone I'm secretly dour.'

'Was that a secret?'

'*Aye*. A right *crabbit auld bastart*, my Granda used to say.' James's mouth quirked. 'But he used to call me a *wee scunner* as well.'

Gabriel didn't know what a *wee scunner* was, but that nostalgic glimmer in James's eye suggested it was fondly meant.

Talk was more businesslike after that, though James's house rules were simple. After tea, James insisted on washing the tea things, so Gabriel retired to unpack his few belongings and choose the best place for his easel.

That done, he stood at his window and looked out across the patch of grass behind the flats; across red brick walls to tight-packed houses, ramshackle sheds, lights coming on in small windows in homes all across Plaistow and West Ham.

No ghosts here, he decided. *I can be safe here. Everything's going to be fine.*

After living for the first few days on Tesco's sandwiches – there was hardly any food in the house and Gabriel was responsible for his own groceries anyway – Gabriel did a proper shop. He returned with provisions to find James watching the news.

Gabriel stared at James sitting motionless in front of the screen, so devoid of movement and colour that Gabriel could have sworn the man was dead. Gabriel had seen dead people in his time, and he knew that nothing living was ever that still.

He'd seen other things that looked dead too, but he'd touched James when their hands had met over his suitcase. James was real, solid flesh, not a wisp of light or the product of a febrile mind. Other people had spoken to James. Baxter and Helene and the estate agent. No way was James a ghost.

Cautiously, Gabriel placed the bags on the floor, walked over and poked James in the shoulder.

James jerked away from him as though scalded.

'Sorry,' said Gabriel, keeping his tone level. 'Just checking.'

'Just checking what?' snapped James.

'That you're real and still breathing.'

'I...'

James's expression tumbled through all kinds of reactions, none of which Gabriel had been expecting. Irritation. Horror. Distress. Shame. That last one made no sense.

'I had a flatmate once,' Gabriel explained conversationally, 'Well, *flatmate*'s overstating it. We went to sleep under the same bridge. I woke up in the morning and he was as dead as a doornail.'

'Oh.'

'Don't ask. It was a bad week and I had to sleep rough, that's all. Denton was 40 going on 300 by then, or his liver was, so it was hardly a surprise. At least he'd had a hot meal for a change. Sometimes,' Gabriel pouted thoughtfully. 'I wonder if it was the pie and mash that did for him, but I couldn't have said no to the poor bugger.'

'Ah. Well. Sorry. Still breathing.' James spread his hands in a demonstrative gesture and took a deliberate deep breath through his nose. 'See?'

Gabriel grinned. 'Well, keep it up. The paperwork for reporting a death is tedious, and more to the point, if you shuffle off the mortal coil, what am I supposed to do for a place to live?'

'If you like, I can leave you the old pile in my will,' said James thoughtfully. 'There's nobody else to take it. Then *you* can have all the fun of scoping out lodgers and making the monthly payments.'

'Now you're giving me motive for murder.'

'I'll take you with me to see my bank manager next time I have to negotiate a delayed payment. Then see how motivated you are to stab me in the gullet.'

'I wouldn't stab you. Too messy.'

'Aye?' James's good humour had returned, and he awaited elaboration.

'Poison, maybe. Or I'd take you for a walk by the canal, smack you with a rock and push you in.'

'You've thought this through.'

'I got bored yesterday. It passed the time.'

James's laughed morphed into a positively infectious giggle, setting Gabriel off. Gabriel liked James's laugh, the more so because most of the time James seemed unspeakably sad. A happy James was a lovely thing.

'So,' said Gabriel. 'How would you get rid of *me*?'

'Fork to the kidney,' said James without hesitation. 'And I'd eat you over a couple of days. Dispose of the evidence in a nice French casserole with peas and tatties.'

'Bullshit. You'd never eat me. You never eat.' Gabriel smirked at James's startled expression. 'Baxter said so, and you've nothing in the house except that half pack of gingernuts he didn't finish nicking off you. In any case, you're a doctor. You'd use me for terrible experiments in the cupboard under the attic stairs. Like Dr Moreau.'

'Sprung,' said James ruefully, but the startlement had fled.

Gabriel unpacked the groceries neatly into the kitchen cupboards while James returned his attention to the TV. That done, Gabriel picked up a fresh apple from the mound he'd stacked in a dusty fruit bowl, dropped into the spare chair and bit into the fruit.

'I googled your stuff online,' said James, muting the program. 'At the Dupre Gallery. Your work's extraordinary.'

Gabriel knew what the critics said of his art; the ones who hated it, and thought it *"cheap emotional exploitation"*, as well as the ones who loved it. *Dare's art*, said one of the favourable analyses, *paints glimpses of street life, homelessness and crime with compassion as well as a palpable sense of danger*. Another had called his work *stark but humanising*. On the whole, Gabriel didn't much care what the critics thought of his work one way or the other, though it was, as Helene said, a relief that some were selling at last. Anything that kept him from having to use his father's money was a good thing.

But Gabriel liked it very much that James liked his work.

'My family would prefer I painted things that were more conventional,' he confessed suddenly. 'They think my work is too dark.'

'The world *is* dark,' said James. 'You find the hope in it anyway. That's important. The capacity to see hope in the darkness is important.' His tone was oddly yearning.

'I think so,' said Gabriel, taking another bite of his apple. He wondered exactly what in James's experiences had made him understand, and long for, hope in the dark and dangerous places of the world.

Over the next fortnight, Gabriel and James settled into a comfortable routine.

True to his word, James didn't pry into Gabriel's odd visitors, who arrived sporadically from Gabriel's third night in his new home. He noticed them, though. Haunted, harried people. Young people who looked out of old eyes; old people who looked out of eyes dimmed with pain. The people from Gabriel's paintings.

Gabriel made sure that James was aware of the visitors, whatever time of the night they arrived, with a soft tap on the bedroom door. James was always awake, betrayed by discreet tell-tales from his small bedroom – the soft footsteps pacing the carpet, the crinkling hush of pages turning, and a low light that glimmered faintly under the door. Other nights, Gabriel would hear his landlord padding about the living room on bare feet. He went out for a glass of water once to see the doctor watching the lamplit street.

As far as Gabriel could tell, James Sharpe rarely ate, either – the half packet of gingernuts remained undiminished, although James drank black tea regularly and an uneaten biscuit often rested on the saucer. He had no friends that Gabriel could see and James never spoke of any.

James had other peculiarities, harder to define. Like the day Gabriel returned from the paint suppliers mid-morning only to find James setting out teacups and biscuits as the door opened.

'How did you know I was coming home?'

'I heard you on the stairs.'

Gabriel hadn't made a sound on the stairs, he was sure.

On top of this was the afternoon he'd taken his sketchbook to the garden to capture the shrivelled ivy vine's patterns on the brickwork. One moment, James was a dozen yards away at the laundry door, and the next moment he was at Gabriel's side, a wasp held by the wings in his pinched fingers.

'It was on your neck,' James explained. 'About to sting you.'

'You've got good eyesight,' Gabriel had noted, determined not to be startled at the speed and unlikelihood of the rescue. 'And quality reflexes, as promised.'

James was *odd*.

Which could as easily describe me, Gabriel thought, and didn't dwell on it.

He had other problems. Some of his street acquaintances had, for want of a better term, *disappeared*.

Chapter Four

GABRIEL LAY AWAKE IN HIS BED, FACTS TUMBLING OVER AND OVER IN HIS head without making the slightest bit of sense. Ben Tiller had gone missing; so had Alicia Jarret. Both of them were old hands on the streets.

The last he'd heard, Alicia had found a bed in a proper shelter, and now *pfft*. Gone. Ben had been doing better, too. His brother, Ethan, had been in touch and while Ben hadn't been comfortable trying to stay in the small, neat suburban house with Ethan and Ethan's girlfriend Jess, they'd connected. They were trying. And now Ben was missing too.

People vanished on the streets all the time, Gabriel was only too aware. Even people who were making progress. But people usually turned up again: sometimes dead of an overdose under a bridge, true, but Alicia was a drunk, not a user.

Ben might have succumbed, but none of Gabriel's contacts knew of anyone who Ben – who was acutely paranoid – trusted enough to buy from while his semi-regular supplier was in stir. It was the absence of a source Ben didn't think was trying to poison him (well, for certain values of poisoning) that had cleaned him up enough to allow the rapprochement with Ethan.

Gabriel's phone rang out with the first few lines of the Mikado's song from Gilbert and Sullivan. *Michael.* Two o'clock in the morning and Michael thought nothing of calling him. As always, an irritating warmth fluttered underneath the more usual testiness that he was calling at all.

Gabriel held the phone to his ear. 'Piss off.'

'Ah, Gabriel,' came the unruffled reply. 'It is always so refreshing to see that the passage of years that in others heralds maturity finds you as juvenile as ever.'

'Michael, it's so delightful to find that, as always, you're cementing your routine as a pompous octogenarian only four decades in advance of the need. Did the foreign office send you on a special course for that, or are you accepting tutelage in Old Fartdom direct from the Chancellor of the Exchequer?'

'I'm not with the foreign office, or the Exchequer, as you well know.'

Talking to his brother, Gabriel fell naturally back into the rhythms and vocabulary of his upbringing. 'No. You skulk around the halls of power in Westminster with the face of a lugubrious turtle and offer a word in season to anyone who looks lost and in need of counsel, which is almost all of those tossers. What is it you do again? No wait. I remember. The secretary to the permanent secretary of the Cabinet Office. It was that or the tea lady.'

'Gabriel–'

'Is there an opening for the undersecretary to the secretary of the permanent secretary, or do you just want someone to help you hand out the biscuits? Because you'll find that, as always, my answer is sod off. Would you like me to help you spell that for your diary?'

'Grow up, Gabriel,' snapped Michael Dare.

'And get old before my time like you did? You're 40, Michael, not 60.'

'And you're 27, not a teenager. Don't you think it's time you got a proper job.'

'No, I don't. I need to make my rent and pay for groceries and all those getting-by things that I've been doing for years without you and without our father. I know it pisses you both off, but what can you do?'

'Are you quite finished?'

'Just about. I want to remind you that I have a job at Wilcott's Art Supplies and my paintings *do* sell. Don't fall off your chair.'

'Marvellous. Before you rally for your final bout of infantile banter, I wanted to let you know that your mother sent a postcard today from Santiago. She sends her love.'

'And you had to let me know this in the middle of the night.'

'First chance I've had to call,' said Michael. 'And I knew you'd be up.'

'How?'

'You're an *artiste*,' said Michael, and Gabriel could hear the sardonic humour in it. 'You keep the hours of a trollop.'

Gabriel smirked, working hard to make sure his much older brother didn't hear his smothered laugh. 'Thanks for the Maternal Update, Michael. You can tell her I'm not dead and thanks for asking.'

'I'll be sure to do so.'

'I know she didn't ask,' Gabriel went on softly. 'She never does. And I know she didn't send me a postcard. But thanks for pretending.'

Gabriel heard Michael sigh.

'I've a roof over my head,' said Gabriel firmly. 'I'm housed and fed, I have a part time job, and my paintings are selling. You don't have to worry about me. And I know the old man didn't ask either, but if he does, which he won't, I'm fine.'

'You won't reconsider the job offer?' Michael asked. 'I could use some help distributing the biscuits.'

Gabriel let his brother hear the laugh this time. 'The civil service would drive me spare. I lack civility.'

'I noticed.'

'See you around, Michael.'

'Chance would be a fine thing.'

Gabriel rang off and put the phone back on the bedside table, allowing a grudging fondness for his brother to taint his thoughts. Michael was a self-important gasbag who would have been happier hobnobbing with Disraeli and Gladstone, but for all his sins, he wasn't a complete twat. Not like their father, who was as complete a twat as nature and disposition could make him.

Gabriel had once tried feeling sorry for his father, but it hadn't stuck. It must have been hard, the old bastard's first wife running off with the accountant and leaving him with a solemn seven year old to raise – a task he outsourced to boarding schools and home tutors. The next wife hadn't even waited to find someone to run off with. She packed her bags when Gabriel was four and, apart from the occasional Christmas and birthday card, never looked back.

Gabriel had been raised, like his half-brother before him, by a succession of nannies to begin with, and then by schoolmasters and tutors – and, thank heavens, by his wonderful Helene Dupre.

Having actually *met* his father, Gabriel didn't blame anyone for taking the first available escape route. He was less forgiving of his mother for not taking him with her, but screw it. She was as much a stranger to him as his father, and it didn't matter, even though Michael thought it did. Michael thought a lot of things that weren't true.

Like the fact Michael thought Gabriel was childish for turning his back on their father's money, and on a high-paying job in the city or the government. Michael had more than once expressed the opinion that they should get something from their connection, even if was just a roof and an education. He thought Gabriel an idiot for choosing to sleep on the streets sometimes rather than accept a penny from their father, and for pursuing art after spending all that time gaining a chemistry degree. As though defiance was the only reason for either.

Irritated again, Gabriel shoved the blankets aside and swung his feet onto the floor. He took a deep breath and listened.

Yes. There it was. The soft, pacing footstep of James in his own room, sleepless as ever.

Gabriel was shuffling, bleary-eyed, to the kitchen in the morning when he caught sight of James darting out of the bathroom, towel wrapped around his hips, moisture dewed in the hollow of his spine and on the tips of his short brown hair. The caduceus tattoo, which he'd glimpsed on their first meeting, was strikingly dark against James's pale skin, the central staff and wings tinted golden, one snake in solid black while its twin was a bold outline. Three red poppies were entwined around the foot of the staff.

More compelling than the tattoo was the way the towel clung to James's waist, thighs and the shape of his arse which, Gabriel noted, continued to be fabulous.

Gabriel cleared his throat, as though that would clear the sudden desire from his system. 'Tea?' he asked, voice rough from lack of sleep.

James turned, revealing the firm musculature and fine swirls of hair of his chest and abdomen, the solid strength in his biceps and shoulders. Gabriel's mouth was instantly dry, and he couldn't stop staring. God.

'Sure,' said James carefully, averting his face from Gabriel's avid gaze. He hurried into his bedroom.

'Yes. Good.' Gabriel unfroze and turned back to the kitchen.

Don't be the creepy flatmate, Gabriel told himself sternly. *He's not interested. Stop staring. You moron.*

Except that Gabriel was pretty certain that James *was* interested, though better at disguising it. He'd seen the flicker of James's gaze taking in Gabriel's low-slung pyjama pants and the bare chest of his slender, wiry physique.

Or maybe, Gabriel thought, James really was straight after all. He'd looked away quickly enough. Gabriel wouldn't have put money on it though. Perhaps it was simply the fact that tall, skinny, bony, weird gits with too-intense eyes and hair that wouldn't stay bloody combed were not James's cup of tea, romantically speaking.

Hell, Gabriel wasn't *anyone's* cup of tea, in Gabriel's experience. Not for longer than a few months, at any rate. By then the novelty of the weird-artist-boyfriend had worn off and it was all, *can't you be more normal? Why can't you get a proper job with that degree of yours? And for god's sake, stop letting* those people *into my house.*

Gabriel generally didn't much like other people after a few months either. Most of them he started to dislike after a week. A *day*. Selfish, narrow-minded, judgemental pricks. They all wanted something without having to give anything back. Some badly judged boyfriends had decided that if Gabriel couldn't afford the rent on a regular basis, he could pay in *other* ways, by spreading his legs and shutting the fuck up about what he did and didn't like that way. The streets were *definitely* better than that.

Gabriel liked James, though. James laughed at Gabriel's black jokes, and made more than a few of his own. He didn't mind that Gabriel was odd in his hours and habits, any more than Gabriel minded James being a bit odd in turn. James never asked Gabriel to justify himself, or made obnoxious comments about his visitors. James would never try to bully him into doing things he didn't want to do.

James, thought Gabriel with exasperation, was bloody lovely, and not bloody interested, and that was bloody that.

That seemed to become even more unequivocally *that* the following evening, after both men had put in a day's solid work at their respective part-time jobs. James dashed in the door from the clinic and changed into a fresh shirt and a pair of clean jeans that clung very nicely to his thighs and backside. Gabriel had to make a point of staring fixedly at his sketch book instead of at James's arse.

'I'm off,' said James, dashing for the door again. 'Date.'

He was dressed nicely, but not *too* nicely. Dark slacks, a checked button-up, a navy and beige plaid blazer. Like all of James's clothes, the outfit was well worn but also well cared for, and he looked good in it.

He looks good in everything, while I... Gabriel fiddled with the hem of one of his usual novelty T-shirts. His battered leather jacket – an Oxfam shop bargain from his university days – was slung over the back of a kitchen chair. *What a style icon. Michael's right. I'm a juvenile delinquent.*

'Do I know him?'

'Sharee, from the clinic.'

'The neonatal nurse?'

'That's her.'

'Oh.' Gabriel was on the back foot for the accumulating reasons of: *he's dating; a woman; definitely not me.* 'Have a good time.' Gabriel tried to be neutral but he thought he mostly sounded snarky.

'We'll see,' James said, as though it were a dangerous mistake to get his hopes up. 'Are you painting tonight?'

Gabriel glanced at his sketchbook. He appeared to have drawn the curves and planes of James's shapely legs and rear. 'Possibly.'

'If you want someone to have a wee peek and cheer you on, I'll be free later.'

'That's pessimistic of you, isn't it?'

James paused at the door. 'Or... not, then.'

Gabriel waved him on, pretending nonchalance. 'Whatever.'

James departed. Gabriel went to his room to paint. He stared at the canvas for half an hour before giving up and pulling out his sketchbook again, where he drew a picture of James's face, with its broad forehead, strong jaw and small chin; the quirk of a smile at the corner of his mouth; and the shadowy sadness in his kind eyes.

Gabriel feathered his fingers over the latter. That happened sometimes. His pencils and paints captured things he hadn't meant to draw. Certainly, James never meant for him to see that expression.

The click of the front door opening and James's soft footfall drew Gabriel away from contemplating the sketch. He glanced at his watch. Not yet 10 pm. Not a successful date, then.

Gabriel put the sketchpad underneath a used palette and emerged from his room.

'James?'

The doctor was standing by an open cupboard, staring blankly inside.

'Are you all right?'

James sighed. 'Yeah, aye. Sharee had to go home to her kid.'

Gabriel considered the comment. 'Did you know she had a kid before you asked her out?'

'Aye. Julian. He's a sweet lad, only six. He likes Lady Gaga and newts. Sharee got a text saying the babysitter was sick.' It was clear James didn't believe a word of it and couldn't be bothered to try.

'I take it she didn't rain check.'

James turned to lean against the counter but he didn't meet Gabriel's sympathetic gaze. 'I don't think I'm her type.'

Gabriel's mouth twitched in disdain at Sharee's lack of good taste. He was on the verge of saying something incredibly stupid like *You could be my type, if you like* and instead said a different stupid thing. 'Plenty more fish, and all that.'

'Fish,' deadpanned James.

'Sure,' said Gabriel. 'Or. You know. Some other aquatic analogy to dating the fickle and clearly deranged.'

That smile pulled at the corner of James's mouth. 'Fickle and deranged now, is she?'

'Well, obviously. What with you being a doctor and ex-army to boot. You have that nice balance of caring and tough, like in those action films with Bruce Willis.'

'The PTSD is just a bonus?'

'Some women love a reclamation project.'

Gabriel thought for a minute he'd pushed it too far, but James laughed. 'Aye, I'm a real fixer-upper.'

'Good basic frame, though,' Gabriel said, grinning, 'And the garden's nice.'

'What does that even mean?' demanded James, merriment bubbling up.

'I haven't the foggiest,' admitted Gabriel, laughing with him, 'But I suppose the next tortured analogy should relate to a splash of paint.'

'Well, you're the man for that.' James's smile faded. 'I guess... bed for me then. See you in the morning.'

'Goodnight. I'm expecting a visitor tonight, by the way. I'll go downstairs to see her. You sleep well.'

James, on his way to his room, hesitated. 'You too.'

Gabriel flicked the kettle on and stared at it, proving that contrary to old wives' tales, the damned things *would* boil while watched. He put a teabag in the cup, then thought better of it and prepared a plunger of coffee. He took the coffee to his room and waited by the window.

Hannah whistled up to him after midnight. Gabriel whistled softly back down, then made his way out of the flat and to the garden in the dark, pulling on his jacket to keep out the chill.

'Hannah. Thank you.'

'Don' thank me Gaby. Ain't told you nuffin' yet.'

'Thanks for coming, anyway,' he said. He placed a hand carefully over hers, moving slowly so that she could see the gesture coming.

Moving equally slowly, Hannah patted his fingers. 'That Daryl Mulloway what dosses under Chelsea Bridge.'

'I know him.'

'He reckons he seen Alicia last week, down the river tunnel, what the Westbourne comes out of in the Thames. He's a liar, but.'

Mulloway was rarely sober, so it was a question of whether he was a liar or just addled.

'Thanks, Hannah. I'll go speak to him.'

'He's a liar an' he pinches stuff,' Hannah said darkly. She tilted her head to one side to regard him critically. 'You done a paintin' of me, dincha?'

'I did. Thank you so much for letting me do that.'

'Dja sell it yet, Gaby?'

'Helene's got it in the gallery. She says someone made an offer.'

'You paid me twenny. You promised me a hundred.'

'I've got it here.' Gabriel drew an envelope from his pocket, but she patted his fingers to halt him.

'Nah. Hang on to it, Gaby. I just git robbed if I got it wiv me. Just gimme anuvver twenny for now.'

Gabriel opened the envelope containing four twenty pound notes, and drew one out for her. Hannah snatched it up and stuffed it down the front of her grimy clothes.

'Daryl,' she said, returning to the previous topic, 'He reckoned he saw our Benny too. Not at the river, but. He don' remember where, he reckons. Liar. Cos he said he'd tell me tomorrer.'

Hannah fell suddenly silent as the back door opened and a bar of light spilled into the garden. She jerked away from the light as Gabriel turned.

James popped his head out of the gap, then hovered uncertainly by the door.

'I know you're busy,' he said quietly into the garden, 'But I thought you might…' He blinked at Hannah, who glared at him with suspicion. 'Sandwich?' he asked, and offered the plate that he held in one hand.

Gabriel stared from the plate of sandwiches, to Hannah's troubled frown, to James's hesitant expression.

'I'd love one,' he said. James approached them, not seeming to notice the coolness of the night in just a khaki tee. Gabriel took a sandwich and bit into it. Ham, cheese and pickle. Nothing fancy, but it was fresh and tasty. 'Here.' He offered one to Hannah, who was always too thin, and after she watched him take a second bite, she shoved half a sandwich into her mouth.

'Beer too, if you like,' offered James in a voice so carefully neutral that Gabriel knew that the doctor was deeply unsure of his welcome. 'Or we've got… uh…'

'I'll take the beer.' Gabriel took the two bottles, noticing that there wasn't a third.

'That's me off, then,' said James, handing the sandwiches to Gabriel. 'Night.'

'Night,' said Hannah around a mouthful of food, which she washed down with a posh German beer.

Gabriel watched her eat most of the sandwiches – from his own kitchen supplies, since James never had anything in the cupboard except tea – and gave her the rest of his beer as they talked about Daryl and the things he said he saw.

'Be careful, Hannah,' said Gabriel at the end, when Hannah had wound down to mumbling. 'If you could come to me after you talk to Mulloway, I'd like that.'

Hannah gave him the side-eye. 'Get your boyfriend to make more sammiches,' she said.

'He's not my–'

But she'd gone.

Chapter Five

HANNAH DIDN'T COME TO SEE GABRIEL THE FOLLOWING NIGHT, OR THE one after. He had two other visitors, though, each with no more than rumour and hearsay for him. Nothing tangible.

James was nowhere to be seen for the first visitor. Gabriel left the flat soon after and was away the whole night. He returned mid-morning the next day, covered in grime, his old shoes caked in stinking mud. He left the fouled shoes in the laundry and went home to shower and sleep.

The next night, however, when Switchblade Roy (so named for the switchblade scars on his cheek) arrived in the small, cold hours, James brought out mugs of sweet milky tea and a plate of biscuits.

'Thanks Doc,' said Switchblade, spraying crumbs through his mouthful. 'Wotcher.'

James withdrew into the flat again.

Switchblade swore he'd seen Hannah that morning, and that she'd sent a message saying Mulloway had disappeared. Then he stuffed his pockets full of biscuits, drank the rest of Gabriel's tea as well as his own, and left.

When Gabriel went back indoors, the light was visible under James's door. Gabriel tapped on it. When no answer came, he tapped again and said, 'James?'

He thought James was going to ignore him, but finally there came a resigned, 'Come in.'

Gabriel pushed the door open and stood in the gap. James was sitting at the open window. He grimaced ruefully at Gabriel.

'Sorry. I didn't mean to interfere. I heard Hannah downstairs the other night.'

Gabriel hadn't thought they'd been speaking very loudly, and remembered again that James's hearing was spookily exceptional.

'She's not one of my patients,' James continued. 'but I see her around the clinic. She doesn't eat properly. Most of our patients who sleep rough don't. I know Roy, though.' James shoved a hand through his short fringe. 'I'm sorry if I interrupted.'

'No,' said Gabriel mildly. 'It was fine. Hannah appreciated it, and Switchblade. He's got a sweet tooth. He loves biscuits, that man, the sweeter the better. Jammy Dodgers were just the ticket,' he added drily. It had once more been his own groceries that James had so freely offered to the visitors, a fact that amused rather than bothered him.

James laughed wryly. 'Yeah. About that. I'll replace them.'

'No need,' said Gabriel. 'I don't mind. It was thoughtful of you.'

'Look, I don't know what it's all about, but if you or they need anything I'm more than happy to help. At least bring them inside.'

'They're not all comfortable with that,' Gabriel said without elaboration.

'I get that. But if it's raining or cold or whatever. They're welcome, if you want to do that.'

'Not afraid some homeless person is going to infect your house or kill you in your sleep?'

'Good god, no,' responded James with genuine scorn.

Gabriel gave James a long, assessing stare. James pursed his lips but endured the evaluation.

Gabriel's gaze drifted from James to take in the whole bedroom – the simple furniture, the uncluttered shelves, the bed that had been lain on but not slept in. A wardrobe, closed, with a belt hanging from the handle. No pictures. No ornaments. It was like no-one really lived here; or like the man who did had no real place in the world. Like he was only temporary.

'Let's have a cup of tea,' Gabriel suggested, wanting suddenly to not be in this lonely room.

There was a beat before James rose from his chair by the window. 'Okay.' He walked past his tenant and into the kitchen, where he busied himself putting on the kettle and throwing teabags into cups.

Silence reigned while the tea was made. James pushed a cup into Gabriel's hands. He sipped at his own tea, steam curling around his face, after they both sat at the table.

'You have questions,' said Gabriel.

'It's not my business,' said James.

'If you're going to have random strangers in your flat at all hours, it's reasonable to know more. More than you've worked out, at any rate.'

'Homeless people. Two or three times a week. You talk to them, sometimes you give them things. Food. Books. Batteries, even. Sometimes after that, you go off for a while. You came back this morning smelling like the Thames at low tide.' James tilted a subdued smile at him. 'It's not a problem.'

'It's not your business,' said Gabriel mildly.

'Like I said,' James shrugged, 'I can see you're helping them, and they're helping you with… is it a missing persons case? So anyway. If I can help, feel free to ask. That includes medical attention, if any of your friends needs a doctor.'

'They can go to the clinic.'

'True, but a lot don't come, not on my shifts anyway. I know it's not straightforward. People don't always trust something official, like a clinic on the National Health. I only keep first aid supplies at the flat, but the offer stands.'

Gabriel nodded, pretending that his heart rate hadn't pushed up several notches. His mind was going through a strobe-flash of *good idea/bad idea/it's under control/it's getting too big for me/they trust me to keep their secrets/people are vanishing, maybe dying/I should do this alone/I promised to help/he wants to help me/he wants to help.*

'Thanks. That could be useful. If it's convenient for all concerned.'

'All right.' James seemed relieved. 'Whatever's good for you.'

Gabriel noticed James's cup was already empty. He reached for it, and James surrendered the cup, almost apologetically, at having drunk it so quickly. Gabriel flicked on the kettle again. He finished drinking his own tea as he prepared a second cup for his landlord, then another for himself.

'You drink a lot of tea,' Gabriel said to James, to have something to say, and felt inane for making the observation. *He bloody knows his own tea-drinking habits.*

James didn't seem to mind. He smiled, a boyish expression that made his solemn face instantly sunnier. 'Aye.'

Gabriel found himself smiling easily back. 'It's very English of you,' he teased.

'I *fake* being English very well. I've painted a birthmark in the shape of Westminster Abbey on my right buttock and I once filled an awkward half hour gap in a conversation with a wounded American soldier with apologies about the weather.'

'Brilliant camouflage,' Gabriel agreed, fetching milk from the fridge. He left the teabag in James's cup for a minute longer than he brewed his own, the way James liked it, and took both cups to the table.

Gabriel set James's cup down right next to his hand. Gabriel's fingers brushed against James's wrist for a second. James's skin was cool to the touch. It made the hair on Gabriel's arms stand up, like with a faint touch of static electricity. It was *thrilling.*

Gabriel skirted around James, closer than he needed to, closer than was polite, so that his flat stomach skimmed past James's strong upper arm and his elbow, before Gabriel sat opposite him.

For a while, they drank in companionable silence.

Then James set his once more empty cup down. 'I see the way you look at me, Gabriel.'

Gabriel made himself keep looking James in the eye.

James's mouth pulled into an unhappy scrunch. 'I'm not good for you. Like that,' he said. He seemed regretful.

'I'm sorry if I bother you,' Gabriel replied, wishing he'd had better control. But they had been laughing together again, and it had been so nice, and frankly, he hadn't been able to help himself.

Well, learn *to help yourself. Idiot.*

'It doesn't bother me. To tell the truth, I like it. But it's not fair on you. I'm not… I'm not in a position to…'

'James, it's fine. I'm not your type. I get it.' Gabriel shifted uncomfortably in his chair. 'Look. I don't want to move out–'

'I don't want you to move out,' said James hastily, 'And it's not that you're not my type.' He pushed his hand through his hair in frustration. 'Inasmuch as I have a type. You're lovely.' He winced. 'You are. Lovely. Gabriel. But I'm not. I'm fucked up. I wouldn't be any good for you. I could hurt you.'

'No you couldn't. I can see what kind of man you are.'

James shook his head. 'I could. I might. I don't know. I don't know what kind of man I am these days, or what I'm capable of. I know I'm… *dangerous.* I could *be* a danger. I should have warned you before you took the room. But I liked you right away, and I needed a lodger. You made me laugh, and I thought… Anyway, I'm sorry. If you want to stay, I'd like you to. I promise that I won't ever put you in harm's way, even if I have to lock myself out of my own flat. But we can only be friends.'

Gabriel took a deep breath, then another. 'I'm not frightened of you.' He'd lived on the streets for months at a stretch, with all the hazards that implied. He wasn't scared of much: of his own mind, sometimes, which had concocted gruesome imaginary friends in his childhood, and the things that had happened to him after those apparitions.

'I am,' said James bleakly. 'I'm frightened of me.'

Gabriel didn't understand.

'But I can help you with your missing persons thing, if you want that,' James continued. 'I'd like to, if you're okay with it. With me. Helping.'

'It'd be good to have some help, to be honest,' said Gabriel. 'Whatever's going on is bad and getting worse. And, well,' here he tried a lopsided smile, 'If you're a bit dangerous, that could be a good thing. To have some of the danger on my side, if you know what I mean.'

Hell, *Gabriel* didn't even know what he meant, but the idea of having James helping him out with whatever this whole mess turned out to be made him feel, if not precisely confident, then less *vulnerable*. The idea of having someone at his back was novel and appealing. That someone being James made him feel he could take on anything.

You're an idiot, Dare, he derided himself, *He's just told you that nothing's ever happening between you. Besides. He dates women.*

Yes, and he also said that you're lovely. And he came home early from that one date. And so what if he's a fuck-up. Aren't we all?

Gabriel inhaled slowly, calming thoughts that were leaping way too far ahead.

'We'd best get back to your questions, then,' he said, in a commendably level tone. 'I'm sure you'd like more background information.'

James tapped the edge of his empty tea cup. 'You lived on the streets for a time, I gather. That's how you know these folk. Maybe it's why they trust you.'

Gabriel leaned back in his chair, displaying a studied, feigned nonchalance.

'My father insisted that I study industrial chemistry, if I was going to study the sciences at all. He'd have preferred business studies, politics and international relations, and I couldn't think of anything more repugnant. When I switched to a fine arts major in my second year, he said he'd disown me if I didn't return to the career path he'd selected for me. I didn't back down. When the money ran out not long after, I kept on with the arts degree with a chemistry minor – it proved handy when I was experimenting with all manner of art media – but things were very precarious. My brother Michael tried the same "play along and you won't starve" bargaining. I told him where to stick it. I even sent him a helpful sketch in case he was confused about the process.' Gabriel smiled tightly. 'And after that I slept on dorm floors until people were sick of me. I sometimes managed to crash in the library for a few days. On and off I was on the street for the night. Or for several.'

Or several weeks or months at a time, but James didn't need to know that.

'That must have made it hard to study.'

'Oh,' said Gabriel airily, dismissing what had indeed been a very tough few years. 'It's marvellous how motivating it can be when you're telling the old man and his heir to go fuck themselves. There are plenty of ways to survive if you plan. Showers on campus, the occasional boyfriend who'll let you stay the night and eat jam sandwiches in exchange for a little light housekeeping.' *And things best not gone into now*. 'People waste a lot of food in the cafeteria. I managed. In my third year I ran into Helene again, and she gave me a hand. She was starting up the gallery then, so she let me sleep in the back room for a while until I found a room to rent. She began to represent my work. I got by.'

'The university couldn't help you with accommodation?'

'According to them, I didn't need help. I had a family with pots of cash. My father liked to remind them of it. He was very keen on me giving up my childish notions.'

'Which only spurred them on,' suggested James with a grin.

'Of course.' Gabriel decided to confess the worst of it, sure that James wouldn't do anything as stupid as pity him. 'The worst patch, over one semester break, had me living in a tunnel for a month during winter. Not an experience I'd care to repeat. My brother Michael said that I was playing at poverty, like I could just go home if...'

Damn. Too much.

'Going home isn't always an option,' observed James gently. 'People don't always see that.'

'No, they don't,' agreed Gabriel, 'It wasn't one for me. I don't... I didn't–'

'You don't have to tell me,' said James. 'Nobody chooses to spend a month of English winter in a tunnel if they think there's an option.'

Gabriel was grateful for the understanding; for not having to explain why he couldn't return to his father's house, his father's authority. 'The closest they came to making me obedient was after that semester in the tunnel,' he said. 'I caught pneumonia and spent the next three weeks in hospital. That's when Helene found me, found out what my father was playing at, and offered me her store room.'

Gabriel pushed away the wearisome memories. His father's house – he never thought of it as home – had never been an option, once he'd escaped from it.

The one time he'd tried to make himself go back, he'd ended up hiding in a pub loo having a panic attack so severe it took hours for the shaking to subside. The days of being sent away to psych wards had long gone, replaced by the combined rigours of bullying, control and emotional neglect, but the fear of it remained. And then there were the other things in the house. The things that didn't frighten him, really, but the consequences of them – hard beds and sedatives and restraints and worse – those things *terrified* him.

One way or another, he had meant to escape, and he'd managed it, with Helene's help and without self-medication. It was a triumph of sorts.

'It was while I was on the street that I began to help my... compatriots of the road. The police can be complete arses if they think they have an easy mark. Being homeless isn't the same as being *useless*.' Gabriel's tone was scornful. 'They targeted a homeless man I knew once, accusing him of an assault that he *obviously* hadn't done. For a start, he'd been in the park with me for the night. For another, his Parkinson's was too bad for him to have held a weapon. I persuaded the senior officer on the case to leave the poor bastard alone. A week later I got Detective Inspector Bakare to investigate an attack on Hannah, when nobody seemed to give a damn about a couple of public school boys being vile shits. It was as well I got there before they got their lighter to work. It turned out they'd already killed someone else.'

James, Gabriel noted, was both disgusted and unsurprised. Oh yes, here was a man who knew what the world could be like.

'After that, people came to me for help with little things. Finding family members, sometimes. Difficulty with the police less often, but they did me the honour of trusting me, and they let me paint them. They live in a hard world, and they're hard people, but they're due as much respect as anyone else. A lot more respect than people like my father, who think they can buy and control and punish anyone who doesn't agree with them.'

Gabriel let out a long, slow breath. He hadn't meant to get that heated. 'So, that's my life story, the highlights reel. Your turn. Why do you even want to help me?'

James folded his hands on the table in front of him. 'I've told you some of it. Grew up an only child with Mum and Granda in Edinburgh. Never met my dad. Came to London after Granda died. I lost my mum in a car accident while I was studying medicine. I graduated, looked for work, and joined the army. I got the bright idea that the infantry was a better use of my skills. GPs are ten a penny. A really good Combat Medical Technician can make a huge difference on the front line. I served in Africa and the Middle East. Things went horribly wrong in Helmand two years ago.' He glanced down to his fingers, saw that they were clenched and made the effort to relax them again.

'Honourable medical discharge because officially I'm a basket case if I'm around large quantities of blood. No use on the front line, not much better at a base. I came back to London eighteen months ago. I put a down payment on this place with what I inherited from Mum and Granda, and I'm paying the rest off as I can. Army pensions, lodgers, and whatever I can manage as a suburban GP. Trying to be useful instead of a useless wreck.'

His tone wavered. *Honesty for honesty* seemed to be his resolution.

'I'm acutely aware that I'm completely fucked up. Everything went to shit in Helmand. Things happened, to me and to... to others, that I can't undo. But I have to believe I can still choose to be who I want to be. Choose who I *am*. I don't have to be a victim of what happened to me and the... the consequences of that. So I choose to be a doctor and help those who need it most. If people are going AWOL and nobody else cares, maybe I can help. I can be more than just this fucked-up ex-combat medic. If that's all right.'

'Fine by me,' said Gabriel. He held out his hand and James, after a quizzical moment, shook it. 'Partners,' Gabriel said.

James smiled, hope brightening his blue eyes. 'Partners.'

James and Gabriel had their first opportunity to work together that evening. No visitors came for Gabriel, but someone threw stones at his window. Downstairs, he found a note scrawled on a used envelope shoved under a stone by the back door.

James appeared at his side and they examined the message together. It read:

Hannah Chelsea Bridge £20

Gabriel turned the paper over and over in his hands. He sniffed the paper and grimaced.

'I wouldn't do that if I were you,' said James with an amused but sympathetic smirk.

Gabriel pressed his lips together. 'Hannah dosses in a place out the back of a strip of curry houses, and Daryl, the one who was kipping under the Chelsea Bridge, smelled a lot more of low tide. It's where I went last night, looking for them. This,' he waved the piece of paper, 'isn't Hannah's handwriting and it smells like–'

'Soot and grease,' said James.

'Right.'

'Fished out of a dirty kitchen?'

'Could be. It doesn't seem right for Hannah.' Gabriel frowned again. 'Maybe she was simply using what was to hand. Oh well. I guess I'd better get to Chelsea Bridge.'

'Want company?'

Gabriel glanced at James's neat dress and highly polished shoes. 'That'd be good, but you'll need to change.'

An hour later – an hour of curled lips and wide berths from their fellow commuters – James and Gabriel had emerged by the river and were walking towards the bridge. Night had fallen and their disreputable get-up was less noticeable from a distance. Both wore sneakers, track pants, old shirts and tatty jackets. James was wearing a spare coat of Gabriel's.

'If we look like we washed up in the last tide, no-one will ask a thing,' Gabriel had told him and, apart from trying to avoid them, nobody had paid them much attention.

'The art of being invisible,' Gabriel had said, 'is merely three square meals, two showers and a roof over your head away.'

James tried not to be distracted by the fact that the jacket he wore, though tatty, smelled so distinctively of Gabriel. *Keep yer heid*, warned Granda's voice. The jacket was threadbare but not dirty. It smelled faintly of perspiration and paint, a little of London exhaust fumes, a little more of the deodorant and shaving gel that Gabriel favoured and slightly more of Jammy Dodger. James pushed his hand into the left pocket and encountered crumbs. It made him smile.

The expression fell away, however, as the two of them arrived at the foot of the Chelsea Bridge and peered into the darkness.

That is, *Gabriel* peered. James could see perfectly well with his uncanny vision, and his whole mind and body were suddenly on high alert. He could see every stone and piece of detritus on the muddy ground. He could make out graffiti on the water-stained and algae-slick stonework of the bridge. He could smell a hundred things at once: ash and mud and murky water and the traffic exhaust and Gabriel's aftershave, and he could taste things in the air too. He could hear insects humming above the low-tide water and waves slapping against a barge moored on the opposite bank, Gabriel's breathing and the crumbling of cindered wood. He had an impression of an unidentifiable *something*, which made the hairs stand up on the back of his neck, like in the war – the sense that something deadly was waiting just out of sight.

James was never sure if this prickling sense of awareness was the same as it had been on the battlefield. He explained his strangeness to people as PTSD, but his body didn't produce adrenalin any more. His heart never varied from its sluggish, lazy lurch and his mostly unnecessary breathing was steady. Was the sense of danger an illusion borne of trauma, or his new senses registering danger before his brain could catch up?

James fell naturally into old army habits. Alert and unhurried, he cautiously approached the pile of ashes he saw heaped up against the stonework. The Thames tide was heading towards its 10 pm low ebb, but by morning these ashes would be washed clean by the high tide.

He didn't *need* to approach the ashes. He could smell it, the burned *meat*. Horribly familiar from missions around Helmand, firefights with the Taliban. James wished he could pretend it was a stray animal, but his night vision clearly picked out the leg, the lined hands, the lumps that had once been torso and head. 'Hold up, Gabriel,' he said, wanting to keep Gabriel from the stench of it, 'I think–'

'Is it Hannah?' Gabriel's throat worked in a dry retch and he held still.

James hunched his shoulders, unhappy that Gabriel had understood what lay in the circle of greasy ashes. *Greasy soot. The letter. God.* 'I'll see.'

'No, wait. We'll call DI Bakare.'

James continued to approach the ashes as Gabriel made his phone call. He crouched and examined the remains, mentally reconstructing height and build. He could see a patch of pale, greying hair. The body's frame was thin and poorly nourished, and the hand, curled into a rigid claw, appeared masculine.

'It's a man,' he said to Gabriel. 'Middle aged, I think. Didn't you say Daryl was an older bloke?' James picked up a broken coat hanger from the coarse ground and poked at the wrinkled hand. The hand was very pale and shrivelled.

James leaned in and inhaled. The body smelled human, and of course if it had been a vampire killed in this manner, the whole thing would be nothing but dust. But the bloodlessness was a worry. James studied the ground and inhaled deeply. He couldn't see any blood. He couldn't *smell* any blood.

Fucking vampires, he thought with disgust. *This poor bastard was bled dry and burned by a fucking vampire.*

And then the next awful thought occurred to him. *Did a vampire send Gabriel a note luring him to a kill?*

His senses snapped back to high alert. As James rose, he tried to detect once more that feeling of lurking threat, as though it was a real thing and not a Pavlovian response learned on a foreign battlefield.

A shape detached from the shadows high above him, from the girders underneath the bridge. It dropped like a stone towards Gabriel, who was talking in an urgent and irritated tone into his phone.

James launched himself at Gabriel, twisting as he dragged him to the ground, so that he took the brunt of the fall as they landed, and sent the phone flying. James twisted again, pressing Gabriel into the mud and pebbles and covering Gabriel's head and torso with his own. Gabriel was finding air to protest as James leapt to his feet, ready to spring at the assailant.

There, by the embankment, nowhere to go but... up. The shape stirred in the dim light and James could see dark hair, pale skin, wicked teeth unsheathed in a voiceless snarl. Its arm lifted, moved and James had time to see the projectile hurtle towards them, so fast it whistled in the night air. A black pebble, spinning, like a bullet, straight for Gabriel as he stumbled to his feet. James stepped into its path and snatched it from the air, hissing as it stung his palm.

'James? What the–'

The shadowed figure had gone. It leapt straight up the embankment to the wall above and disappeared.

James turned towards Gabriel, shaking the sting from his hand as he dropped the stone. 'Are you all right?'

'Fine, given the rugby tackle.'

'Sorry about that.'

'Where did he come from?'

'Who?'

'Very funny. That man. Nice catch, by the way.'

James's glance flicked to the pile of ashes and the body.

Gabriel followed his gaze. 'Oh.' He flexed his hands and clenched them again. He spotted his phone, screen glowing, in the mud, and snatched it up. He wiped the instrument off on his shirt and pressed it to his ear. 'Vic?'

James could hear the waspish buzz of a voice in reply.

'Yes, well someone attacked us a minute ago... yes, *us*. I'm here with a friend.'

James was listening for any noise heralding imminent attack, but they were alone in the darkness.

'You're hilarious, Vic. Are you coming? I think we've found Daryl Mulloway...It's too late for an ambulance. Forensics better come fast, though. The tide's coming in.'

Detective Inspector Victor Bakare and his team were with them fifteen minutes later. Bakare took in their shabby track suits with no comment but a sardonically raised eyebrow. Gabriel told the policeman what he knew of Hannah's disappearance and the circumstances that had brought him to Chelsea Bridge. Gabriel appeared calm, but James could hear his heart thundering, and see the horrified glances he darted towards the corpse.

James didn't look at the body. All of his other senses were too well aware of it. Instead, he watched the police investigating the scene, taking photographs, measuring things, and bagging up potential evidence. One officer in particular was staring at the two of them; staring at *him*. She was a plainclothes detective, her dark brown eyes glared at him in a strange fashion – both judgemental and pitying.

The looks she gave Gabriel were harsher still. Suspicious and angry. James knew she had it the wrong way around. If she'd understood anything about them at all, she'd have known that James was the one deserving of suspicion and rage.

He returned his attention to Gabriel and the DI. Bakare was giving James pointed sidelong looks.

Gabriel, with a sigh, took the hint. 'Detective Inspector Victor Bakare, this is Doctor James Sharpe.'

Bakare arched an eyebrow at James without offering a hand to shake. 'And you're Gabe's what? Jogging partner? Street buddy? Boyfriend? Parole officer?'

'I'm his landlord,' said James, deadpan.

'His *landlord*.' Bakare packed an awful lot of scepticism into three syllables, a talent for which he thanked his Nigerian forbears.

James offered a mild smile. 'I take the vetting procedure very seriously. Tomorrow, I'm following him to the gallery to decide whether he's a good enough artist to stay under my roof.'

Bakare was unimpressed. 'I do love a comedian,' he said flatly. 'Especially at a murder scene where someone's been butchered and burned to death.'

James sighed ruefully. 'Dr James Sharpe. I work at the Lester Avenue clinic. Gabriel does rent a room from me, and I offered to accompany him when he got the note to come here.'

'More than a landlord then, eh?'

'Friends,' asserted James.

'Plus,' interjected Gabriel lightly, 'trustworthy tenants are hard to come by, I expect, and James didn't want his new one to be murdered all alone under Chelsea Bridge if he could help it. I've only just settled in.'

Gabriel's eyes met James's and there was that flash of humour again.

'He's paid ahead,' said James drily. 'So I'd have had some breathing space. Still. I like him a lot better than the last tenant; I'm hoping not to have to replace him soon.'

Bakare rolled his eyes at the pair of them. 'You two were bloody made for each other.'

Gabriel turned away from them both. James looked at the dark ribbon of the Thames, with the lights glinting off the inky black. 'Tide's coming up.'

'So it is,' Bakare agreed. 'Why don't you go home, and come into the station tomorrow to sign your statements.'

'I'm at my clinic tomorrow,' said James. 'I'll come after work.'

'Good. Ask for me or Sergeant Datta.' Bakare indicated the dark-eyed, dark-skinned woman who had been giving James and Gabriel the unfriendly appraisals. 'See you first thing, Gabe.'

Gabriel was watching the forensics team work on the site. 'I won't talk to Datta.'

'Gabe…'

'Vic, she doesn't *like* me. She wants to pin this on me already and I didn't bloody *do* it. I've been trying to *find* Hannah. Ben Tiller and Alicia Jarret too… what?'

Bakare hadn't covered his surprise quickly enough. 'This Alicia Jarret you've been looking for,' he said, 'Tell me about her.'

'She went missing a week ago,' said Gabriel. 'She'd found a place in a shelter and then she vanished. One of her friends asked me to keep an eye out for her. No-one's seen her, or heard a whisper. She didn't show up on her usual corner to sell *The Big Issue*, she didn't go to her clinic appointment. Nothing.' Gabriel drew a breath. 'She's dead, isn't she?'

'Found the body this morning.'

'Like Mulloway?'

'Not burned like him, no. I'll have to get the autopsy report before I can say anything else.'

Gabriel swore. 'Wasn't me,' he said fiercely, 'whatever your precious Sergeant Datta thinks.'

'Why would she think you had anything to do with it?' Bakare asked blandly.

'You'll have to ask her,' said Gabriel. 'The unreasonable prejudices of the Met have always been a mystery to me.' He glanced over his shoulder to highlight the way Datta was glaring at him with her lip curled. He grimaced and waved at her.

She sneered back at him, then frowned at James.

James stepped closer to Gabriel. 'Let's get home,' he said.

Gabriel jammed his hands into his pockets and glared at the policeman. 'You're going to investigate this properly,' he demanded more than asked, 'you're going to find out who killed these people. They weren't *nothing*. They deserved better. They deserve an *effort*, at least.'

James thought that Bakare might be outraged at the smear on his professionalism, but the DI didn't react. 'I'll do everything I can, Gabe. I promise.'

Gabriel nodded curtly then strode up the banks, away from the incoming tide. James cast a final glance back at the unfathomable Sergeant Datta, and followed his friend away from the bridge.

Chapter Six

JAMES SLID THE NEEDLE SMOOTHLY UNDER THE WOMAN'S SKIN AND INTO the vein. He could smell the blood, and hear its steady whoosh in the circulatory system when he listened closely enough. Those abilities, along with his preternaturally steady hand, made him a favourite at the clinic for taking blood samples.

He filled the two vials and withdrew the needle. He surreptitiously licked his thumb and passed it over the small puncture wound, so that it began to heal up almost at once. The healing properties of vampire saliva were pretty much the only advantage he'd gained from the transition. Mrs Kapur tended to bruise easily, and this was a simple thing he could do for her comfort. She was 72, and a good-hearted soul, and he figured she deserved any consideration that was so easy for him to give.

'That's all, Mrs Kapur. We'll be in touch with your results.'

Mrs Kapur patted his arm. 'Lovely, thank you, Doctor Sharpe.' Then she giggled. 'That's the wrong name for you. You should be Doctor Gentle. I never feel it when you're using the needle.'

'All part of the service,' he said, smiling at her as she left. Once the door was shut, he labelled one vial then he pulled the stopper out of the second and drank it.

Thyroid function down, and I'll need to up her heart medication.

He scribbled a note to transfer later to Mrs Kapur's computer records. First, he had to get to the police station to sign his statement from last night's incident.

He straightened his suit and tie as he left the clinic. Gabriel was there, striding in rapid, agitated steps up the path to the entrance, brow furrowed unhappily. His leather jacket was drawn close around his body, and the dark green scarf he wore was wound firmly around his throat. It was like he had armoured himself in wool and attitude.

'Everything okay?'

Gabriel shrugged jerkily. 'I still need to give my statement.'

'I thought you went in this morning.'

'Bakare wasn't in this morning. Datta was. I don't talk to Datta. She acts like I murder people on Bank Holidays for a hobby.'

James's hand flexed into a fist, then splayed out as he forced the tension out of his joints. 'Let's go find Bakare, then.'

Gabriel jammed his hands in his pockets. 'Do you think she's right?'

'Of course she's not bloody right. You're no killer.'

'How do you know?'

Takes one to know one. James quashed the notion. He had more factual reasons for knowing it to be true. He'd have smelled the blood on Gabriel, for a start. He'd have smelled the burned meat on him, if he'd killed Daryl Mulloway. That kind of stink took a long time to wash clean. He'd been to burned-out villages where the stench of firebombed homes lingered for months.

'I've met killers.'

'Feel free to be a character witness for me, then. Datta aims to pin something on me if she can.' He fell into step beside James and they walked together towards the nearest bus stop.

'Aren't you going to ask why she doesn't like me?' Gabriel prompted.

Dinnae care, do ye, Jamie? Ye like the braw lad plenty for everybody.

63

'I assume she's fickle and deranged.'

The reminder of his words about the failed date washed the tension out of Gabriel. 'Maybe. I've never understood it, otherwise.'

Fortunately, Bakare was in when they reached the station. Less fortunately, he was on his way out, Datta in his wake. 'We've got another body,' Bakare said through gritted teeth, 'You'll have to come back tomorrow if you–' Then he pulled up short. 'This Ben Tiller you were looking for. Can you give me a description?'

'Twenty-two. About James's height. Dark hair, hazel eyes. He's got a scar on his...' Gabriel waved indicatively towards his own chin. 'He was glassed by a gang of pricks in a park last year.'

'Think you could ID him?'

Gabriel's fists clenched. 'Yes.'

'Come with us, then.' Bakare regarded James sourly as he fell into step with them. 'Don't recall inviting you, Doctor Sharpe.'

'You want to take Gabriel to a crime scene to identify a body and you're telling me you want him alone?' James's voice was calm, but his posture was military-rigid, his eyes hard. 'I can always call his lawyer if you don't want me along.'

'Fine. Get in the car. Do what you're told when we get there and stay out of the way. Datta, take your own car.'

With a glare at both James and Gabriel, Datta obediently went to her own vehicle.

James wondered what the hell he was doing, drawing attention to himself this way, but Gabriel's small nod of thanks settled the matter. James would be damned if he let Gabriel get dragged off to a murder scene in the company of one, and possibly two, police officers who seemed to think him guilty of a gruesome crime.

James slid into the back seat of Bakare's car beside Gabriel. 'Should I be calling a lawyer?'

'Not yet,' replied Gabriel quietly. 'There's nothing they can charge me with. *I didn't do it.*'

'I know.'

Gabriel drooped his lanky frame against the seat, long legs bent and his angular face pensive. He closed his eyes. He looked terribly vulnerable, with his dark hair in customary disarray and mouth pursed. When he opened his green eyes again, his gaze met Bakare's reflected in the rear vision mirror.

Bakare's brown eyes crinkled apologetically. 'Gabe, I don't think it's you. But you're the only link so far.'

'Me and the fact they're all living on the streets. I think you'll find a lot of other links if you bothered to look.'

Bakare scrubbed his hand through his thinning hair. 'Let's eliminate you from the suspect list, shall we? Then I can get Datta off my back about you and we can follow the other leads'

James wanted to take the DI to task over it all – the irregularities and lack of proper protocol, Datta's clear prejudice, the idiotic assumptions. He was sure that Bakare was aiming to observe Gabriel's reactions, and attempt to catch the artist in a cover-up or lie, and it simply wasn't going to happen. Gabriel was innocent.

More to the point, if vampires had killed Daryl Mulloway, vampires might also be involved in the deaths of Alicia Jarret and this new corpse. Gabriel Dare was no vampire. He hadn't even recognised James as being one.

James very much wanted to see, first-hand, if this new corpse had been killed in the same way as Mulloway. Because if it had, some arsehole vampire was on his patch and he was *not fucking having it*. Not for one hell-damned second longer.

Aye, I'll feckin' skelp the bastard.

Fifteen minutes later, the DI's car, then Datta's, pulled up in a small square of park next to a boarded-up shop and a derelict garage. Soon after, James was standing next to Gabriel at the tape barrier, staring up into a tree.

A body was draped between its branches, head hanging back. The dark hair fell away from the young man's face, which was frozen in a rictus of horror. A scar ran from beside his mouth to just underneath his chin from the glassing. The faintest rust red was smeared on his lips and teeth. His throat had been gashed open on the left, but there was no other blood at the scene.

Gabriel stared at the body. 'That's Ben,' he said dully.

Bakare looked at Gabriel, at the body, at James. 'You're going to give an alibi to Gabe, aren't you?' he said.

'Of course I fucking am,' snapped James. 'We were together at home all evening, except for those few hours under the Chelsea Bridge. Then we went home.'

'You can vouch for him all night?'

'Yes.'

'He could have slipped out while you were sleeping.'

'I don't sleep. I'm an insomniac.' When Bakare didn't look convinced he added, 'Ex-army, active front line service in a warzone. I don't sleep well at the best of times. Last night was not the best of times. I was awake all night. Gabriel didn't leave the flat after we got home. Happy now?'

'Yeah. Pretty happy.' Bakare cast a glance at Gabriel, who had not taken his eyes off the body in the tree. 'I'm sorry, Gabe. It's my job to ask.'

'Fine. Go ask some other people. Find out who's doing this. We're done here.'

James regarded the corpse in the tree closely. He tilted his head and inhaled deeply, passing it off as the settling of nerves, but he could smell it, even from here: the vampire blood in Ben Tiller's mouth. Not enough to turn him, even given there was no guarantee a turning would work. Ben had bitten the vampire who murdered him.

Brave lad. Poor brave, terrified boy. It took courage to bite a vampire. Not much damage caused, but he'd drawn blood, with its distinctive scent for those with the power to detect it.

What made James particularly angry was knowing that murder wasn't *necessary*. There were clubs for this sort of thing, with willing volunteers who offered their throat to the beast and off they went, happy as crazy, crazy Larry. Vampires didn't need that much blood in a sitting. Even for the greedy, a mouthful from each of a dozen volunteers provided sustenance without hard-to-hide deaths. Too many of those and the police investigations would start, and those were, James gathered, irritating and *inconvenient*.

James hardly thought that London's vampires would bother acting against this particular killer, though, no matter the inconvenience. It wasn't as though vampires had any real hierarchy. As far as James had learned, the individuals in London's small vampire population had their petty domains and were very selective about who they brought in. No. London's vampires, like London's constabulary, probably wouldn't be arsed to act in this matter unless it threatened them directly.

The murders were unnecessary, James reflected, which mean that the vampire committing them was possibly doing it for fun.

It was exactly the sort of thing that gobshite, Major Cael West, would have done.

James clenched his jaw. He could hardly suggest *that* to anyone. No-one would believe him for a start. Well, they might if he fanged up in front of them, but James couldn't think of a single scenario where that ended well.

'You said you'd found Alicia Jarret too,' said James suddenly to the DI. 'Was she like him?' He gestured towards the corpse. 'No blood?' At Bakare's look he added, 'I'm a doctor and I was a combat medic for six years. Give me some credit.'

Bakare blew out his pent-up breath. 'Yes she was. Stuffed into a drainage outlet. Throat lacerations. No blood.'

Gabriel trembled. James could practically feel him vibrating from where he stood. He took Gabriel by the elbow and steered him away from the horror.

When James noticed that the scent of vampire blood was following them, he realised that they were in fact following *it*. He peered around and saw the smudges of blood along the footpath, dripped against the kerb as well. He tried to lead Gabriel away from the path he was unwittingly following, but Gabriel wouldn't change course.

'He bit his attacker, did you see?' asked Gabriel.

'What?'

'Ben's mouth had blood on it. All in his teeth. Well, I think it was blood. Odd coloured, dark, but blood I think.'

'How did you see that?'

'I'm an artist, James. I notice things, especially colours where they shouldn't be. Ben's mouth was all smeared with the wrong kind of red. You did see, didn't you?'

Well, bugger. This is turning into a right guddle, isn't it, Granda?

'Aye.'

'Good, because there's more of it all along this street.' Gabriel nodded at the smudges of blood on the concrete.

James realised with alarm that their path was not coincidental after all. 'We should leave this to the police.'

'Right. Yeah. Because they're so keen to find out who's actually doing this and stop the killing. *Obviously* it should all be left in their safe hands.'

'Gabriel–'

'Datta has had it in for me from the day we met, and it's so bad now that Bakare stopped to eliminate me first before doing a proper investigation. Do you know how many people have gone missing from the streets in the last month? *Six.* Six people, James. I didn't know all of them, by the way, if you're asking.'

'I'm not asking.'

'But Ben knew some of them. So did Hannah. Now Daryl Mulloway, Ben and Alicia are all dead and Hannah's missing. Whatever is going on isn't stopping, and Bakare and his team don't give a shit. Nobody will give a shit until it's someone they think *matters.*'

'You think that someone has to be *you*?'

Gabriel snorted his opinion of that comment. 'I'm nothing to them, James. You can see that. But I'm fucked if I'm going to just sit around and wait for the next murder. We've got an opportunity here. A literal *trail*. I'm going to bloody well follow it and see if I can give Bakare something concrete to chase, at least. You don't have to come if you've got something better to do.'

Gabriel strode off, keeping his eye on the drops of blood as they led him into a side street.

James followed, hoping that Gabriel would lose the trail, but he didn't. That worried James more than everything else combined, because he was pretty damned sure that nobody could follow a vampire's trail unless the vampire *wanted* to be followed. Hell, a human bite would hardly still be bleeding this far away from the scene in normal circumstances.

Normal. Christ. What does that even mean anymore?

James kept at Gabriel's heels, wondering what the hell to do with that thought. They were being led into a trap. But why was someone baiting Gabriel like this?

And it had to be *Gabriel* they were after. They were targeting Gabriel's friends. Even with the whiff of Cael West about the whole hideous thing, West had no connection with Gabriel. Anyway, West was in Afghanistan, if he was around at all. And if he wasn't, he'd be after James, not James's new tenant. It didn't make any bloody *sense*.

'*James*, are you coming or not?'

James didn't pick up his pace. 'They'll be long gone, Gabriel.' But he wasn't optimistic.

'No, no, the blood's fresh. Oh, through here.' Gabriel darted into an alley. James followed.

The fact that the sun was setting was neither here nor there, James knew. Vampires were perfectly capable of operating in the daylight, supernatural strength and senses undiminished. Being a vampire didn't stop you having psychosomatic health problems, either. Being a vampire didn't make you as all-powerful as it looked in all those stupid films. It didn't make you smart.

But being a vampire did make you fast, and deadly.

Gabriel vanished in front of James's eyes, plucked straight up into the air, feet kicking against the sudden pull, hands scrabbling at his scarf tightening around his throat.

James took three running steps and leapt straight up, wrapping one arm around Gabriel's waist, the other hooked into the scarf to keep it from choking its owner. James twisted his body as he seized Gabriel, an action that wrenched him from the grip of the man on the roof of the lock-up and they fell together, spiralling six feet to the street.

James landed first and bent his knees into the landing, absorbing the shock and bringing Gabriel down with him. He heard the other vampire land behind them and released Gabriel instantly, whirling to face the threat. There was nothing for it. Gabriel would see whatever he would see, because it was too late and too dangerous to hide anything now.

The vampire leapt at him, and James, instead of ducking, threw himself shoulder-first to meet the attack. The vampire grabbed his arms and used the leverage to flip himself right over James's head, landing elegantly in front of Gabriel Dare and sending James sprawling.

'Hello, Mr Dare,' said the vampire in a silken voice. 'You finally found the trail. It took five killings for you to notice one I'd laid.'

'A trail,' Gabriel repeated, puzzled, before his voice flattened to a darker tone. 'A trap. For me?' He scowled. 'You've been killing them to get to *me*? You utter fuck.'

James scrambled up. *You'll have noticed his teeth by now. You should be terrified. But of course you're not. You have no idea what you're looking at.* He cast about for a weapon, preferably something pointy, but anything would do.

'Well, you're a stop on the way to where we want to get,' the vampire was saying, 'and the opportunity for proper kills for the first time in a hundred years was too good to pass up. I love the struggle from the feistier humans. I have so missed the taste of that, and feeling really, properly, *full.*'

'Human?' Gabriel was unable yet to make sense of it.

Any answer was lost when the vampire took an impossible vertical leap as James's fist, wrapped around a discarded crowbar, whistled through the space he'd occupied a moment ago.

'James, what–'

'Down!'

Afterwards, Gabriel was able to reconstruct events from strobe-like memory.

How the stranger landed beside him, grabbed his shoulders and bared long, sharp teeth as he lunged for Gabriel's throat.

How James thrust his arm between those fangs and Gabriel's neck, taking the bite in the forearm, and swinging a crowbar with his free hand onto the assailant's skull.

How the assailant, snarling, tore his teeth free from James's arm and how James pulled them both backwards, away from Gabriel.

How the assailant drew a short wooden spike from an inside pocket and plunged it into James Sharpe's chest, right through his crisp, white cotton shirt.

How James grunted, hissed, 'Missed, ye walloper', wrenched the spike out of his diaphragm and in turn smashed the primitive weapon, point-first, into the left-hand side of the assailant's chest.

And how the assailant exploded into a storm of dust that sprinkled gently onto the street.

'James?'

'You right, Gabriel?' James was clutching at the wound in his torso, the hole surrounded by dark blood. 'He… he didnae bite you… while I was down? Wouldnae… change you, obviously… but it's… nasty. Filthy wounds, bites.'

'James, what just happened?'

'Oh.' James's knees wobbled, 'Stuff. It's… hard tae… Damn.'

His knees buckled and he folded to the ground. Gabriel was instantly at his side, pushing aside James's suit jacket and pulling up his shirt to inspect the ghastly wound.

Gabriel made a peculiar noise in the back of his throat and began to tear off his scarf to have something to press against the oozing hole in James's pale chest.

'No, no Gabriel, it's f-f-fine.' James tried to reassure him, but although the bastard had missed his heart, being staked hurt like a bitch.

'God, James, you're not fine, you're… you're…' The panic faded from Gabriel's voice, replaced with bemusement, 'You're hardly bleeding.'

'Aye. S'all right. Side effect. One of the better ones. Feck.' A piercing twinge of pain made him gasp at air that, strictly speaking, he didn't need any more, except to talk. Right now, he couldn't think of anything to say.

Gabriel rucked up James's sweater again to stare at the wound.

'Gabriel.'

'James, what…?'

'Gabriel, it hurts. I need tae get up. I need home. I need blood.'

'And you have… you have *blood* at home?'

'Nae, but I can rest. I can… please. I'll explain. Later. I just…'

'You're a-a-a *vampire*, then.' Gabriel said it like he was trying out the idea for size, and finding it an uncomfortable fit.

James closed his eyes and wished the world would go away. 'Aye.'

A right guddle, aye. What a mess.

'And the man who attacked us? Also a vampire?'

'Aye.'

'Like the man under the bridge.'

'Aye.'

The silence continued and James, eyes still closed against the unbearable world, began to shudder with the pain.

'Please. Gabriel. I'll nae hurt you. I swear I willnae hurt you. Just get me home, please. Then you can pack and leave. I won't stop you. I understand. But please, believe me. I wouldnae hurt you, ever.' He was shaking so hard his teeth were chattering.

Against all expectation, James felt fingers brush across his cheek. 'Of course you wouldn't hurt me,' said Gabriel softly. 'You've been promising not to all this time. And you haven't. You've looked out for me.'

James's eyes were scrunched shut now, and if he were capable of producing tears anymore he might have been crying. 'I'm sorry,' was all he managed to say, before another bout of pain reduced him to speechless shaking.

'No. It's all right.' Gabriel cradled James's body. James couldn't understand how Gabriel could be so calm, and speak so gently, to the monster he held. 'Well,' Gabriel amended, 'it's clearly not all right. But you've just saved my life, possibly for the second time. I wish I knew the first thing about… about your biology. You need blood to heal, though, is that right?'

This time when James shuddered, a whimper escaped his clamped teeth.

'Fuck, I'm sorry, banging on instead of helping. Here, bite that.'

James opened his eyes enough to see that Gabriel held his arm out to him in an unmistakable offer.

James flinched. 'No.'

'Don't be an idiot, James. You're seriously hurt and you're in pain. I expect the woman who's watching us from her bathroom window has called the police, and I haven't a clue what we're supposed to say to them. And… and ashes-to-ashes there was talking in the plural, "we". If his mates show up, I won't stand a chance without you. Your being noble could get us both killed.'

James tried to form another protest, but a wave of pain shuddered through him. 'Gabriel. I promised… I'll nae… I won't hurt…'

'Just do it,' said Gabriel tensely.

James let the pain take him, triggering the small but necessary change. He bared his new-descended fangs and, as gently as possible, bit the offered forearm.

Gabriel stifled a gasp, but held still as James's teeth pierced the skin.

James bit to open the small wounds further, then sucked at the flow. A few mouthfuls. Nothing more. He didn't need more. He refused to take more.

Then he swirled his tongue over the two holes and felt them close up. Done, he pushed Gabriel's arm away roughly, as though placing it firmly away from temptation.

'All right?' Gabriel's tone was steadier.

'In a minute.' James wiped the back of his hand across his mouth, then licked the smear of blood from his hand. No point wasting any.

'Do you normally drink human blood?' Gabriel asked, suddenly uncertain.

'Not often, and not directly, like that. I drink animal blood from time to time.' James didn't think that was as reassuring as he tried to make it. He made his teeth retract safely away. He didn't like to think about Gabriel watching his teeth while he talked. He didn't want Gabriel worrying about what they meant. 'Mostly, I drink tea.' He tried to laugh, to make it seem normal.

'Is that what all the tea is about? Crushing the craving?' The questions came rushing out, anxiety spilling into curiosity. 'What about tea does that? How effective is animal blood for the… I suppose you get cravings. Do you? Is that what it's like? Do you spend a lot of time looking at my neck?'

Of course Gabriel would go thinking exactly along the lines where James didn't want him to go. 'Actually,' said James, peeved, 'I spend a lot of time looking at your hands.'

'My *hands*?'

'You have beautiful hands.' James could feel his strength returning with the gift of Gabriel's blood, along with the slight itch of the wound in his chest mending.

'Oh. Well. That's a relief.' Gabriel's grin at him was something in the order of a miracle.

'Not weird, then?' James asked, with a trace of their old humour.

'*Quite* weird,' Gabriel's mouth twitched in a tentative smile. 'But more reassuring than you obsessing over my throat.'

'I do not spend time pining over your carotid artery, you plonker. When I need human blood, I sneak blood samples at the clinic. Things go missing at the NHS all the time. What do you take me for?'

Surprisingly, Gabriel seemed heartened by the irritated outburst. 'You're feeling better.'

James lifted the jumper to inspect the damage. The healing had accelerated and his diaphragm showed only a minor and vanishing scar.

'Time to go.' Gabriel held out his hand and helped James to his feet. James didn't need the help, but took it gratefully. That way, he could pretend for a little longer that everything would be okay with him and Gabriel.

James buttoned the suit jacket over the tear in his shirt and straightened his tie. They jogged away, sticking to shadows, darting from street to street, but they weren't followed and they weren't found. At the main road, they flagged a cab. It was an extravagance, given the state of their mutual finances, but neither of them could face either public transport or a walk.

James was pensive on the way home, waiting for further questions that didn't come. All Gabriel said was, 'Your accent comes out when you're stressed or hurt. Did you know?'

'I know.'

'It's gone again.'

'I'm fine now.'

After that, Gabriel lapsed back into contemplative silence and James waited.

Then, two steps through the downstairs door to Ivy Gardens, the questions and comments started again, so rapidly fired that there was no time to answer a single one.

'How long have you been a vampire? Is that the right term? How did it happen? Who did it to you? What are the rules? Those movies are stupid and never make sense. Can you turn into a wolf? Of course not, stupid question, sorry. Where do your teeth go? You still breathe – do you need to? Do you have a heartbeat? What's the deal with your saliva? I felt how it worked on the cuts when you bit me and there's not even a scar now. I could take samples, and the saliva, skin and hair as well, and do some tests–'

Gabriel stopped, hand on the open door, when he realised James was still standing, grim-faced, at the top of the stairs. 'What is it?'

James's jaw worked until he found his voice. 'Gabriel, this isn't a Boy's Own Adventure. I'm not a school project. I'm a vampire. I'm a *monster*.'

That snapped Gabriel out of his excitable blathering. 'Of course you're not a monster.' He entered the flat and waited for James to follow.

Sensing that the top landing was not the place for this conversation, James stepped across the threshold and shoved the door shut. 'Gabriel, are you paying attention? I'm a *vampire*.'

Gabriel exhaled a slow breath. 'You know, James,' he said carefully, 'I lived on the streets on and off for the better part of a decade, and I've become a good judge of character. I had to. And here's something else. I'm now certain I've met vampires before. In fact, I think some things I thought I'd imagined over the years, maybe I really did see.'

He'd gone from giddily fascinated to oddly sober. 'For years, I've thought I was crazy. Not in one of those "oh I'm zany, good for a laugh, me" ways. I mean "psychotic, seeing things, shadows in my head" crazy. I tried to tell myself instead that I was imagining things. But I knew that I saw them, the way I used to see things when I was small. But I was damned if I was going to let anybody start dosing me up on neuroleptics again, so I shut up and explained the weird shit I saw as hunger, or the cold, or tricks of the light. But here you are. A vampire. *Real*.'

'That doesn't make me *safe*.'

'No. But I've just told you, I'm an excellent judge of character. Frankly, there are human beings who've been a long way from safe for me. I don't doubt you, James. I might have only met you a month ago but I *know* you. You don't scare me.'

James regarded Gabriel with a mixture of wonder and curiosity. Then he frowned. 'Who the hell put you on neuroleptics? That's an anti-psychosis medicine – and you were a *kid* when that happened?'

Now it was Gabriel who looked like he wished James didn't make beelines for the one topic he'd hoped to avoid. 'My dad thought I was bonkers when I was a kid,' he said. 'Actually, he still does.'

James's expression changed to one of concern. 'What did you see? When you were little.'

Gabriel moistened his lips nervously, then figured that if confessions were to be made this evening, they had to be made in full.

'Ghosts. I used to think my house was haunted. Nobody ever believed me. My father said I was over-imaginative, and that I made up invisible playmates because I was in that huge house on my own so much. Then I described one of my imaginary playmates as having her entrails spilling out of her stomach, and the boy in the coal cellar had rope around his neck and his tongue was black and stuck out of his mouth like a sausage, and that the creepy baby would cry and cry and cry until the lady in the white dress picked it up and smashed its head into the fireplace.

'My father said I was sick in the head. He sent me to a lot of psychiatrists and the occasional institution and he fed me a lot of fucking *pills* before I learned to keep my mouth shut.'

Gabriel leaned towards James. 'What you did tonight. That's the first time in twenty years I've thought maybe I'm not deep-down crazy. Maybe my house really *was* haunted. You don't understand what this means to me.'

'Gabriel…'

'Because if you're real, then the ghosts were real. And if they're real, I want to know what they are. Ghosts and vampires, and those other things I thought I saw. I want to know everything that can be known about it, because it'll keep proving I'm not mad and I never was.' The relief in his expression, the hope in it, was nearly heart-breaking.

Then Gabriel, fierce and earnest, wrapped his long fingers around James's blunter ones. 'You're not a monster, James. My father is, sometimes, but not you. You're a good man. You saved my life; in more ways than one. And I want to find out exactly what it means. Being a vampire. You can tell me how it works. There must be rules–'

'I don't *know* how it works,' James snapped. 'I didn't come with an instruction manual. I woke up as this *thing*, and was left to work it out on my own.'

'I could *help* you work it out. I'm a chemist, remember. We've got somewhere to start.'

'I'm not a science project, Gabriel. Don't make me into one. I couldn't stand it.' *Not from you.*

'Don't you want to *know?*'

To know what West turned me into? The myths are no good. So much of what's in the movies and books isn't true. I don't know what I am. I don't know what this is or what it means.

'Of course I do.'

'And of course you won't be a *science project*. How could you think you would be? James, you're my *friend*.'

James saw no fear in Gabriel's eyes. He saw burning curiosity, yes, but also warmth. Pleading. He saw something he had not seen since before that day in Helmand. A friend, offering to help.

'I've never seen a ghost,' James admitted slowly.

'You don't believe me?'

'That's not what I'm saying.' James grimaced. 'There's so much I don't know.'

'Then let's find out together.'

'All right.' James swallowed. 'Aye. That'd be good.'

'It *would* be good,' Gabriel agreed. 'We'll be pioneers in the field. That's fantastic, that.' He grinned broadly.

'It's mad, is what it is.'

'Bloody mad,' Gabriel agreed.

Their eyes met and then they were both giggling in fits.

James felt like something had been unlocked inside. With this secret gone, he'd be able to help Gabriel find out what the hell was going on – because Gabriel was right. The police wouldn't do much here. They couldn't. Not if they spent their time seeking a simply *human* reason for it all.

And, James couldn't help thinking, with a fluttering sense of hope, he could finally have more of his life back. *You were always right, Granda. It's a lang road that's nae got a turnin.'*

'So. Do you have a cape?' Gabriel asked cheekily on the way to the kitchen.

'Opera cape,' James replied, deadly serious. 'And spats. I'm like Bela Lugosi when I frock up.'

'You're much better looking than Bela Lugosi,' Gabriel protested. 'You're like a paler, blonder Frank Langella.'

'I don't know who that is.'

'Yeah, you do.' They reached the kitchen and Gabriel poured and gulped down two glasses of water. James sank onto a chair, everything as superficially normal as usual.

The pensive moment froze.

Gabriel broke the silence. 'Will you still help me find out what's going on? Despite what happened tonight? We have to find out who's doing this. That… vampire said I was a step on the way to something else. What do *vampires* want with *me*?' He looked suddenly young and fearful.

James rose, but he was afraid to reach out – although it was the *only* thing he wanted to do. Reach out and press a comforting hand to Gabriel's shoulder; to pull him into an embrace.

'I swear to you Gabriel, we'll find out, and we'll stop them. I won't let anyone hurt you.'

Gabriel's gaze dropped to James's torso, where the stake had torn a hole in his body; where the mouthful of Gabriel's blood had made that wound heal like a miracle.

'Don't let…' Gabriel cleared his throat. 'Don't let any of the bastards s-stake you, either. I don't want to lose you.'

It seemed too early for a declaration like that. Too early, or much, much too late, James thought. He did succumb to the impulse to reach out, though, and squeezed Gabriel's shoulder gently.

Impulsively, Gabriel pressed a kiss to James's cheek, and then vanished into his room.

James pressed his fingers to the spot. He could feel the shape of Gabriel's lips on his skin; and he felt it there, warm and tingling, all the long and wakeful night.

Chapter Seven

GABRIEL GAVE UP ON HIS ATTEMPT TO CAPTURE ELUSIVE SLEEP. HE STARED at his clock, the digits glowing 03:52.

He wondered if James was awake, then grimaced at his own idiocy. Of course James was awake. James was *always* awake, and now Gabriel knew why. Or *part* of the why. He didn't know why vampires didn't need to sleep. Maybe they did. Maybe James slept upside down in the attic when Gabriel wasn't around.

'Twat,' Gabriel muttered at himself. He pushed the bedding aside, put his feet on the floor and wriggled his toes against the carpet, grounding himself in the texture of the cheap pile on his skin.

He walked out to the kitchen, which was in virtual darkness. There, as predicted, was James, dressed again in his jeans and khaki T-shirt, the tail end of the caduceus tattoo just visible under the sleeve. He sat at the table, staring at a partially filled glass vial of dark red fluid which rolled sluggishly around the receptacle. On the table, sitting in a clear tumbler, were five similar vials, each stoppered with rubber. A pen lay beside an open, blank notebook.

'Thought I'd make a start,' James said, the calmness of his tone belied by the swiftness with which he'd set about drawing his blood for the experiments they'd only just agreed upon conducting.

'The damned stuff is even harder to extract than it was when I first turned.'

Gabriel sat beside him and stared at the viscous substance in the vial. It was the consistency of mercury and the colour of dried blood, except this blood was fresh and liquid. *Carmine*, Gabriel's palette memory supplied, *hex triplet 960018*. He'd memorised the codes for two dozen reds during an experimental phase in digital art he'd abandoned back at university. He preferred art he could touch and smell. But the hex triplets had stuck.

Gabriel lifted up one of the vials, swirling it around as he examined it. 'We should check the folklore and literary tropes first,' he said, pulling the notebook and pen over to draw a simple grid. 'We'll need silver, garlic, holy water, I suppose. I can find that later, but we'll use tap water and distilled water as controls. Wasn't there a TV show that threw salt at everything as well? Iron, too.' He caught James looking at him quizzically. 'What?'

'Isn't silver for werewolves; iron for fairies?'

'Worth checking. Elimination is as important as confirmation. Though I'm pretty sure you're not a fairy.'

James actually smiled. 'God. This reminds me of medical school.'

'We can make time for a cadaver lesson,' said Gabriel with a sardonic quirk of his mouth, 'Since technically I suppose you are one.'

James regarded him gravely.

Fuck. I've gone too far.

'They used to prank the first years,' said James. 'They'd bring us in to watch a senior year student perform a dissection. We're all sitting there, trying not to be squeamish, quietly freaking out, and we'd see what we thought was a scalpel making an incision in the cadaver's chest, and then... *AAARGH!!*' James shrieked and jumped up, waving his arms.

Gabriel almost fell out of his chair. He righted himself and glared at James, who was sniggering away.

'The look on your wee face!' cackled James.

Gabriel's glare morphed into a pursed mouth, then an answering grin. 'What did *you* do?'

'I fell out my chair, of course, like a numpty,' admitted James. 'Then I laughed my arse off.'

'Of course you did.'

'In my senior year, I got to play the reanimated corpse. Prescient, now I think on it.' He grimaced. 'I'm half inclined to believe it really was a portent, nowadays.'

'I'd call that superstitious nonsense,' said Gabriel. 'But, well.'

'Fucks up your world view, this vampire thing.'

Gabriel picked up the pen again. 'Let's get on with constructing a new world view then.'

They spent the next few hours, side by side. They established a few baselines: James's temperature was a steady 32°C; his heart thumped at a leisurely eight beats per minute; and it turned out that while his breathing was a reflex, he really did need to inhale once every hour or his heart rate slowed further and he began to drift into a sort of sleep.

James refused to repeat his own early experiments which proved the only food he could ingest was black tea, water or blood. Solid food came up as quickly as it went down and, James said, he didn't really need to go through that again with witnesses.

For further tests, they syringed drops of vampire blood onto clean saucers. The stuff, as James had noted, was difficult to extract. It evaded the needle and then resisted being squirted onto the dish; not with any great force, but the sensation of resistance remained. They made notes to devise tests to determine if the strange effect was a physical property of the blood or a psychological resistance on behalf of the person extracting it. If the latter, whether it affected them both equally, or whether Gabriel's impulse emanated from an evolved human response to vampire blood.

Tap water had no effect on the stuff. Salt water made it skim around the depression in the saucer but no other change was visually discernible.

Gabriel had bought garlic but not yet used it for cooking. He crushed it, to find that James instinctively recoiled from the smell. Speculation that this was merely the response of hyper-sensitive olfactory abilities was dismissed when the smallest drop of garlic juice made the vampire blood coagulate into an awful, thick, blackened slurry. A piece of the garlic made the slurry thicken almost to solidity.

Before continuing, Gabriel found an empty jar and sealed the rest of the garlic tightly inside it. He washed his hands six times in hot soapy water before coming back to the experiments.

'Put latex gloves on the shopping list,' he noted, 'and don't let me shake hands with you for at least a day.'

'Because holding hands is what we do so much of here at Ivy Gardens.'

There was an odd, awkward beat of silence before they both ploughed right on past that notion.

Finding silver for testing proved a challenge, until James remembered he had his mother's mismatched set of silver-plated cutlery in the cupboard. He'd retrieved it from storage with his other belongings on his discharge, but had little call to use it. 'The handles made my hands itch, so I got some cheap stainless steel ones.'

They placed the tip of a silver-plated knife into a drop of blood, and the blood fizzed mildly.

Curious, Gabriel stabbed the tip of the knife into the jar of garlic, and placed it in the blood. The blood fizzed, coagulated and gave off a terrible stink.

'Better toss the silverware out too, then,' he said.

James, who had pushed well back from the table, shook his head. 'Keep it in your room.'

Gabriel was inclined to argue the point, but James was staring at the dish of blackened vampire blood in fascinated horror.

'We don't have to do this now,' Gabriel offered gently.

'We have to find out, don't we? Apart from anything else, you need protection. You may one day need it from me.'

'Don't be ridiculous.'

'I'm not being ridiculous. You don't… you don't know what I… You don't know.'

Gabriel reached for James's shoulder, echoing James's earlier solace.

'I'm an excellent judge of character, remember? If you can't trust yourself, trust me. I lived with a father who did his best to grind me into the dirt to get back at my mother; a man who medicated me from the ages of eight to twelve and packed me off to psychiatrists and institutions rather than try to listen, let alone understand. I lived on the streets, and I've fought for my independence my whole life. I know what people who want to hurt me look and sound like. You're not like them. You don't want to hurt me.'

'No. I don't.'

Gabriel's leaned across the table to kiss James's mouth. Their lips met, soft and chaste and sweet. James's skin warmed under Gabriel's tender touch. He didn't kiss back, exactly, but with his head tilted up, his whole stance softened, relaxed, held still, and he received the kiss like a benediction. When Gabriel drew away, James's eyes were closed.

'James.'

James's blue eyes opened, and they were full of longing and sorrow and fear. 'I don't want to hurt you. That doesn't mean I won't without meaning to. It's happened before. When I first woke like this. A vampire. I didnae know what I was yet. But I was so thirsty and… I did monstrous things, Gabriel.'

'But you're not a monster. Trust me on this.'

'Eight hours ago, you didn't know that vampires could exist. Now you're telling the one you live with that you trust him.'

'Yes.'

'With your life.'

'Yes.'

'You're daft. But please. Even if you can trust my intent, you can't trust the thirst. Promise me you'll defend yourself if I… if I forget myself again.'

'I promise.'

By the time dawn arrived, ten pages of the notebook were filled and they had plans to find equipment and materials to conduct further tests, including experiments with religious symbols in a variety of materials. Gabriel had made a list of things he'd need to obtain from Helene's storeroom.

'If you need to store blood from the butcher in the fridge, you should do that. I don't mind. Can't be worse than the urine samples one bastard kept in the fridge at university, right? It's several degrees of magnitude better than some of the stuff I slept beside while I was between roofs.'

'You're taking this very well.'

'I thought about having a panic attack when I went to bed, but to be honest, it makes parts of my life make sense for the first time. And I like you. So.' He shrugged.

James regarded him with soft-eyed wonderment. 'You really are something special.'

'Not so much.'

James patted Gabriel's wrist. 'You are to me.'

A sharp rap on the door interrupted whatever Gabriel intended to say next. A uniformed constable had arrived to escort Gabriel and James to the station to make their belated statements.

'I have work,' said James, annoyed.

'You can call them, I'm sure, sir,' said the constable, too firmly to encourage argument.

James would have argued anyway, but he wanted the damned thing done and out of the way. He phoned the clinic while Gabriel dressed, then pulled on his dark green field jacket and suffered to be put into the back of the police car with Gabriel.

James made his statement covering the discovery of the body under the bridge and the business at the Tiller crime scene (though not what happened afterwards) and then signed it. DI Bakare urged him to return to work, but James had already decided he wasn't leaving until Gabriel was done. This whole urgency to get them into the station, to separate them as soon as possible, left him uneasy and stubborn.

'I'll wait for Gabriel,' he said firmly, at Bakare's third insistence that it could take time.

Bakare returned with ill-concealed irritation to the desk where Gabriel was giving his statement.

James took up a watchful position by the water cooler, watching Gabriel being interviewed – his posture stiff, Bakare being awkwardly solicitous – when Sergeant Datta came alongside. He cut a quick glance at her, then returned his gaze to Gabriel.

'Don't trust him,' Datta said in a low, urgent voice.

'Thank you for the tip, Sergeant, but I believe I'm old enough to choose my own friends.'

'I mean it. He's not quite right. He's dangerous. He's dangerous to *you*.'

Her earnest tone was puzzling. She wasn't being cold or malicious. Her heartbeat was elevated and her irises dilated. Sergeant Datta was genuinely anxious.

'What makes you say that?'

A chair scraped and they both looked up to see Gabriel rise and walk their way.

'Just keep it in mind,' snapped Datta and she skulked away.

James stepped towards Gabriel. 'Everything all right?'

'Apart from all the dead homeless people?'

'Apart from them. No news of Hannah?'

'No.'

'That's a start, then. We can look for her again tonight.'

'What makes you think we'll have better luck?' They'd pushed through the doors and onto the street.

'I won't have to worry about you seeing me do weird shite while we're looking.'

'Oh? Such as?'

James tapped the side of his nose. 'I've an excellent sense of smell, and you'll have to admit that, whatever else Hannah may be, she doesn't get many opportunities to be fussy with her hygiene.'

'There is that.'

In the late afternoon, James phoned Gabriel with a rain check.

'We'll look for Hannah later, I promise, but I completely forgot I was supposed to take Carrie Anne out last night.'

'Carrie Anne.'

'From the pharmacy.'

'You're going on a date.'

'Coffee,' amended James, half sheepish, half… Gabriel didn't know what. 'I need to make it up to her a bit.'

'I see.'

'No you don't. You're pissed off. So's she. It'll only be coffee. When I get back, we'll head out.'

'Sure. Fine. Whatever you want.'

Gabriel hung up before James could make any further justifications, then sat around swinging between feeling offended that James could abandon the search for Hannah on such feeble grounds, and feeling like a jealous, shitty friend.

Late in the afternoon, Gabriel heard the downstairs door open and shut. He heard the soft footsteps measuring the stairs to the flat. James had a light tread, and could be almost soundless when he so wished, but now his footfalls were heavy and slow.

The door opened and James entered. He hung his plaid blazer while Gabriel watched.

'Have a lovely time with Carrie Anne?' he asked, and winced at his own bitchiness.

'Not that you'd notice,' said James, not rising to the bait.

Gabriel levelled an angry glare at James's back. 'I don't understand why you persist.'

'No. You wouldn't.' James pinched the bridge of his nose.

'You insist on dating women every week or so, never the same woman twice, and whether you return at nine or at midnight, you come back miserable. Why do you expect each time to be different?' Gabriel shoved the papers he'd been working on to one side.

'Christ, you're a real pep-talker.'

'Jesus, James. You're *unhappy* and you keep doing something that makes you *more* unhappy. I don't understand,' His curtness softened into concern. 'Is it for the sex?'

'It's not about the sex,' said James.

'So you *are* having sex.' Concern became curtness again.

'No.'

'Sorry. None of my business, I know. God. I just… why do you keep doing this to yourself, if not for the sex?'

James wiped a hand over his face and collapsed into his chair. 'Fine. You want to know why? When I was first trying to understand what I was, masturbation was among the first experiments I tried. I believed I was a danger to any potential partner, but I wanted to see if it would distract me from the blood cravings.' He looked away, not wanting to meet Gabriel's curiosity, then looked back, because fuck it, he was a doctor and he could discuss this as an adult, 'So, aye. I can achieve an erection, more or less. I can't orgasm, though. There's no ejaculate – my body doesn't produce fluids like sperm or tears or snot any more. Genital manipulation isn't unpleasant, but it's not particularly stimulating. Basically, I no longer experience sexual desire.'

He wished Gabriel wouldn't look at him like that. Like he was *sorry*.

'You still look at women,' said Gabriel, in an even tone, 'and men.'

And at you, James thought. 'I *remember* desire, but I don't *feel* it. I crave blood, sometimes, but that's not the same thing.'

'Then why…?'

'Even when I was human, it was never just about the sex, Gabriel. It's about companionship. Connection.'

'But why date *women*?'

Because they don't make me think of you.

'I find that, more often, women are less bothered if the first date doesnae end in sex.' James studied his hands. 'I only want some company. Closeness. Touch. I miss being touched, Gabriel.' He looked up again. 'And I don't mean sexually. My penis doesn't have to be involved.'

'Is that why you're always home early from your dates? They don't touch you?'

James sighed. 'Sometimes they do. That's usually when it falls apart. Holding and touching hands, that's not so bad for them. They think it's funny, that my hands are cold. They make jokes about warming me up. If the date's going well – if we've got through dinner without them noticing I'm not actually eating anything – there might be more. There might be kissing, they might want to undo a few buttons. Every now and then it gets further, but mostly... mostly it doesn't.'

'Your lower body temperature puts them off?'

He shouldn't have been surprised that Gabriel had noticed that aspect. Gabriel noticed a lot; usually too much. 'For starters. The signals they get from me are all wrong. My skin is too cool. My mouth is too cold for kissing to be pleasant. My low heart and respiration rates are noticeable and *weird*. The whole package is off-putting.'

He sighed. 'The worst part is I think the human instinct knows what I am even if the conscious mind doesn't. They all find a reason to go home in a hurry soon enough.'

'And so you come home, too. Miserable and alone.'

'Aye.' James slumped back in his chair and stared at the ceiling. 'So cheers,' he said, tone flinty, 'getting that out helped a lot.'

He heard Gabriel move, but wasn't expecting it when Gabriel kneeled by his chair and took his hand. Gabriel pressed the fingers of his right hand to James's cheek, less a caress than a way to frame James's mouth, at present unremarkable.

'Show me?'

James rolled his eyes to conceal his discomfort, but Gabriel didn't back down, so he allowed his fangs to descend. The tips of them pressed lightly into his lower lip.

'You grew calcium deposits over your canine teeth. They formed into hollow points that descend and retract in response to stimuli as well as your own will,' said Gabriel. 'That's what makes sense, anyway.'

'You work that out with your chemistry degree? And your point?'

'I'm biologically fully human and fully aware of your condition, and I'm not repelled.'

James tilted his head to one side, as though that would help.

'Michael and I were raised,' continued Gabriel, going even further off topic, 'by a man who believed in education and discipline and not much else. Not, for example, the value of touch.'

'So you're saying I should get over it.'

'No, you idiot,' said Gabriel affectionately, 'I mean that I *understand*. I know what skin hunger *is*.'

'Oh.'

'Stand up.'

James stood.

'We're friends,' said Gabriel. 'We can do this and still be just friends. Can't we?'

'Aye,' said James softly, filled with sudden yearning and hope. 'I think we can.'

'All right, then.'

Gabriel wrapped his long arms around James's broad shoulders; pressed his tall, slender body against James's shorter, stockier build. He pulled James close and laid a pale cheek against a paler brow.

James swallowed, and if his body had still been capable of producing tears, his eyes would have been wet. He leaned into Gabriel's embrace and wrapped his arms around his waist.

James's face was of a height with Gabriel's warm throat. With all his senses he could feel Gabriel's blood pulsing under the surface. He sensed his teeth descending in response to the stimulus and made the effort to retract them. 'Sorry, I'll–'

'You don't need to do that,' murmured Gabriel. He hugged James more firmly, to emphasise the point. 'I trust you.'

Rather than fight about it, James let it go, keeping tabs on his responses. His teeth descended, but he felt no need to bite. He nestled into the hold, enjoying the warmth. 'I'm not too cold, am I?'

'No.'

'You don't have to–'

'James. It's fine.'

James subsided and rested his head on Gabriel's shoulder. The artist's height, his lean strength, felt… sheltering. *Even predators need a place to be safe.*

Gabriel hugged him harder. 'I know this can't be the life you wanted, James, but you don't have to be unhappy.'

'I'm not,' said James, because somehow, suddenly, that had become true. It wasn't the life he'd planned, but it was turning out… okay. If he only had one friend, one person who knew almost everything about him, he was glad it was Gabriel.

Slowly, they drew apart. More slowly still, their hands dropped from each other's shoulders. Their matching grins were slightly embarrassed but mostly content.

'Does this mean you're giving up on dating?' asked Gabriel.

'Oh god, yes, please,' said James.

The search for Hannah didn't go well. They inspected Chelsea Bridge again, keeping well away from any police units moving up and down the river. James could smell the ash and grease of the gruesome fire under the bridge, overlain with brackish river water and oily flotsam deposited on the bank during high tide. He detected nothing that could be ascribed to Hannah. He heard nothing that could help, either: seagulls and mournful boat horns and the *lap lap lap* of the Thames against the embankments. A squeaking river rat was found to be fleeing from a battle-scarred tomcat. Carrion crows squabbled over the corpse of a pigeon but nothing worse.

After the riverside, they checked her known haunts. No sign. She had vanished.

On the prowl, James also kept his senses alert for any trace of a vampire on their tracks. That, too, was futile, though James was somewhat relieved.

At home, exhausted and dispirited, they conducted more tests with household chemicals, singly and combined, and various metals. Gabriel wrote up the results in his notebook.

James made tea for them both, and shared gingernuts from a fresh packet. It transpired that he bought them for the familiar, favourite scent of them; and that he didn't mind at all that Gabriel was also partial to dunking them into strong tea.

Today, Gabriel was forgoing the pleasures of dunking in favour of worrying his lip, mouth pulled tight in a moue as he gnawed at the skin and jotted results in the book.

'You know,' said James lightly, 'you have very artistic handwriting.'

Gabriel shot James a mildly offended glare. He dropped his gaze to the page, with its neatly partitioned tables filled with his free-flowing script. 'Are you saying my handwriting's illegible?'

'No. I'm saying that it's very artistic. Is legibility meant to be a feature?'

'As long as people can tell who did the paintings, does it matter?' In demonstration, Gabriel signed the bottom of a page with the signature he used on his art. A huge *G* that fell to a legible lower case *a,* which turned rapidly into a squiggle, an oval that was meant to be a *D* and final squiggle. 'See? Took me years to perfect that. Looks better in paint, mind.'

'It looks like a small snail and a baby snail being stalked by a turtle walking on its hind legs.'

'You can talk. Have you actually *seen* your own writing? You're an unspeakable cliché about the unreadable scrawl of the medical man.'

'I'll have you know that Medical Scribble 101 was a compulsory course for all medical students, and I was the first to achieve Honours. They ought to put up a plaque, but they couldn't read my work well enough to spell my name.'

'That's criminal neglect.' Gabriel immediately flipped to a blank page and sketched out a shield, in which he printed James's name clearly. He added a line that might have read "For services to medical penmanship" in a fair approximation of the doctor's crabbed handwriting. It made them both laugh.

Gabriel scrubbed at his eyes. 'I don't think we can do any more tonight. It's–' he peered at the clock. 'Shit. Almost 3am. I have a half day at Wilcott's tomorrow. Better grab a few hours or all the paints I mix will turn out sludge brown.'

The two men hugged goodnight, holding on a shade longer than "just good friends" would – but, Gabriel thought later, perhaps long enough for two people who had at last found a friend.

Chapter Eight

JAMES RETURNED TO THE CLINIC THE NEXT MORNING, TAKING ON A SHORT extra shift to make up for having missed so many hours the previous day.

Gabriel managed to get to Wilcott's, off Ilford's High Road mall, in time for the 8am start. He spent four hours mixing paints, advising a regular client on the use of resins, and wishing he was still in bed. It was nice having a bed, even if he spent all his time in it alone. At least he also had a kitchen now, and someone to share it with.

When he got home, Gabriel cleared the previous night's experiments from the table. He gathered up most of the silverware in the house and put it in a plastic container, though he left one experiment – a silver letter opener steeping in silver-nitrate-infused garlic – on the sink. They'd determine that silver made James's skin itch, and that longer exposure inflamed the epidermal layers, before Gabriel refused to let James use himself as such a direct test subject any more. Gabriel also located a more airtight container for the garlic, which he had split into cloves and a teaspoonful of mash while wearing latex gloves, ready for further tests.

A quick cheese and chutney sandwich later, Gabriel was at his easel by his bedroom window. Annoyingly, he found that the image he was trying to capture kept turning into James. The calming, broad-shouldered solidity of him. The severe cut of his brown hair contrasting with the compassionate but wary look in his blue eyes. A hint of sharpness around his mouth, which could soften so handsomely with his rare open smiles, but his hands were offered, palm up, as though in supplication.

When Helene phoned and wanted to come by, Gabriel thought it wise to stop working. He put the canvas on the floor, draped a paint cloth over it, and propped one of his other works-in-progress on the easel.

The tea was brewed and ready to pour when Helene arrived. She presented a box of tiny macarons, looking like a set of highly coloured buttons for a giant toy bear, with a flourish.

'You should have called,' she said.

'About what?'

'Gabriel.'

Gabriel began rearranging the macarons on the plate in order of the colour spectrum, eating the creamy-beige one absent-mindedly when it didn't fit the pattern.

'How can I help you when you don't let me know what's happening? I can get you a lawyer.'

Gabriel coughed on the beige macaron, eyes watering. He swigged his tea before glaring at her. 'I don't need a lawyer.'

'You do,' Helene said. 'Because you are innocent.'

'How do you know what's going on anyway?'

'That Detective Inspector Bakare.' She smiled slyly. 'He's bought two of your pieces, did you know? Small ones. He would like to buy larger ones, but he can't afford them. He told me not to tell you, but honestly, the man is a fool sometimes and doesn't know what he's thinking. He's on your side, Gabriel, or he wants to be, but he is a policeman. There are limits to what he can do. Rather, there are things that he must be seen to do.'

Gabriel scowled and rearranged the remaining macarons in a

pattern that reflected his fractious thoughts. He stopped when Helene laid a hand on his wrist.

'Gabriel, darling. What can I do?'

'Do you remember those ghosts I used to see when I was a kid?'

Helene patted his hand. 'Of course.'

'What would you say if I told you they were real? What if I said they weren't the only real things? What if I told you there really are monsters?'

'I've met your father, my darling boy. I know monsters are real.'

Gabriel's sigh was aggrieved. 'That's not what I mean.'

Helene rubbed a thumb across the back of his hand. 'You were a very intense little boy,' she said, 'always thinking so much. Always seeing so much. I worried about you. It seemed that if you thought you saw such terrible ghosts, you must have been frightened of the world, but that's not how you were. You were curious. You felt sorry for them, I believe.'

'I did. They were so sad. And trapped. Just like me.'

'But you stopped seeing them,' said Helene, with a hint of hopefulness in her voice.

No. I pretended I didn't until I believed it. And now I know they were true but I can't see them anymore.

'Did you ever see any ghosts in that house?' he asked instead of replying.

Helene's delicate pout suggested... he didn't know what.

'It was a strange house,' she said at last, 'and I do not miss it. Now, tell me what you think of the macarons. They are Pierre Hermé.'

With the subject definitively dropped, at least for the time being, Gabriel selected a macaron whose colour most jarred in tone and intensity with the others. He dunked it into his tea.

Helene pretended to be scandalised. 'Have you any idea how much those cost, Gabriel?'

'I like 'em dunked,' he said through half a mouthful, and grinned at her, the twinkle back in his eye.

'I know you do,' she replied, with a theatrical long-suffering sigh. 'And how is it working out with James as a landlord? Mr Bakare says he's taking care of you.' The double entendre was unmistakable.

'Not like that,' Gabriel protested. 'We're just friends.'

'You'd like it to be more, though.'

And damn her for knowing him so well. 'There are some obstacles to that.'

'Well, be careful. I like him, but I think there's something damaged about him. A man like that can hurt you without meaning to.' Before he could show his irritation at that, she added, 'And you can hurt him too.'

'Well, we're both damaged goods then,' Gabriel said, irritation vying with resignation. 'Doesn't that cancel it out or something?

'Or make double the mess.'

Gabriel had to admit to the truth of that.

Finally paying attention to his reluctance to speak of the killings or James, Helene changed the subject to talk of art, Gabriel's progress with his latest works, whether he needed more supplies yet. They drank more tea and Gabriel ate all but one of the macarons. Helene handed over two more cheques, one made out to James for the rent, the other in Gabriel's name.

'Don't you think you'd better hang on to that for bail?' he challenged.

'If you need bail, I will pay the bail,' said Helene sternly. 'But it won't come to that.'

Gabriel wasn't convinced, but he let the matter rest.

'I must be off, Gabriel. Don't see me out, I know the way.'

'Did you leave a trail of crumbs?' he asked with an arched eyebrow. 'It's such a vast, palatial residence you might get lost.'

'Don't be so grumpy,' Helene admonished him mildly. 'You like this flat and it is palatial enough for you. You need to relax. You should see if your James will have sex with you.'

'I thought you said I should steer clear of him.'

'You should,' said Helene with an impish and sympathetic crinkling of her eyes. 'But you won't.'

'Off with you, wicked woman,' Gabriel said, shooing her out. 'I have painting to do.'

Helene skittered ahead of him, laughing, while Gabriel carried the dishes to the sink. He heard the door open and Helene's sudden *oh*! before a low voice rumbled something inaudible.

Then he heard Helene say, 'Well if he's expecting you, do come in.'

He heard the door shut and the skin along his spine, his neck, his scalp, prickled with apprehension.

Gabriel turned from the sink, clutching the letter opener, the only implement at hand. He relaxed marginally when he saw a very pale man regarding him with supercilious disinterest.

'I'm not in to visitors. I'm working,' said Gabriel.

'I am here for Doctor Sharpe,' said the man. His accent was cultured. Mannered, even. Gabriel suspected it was not the man's natural accent.

'James isn't home.'

'I will wait.'

The stranger walked into the living room and perched on the sofa. He arched an eyebrow at the cushions as though suspecting them of harbouring bedbugs. Gabriel decided that, whatever else he was, the stranger was a poser, a wanker and an insufferable snob.

'I'm working, and you're leaving.'

'I am not leaving.'

And god, what was with all the refusal to use contractions? All that waxy pale skin and stilted speech made the git sound like a cheap TV vam–

Oh.

Gabriel refused flatly to be frightened. 'Deathly white skin, precise speech patterns, standoffish mien,' he observed, 'I assume you're here on vampire business?'

The stranger arched an elegant eyebrow at him. 'Pale skin and standoffishness equally apply to you, Mr Dare.'

Gabriel registered the lack of response to *vampire business*. 'Except that I have a pulse.'

'I have,' said the stranger, smiling ferally, 'noted that. Yes.'

Gabriel held very still, considering how his familiarity with James's state, and his lack of real familiarity with any other vampire, might have led him to this miscalculation. Then he gave the vampire a slow smile of his own. 'Don't imagine that I'm not prepared. I *live* with a vampire.'

'A *tame* one,' sneered the stranger.

Before the exchange could go further, the door opened and James walked in.

To be fair to the visiting vampire, James – in his habitual neat-casual attire and carrying a Tesco's plastic bag of milk and teabags – looked every bit as tame as a rabbit.

James took in the scenario, nodded a casual greeting to Gabriel, and crossed the room with the economical grace of a tiger to put the meagre groceries on the table.

Tame, my arse, thought Gabriel with satisfaction. The stranger appeared surprised as well, though he covered it swiftly.

'Doctor Sharpe,' he said, rising. 'I am Mordecai Grimshaw.' He waited expectantly.

James folded his arms. 'How very nice for you.'

Now it was Grimshaw's turn to be put out. 'Of the Grimshaw Coterie,' he elaborated stiffly.

'Again, cheers, so pleased for you and your wee kingdom. Hope the weather stays fine for it. Goodbye.' He turned and started to unpack the bag.

'*Doctor Sharpe!*'

The good Doctor Sharpe ignored the commanding tone and stowed the milk in the fridge, next to two vials of his own blood.

'Doctor. Sharpe.' The name was spoken through gritted teeth that time.

James turned, raised an eyebrow. 'You still here?'

'I need,' said Grimshaw through rigid jaws, 'your...advice.'

'Why didn't you say? Take two aspirin, call me when you're dead.' A beat. 'Deader.'

'You do not make this easy, Doctor.'

'I don't intend to make this *easy*, Mr Grimshaw. I made it clear on my return to London, when I was approached by no less than *five* vampires with delusions of grandeur, I'm not joining anyone's little vampire enclave. I'm not having any part of your silly power plays and those incredibly ridiculous standoffs where people in the undead equivalent of a posing pouch sneer and throw a perfumed hanky at some other moron with teeth and an inflated opinion of their own importance. I'm not interested, full stop. Not unless you've decided to start killing people instead of drinking delicately from those volunteers who've mistaken you for the lead character in a romance novel. I'll have plenty of interest if that's the case, and you won't enjoy it. If you're not here with information about these killings, you can get out of my house.'

Grimshaw blinked. He blinked again. 'What killings?'

'Right,' said James. 'Out.'

'Doctor Sharpe.'

'I don't plan to repeat myself,' said James, 'Who let you in, anyway?'

'Helene,' said Gabriel, who had been enjoying the exchange immensely.

'Better ask her not to do that anymore.'

'I had no intention of harming your... thralls,' said Grimshaw in a voice dripping with acid and honey. 'Merely inviting you to ally your own *wee kingdom* with my own.'

'You're starting to really piss me off.'

Grimshaw, not used to such defiance, reached the end of his tether. In a vampire, that took the shape of him, teeth bared, snatching Gabriel by the throat with supernatural speed and reeling him in, nails biting into his skin.

An instant later, Grimshaw was howling in agony and hopping on one leg. In the other was buried the solid silver letter opener that had been dipped in silver nitrate and garlic, which Gabriel had plunged into the nearest bit of meaty muscle. The only reason Grimshaw wasn't falling over with the pain is that James had hold of his hair and was yanking it towards the ceiling. James's teeth had descended too, vicious points close to Grimshaw's face.

'Two things, ye turnip,' said James with deadly calm. 'One: it turns out silver isn't only for werewolves. Combined with garlic, it hurts like a motherfucker for vampires as well.'

Grimshaw whimpered. He groped for the knife handle, but James seized one of his wrists in a grip like steel and squeezed until bones creaked. Grimshaw waved the other in the air in a feeble gesture of surrender.

'And two: *I. Don't. Like. You.*'

'Please,' sobbed Grimshaw. 'Take it out. Take it out. It burns.'

'Could he actually burn?' Gabriel asked, his perturbation at Grimshaw's reaction buried under a veneer of scientific curiosity. The wound was swelling nastily.

'I don't think so.' James frowned. 'Not unless we set fire to him.'

'Not a good idea,' said Gabriel, matching James's tone with bravado. 'We might set fire to the curtains while we're at it.'

'They are ugly curtains,' offered James.

Grimshaw whimpered again.

James, taking pity at last, hauled Grimshaw upright. 'I'm going to take the knife out, ye Jessie,' he said. 'And I'm going to treat the wound. And you are going to go back home and never come here again.'

Grimshaw nodded frantically. Satisfied, James dropped him onto the sofa, tore the cloth of the expensive tailored trousers to get to the injury and pulled out the knife. A gush of sticky, almost black blood came with it, curdled by the garlic and silver.

Gabriel stood guard over Grimshaw with the gory knife while James cleaned the cut, flushing the gash with water. When it was clean, it began to heal of its own supernatural accord.

As the pain receded, Grimshaw stared from Gabriel to James in disbelief.

'You know what that knife can do, and you let the human carry it?'

They hadn't formally discussed Gabriel being permanently armed with the thing, but it struck James as an excellent idea. 'I insist that he does.'

'But why?'

'Because,' said Gabriel with a wicked gleam in his eye, 'he likes to live dangerously.'

Unexpectedly, James laughed, vampire canines nowhere in sight. 'You,' James, sobering, jabbed a finger at Grimshaw, 'go home. I never want to see you again. You don't want to see me, either. You don't know what other surprises we've cooked up.'

Grimshaw eagerly agreed that he did not. He struggled to his feet. With great dignity and a very strained voice, Grimshaw slipped his fingers into the breast pocket of his suit and withdrew a business card.

'Should you change your mind, Doctor Sharpe, you may find me at home.'

James didn't take the card, and Grimshaw was forced to place it on the coffee table.

'We may be able to help each other,' he said.

'I doubt it.'

'Your stubbornness and prejudice against your own kind are foolish. We are not all like–' His teeth snapped shut. 'Good day, then, Doctor Sharpe.'

'I'd make a move on that pissing off now, if I were you.'

The vampire walked out with studied poise and majesty, an effect undermined by his torn trousers and persistent limp.

James watched him leave, all the way down the stairs, from the doorway and then from the window. His nostrils flared, as though he could smell something nasty.

Gabriel was scrabbling among his papers for his notebook so he could dash down his new observations.

'You'd better clean and re-garlic up that thing,' said James warily. 'Just in case.'

With an *aha!* of triumph, Gabriel found the notebook and sat to write in it furiously. He drew an excellent and accurate depiction of the swollen knife wound from memory.

When he was done he found James, arms folded, regarding the floor with a troubled expression. 'What's up?'

'Grimshaw's coming here is no coincidence.'

'What does that mean?'

'I think Grimshaw was sent here by the vampire that made me.'

Gabriel stared at him. 'How could you know?'

'I could smell West, faintly.'

'Smell?'

'Vampires have an acute sense of smell,' said James with a grimace, as though it were a disgusting failing. 'And Major Cael West always smelled of stale tobacco, onions and old blood even when I only had human senses.'

At Gabriel's continued consternation, James went on.

'He was in Afghanistan, last I knew. That was getting on for two years ago. I tried to kill him there. I failed. I thought he was still in the Middle East. Plenty of scope for a vampire in a war zone.'

'Do you think he's got something to do with the murders?'

'I think it's inevitable he has,' said James.

'Do you think it has something to do with *you*?' But Gabriel's tone was curious, not accusatory.

'I can't see how, but I can't rule it out. If West has come back to England, he hasn't tried to find me before now. I made it clear how I felt about his offer back in Helmand.'

'What offer?'

James shifted uncomfortably again. 'After I woke up… changed, he said he'd done it because he had a job for a medic. He wanted me to join his little band of blood-sucking psychopaths.'

'And you declined the offer?'

'By trying to stake him, yes.' James glanced away, and Gabriel thought that there must be more to the story.

'I wasn't a match for him. He got away.' James shook his head. 'If I'd managed to kill the bastard then, these murders wouldn't be happening.'

'This is not your fault,' Gabriel told him. 'Don't you go taking stupid guilt on with everything else. You said this guy, West, had a gang of vampires. Even if you'd killed him, this scheme, whatever it is, may have gone ahead anyway. There must be a larger purpose to it than that one bastard. It's… it's too strange and pointlessly focused on me to be a simple case of thrill killing.'

'It's not down to you either, Gabriel.'

Gabriel released a pent-up breath. 'No. Right. It's down to this prick, West, and his *gang*.'

James picked up the business card from the coffee table. 'Maybe we'd better go talk to Mordecai Grimshaw after all.'

Gabriel reached for his wallet and keys, but James stayed him with a gesture. 'Not right away.'

'Why not?'

James sighed. 'There are so many things I haven't told you yet.'

'Such as?'

'I lost the last time I faced Cael West. I don't dare risk a confrontation again without being at my peak.'

'What do you need?' asked Gabriel instantly.

'I need to rest. It's not sleep, more like being dormant.'

'Like a volcano?'

'Heh. If you like.'

Gabriel's eyes widened. 'I knew it. You really do hang upside down from a ceiling.'

'You're a funny bastard, Gabriel Dare.'

'I am,' Gabriel agreed with an unrepentant grin. 'You're lucky you're getting me for free now instead of having to line up at the Edinburgh Festival like everyone else.'

James shook his head, but the corners of his eyes were creased with amusement. 'It's been a long couple of days and nights, and if there's half a chance Cael West is waiting for us, I need to be rested. Give me two hours. And I should,' he grimaced, 'eat.'

'Oh,' replied Gabriel, stunned. He pushed up his shirtsleeve. 'I can... we can sort that...'

'Pig's blood,' said James firmly, taking Gabriel's hand and tugging the sleeve down again. 'I can get some from the butcher near Spitalfields.'

'*I'll* get some from the butcher near Spitalfields,' said Gabriel.

James hesitated, then said: 'If you can't get pig's blood, cow's blood will be fine, or sheep. Chicken'll do in a pinch.'

Gabriel was matter-of-fact, like this was the usual shopping-trip request. 'Got it. You rest up. Or hang around. Whichever it is you do, and I'll be back soon.'

'When you do, don't worry if I seem a bit...'

'Dead?'

'Startled, I was going to say,' but there was humour in it. 'I'm not used to anyone being around when I zone out.'

Gabriel's teasing vanished. 'I'll wake you up gently.' He wrapped his arms around James and hugged. 'Don't worry.'

Holding James like this felt good. Damn, but the man *fit* in his arms. For all that James was shorter, he was broader across the shoulder, his compact physique filling the space between Gabriel's long arms. Thin and gangly, so much in Gabriel's life had made him feel insubstantial: as a boy nobody had listened, as a young man on the street he'd been invisible. Yet here he was, heard and needed. James's solidity, the weight of him in Gabriel's arms, was a welcome anchor.

When James squeezed his arms gently around Gabriel's shoulders, Gabriel couldn't help smiling, and he couldn't help turning his head to press a kiss to James's temple.

James held very still, then relaxed. So Gabriel kissed James's temple again. When James turned his face towards him, he placed a soft, undemanding kiss on James's mouth.

James, cautiously, uncertainly, returned the kiss. Then he sighed. 'I don't think I can be what you want,' he said. 'I know I can't be what you need.'

'You don't know what I want or need,' said Gabriel. 'You haven't asked.'

'I've explained about... about sex.'

'You say you don't experience desire,' said Gabriel. He rubbed his hand against James's back. 'But you desire *touch*. If sex gives you no pleasure, we don't need that. This is good. This is nice.'

James met Gabriel's eyes but, tellingly, he didn't pull away from the embrace. 'I don't even know if I'm capable of love any more. I don't know if I have a soul.'

'I don't know if I have one either,' said Gabriel reasonably. 'But you like me, don't you?'

James's fingers flexed against Gabriel's arms. 'Aye. Yes, I like you a lot.'

'And I like you a lot,' said Gabriel. 'Isn't that where most people start?'

'I suppose it is.'

'Then let's start with that.'

James's Adam's apple bobbed. 'All right.'

'Can I kiss you again?'

'Aye, I'd like…'

Gabriel cupped James's jaw in his hand. He breathed warm over James's cheek, his lips. James tilted his head up to meet him.

James's mouth was indeed cool and strange. And perfect and wonderful. Their lips parted and, tentatively, Gabriel ran the tip of his tongue over James's lip, over the edge of his tongue. James made a lovely, tiny moan, restrained, yet with the hint of longing.

Gabriel drew away. James reluctantly let him go.

'I won't be gone long,' Gabriel said.

'Be careful,' said James. 'Take the knife. If West is mixed up in this, we can't know what to expect.'

Gabriel took the knife.

Chapter Nine

Dormancy was an odd thing. In lieu of human sleep, vampires went utterly still and their minds withdrew into rest. While in that vulnerable suspension, their altered bodies assimilated ingested blood, repaired damaged cells, and grew stronger.

Their complete stillness made them hard to detect: their only defence while dormant. Vampires were predators, but also prey. Humans had spent thousands of years learning to protect themselves, after all.

James suspected that staking vampires in their dormant state was the only way humans ever manage to kill them. He lacked empirical data for his theory, but he found logic in it. When dormant, he was aware of but didn't engage with external stimuli. He roused slowly and sluggishly if he heard anything alarming.

Sneaking up on a sleeping vampire was definitely the way to kill them. It's how *he* would have done it. It was hard to imagine any but the most extraordinary of human beings winning a fight with an alert vampire, with all that supernatural strength and agility, all those hyper-vigilant senses and instincts for survival and the hunt in their favour.

James would normally have stretched out on his bed to go into his dormant state – with a chair propped against the door to keep it shut for good measure. But he now shared his home with someone he trusted.

It felt so strange to trust someone again; and he trusted Gabriel more than he trusted himself. He hadn't trusted himself since he'd effectively died in that village in Helmand two years ago. For God's sake, Gabriel actually *teased* him about what he was, even after seeing the creature he'd become.

I knew it. You really do hang upside down from a ceiling!

Cheeky beggar. Of all the reactions James had expected when someone finally learned his secret, *playfulness* hadn't been among them. Gabriel was either a certifiable lunatic or a certified miracle.

So he wants to see a vampire hanging upside down from the ceiling, does he?

The flat didn't offer anything useful to hang from, but the armchair had a high back. James knew Gabriel would get the joke, and it wasn't as though he'd be inconvenienced by anything like a rush of blood to the head.

James arranged himself on the armchair, knees bent over the back of it, his back barely skimming the seat, head hanging over the edge of the cushion nearly to the floor.

In this inverted position, with his arms folded across his chest (good old Hammer Horror *Castle of Dracula* style) James contemplated the wonder of Gabriel's warm mouth pressed on his. The wonder of how, instead of flinching at it, Gabriel had deepened the kiss, as though wanting to chase away the cold; to take it into himself and give warmth back. He focused on this cautious miracle and instead of fearing how soon it would end, indulged in the knowledge that, for the first time in a long time, he didn't feel like an exile from humanity.

Holding to that thought, James ceased his reflex breathing and willed his body and mind to stillness.

James was aware of a voice he trusted speaking his name, but distantly, muffled. The voice wasn't a threat, so it didn't rouse him from his detached state.

A door opened, and that didn't rouse him either. The sound, familiar enough, was followed by... a silence.

He registered the faint snick of something that part of his brain identified, but the context was unclear. This noise was as much about security as danger. It heralded wariness, but didn't make him stir yet. He remained deep in the sluggish dark.

A second voice, a woman's, encroached on the periphery of his consciousness in a whisper. 'You stay right where you are, Dare.'

The one he trusted said, 'It's not what you think.'

'Oh my god,' said the woman, voice filled with horror. 'I told you, Victor. I *told* you, and you didn't believe me. My god. The poor, stupid bastard. I *warned* him.'

A third voice joined the conversation that was finally registering in James's drowsing vampire brain.

'It may not be what it looks like.' This voice was older, troubled, but trying for calmness. 'Maybe he's unconscious.'

'His fucking eyes are *open* and he's not *breathing*,' said the woman, both horrified and ringing with vindication. 'And I told you to *stay put*, Dare.'

The origin of that wary sound from before finally coalesced into a thought. *Weapon drawn from a leather holster.*

James began to emerge from his inertia.

He became aware, distantly, and then more urgently, of two fingers pressed against his wrists; then hard against a carotid artery that had nothing much to report.

'What the hell are you doing, Sergeant?'

Datta shrieked and backed off so fast she fell over the carpet and landed hard on her arse. Any mortification she felt was tempered by the fact that her DI had yelled and jumped a foot straight back as well, colliding with Gabriel Dare, who swore and dropped a double-bagged tub of something liquid on the floor.

'Oh, for God's sake,' James grumped. 'What's wrong with you lot?'

'You didn't have a pulse,' gasped Datta. 'You didn't... you're cold and you didn't have a pulse.'

James glared at her – it would've had more impact if he hadn't been upside down with his knees crooked over the back of an armchair.

'And what the fuck are you doing hanging there?' Her tone was accusatory.

'Yoga,' he sniped. 'It's meant to be *relaxing*.' He took his weight on his arms and curled his feet down to the floor.

'You were *dead*,' Datta persisted, as James rose and stretched.

'Can't get more relaxed than dead, I suppose,' said Gabriel peevishly. 'But I think death is meant to be incurable, isn't it? Just as well you're not with forensics, Datta. You'd be neck deep in murders that turned out to be bad cases of tantric meditation.'

Bakare was mildly shocked and largely annoyed, as if they'd been playing a horrible practical joke on his staff. Datta glared stormily at James, like not being dead was a personal affront to her theories on the dangerousness of Gabriel Dare.

Gabriel regarded James contritely. 'Sorry to barge in on the yoga, James. They were bloody insistent and didn't give me a chance to let you know we had company.'

'Not your fault. Did you get the–'

'I did, but....' Gabriel was gathering up the bags from the floor. The container had split, spilling blood through the plastic bags and all over the kitchen linoleum.

'Is that blood?' Bakare asked, aghast. Datta reached for her nightstick again.

'It's pig's blood,' sighed Gabriel, 'from the Italian butcher in Spitalfields. I can show you the receipt if you like. I was planning to show James how to make traditional Portuguese blood sausage, but there goes that idea.' He mopped up the gory mess with tea towels and deposited the lot in the sink with a nasty splotch.

James watched the blood swirl in the sink and felt his fangs descending. He hadn't eaten in a few days, and hadn't realised how hungry he was. Too late now. He'd have to manage until the Yard detectives had pushed off. They'd go to the butcher again on their way out to investigate Grimshaw. It'd be all right.

'Cooking lessons?' asked Datta scathingly. 'You?'

'What? I cook. It's only chemistry.'

'He whips up a terrific soufflé,' James threw in, stepping away from the compelling smell of blood in the sink. 'He makes a Jaffa Cake bread pudding that ought to be illegal.'

He and Gabriel exchanged half grins, semi-surprised at how well they worked as a double act, as though they'd known each other for years rather than weeks.

'So, are you here solely to mess up my afternoon, or have there been developments?' Gabriel asked Bakare.

'Well, it's not a goddamned social call,' sneered Datta.

'That's all your social graces wasted then,' observed James drily. 'I suppose you'd best state your business.'

'Do you know this man?' Bakare shoved a grainy photograph at them, of a wiry, red-haired man passing through a tube station pedestrian tunnel. He looked like he'd either prematurely aged or, alternatively, was an oddly youthful 40 year old.

'No,' said James. Gabriel shook his head.

'How about this guy?' A second photo, of a taller, older man with buzzcut hair, passing through the same tunnel.

James stilled. 'Who is he?'

'We don't know yet. CCTV footage picked them up the night Ben Tiller died. These two show up here and on the cameras around the intersection where Alicia Jarret was last seen alive.'

'So you have actual suspects,' observed Gabriel.

'I wouldn't go that far yet,' said Bakare. 'You don't recognise them?'

'They're strangers to me.'

'The tall one looks military,' said James.

'That's what we thought. Fine. Well, we'll leave you to your yoga and cooking lessons, gentlemen.'

Gabriel ushered them out, meeting Datta's glare with one of his own. When he returned to the living room, he folded his arms.

'Who the hell is that in the picture, James?'

'I...'

'I know you. You recognised him. Why didn't you tell them?'

James rubbed a hand over his chest, over his sluggish heart, distractedly. 'That's Major Cael West, and I have no idea what they'd do with the information.'

'They could hunt him down.'

'Gabriel, the man's a cold-blooded murderer, and a vampire. He won't hesitate to kill anyone who confronts him. I'm not sure I should send the police after him without all the facts, but I haven't the first idea how to give them the facts.' He rubbed the side of his neck instead. 'I need to think about this.'

What James needed to do was to find that son of a bitch and stake him to dust, if he could. But he didn't want to share that particular thought with either Gabriel or the police.

'We should check out Grimshaw soon, then,' said Gabriel quietly. 'See what he knows about it. Unless you think he was here on West's business.'

'West might have put him up to it, but it's hard to say. Vampires tend to work alone or in small groups. He might have been here under duress. He was inviting me to join his stupid little court, which probably just involves Grimshaw and whatever blood donor he's drummed up lately. I got the feeling he wanted an ally.'

'Wouldn't that be a good thing?'

'Bollocks, it would,' said James. 'The main thing I've noticed when vampires want other vampires as allies is that they're aiming to start turf wars with some other prick of the night.'

'If that prick of the night is behind these murders…'

James stepped further away from the scent of blood in the sink. 'You're right. Christ. Sorry. I try to steer clear of them. I should have thought about it before turfing him out.'

'Let's see what he wanted. We can go by the butcher again.'

James checked his watch. 'He'll be shut now. I'll go in the morning. It's fine.' He headed for the door. 'Come on then. Might as well get it over with.'

They went to the address on Grimshaw's card, one of a set of old terrace houses in need of maintenance. On one side, the houses were bordered by the tail end of Wandsworth Common; the prison was at the end of the street.

The overgrown garden of Grimshaw's house was barely restrained by a low, cracked, brown brick wall, half smothered under ivy which also climbed up the plane tree that shaded the front window. A briar rose bush hugged the house beneath the front window which was curtained not with drapes but an old striped sheet. Blackbird chicks peeped frenetically from a nest in the plane tree, but the hen was nowhere about. No sign either of insects or mice. Only that desperate cheeping.

The front door was ajar. Walking right in would have been simple, but James stopped as though a force field held him back.

'Do you need an invitation?' Gabriel asked, pushing the door open with his hip and stepping over the threshold, 'Come on, then. I invite you in.'

James's nostrils flared. Every sense in him was taut and ready for flight, triggered by the smell. The smell that Gabriel hadn't registered yet. A raw, fresh, intense, overpowering smell that had driven away the mice and the blackbird, and sent her brood peeping in wild distress.

James knew he'd had too many days without blood of any kind – ordinary food did nothing for him, didn't even stay in his body for more than a few hours. Tea he could drink. Red wine. Black coffee. Water. But his metabolism was fussy. It wanted *blood*. Human blood. Not much, not every day, but blood. The dark fluid that ran in his veins needed it. Animal blood would do in a pinch, to get what he needed. Erythrocytes and leukocytes and thrombocytes and plasma, the latter with its lipids and proteins and *oh god*, he could smell it and damned near taste it, and his fangs descended and he didn't even try to stop it.

'James?'

James shook his head to free it from the greedy buzz. He made the effort to retract his fangs. *Ye shouldae fed earlier, Jamie.*

Feck off, Granda.

So he had cravings. That didn't have to mean he gave up all control to the beast. He wasn't a new-turned vampire with no idea what was going on, and this was not Afghanistan.

'Fine. I'm fine. Can you smell it?'

Gabriel lifted his head to sniff. 'Oh. Hell.' He looked at James again. 'Are you all right?'

'Of course,' said James tightly, 'Come on.'

James and Gabriel stepped into the hallway and made their way to the sitting room leading off to the left. James had a few moments to see what was there, before he was overwhelmed.

The boy hung upside down from the ceiling (a grotesque mimicry of how he had spent the afternoon, hanging upside down from the armchair, wanting to make Gabriel laugh) and his throat was cut and the blood from that second, gaping mouth painted the boy's face and the floor and the carpet and the floorboards leading to the kitchen and under the sofa and under the sound system and under and over and *oh god oh god oh god* so much blood, so much blood, all of it and the smell and *all of it* and it was wasted *wasted*, all that blood *going tae waste*, spreading and cooling and congealing and it was *god what a terrible terrible waste and he was so so so so so so fucking thirsty*.

He couldn't hear a thing but the blood rushing in living veins, right next to him, right at his side. James didn't know why he was kneeling on the floor, hands over his ears, trying not to listen, eyes screwed shut, trying not to see, but his tongue darted out and over and out and over his lower lip, over the tips of his teeth and he was producing saliva, all ready, ready to bite and heal, bite and heal, bite and bite and bite and fucking *drink* he was so thirsty so thirsty so…

There were noises in what he thought was a language he used to speak. None of it made sense. *Noise noise noise.*

Fuck. He was *so. Thirsty.*

'James. James. James, talk to me. Look at me.'

James bared his teeth and he may have hissed. There was another smell, strong. Chemicals. Paint and canvas. Tea and biscuits. The nest. The nest and home and tea and…

'Gabriel.' His voice rasped. James realised suddenly that Gabriel was wrapped around him, that the blood he could hear in living veins belonged to Gabriel. Gabriel. The nest. Home. Not food. *Home.* James shuddered and pressed into the arms wrapped around his shoulders, pushed his forehead into the chest that blocked his transformed face from view. 'Help me.'

Gabriel pulled James to his feet and James stumbled up, hiding his face in Gabriel's jacket, trembling with the effort not to bite, or to fall to the floor and *lick lick lick lick what a waste of all that blood*. He couldn't suppress a whimper as Gabriel dragged him out the door and onto the street again. Into the tiny, overgrown garden, between the house and the street with its sounds and scents of passing people/food/*not food/people*.

Hands pulled him to the ground, cradled his shuddering body between the shelter of the plane tree and the briar rose.

James clung to Gabriel and pushed his forehead against Gabriel's chest. 'Too much. Too much,' he muttered, 'I havenae... I havenae eaten. Too much. It's too much.'

'I'm sorry,' Gabriel stroked James's back, and his hair. 'I dropped the blood. I shouldn't have washed it away. We could have...'

'Mae fault,' said James, with a curious lisp because his teeth wouldn't retract; were longer than usual, aching with the wanting to *bite*. 'Mae responsibility. Mae...' He groaned and leaned further into Gabriel's hold.

'If you drink now, will you be all right?'

'I-I-I need...'

'James, if you feed a little, can you cope? We need to find Grimshaw, but we'll get a cab home instead, if that's what you need.'

A dry, hacking laugh escaped James's watering mouth. 'Might eat... the cabbie.'

Gabriel bent and wrapped himself further around his friend.

'Maybe,' rasped James.

'Maybe what?'

'Maybe. If I. Feed. Maybe. I can. I can. Maybe.'

The lack of coherence wasn't good, but Gabriel didn't hesitate. He pushed up a sleeve and shoved his forearm in front of James's mouth.

'Nae,' James keened, even as he pulled Gabriel's arm up to his teeth.

'Well, I'm not going to let someone else do it,' Gabriel admonished him, wincing as the fangs slipped into his skin.

James sucked strongly on the wound. He drank for almost a half a minute this time. As Gabriel began to wobble dizzily, James pulled away with a grunt of effort. He licked the blood from around his mouth, and opened his eyes to look at Gabriel like a lost boy.

'Sorry. I'm sorry.'

'It's all right.'

James furtively licked at the glistening red holes in Gabriel's arm, then shoved the arm away again, averting his eyes. Full of shame.

Gabriel watched, fascinated, as the wounds healed. In his arms, James rasped like he was labouring after a marathon. Gabriel pulled James into a close embrace again. It wasn't like he actually needed to breathe, after all.

'Ye shouldnae…'

'Shh, James, shh. I'm fine. You're fine.' He kissed James's brow and finally, James abandoned any protest. He went still and might have been an actual corpse, if it weren't for his fingers flexing minutely against the worn leather of Gabriel's coat.

'Thanks,' said James at last.

'We should go home.'

'No. We need tae go in. Find Grimshaw and West.'

'I know, but–'

James hauled himself to his feet and straightened his collar, his jacket, checked for bloodstains on his mouth and clothes. His fangs disappeared. He carefully scrutinised Gabriel too, anxiously inspecting his unblemished arm for any sign of lasting harm.

Gabriel placed a hand reassuringly over James's. 'No blood spilled,' he said, meaning none on his clothes or skin.

'No. It's too precious to waste,' said James seriously. Then, changing the subject, he said, 'There's something not right in there.'

'Apart from the spectacular exsanguination?' Gabriel hid his horror beneath a determination to be unwavering, for James's sake.

'Apart from that, aye.'

'Shall we, then?'

They walked back inside the house, bracing for a repeat of James's meltdown, but he was calm, and in control again.

'You okay?' Gabriel checked anyway.

'Aye. It's intense, but,' he smiled oddly, 'I have *precious* blood in me now, given freely. That means something.'

'Being a vampire is metaphysical as well as physical?'

'Yes.' They reached the living room, and James ignored all the wasted blood and inspected the body.

'Oh Christ. It's Blue,' said James staring fixedly at the boy's face.

'Blue?' Gabriel hugged himself and kept his eyes on James rather than on the carmine-soaked room.

'A lad from the clinic. Peter something. A street kid. He came in for blood tests and a check-up; said he'd found someone to take care of him. I shouldhae realised he was setting up with a vampire. But this doesnae make sense. No vampire would waste blood like that without good reason. I have tae talk to Grimshaw. He must be here somewhere. I can *smell* him.'

'This is his... coterie, then?'

James snorted humourlessly. 'Such as it was.'

Gabriel grimaced. "Coterie" was a grand name for a vampire and a young man living in a perfectly ordinary middle class terrace house in Clapham.

James paused. Raised his head. Sniffed.

'Fuck.'

'What?'

'West. It's faint, but he was here. I wouldn't be surprised if he killed Blue to punish Grimshaw for doing such a piss-poor job of luring me in, or for trying to ally himself to me behind West's back. That'd be his style – killing Grimshaw's blood supply. Wasting it.'

Gabriel started to speak, but James held up a hand. He cocked his head, listening intently.

'West?' mouthed Gabriel.

James shook his head. 'West's long gone.' For a man already bloodlessly pale, he looked ill. 'We need to get into the space above the sitting room.'

They found the hatch into the crawlspace between floors, above the kitchen door. James pulled a chair underneath the hatch, opened it and climbed into the space. Once inside, he offered an arm to Gabriel and pulled him swiftly up.

'Stay behind me,' he murmured. 'Though if this is what I think it is, feel free to stay in the kitchen.'

Gabriel had no intention of leaving James to face whatever this was. He crawled along behind as the vampire made his way across beams in the direction of the living room.

The body James was seeking was propped up across the beams. Where its head rested, several holes had been drilled.

'Grimshaw?' James's voice was very quiet.

The body made a noise – a groan or a hushed wail. James put a hand out to the head that made the sound without touching it.

'West,' breathed James. 'Fucking sadist.'

Grimshaw groaned in despairing agreement.

Gabriel didn't have supernatural eyesight, but soon his eyes adjusted enough to see what James had found.

Grimshaw – he had to assume it was the Mordecai Grimshaw who had visited their home scant hours ago, because he was almost unrecognisable – was pitiful. He evinced *pity*. Gabriel wouldn't even attempt to deny it. Not with the man himself – and he had once been a man, Gabriel reminded himself – lying there, unable to move.

Legs and arms hacked off; the ragged, unbleeding wounds suggested a simple saw. Eyes intact and permanently staring, with the lids sliced off, maybe with a hard, sharp vampire thumbnail; the same method could have been used to slit Blue's throat. Tongue cut out, or pulled. A pair of pliers on a crossbeam suggested as much.

The vampire was toothless as well, every tooth gone, but most obviously the ones that a vampire used to feed. This maiming had been vicious and vindictive.

Piles of ash heaped around the crawlspace suggested that the removed limbs and organs had reverted to dust soon after each procedure.

Gabriel, aware suddenly that his knee was embedded in what may once have been an arm, recoiled. Dust puffed up and he tried not to inhale. After that, he remained still, his skin prickling with horror.

Grimshaw had been maimed and propped up in the roof cavity; holes cut in flooring and his eyelids removed so that he had to watch the murder of his... pet? His friend? As he was James's?

James spoke softly to Grimshaw. 'I can end this. If you want. I'm sorry. I'd no idea he'd do this.'

Grimshaw moaned softly. He said, 'Paaaaaahh,' which Gabriel, nauseated, supposed was what "please" sounded like when you had no tongue and no teeth.

Gabriel would have preferred to get away as far and as fast as possible, but there was a reason for all of this, and he had to know. If there was a way to do it, they had to stop West's bizarre vendetta. Six people dead. Seven, with Blue. And now this poor bastard. Gabriel's flesh crawled right down to the bone with how cruel this was; with how cruel he'd been himself, making snarky comments while Grimshaw writhed with pain in their living room, a garlic-slicked silver blade in his leg.

'Can you tell us anything about West?' asked James. 'Where he is? His plans?'

Grimshaw stared at him. 'Baaaaaw,' he said. 'Haaaa'wa'weeeem Baaaaw. Ahhhwwp Baa'eeee.'

James patted Grimshaw's head soothingly. 'It's all right. Shh.'

'I think he's saying Halloween Ball,' said Gabriel grimly, who had held conversations with the toothless and impaired before. 'A Halloween Ball.'

'Aaaahhth,' agreed Grimshaw, nodding.

'Where?' Gabriel asked.

Grimshaw tried to oblige. 'Ahhhwwp Baa'eeee,' he repeated.

Gabriel rolled the other sounds round his mouth, holding his tongue out of the way, trying to discover the originating words. 'Or?'

Grimshaw scowled. '*Ahhhwwp* Baa'eeee.'

James tried. 'Not "or". There's a final consonant. Orb? All?'

'Awwwwb. *Waaaaawb*. Bwaa'heee.'

'Ward?'

For someone so physically ruined, so appallingly disfigured, Grimshaw managed to convey his disgust and irritation very well with a contortion of his expression. He closed his mouth and hummed instead – an old hymn that made him wince to sing.

James hummed along, before singing, without similar signs of pain, '*In pastures green, he leadeth me, the quiet waters by…*'

'*The Lord's My Shepherd*?' queried Gabriel. At Grimshaw's relief, he said, 'Lord? Lord someone? What Lord? There are hundreds of the bastards.'

'*Bwaa'heee.*' It might have been blackly hilarious if it weren't so completely ugly and awful.

Gabriel rolled the sound around his mouth. A Lord having a Halloween Party. Lord… *Baa'eee. Bwaa'hee.* If Waawb was Lord, then… Gabriel tried jamming an L in place of the W. *Blaa'hee.*

'Christ, you don't mean Lord Blakely's annual shindig, do you? Anything else?'

Grimshaw gave him a look of pure poison.

'And West is up to something there.'

The tension left Grimshaw's brutalised body, now that he'd finally made himself understood.

James turned back to his patient. 'Do you want us to get you out of here?'

Grimshaw shook his head.

'You want me to…? Are you sure?'

The pure poison was turned on James then.

Gabriel had learned from James that vampires could heal quickly. Any cut, any crush injury, any bullet hole, and a vampire's body could repair itself. Even the silver-and-garlic wound Grimshaw had suffered that morning in his trespass at

Ivy Gardens had healed once the offending substances were cleaned from the wound.

But a vampire couldn't replace a severed limb or a removed organ. Granted, most of its organs weren't necessary to its existence, except the heart and brain. But limbs were quite important. The teeth were vital.

James patted Grimshaw's skull again, and Gabriel marvelled at how James Sharpe could still be a doctor while at the same time being a vampire.

'I'm sorry. But I swear, we'll stop him.'

Grimshaw gave a shuddering sigh.

'Gabriel, you have the knife?'

Gabriel pulled the silver blade from his pocket. James took it gingerly and wrapped a handkerchief around the hilt so he could hold it without it itching.

'This will hurt. I'm sorry.'

Grimshaw rolled his eyes with irritation.

'Gabriel, cover your mouth.'

Gabriel, keenly not wanting to inhale dead vampire, pulled his scarf up over his mouth and nose. James waited until he was ready, then put his hand over Grimshaw's chest. Once he was happy he'd found the right place, he looked Grimshaw in the eyes.

'I'm sorry about Blue, too.'

Before Grimshaw could grimace at him about that as well, James plunged the knife in, hard, fast, straight through skin and muscle and into the bloodless heart. He twisted as he stabbed, and pulled out just as fast, destroying the organ. He sat back on his heels.

Grimshaw's body quaked briefly then dissolved into dust.

James frowned at the pile of ash where a person once had been. 'Right,' he said, 'let's get the fuck out of here. I need a shower. And a cup of fucking tea.'

They made their way back to the hatch and into the kitchen. James wiped down the surfaces they'd touched, grateful that neither of them had touched the front door handle. He didn't want to go past Blue again.

'Maybe we should see if we can get out the side way, or over the back fence,' suggested Gabriel.

They took the back way out.

Once home, James retreated to his room while Gabriel showered Grimshaw's dust off his skin.

The backyard retreat had been necessary, both of them reluctant to be confronted again with that sweet-stinking bloodbath. For James, it wasn't only fear of triggering the thirst frenzy. The shame he felt was not solely about having lost control at the Clapham townhouse; or about having fed from Gabriel.

He could have explained it to Gabriel with a half-truth.

A house on patrol. The Taliban had killed everyone. Men, women, kids. Blood everywhere. Walls painted red. So much blood.

But James didn't know if Gabriel would understand, let alone forgive, the whole truth.

Cael West killed that family. He offered them to me alive and the father begged me to let his children live. He offered me his throat and I didn't mean to be the death of him. I only meant to drink a little. I took more than I meant. He was nearly dead of blood loss when I stopped. Too late to save him, but I stopped.

'Yer doing but nae yer choice, Jamie,' he heard his grandfather's memory-ghost say.

But West wasn't happy with that, Granda. When I refused to finish draining that poor bastard, West killed the whole family, for spite, weans and all. So fast. So fast. He was full of blood and at the peak of his power, and I was a half-starved new vampire and I couldnae stop him. The walls dripped red with wasted blood because I refused to kill.

'Nae yer fault, lad.'

I tried to kill West. I was so angry. Too angry. I didnae kill him. I missed. He pulled the stick of wood I'd missed with from his gut and told me he had plans. 'We could have used you in my team,' he said to me. 'We've got plans back home, we have, me and my mate. You could have been part of it. Remember that, Doc. When it's too late for you to be part of it.'

Then the sick shite laughed at me and left me wi' the dead. Walls painted red. So much blood.

I failed, Granda. All of these murders and whatever he does next, that's mae *fault. I shouldae killed him and I failed.*

Granda's memory had nothing to say to that, it seemed.

James pressed the heels of his hands into his eyes, but that never did anything to wipe the blood-soaked memories.

Well, to hell with all of that blether.

Cael West was going to a posh Halloween party at a Lord's house next week, and James Sharpe was going to be there to put a stop to him.

James's fangs and clenching fingertips tingled in anticipation.

Chapter Ten

'GABRIEL. THIS *IS* UNEXPECTED.' MICHAEL IN FACT SOUNDED FAR FROM astonished to hear from his brother, 'Everything working out splendidly at your new abode?'

It annoyed Gabriel, how unsurprised his brother could appear on the rare occasions when Gabriel initiated contact. But he couldn't afford to be annoyed. He needed information.

'Better than splendid, as if you didn't already know.' Not a great start. Annoyance was a default setting, apparently, and Michael was always keeping bloody tabs.

'Indeed, but it's good to have confirmation. What is it you want?'

'Why would I want anything?'

'You have called me precisely three times in the last twelve months. Once from a gallery exhibition to state that, despite expectations to the contrary, someone wanted to buy your paintings and would I please tell the old bastard to stop trying to buy you back with family money you didn't want. Once when you were drunk to tell me that our father is a complete prick, which I know. And once to get me to send you some of your old clothing that was gathering dust in the attic. You're not drunk, so you must want something.'

'Fine. I've heard that twat Tony Blakely is holding his usual Halloween party next week.'

'Do you mean our county neighbour, Anthony Blakely, Earl of Winchester and Secretary of State for Environment, Food and Rural Affairs?'

'That's the twat,' confirmed Gabriel. 'Is he still a prize tosser who thinks homeless people should be rounded up in camps in Slough to keep London a city fit for heroes?'

'What about the party, Gabriel?'

'Is it at his bloody great mansion in Kings Worthy, or his town residence?'

'Why do you need to know?'

'A customer at the gallery who bought one of my paintings mentioned it. He wants me to bring Helene along to meet some people who want to buy my stuff, support the gallery. I'd rather fry my own bollocks in yak butter, but it'd be good for Helene. I figured if I at least knew which of his gilded halls I'd have to go to, I can plan my escape routes accordingly.'

'Plus you would be delighted to sell your paintings under the nose of the Slough-centric, titled twat?'

'Would I?'

'The function will be held at Kings Worthy. You'll need an invitation.'

'Maybe I can slide out of the whole rank affair after all.'

'Let us all fervently hope so. Is that all?'

'Until the next time I need something. Or I'm drunk.'

'Quite.'

But before either of them could hang up, Gabriel surprised even himself with, 'Michael, wait.' Spoken abruptly, with sudden, unexpected urgency.

'Yes?' Michael's tone was cautious.

'Do you remember when I was a kid, how I used to see ghosts?'

'Yes. Of course I do.'

'Did... did you ever see any?'

Gabriel was the one to break the very long silence. 'Because I was thinking the other day that sending me away for shock therapy and medication every time I mentioned it was a bit extreme.'

'It was.'

'You weren't home for most of that.'

'No.'

'Our old man's a cockweasel.'

'Yes, Gabriel. He is. And in answer to your question – perhaps. You may not credit it, but I had a very vivid imagination when I was small. Father wouldn't stand for it, of course, and I stopped seeing them.'

Gabriel was not sure what to make of that answer, so he ignored it. 'Right then. Bye.'

For a time after they'd rung off, Gabriel stared at his unfinished canvas of James Sharpe, and wondered whether or not his older brother had seen the ghosts in their childhood house. And whether he had ever believed they were real.

James made a few phone calls of his own, to people he hadn't spoken to in a long time. Old army buddies, mustered or invalided out both before and after his own medical discharge. Most of them didn't mention the long intervening silence. Everyone knew that war service, and coming home, hit people in different ways.

Few of them could help, though. Only one had seen Major West in London since their return.

'I thought I saw him hanging around with some squirly Geordie near the British Library one week,' said former Corporal Sunil Juhekar, 'But I had to be mistaken. Wasn't West killed in an ambush like the one that did your head in?'

'They never found his body,' James said.

'Yeah, well that was West all over, wasn't it? Creepy bastard never did anything by the book, unless he thought he could do someone over with it. We used to pray he'd get his head shot off on patrol. I'm sure he got Howie and Kele killed that time. Thank fuck

General Penry pulled him in to HQ before he got the rest of his unit blown up.'

Or drained them, James thought, thinking bitterly of the men's more likely fate.

'Why're you asking, anyway?'

'I thought I saw him the other week,' said James, 'And I thought if I wasn't seeing things, he might have been around London for a while.'

'I suppose if anyone could have crawled out of that firefight and buggered off without a trace, it'd be West. I wouldn't put it past him to be AWOL either. If I see him again, Jim, I'll give you a buzz. How've you been, any rate? Feeling... better?'

It was, James reflected, a kind way to ask whether he was still stark raving bonkers.

'Still mildly loony, but doing well, thanks. Working part time as a GP in the East End. Mostly head colds, liver complaints and hypochondriacs. Nice and quiet with no loud noises. You?'

'Oh, you know. Rehab's going well. I'm learning to type left-handed and I'm being fitted for my prosthetics on Friday. I'm trying to convince the doc to give me a peg-leg, a hook and a parrot, but you know army services. "If you wanted to be a pirate, you should have got yourself blown up in the navy".'

'No imagination, those army types,' agreed James.

'Sad but true. Hey, when I've got my running legs back on, how about a curry and a pint?'

'That'd be good, aye,' said James. He hated the idea of trying to pretend to be anything like normal, but he hated the idea of Sunil thinking he was being abandoned.

'Jim.'

'Aye, Sunil?'

'I know what it's like. How lonely it is. Nobody gets it if they haven't been there.'

'I'm all right, Sunil. I've got friends.'

'Name three.'

'Sunil.'

'Nobody's heard from you in over a year. We've been worried, Jim.'

'I'm fine.'

'You seeing a therapist?'

'Sunil, I said I'm fine.'

'Sorry. Sorry, but maybe you heard. We lost Adrian last week. Hanged himself.'

James hadn't heard. 'Gabriel,' he blurted.

'What?'

'I can name one friend. Gabriel. He's an artist. Has a bit of history. He understands more than most.'

'Hey. That's good. I'm glad.'

'Aye. Me too. So. Maybe. Coffee. When you've got your running legs back on.'

'I'd like that.'

'We'll talk.'

James emerged from his bedroom, where he'd made the call, to find Gabriel in the kitchen with a tub of pig's blood, picked up that morning from the Italian butcher.

'I don't know how often you need this,' Gabriel said, reaching into the cupboard for a ceramic cup. 'But I thought you'd want something before we go looking for Hannah again.' He raised an eyebrow at James, who was staring at the cup as though it was loaded. 'What? Oh. Do I need to microwave it?'

James's expression was somewhere between shame and horror. 'You don't have to...' He petered out.

'I don't have to what?'

'Do that. Be here. For... that.'

Gabriel peered at him, at the container of animal blood and the cup, and then back at James.

'You know, I've seen grosser things than a tub full of blood.'

'Have you seen grosser things than someone drinking it?'

'Pretty sure I have.'

'You act like this is fine and normal.'

'You act like I give a toss that it isn't.'

Silence filled the space as they stared at each other.

'So. How long in the microwave?' Gabriel asked.

'Ten seconds is fine,' said James. 'Takes the chill off.'

'Right.' Gabriel decanted the blood into the coffee cup and put it in the microwave. They stood side by side and watched the cup circle around and around while the seconds counted down. The oven pinged. Gabriel retrieved the cup and handed it to James.

James stared at Gabriel. At the warm, thick liquid in the cup. Back at Gabriel. Down again. He sipped the blood. It smelled, as always, odd but compelling. He sipped it. Took another sip. Licked his lip to remove the smear of blood left there. He felt Gabriel looking at him expectantly.

'Mmm,' he said. 'Good. Just right. Thanks.'

Then he met Gabriel's gaze, his single upraised eyebrow, and they both started to giggle at the incongruity of it all.

'Well, what am I supposed to say?' demanded James.

'Nothing,' said Gabriel, reaching for the tea he'd left brewing. 'I'm pretty sure Debrett's doesn't have a chapter covering small talk over a cup of warm blood.'

'A shocking oversight.'

'I'll write them a strongly worded letter about this awkward social situation as soon as I get a moment.'

The tension broken, they sat on opposite sides of their table to drink their beverages.

'This is easier,' said James. 'Doing this out here. Not having to wait till you're asleep or out.'

'Good. And by the way, I have.'

'Have what?'

'Seen much grosser things than you drinking a mug of blood.'

James wished that Gabriel wouldn't keep being so blunt about it, and then decided he was glad for the bluntness. Euphemisms wouldn't change what he was, or what he did. Gabriel was meeting that head on. It was, he hoped, a healthy sign.

'No details while I'm drinking,' he said.

'You're squeamish? That must be a handicap.'

'You have no idea,' James deadpanned back at him.

'Let's talk about Hannah, and this Blakely party.'

The Halloween party at Lord Blakely's Kings Worthy property was five days away, which gave them very little time for learning the lay of the land and making plans for getting in, finding West and working out how to make him tell them what he was up to. Other preparations would have to be made as well, to ensure they had some kind of defence if necessary. They divided tasks for that venture between them, washed their cups and headed out to see if there was news on Hannah.

They found Switchblade Roy hanging about the Queen's Road off-licence a few roads from the clinic.

'Wotcher, Doc,' he greeted them. 'Gabe.'

'Hey, Roy,' Gabriel replied, tossing the man an unopened packet of Jaffa Cakes. Switchblade Roy caught them with a brief fumble and clutched them to his chest.

'Ta, Gabe. Them's me favourite. Easy on the teeth an' all. Though Pink Wafers is good too.'

'Wafers next time,' Gabriel promised.

'An' maybe them Bourbons? They were me gran's favourite.'

'Sure,' agreed Gabriel readily, still not asking what they had come to ask.

'I heard news about Hannah,' Switchblade offered at last. 'Fat Betsy, what knows her from around the dosshouse on Curzon Street, she says Hannah come in, grabbed a hat from lost and found and lit out of town. Reckons she had a niece down Bournemouth she was gonna see.'

'Did Betsy say why?'

'She said Hannah had the wind up pretty bad. Saw something nasty under the Chelsea Bridge, and said she wasn't waiting around for the same thing to happen to her, so she took off.'

So that, for the moment, was that. Gabriel pressed a folded five pound note into Switchblade's fist and thanked him. 'See you next week with the Wafers,' he said.

'And the Bourbons.'

'And the Bourbons.'

'Right you are. Wotcher, Doc, see ya at the clinic sometime.'

James and Gabriel watched Switchblade Roy leave, cheerfully chewing on a stuffed mouthful of Jaffa Cakes. James thought a vegetable or two might have been a better offering, but Roy's teeth were in terrible shape. A stick of celery might break another one.

'Think Hannah's clear of it?' he asked.

'I hope so. Depends on whether her niece exists, and if she'll help. It's bloody cold in Bournemouth in October if she has to stay on the streets, and she won't know the local safe places. I mean, relatively safe places.' Gabriel shook his head. 'Safer than here, anyway.'

'Right. Okay. Let's get to work on the other stuff, then.'

Other stuff included ongoing experiments with James's biology. Besides the experiments on his blood, James became curious about his body's capacity to heal quickly. Gabriel was both horrified and fascinated when James cut a stripe into his arm with a steel knife, only to have the wound knit up before their eyes. He cut a second, deeper wound, and it healed as quickly.

'No more of that,' said Gabriel gruffly, putting his hand over the newly unblemished skin.

'It stings, but not much,' James said, gently. 'It heals right up.'

'No,' said Gabriel, bothered more than he could say. 'Please. I don't like to see you doing that.' He swallowed. 'It's like what happened to Grimshaw.'

James pushed the knife away. 'There, gone. No harm done.' He knew he wasn't invulnerable. Grimshaw's fate made that clear. But it warmed him that it mattered so much to Gabriel.

On impulse, Gabriel lifted James's hand so he could drop a kiss on the skin that showed no sign of scar or bleeding.

James, just as impulsively, lifted a hand to pet Gabriel's head, to slide his fingers through the locks of Gabriel's dark, unruly hair.

The next round of experiments with James's healing ability began the next day, when Gabriel had warmed up a cup of blood for James and made tea for himself. He jumped up too quickly to answer a phone call from Helene, upsetting the teapot and spilling scalding tea all over his hand. He dashed to the sink, swearing, to plunge his hand under a torrent of cold water, and swore again when James inspected the damage. Gabriel snatched his hand away, hissing with the blooming pain of the burn.

'For God's sake, Gabriel, hold still. Let me see it. I'm a *doctor*.'

Gabriel, wincing, allowed James to inspect his hand. His index finger was blistering, the skin around it red and puffy already. He was not expecting it when James bent to the injured finger and licked it. He licked it a second time, then put it in his mouth. Gabriel stared in astonishment when James swirled his tongue around his finger, wetting it thoroughly with saliva, then withdrew it to lick all around it.

He gaped at his finger and hand, no longer red; looking perfectly healthy and unharmed. 'So it doesn't only work on the bites you make,' he accused.

'No,' said James sheepishly.

'It's magic doctor spit.'

'To be technical, it's magic *vampire* spit.'

'So technically, if you kiss me, you really will be kissing it better.'

James began to laugh. 'I suppose, technically, yes.'

Gabriel beamed. 'Nice.' He offered his cheek and James, with great ceremony, pressed a soft, lingering kiss to it. Gabriel tilted his head so that his lips met James's. Their eyes met, warm and delighted, then drew apart, not wanting to push too far.

Then James reached for Gabriel again, his hand sliding around Gabriel's waist. They touched these days: they could hug, and he liked that. He had missed that, and he'd missed this, the warmth of kissing another person. He liked kissing Gabriel. He liked how he felt, as though he were alive again, still human, still capable of loving and being loved.

He stretched up and pressed his mouth softly again to Gabriel's, holding to his waist gently, giving Gabriel every chance to draw away. Instead, Gabriel wrapped his arms around James and returned the kiss, softly, too, at first, then harder, more demanding.

James lifted his free hand to Gabriel's jaw, rubbed his thumb along the line of it, loving the texture of stubble on his fingertips. His fingers continued along to his hairline, and James's hypersensitive skin felt every strand of Gabriel's dark hair that bore the splendid scent of oil paints, Gabriel's lemon-scented shampoo, and his own clean maleness.

Gabriel made a low, sweet sound and tentatively brushed the tip of his tongue along the inside of James's lip. James sighed low himself as he deepened the kiss, wanting no breath in him but Gabriel's. Gabriel didn't shy from him, but kissed him more deeply still.

As Gabriel's heartbeat quickened, as he became warm and pliant with the kiss, James treasured the willing surrender. Trust and need tasted like this. Like belonging.

When the kiss finally ended they stayed in each other's arms.

'See?' said Gabriel languidly. 'All better.'

Chapter Eleven

TOWARDS THE VERY END OF JAMES'S CLINIC SHIFT THE NEXT DAY, THE staff and patients heard the sirens. Someone came in with the word. Something terrible had happened at the Donal house, three streets away; his dodgy business interests coming home to roost in the most dreadful way. *Even the kids*, was the horrified, salacious whisper.

James wondered if this latest tragedy related to Cael West's vicious doings. He detoured by the Donal's street on his way home. There was crime scene tape, cars with flashing lights and both uniformed and plainclothes cops all over the place. James listened and inhaled deeply, but no scent of West greeted him – only blood masking the usual suburban smells. The conversations he heard didn't indicate anything strange.

But he could hear a grown woman crying.

Concerned, James followed the sound to a narrow service alley half a block away from the Donal house, beyond the cordoned crime scene.

He knew Sergeant Tavisa Datta by her scent before he saw it was her. He was tempted to walk on by, but whatever else he was, and however angry she made him, he was still a doctor, and she was a person in distress.

James stepped down the service alley.

Datta was hunched against the wall, hands clutched in her hair, hiding her face. Every now and then, she emitted a sharp sob. She was clearly trying her hardest not to cry and failing terribly.

She glared up at him. 'What are you doing here?' Her voice shook.

'Walking home. I live a few streets that way, remember?'

She pressed her forehead against her knees. James could hear her teeth chattering.

'Sergeant Datta–'

'Four dead,' she said in a voice that was almost a moan. 'Mother. Father. Son. Daughter. Mum, Dad and the boy have their throats slashed. The son will be in the front hall. He tried to run. He was only 12. The father will be in the back garden. There'll be fourteen stab wounds. The killer really, really hated him.'

Her next breath juddered in; hissed out. 'The mother will be upstairs in the daughter's bedroom. The blood will have soaked into the duvet. A Wonder Woman duvet. It's pooling on the floor against the doll's house. A big plush teddy bear is soaking it up. So much blood, Doctor Sharpe. The smell of it. *The smell of it.*'

James knew exactly what she meant.

'I don't want to do this anymore,' she said, and wept.

'Sergeant?'

'I haven't been to the scene yet. But I know what's there.'

Many years ago, James Sharpe would have assumed fatigue or drugs or psychosis. That was before Afghanistan and Cael West, and waking up dead.

He wondered which kind of monster Tavisa Datta would turn out to be, and why he'd never noticed before.

'I dream things,' she said. 'And they come true.'

Oh. That kind of monster.

'You don't make them happen,' he said, as kindly as he could.

'How do you know?'

'How could you possibly cause them with a dream?'

'I couldn't,' she decided. 'But I can't stop it either. I don't know why I see these things if I can't stop them.'

'Things don't always make sense. They're not always for a reason.'

'*That. Doesn't. Help.*'

'I know.'

She glared at him with as much fear as ferocity. 'He's going to hurt you, Doctor Sharpe. Kill you. Gabriel Dare.'

'No he won't.'

'It's what I see. When I see *you*, all I see is a dead man. Which is horrible, I know. I'm sorry. But you look dead to me. I can't see what you look like alive any more. Too pale. Like you don't breathe. Just a trick of the brain. This crazy brain.' She tapped her temple with her forefinger and tried to pretend it was a joke, but she was crumbling to pieces instead.

James wondered what the hell he was supposed to say next, but Datta hadn't finished. The anger rose up over her fear.

'I keep *telling* you. Gabriel Dare will kill you one day. *I saw it.*'

'What did you see? Him killing me? My body?'

'Yes. No. Yes. I don't know. But your body is there. There's a body, covered in blood, and you're next to it, not a mark on you. Sitting there. Not breathing. Pale as death. No pulse. You're next to the body Gabriel Dare killed and you're dead, with a look on your face like you've been betrayed, or like your best friend died, because you know. You *know*. He's going to be the death of you. Get out while you can. Please. Please.' The rage was gone again, leaving only the despair. 'I know I'm a freak, I *know* it, but I've *seen* this. I dreamed that body two years ago and I know Gabriel has something to do with it. I've never trusted him. He's going to become a killer. When I saw you with him, I realised you were the one I'd dreamed of. And now when I have that dream, I know what's coming and I can't...I can't *stop* it.'

James remained steady in the face of her certainty. After all, he was the one who knew he was already dead. 'I believe you, all right? I believe you see what you see.'

She gave him a sceptical look.

'I've seen a lot of the world, Sergeant Datta,' said James. 'I've seen a lot of strange things that can't be explained by science.' *Done a few by now, too.* 'One bloke I served with in Afghanistan dreamed things exactly three days before any IED incident. So I believe you when you say you're having precognitive dreams. But it's a *dream*, open to interpretation. You're not interpreting it correctly. You can't be. Gabriel won't kill me. He can't kill me.'

'Don't be stupid. You're flesh and blood like anyone. Being ex-military won't help you. Thinking he's your friend won't save you.'

Being dead already might. But he didn't say that. 'I'll keep it in mind, then. But it doesn't mean what you think it does.'

She shook her head. Slowly, like every bone ached, she stood and scrubbed her face with her hands until the tears and despair were gone, and only the distrust and rage were left.

'I have to go. The DI needs me.'

James stepped back to give her space. 'What about the daughter?'

'What?'

'The daughter. You described everyone else. Where's the daughter?'

Datta scowled. 'Leave it.'

'Not in her room?'

'No,' she snapped, 'She's not in her room. She's in the dark. Surrounded by blood and eyes. And she's dead. Like the rest of them. I'm going to get there too late.'

At James's searching look, her scowl twisted into an expression that betrayed her despair again. '*That's what I see.* Eyes and red and darkness and she stops breathing. She's five years old and she stops breathing before I find her.'

James met her despair with a challenge. 'Let's go find her alive, then. Prove your dream a liar.'

'They haven't lied before.'

'They haven't met me before.'

Sceptical, yet desperate for hope to hang onto, Datta clenched her jaw, drew herself up tall, and walked down the street into her nightmare.

DI Bakare started in on her immediately with, 'Where the hell have you been?'

'Sorry sir,' said Sergeant Datta tersely. 'I was held up and then I bumped into Doctor Sharpe. Any developments?'

'Still trying to find the daughter, Penny,' said Bakare wearily from where he stood beside the body of a young boy in the hallway. The child's throat had been slashed. The DI glared at James. 'This isn't a sightseeing tour.'

'I'm a doctor. I caught the basics from the Sergeant and thought if you found the girl I might be of use.'

Bakare conceded the point. 'It's an ugly crime scene.'

'I'm an Afghanistan veteran,' said James, 'I think I can handle it.'

'All right, but keep back. Don't want the crime scene contaminated.'

'So what's going on? You're sure the girl wasn't taken?'

'Sure as we can be without witnesses, but we have to keep looking,' said Bakare.

Datta flinched, then squared her shoulders and scanned the scene.

'There's a ladder lying across the back garden, broken like it was dropped from a height, but it's too short to reach the first storey from outside,' said Bakare. He led them to the back of the house where a middle-aged man was sprawled in a pool of coagulating blood from multiple stab wounds. Exactly as Datta had predicted.

'Could the ladder have been used inside the house and thrown out the window?' said Datta.

'Perhaps – but by who, and why?'

'Is the mother upstairs?' she asked.

Bakare gave her a piercing look. 'Yes.'

Datta went upstairs, her DI and James at her heels, like she was walking to her own execution.

On the second level, a short corridor led to three bedrooms: the master bedroom, the boy's room at the front of the house, and the girl's bedroom at the back.

Bakare and Datta examined the body of the dead woman in the back room. Her throat was slashed, the blood soaked into the bedclothes. *Wonder Woman duvet.* It pooled onto the floor and the thick mess of it spread around a doll's house and into the feet of a teddy bear. *Big plush teddy bear.*

The smell of it was thick. James was glad he'd eaten well recently. It made his teeth itch.

Datta was practically quivering with rage, her teeth clenched. James could hear them grinding.

Bakare strode past it all to examine the window and study the sill, the handles, the tangled teddy-bear mobile that dangled from the curtain rod. He squinted into the garden; at the broken ladder below. He looked around the room and up at the ceiling.

'What?' James was puzzled but alert.

Bakare picked his way past them to peer in the wardrobe but was unsurprised to find it yielded nothing of interest. Then he stepped back into the hall and looked up at the high ceiling.

'Datta!'

James and the Sergeant joined the DI, who showed them the hatch in the ceiling – the kind that usually led to an attic. It was too high to be reached under normal circumstances. As James watched, Datta strode two steps into the hall and examined the wall beside the stair.

'Think you can get up there if I give you a hand, Sergeant?'

'Yes, sir.' Datta looked as though she would be ill.

James cocked his head and listened. Rustling. Maybe rats.

Maybe *not* rats.

'Here,' said James. 'Let me.'

To hell with witnesses. Whatever else was up there, Datta's dreamed *darkness* was part of it. He pulled his tie off and folded it into his pocket, removed his suit coat, which he left folded on the floor, and undid his top buttons. From a standing start, James leapt up and knocked the hatch open, hanging onto the edge with his fingers. He began to pull himself up into the space. It was an impressive physical feat to anyone watching, if they didn't know he was a vampire.

'The ladder used to rest here,' Bakare explained, fingers brushing over the section of paintwork that had been rubbed thin by the ladder. 'Positioned to easily use it to get up there.'

James leaned down through the hatch and offered his hand to Datta. She took it, not daring to hope, and with his easy, unnatural strength, he pulled her up into the dark and the dust with him.

'What are we looking for?' asked James, releasing Tavisa's hand. He was trying to listen, but there were too many noises. All those beating hearts, all those heavy breaths. A muddle. 'What did you see in your dream?'

'Eyes. Eyes and red.'

'What do you mean by 'red'?'

'Blood,' she said.

'No,' said James. He could smell no spilled blood up here. 'You'd have said blood if that's what you meant. Blood is what *red* makes you think of. What do you actually *mean*?' James, with his uncanny vision, was scouring the attic space, which was full of junk. Boxes and old furniture, bags of clothes, suitcases, a seamstress's model, an old exercise bike.

'I said *blood*.' Datta's voice was hard.

'But then you said *red*,' James replied, '*Eyes* and *red* you said.' He listened for breathing, for heartbeats. There were many small, rapid heartbeats further up in the roof. Rats, probably. In this room it was harder to hear. Datta's. Something else, maybe. Muffled. Too fast.

'Hurry,' James said. 'We're running out of time.'

'The red is… soft,' Datta bit out. 'Soft and silky. It flows. And it's very, very red. Scarlet. '

'Blood isn't soft and silky,' said James. 'It's wet and sticky, especially when it's coagulating. It's not scarlet either. Bright red when oxygenated, dark red, more carmine, without oxygen. What did it smell like? Did it taste like anything? Copper? Was it sweet?'

Datta grimaced disgust at him, but tried to remember. 'A bit sweet and it…. It smelled like lavender.'

'Lavender? Not cedar as well, by any chance? Or cloves or cinnamon?'

Datta's nose wrinkled at the dream-memory of scent. 'Very faintly.'

'My Granda used spices instead of mothballs. I think we're looking for a storage box or a trunk. Large enough for a child to fit into.'

James could hear it now, separated from Datta's own rapidly thumping pulse. The breaths were coming more harshly, and he could see a trunk in the darkness, behind a pile of suitcases.

'Here!' James started towards the trunk. 'You can see in the dust where everything's been moved!'

The two of them were throwing things out of the way, Datta not answering Bakare's demands from below to know '*what the hell is going on?* '

They reached the huge wooden trunk, stained and dented, old and heavy. From its seam, where the lid met the body, a scrap of scarlet cloth had escaped.

James threw the heavy lid open with ease. Inside the trunk, a pale face pointed up at them, surrounded by abandoned soft toys and old clothes for dress-ups, including a scarlet ball gown. The girl looked like a painting of the death of innocence.

Datta's sharp cry was desolate as James pulled the child out of her hiding place. She was tiny in his arms as he laid her on the floor.

'She has a pulse,' he declared, ensuring the girl's airways were clear before beginning CPR.

Datta stumbled, a fist shoved in her mouth to stop her own cries.

James breathed into the girl's lungs a second time, a third, a fourth, and on the fifth, there was a cough. A cry. James pressed fingers to the child's throat, even though he already knew her pulse was getting stronger.

The little girl opened her eyes, saw James, and screamed.

'It's okay honey,' said Datta, crawling forward to her. 'Penny. Sweetheart, it's okay.'

Penny's frightened gaze went to the sergeant and in the next moment, the five year old lunged away from James and fell into Tavisa Datta's arms.

James sat back on his haunches then leaned over to shout at those below: 'We've got the girl. She's alive.'

Datta had scooped the crying child into her arms and was rocking her back and forth, saying over and over, 'You're all right. You're all right, Penny. We found you in time. We found you. I found you.' The two of them, woman and child, cried through the ending of their terror together.

Penny Donal's auntie had been fetched, and she travelled with the girl in the ambulance as Datta and Bakare finished fitting together their theory.

The location of Mrs Donal's body in her daughter's bedroom indicated that she was the one who had taken the girl into the attic and hidden her in the trunk. She'd taken the precaution then of throwing the ladder into the garden through the bedroom window. Probably she had already found her son's body and had been frantic to keep Penny from harm. She can't have realised the lid would be too heavy for the girl to lift herself; or else thought she could persuade the killer to leave them alone. Perhaps she hadn't thought it through at all. She hadn't had much time.

Bakare peered past the ladder-scratched window sill into the garden, where Mr Donal's savaged body lay, not far from the broken ladder. 'Maybe if she hadn't thrown it, the killer wouldn't have realised she was up here and come to cut her throat.'

James stood as far from Mrs Donal's body as he could get and put his coat back on. The smell of the blood was getting to him. He was keeping his fangs sheathed with effort, and his hands were beginning to shake.

'You okay, Sharpe?' Bakare peered at him.

'Been better,' he said, jamming his hands into his pockets. This could have nothing to do with the other killings, he was sure. No scent of vampire anywhere. Only the blood. All the blood. *All the wasted blood.*

He shook his head to clear it. 'I should head home.' He started for the bedroom door, almost flinching as he passed by Mrs Donal's body and the blood-soaked bed.

'Don't worry,' said Bakare kindly, mistaking James's reaction, 'We'll have this bastard soon. Donal was known to us – small time drug dealer. He's been playing with the big boys, and it looks like the big boys didn't like his game.'

'We'll get him,' Datta said earnestly to James as she followed him down the stairs. He edged past the boy as well, and once in the street took deep breaths to clear his nose and head of the scent. He could still smell it, but it wasn't as bad outside.

'Are you all right?'

James opened his screwed-shut eyes to see Datta regarding him with concern.

'Too much blood,' he said without thinking.

'Yeah,' she agreed, but she smiled at him. *Smiled.* James had never seen her smile before.

'I'll be fine.'

'Well. Take care, anyway, and thank you.'

'You're welcome. I told you, those dreams don't tell the whole story.'

Datta grimaced. 'I like to think not. I joined the force because of those dreams, you know. Thinking I could make a difference. Until today, I never have. Perhaps I can again.'

'I'm sure you can. You weren't wrong in what you saw. You weren't right either.'

'I suppose. But be careful.'

'I don't need to be careful of Gabriel,' said James, exasperated.

'There's something out there,' she said darkly. 'It involves him, and it doesn't look good for you.'

'For either of us, I suspect. But I'll be careful of whatever's coming. Your dreams aren't inevitable. We simply have to work out what they mean.'

Gabriel was waiting when he got home, having returned from one of his sporadic days at the art supplies factory. He took one look at James and prepared a mug of warmed pig's blood for him, tea for himself, and sat them both at the table.

James's hands slowly lost their tremor as he sipped and told Gabriel about the murders and, more importantly for them, Datta's precognitive dreams – the driving force behind her antipathy towards Gabriel.

'She started having that dream before you and I even met,' said James.

'I could never kill you.'

'You could, you know, if you had to. Our research…'

Gabriel scowled fiercely. 'I *wouldn't,* then. And in any case, if I killed you now, you'd be dust, not sitting next to a corpse in the street looking tragic.'

'There is that,' James conceded, his hand resting on Gabriel's.

'She thinks she perceives me as dead because she's seen me dead in a dream. She's no idea she's seeing me as I am.'

Gabriel turned his hand palm-up and clasped James's in his own. 'I wonder what that dream's really showing her.'

'That's the million pound question, isn't it?' James squeezed Gabriel's hand gently.

As they finished their respective beverages, they continued to hold hands like it was the most natural thing in the world.

Chapter Twelve

JAMES DIDN'T NEED MUCH REST, BUT ON THE THIRD DAY OF PREPARATIONS, when Gabriel had to go out for more garlic, James took the opportunity to lie dormant for a few hours. He'd been ingesting blood more regularly and needed time to efficiently metabolise it. He locked up the flat, lay on his bed and closed his eyes.

It was dark when he opened his eyes again, stirred by a faint notion that something wasn't right.

That something was Gabriel's continued absence from the flat, hours after he should have returned home.

James tried to convince himself he was being alarmist. *Gabriel's a grown man. He'll be fine. Probably met a friend on the way to the grocer.*

Or Cael West has killed him.

Although his body didn't produce any burst of adrenalin, his brain remembered what alarm felt like, and James found himself panicking anyway.

If you've touched Gabriel, West, you gobshite, I will hack you limb from limb, like you did to Mordecai Grimshaw. Granda's voice of encouragement was notably absent, and had been ever since the incident at Grimshaw's house. *I will turn you to ash a piece at a time, you fucker, if you even think of hurting him.*

James decided he was fine with being alarmist. He'd apologise for making a tit of himself later if he had to. He grabbed his coat and keys and ran out the door.

He headed towards the grocer first, at a purely human speed, senses alert.

It was a grey day, the diffuse light gleaming off pale grey clouds from horizon to horizon. All the waterways of London were on the breeze; the bilgy swill of the dockyards, the dankness of the rivers trapped underground as their run-off spilled from narrow tunnels into the Thames; the whiff of Crossness Sewage Works; the salt tang of the distant Channel. The dampness in the air carried all kinds of smells, and obscured others. Hanging in it was the tantalising insinuation that Gabriel had passed this way, so faint he began to fear he was imagining it.

James stopped and asked an old man sitting, smoking, on a low brick wall if he'd seen 'a tall bloke, skinny, messy hair, green eyes. Good looking. Smells like paint.'

The old fellow gave him a piercing stare then a sly grin and pointed with the cigarette between his knuckles. 'Your boyfriend met some blokes down there,' he said, gesturing towards a narrow alley alongside the minimart. 'Hope he ain't cheatin' on ya. Though mebbe he's earning a bit o' cash on the side for the *rent*.'

James didn't dignify that comment with more than a half-animal snarl. In his shock, the man dropped his cigarette in his lap, making him leap up and dust the embers from his crotch.

There was nothing in the alley, narrow and squeezed in between high brick walls. The place smelled of piss and mud and fresh blood.
Fuck.

With a quick glance to ensure no-one was watching, James crouched, sniffing. When he found the few drops of blood, he sprawled on the stones, getting nearer to the source of the scent. He loomed over the blood spatter, less like an animal and more like an insect, balanced on the toes of his shoes and the tips of his fingers, practically licking the filthy cobblestones under his face.

He sniffed deeply, filtering out the stink of the refuse, of piss and vomit and decay. His tongue ghosted over the spots of blood amongst the debris. Some of it was unknown but human, the rest was definitely Gabriel's. He'd know the taste of it anywhere. Another flavour tainted his tongue as well – a sedative in Gabriel's blood.

Of the other scents, nothing reeked of Cael West. That was something, at least.

James knew it wasn't appropriate to go about town killing everyone who threatened Gabriel. But so help him, if the bastards who'd taken Gabriel had harmed him, they'd wish they hadn't been born. They'd certainly wish they didn't know how bones could look so white when *sticking out of their own fucking skin.*

His expression was no less disturbing than his thoughts. Blue eyes flat and bleak, mouth a hard line, he looked like a killing machine waiting to lock on to a target.

They cornered him here. He fought; was injured and bled, but not much. Got a bloodletting strike in too, good man. They drugged him and dragged him off. Within the last four hours.

He took off after the blood trails at a swift, loping gait that no human could match, no matter how drug-enhanced.

The trail led him to a row of grubby workshops, used mainly for automotive repairs. The odour of grease and rubber was pungent. He could smell Gabriel, olfactory neon in the stench, and he followed the scent to a locked metal door. James turned the handle; lock and all twisted clear of the door like so much tinfoil. James threw the mechanism aside and stepped into the darkness.

He stole quietly down corridors, past empty rooms with doors ajar. He stopped to sniff things. When he came to a set of stairs, he followed them down.

James came to a vacant chair, a crumpled newspaper beside it, and edged further down. He heard running water. Crinkling plastic as a packet of biscuits was opened. The rumble of a boiling kettle.

The tea-maker stared at James in surprise, opened his mouth to yell and found any sound cut off by the cold grip clamped around his throat.

'Where is he?' snarled James. His fangs were showing.

The man, unable to speak, rolled his eyes frantically towards the door. The sour smell of urine rose up as he pissed himself in terror. He tried to speak and couldn't, so James loosened his grip a fraction. 'Down the hall,' the man gasped out, 'We was just paid to bring him here, keep him harmless. Please. Please, don't kill me.'

James pushed his face close to the man's. 'If he's hurt, I'm coming back for you,' he said, vicious.

He dropped the man, who clutched at his bruised throat but did not take his eyes off James.

James crept further down the hall.

James didn't need his acute vampire hearing to identify Gabriel's laugh as it came ringing out of the room two doors down.

'You have a fabulously ugly face,' Gabriel crowed in delight. 'You would be a dream to paint. All those crags and shadows. Scars are hard to get right, did you know? They end up looking painted on, which they are, but they shouldn't *look* it, they should grow out of the skin, which they sort of do. I have painted a lot of scars. I'm getting much better at it. I'd rather there weren't scars to paint. My sitters would too, but that's life. That's the life I'm trying to show people. I could show people your life. Ugly, scarred, messed up. You'd be a fantastic subject. Only I prefer showing the hope. You're a mess. You gave up a long time ago.'

'Shut up,' snarled a voice. 'Will you shut the fuck up?'

James splayed his hand on the closed door and listened.

'Your mate there is less interesting, but I suppose having a boring face is a challenge on its own. I could do his posture more than his face. He's a homunculus with the face of an accountant. That's weird. That's weirder that most of the shit I've seen. And I've seen a lot of weird shit.'

'Shut up!'

James used all his senses to piece together the layout beyond the door. Besides Gabriel, there were the two men – Ugly Scar and Homunculus. James could smell gun oil and dried blood. Under Gabriel's run of odd commentary, he could hear a chair scrape, and impatient shuffling. One sitting, one standing. They smelled human.

'Is this a typical reaction to ecstasy? Is it? I don't generally take drugs and you shouldn't have shoved it down my throat like that. I'm not a cat. Is it supposed to make everything effervescent? *Eff-erv-escent.* You're all bubbly on your outlines. I should paint that, too. I smoked pot a couple of times at university. It was boring. Didn't do much except make me babble. I babble like a Babylonian. Ha! I'm funny. James would laugh at that.'

James was ostensibly unarmed, but he had teeth and he had two hands that could rip a human body to pieces. He hadn't done that to anybody yet, but he'd seen West do it. He knew he had the strength, if he had the motivation, and right now he was feeling pretty fucking motivated.

'Have I told you about James? He's *wonderful*. Smart, funny. Hot. He is so hot. Fantastic arse. But we're just good friends. He let me kiss him. It was lovely. I hope he lets me kiss him again. If he doesn't want sex that's okay. I like being with him. I liked kissing him, but we can just watch TV together if he wants. He's lovely. He's lonely. Like me. But he's so so so so so so wonderful. He's my *friend*. Way better than all of *your* friends. You need so many, and none of them are worth a fraction of James. Not even when you add them all up.'

James braced himself and put his weight back on his heel, ready to kick.

'You should meet him. Or not. Probably not. Definitely not, actually, you're not nearly good enough for him. But he's absolutely the best person I've ever met. Dead or alive.' Gabriel burst into uproarious cackles at his own private joke.

'Will. You. Shut. Up!' The sound of a chair scraping and someone standing up.

James kicked the door in and made straight for Gabriel, so that when the irate captor took his swing, suddenly a completely different face was in the way of the gun butt.

A completely different face that took the brunt of the blow with hardly a flinch and then delivered the most bowel-watering snarl of rage that the attacker had ever seen or heard in his life. He stumbled backwards, tripped over the chair and fell on his arse. James snatched up the dropped gun. Almost too swiftly to follow, he detached the magazine, shook out its cartridges and the one in the chamber, separated the slide from the body and dropped the halves on the floor.

Meanwhile, Captor Number Two, who had been leaning against a wall watching the proceedings while sharpening his hunting knife, lunged at James with the weapon.

James prised the hunting knife out of the man's grip as though taking a rattle from a child, wrapped his hand around the man's wrist and twisted. The snap of bone was audible even through the sudden, awful scream of pain. James shoved the man back over his already fallen comrade.

'Stay down,' he said, teeth showing. 'Or I'll put you down for good.'

With the captured blade, James cut Gabriel out of the ropes that held him tied to the metal rings in the wall.

'*Jaaaaames,*' crooned Gabriel. '*Helloooooo.*'

'Hello,' James gritted out, sawing at the ropes and catching Gabriel as he slumped. 'Sorry it took me a while to find you.'

'Have I been here long?'

'A few hours,' James confessed, holding Gabriel and checking his pulse, his pupil dilation and his breathing. 'I woke up an hour and a half ago to find you'd vanished.'

'Woke up? But you don't– Oooooh. *Ooooooh*,' Gabriel repeated, suddenly aware that something ought to be concealed from the strangers present. He draped his arms over James's shoulders. 'Sleeeep. I bet you're cute when you're asleeeeep.'

James shifted Gabriel in his arms, as though his tall friend weighed no more than a kitten, to inspect the contusion on his cheek, and the ones on his knuckles. He inspected the red swelling in the side of Gabriel's neck, too, where the hypodermic had gone in.

'Are you hurt anywhere else?' James demanded.

'My *priiiiiiiide*,' Gabriel drawled, trying to stand upright and failing. His knees sagged and James held him tight. He giggled. 'I survived on the streets for years, I can fight when I need to. I don't fight fair either, can't afford fair out there, nooooo, but they *snuck up on me*.'

Gabriel moaned and buried his face in James's shoulder. '*I'm so embarrassed*,' he wailed in a harsh whisper. 'One of them stabbed me in the bum.'

James arranged Gabriel against his chest and looked down. Gabriel's black jeans were cut near his right hip and blood stained the tattered edges of the cloth. James pried the cloth apart to reveal the small wound, barely a centimetre wide and very shallow. Blood had dried in a smear around the skin.

'Won't need stitches,' James reassured him. 'At least you bled enough to leave a trail.'

'Excellent,' said Gabriel, his voice at last beginning to slur. 'My bleeding arse left a trail. Like Goldilocks. No, not that one, the other one. Hansel and thingy. Can I be Gretel?'

'You can be whoever you like. Here, look at me. How many fingers am I holding up?'

'Three,' said Gabriel. 'I can see six, but that's the drugs talking.'

'Right. Hospital for you, then.'

'Oh Christ, no. Hate hospitals. Hate 'em. Sometimes they put electrodes on my head and make me…make me…' Gabriel began to twitch and clutch at James in fear. 'Don't make me go back. Don't let Daddy make me go.'

'Okay,' said James gently, 'We'll go home.'

'Home,' repeated Gabriel in a dazed, little-boy voice. He hugged James, snuggling in. 'You're my best friend,' Gabriel said, wilting into an exhausted, addled mess onto James's chest.

'You're mine too,' James said, holding him. He looked at the two men tangled together on the floor. Ugly Scar had the broken wrist; Homunculus was stretching for a firearm on the table.

'Don't,' said James. 'It won't kill me. You'll just piss me off. More.'

The man stopped.

'Who did this?' James asked.

Homunculus blinked rapidly and said, 'Don't know. We got the job through a third party, a bloke we do business with from time to time. He's a middle man, like. Grab the painter, he said, fill him full of happy-tabs to keep him quiet, wait for pick-up, we was told. Cash on delivery. Said a bloke named West would come for the little queer tonight.'

James lowered Gabriel gently to the ground, and then faster than the eye could see, he had a hand around Homunculus's throat. The man's eyes bugged out as he struggled for breath.

'Be very clear,' said James, his eyes black and his voice deadly calm, 'I love this man. If anyone touches him again, they'll answer to me. Nod if I have made myself clear.'

The man nodded frantically.

'Spread the word. To your contact. To anyone you know who might try again. Next time, I'll *kill* whoever hurts him.' James let him go and bent to help Gabriel up again.

From Gabriel came a giggle, muffled against James's chest. He regarded his former captor with a dopey grin. 'He loves me. Did you hear that? He loves me. And I love him.' He subsided back into a sleepy cuddle against James's shoulders. 'I want to go home. Let's go home James, and I can kiss you again.'

James scooped Gabriel up in his arms and walked out of the warehouse. He began to walk home, despite how conspicuous they were. It was no special effort for him, and he gave not a single fuck about the speculative glances that came his way.

However, he didn't want to draw the attention of the police, so after half a block James put Gabriel carefully on a bench and hailed a cab. He helped him into the back seat when the vehicle arrived. 'He's not feeling too well,' he said to the driver. 'I need to get him home.'

As the cab took them away, James kissed Gabriel's cheek – surreptitiously licking the contusion, covering it generously with vampire spit. The injury began to heal immediately. Carefully, he did the same to Gabriel's scraped knuckles, more concerned with healing the skin than the taste of blood, though the taste of him was comforting.

James couldn't provide the same treatment for the shallow knife wound in Gabriel's backside until later. He giggled at the idea of licking Gabriel's rump in the back seat of a taxi. He recognised the giddy relief in his reaction, but decided not to care. He *was* giddily relieved. Gabriel was alive, and relatively unharmed, and loved him.

Oh.

But that was definitely what Gabriel had said. Right after James's own unthinking confession.

He loves me and I love him.

James pulled Gabriel against him and pressed his nose against Gabriel's messy hair, inhaling his scent. Gabriel hummed happily and snuggled. James embraced him more closely.

It didn't solve anything, this sudden knowledge that yes, he could feel love, that he did in fact love Gabriel; or that Gabriel loved him back. James was still a vampire, with all the dangers and obstacles that implied. They were still in trouble that they didn't yet understand. Everything was still dangerous and impossible.

But I love him and he loves me, thought James, and right then and there, the knowledge made him strong.

James paid the driver – this life with Gabriel was getting expensive; James would have to save funds elsewhere this month – and carried Gabriel from the street to their building, up the stairs and into Gabriel's own bed. He fetched a jug of water and made Gabriel drink two full glasses before tending to his other needs.

James stripped Gabriel of everything including his pants, despite Gabriel's consistent giggling and claims of being ticklish, to check all the other minor wounds. Gabriel's body was distractingly beautiful – whippet-lean and strong. James very determinedly put on his Doctor's Hat and refused to let his gaze linger on anything except the injuries.

James began by pooling spit in his hand and rubbing it gently over Gabriel's cheek and knuckles again, to be sure they'd healed. Gabriel watched with an incongruously adoring half-smile. When James went to rub spit-moistened fingers on the hypodermic puncture wound in his neck, Gabriel instead stretched his chin up.

'Kiss it better?' he asked with a boyishly smirk.

James placed his mouth over the small wound. He licked at it with the tip of his tongue. Under his mouth, he could feel the fluttering rhythm of Gabriel's pulse, but he had no urge to bite. He licked the wound again, kissed the spot and sat back.

'You should fix my bum,' said Gabriel, turning over to bare the small wound in his naked backside, 'You can kiss that too if you like.'

'Did you just tell me to kiss your arse?'

Gabriel glanced over his shoulder, alarmed, but he grinned

suddenly at the humorous twinkle in James's eye. 'Just a bit,' he urged, waggling his bottom.

'You think because we've kissed now, I'll kiss you everywhere.'

'You don't have to,' said Gabriel, eyes wide. It had somehow stopped being a joke, even though it was still ludicrous.

James patted Gabriel's bare hip. 'Another time,' he said softly, 'When you're not out of your skull, eh?'

Gabriel sighed. 'Okay.'

James spit generously onto his thumb and rubbed it over the shallow cut. Gabriel giggled.

'Your hands are nice.'

'My hands are cold.'

'They're still nice. Gentle. I like your hands.'

James patted Gabriel's hip again. He helped Gabriel, too dozy now to help, into pyjama bottoms, then pulled the sheet and blankets up over him. 'You rest up. I'll be right here.'

'Thanks,' mumbled Gabriel, falling into sleep.

Gabriel woke later in the evening with a headache and a horrible thirst, but otherwise fine. After downing two more glasses of water and a couple of painkillers, he acquiesced to another swift, clinical examination from James, who declared him fit. 'But you should get more rest. It's late anyway. We'll get back onto this business in the morning, when you're fighting fit.'

Gabriel, too groggy and weary to argue, went back to bed. He slept fitfully, waking up periodically from formless dreams in which threatening shadows crowded round him, only to be driven back by the arrival of a shaft of intense white light, hard like a blade and as illuminating as the sun.

The fourth time he woke, Gabriel lay in the dark, listening. Even though he couldn't hear a thing, there was a quality to the silence that was familiar.

'James,' he called out so his voice would carry through his closed door.

Nothing.

'James, it's three in the morning.'

More nothing.

'James, it's not like I don't know you're out there.'

The door opened and James stood sheepishly in the doorway.

'I'm fine,' said Gabriel, spreading his arms to indicate how entirely he was physically fine.

'I see that. Aye.'

'But you keep checking on me,' he said, suddenly realising why he kept waking from his bad dreams.

'Aye,' James conceded, 'Am I keeping you awake?'

'No. At least. I don't mind. You make the nightmares push off. That's good.'

'Good.'

'Do you need to rest?'

'I'll be fine.'

'You need to though, don't you? Not resting can be as bad as not eating, for you.'

'Not quite that bad.'

'But not good.'

'Makes me a wee bit slow, I admit.'

'So. Rest up. I'm fine.'

'Right. Yes. Good idea.'

James didn't budge.

'Are you going to stand there all night?'

'Ah. No. Sorry. Sorry, I'll go.'

'Don't be an idiot. Come in here.'

James remained where he was, hand on the door handle. 'No. Really. I'm being stupid. I'll go.'

'No, you won't. You'll come in here.'

James sighed and neither came nor went.

'You think I don't know,' said Gabriel softly.

'I think you probably do,' countered James. 'Doesn't make it not stupid.'

'What I think is that it's frankly astonishing that you ever go into your dormant state when there is no one to guard you at your most vulnerable.'

'Gabriel–'

'And then today, you went into your dormant state to rest, and when you woke up, I was missing.'

James frowned.

'It's a measure of how remarkable you are,' said Gabriel, 'that you're putting off re-entering your dormant state tonight because you're worried, not about *your* safety, but about *mine*.'

'I know you're all right. Really. But I–'

'You don't have to justify a damned thing to me, James, and there are better options than enduring that which doesn't have to be endured.' Gabriel patted the bed. 'Stay here.'

James took a step towards the bed before he'd even thought about it. Then he took the remaining steps and sat on the edge of the bed. Gabriel arranged himself more deliberately and patted the space between his knees.

'I could go on the other side,' said James.

'You could,' agreed Gabriel, but he didn't adjust his posture. 'I'm not trying to have sex with you,' he elaborated at last. 'It's more I think you'll feel better this way. Safer. You said you can hear things while you rest. I know you can rouse quickly if necessary. So why should you be dormant, on your own, and vulnerable, when you can stay here with me? I'll watch your back and you can watch mine. This keeps us both safe.'

'It's hardly conventional,' James offered.

'Yes. Because you and me, we're all about convention,' replied Gabriel with a sardonic lift of the eyebrow. 'Anyway, you've already seen me naked. At least I've got pyjamas on now.'

'Well, with logic like that…'

'Exactly,' agreed Gabriel.

James, dressed but barefoot, crawled onto the bed and between Gabriel's knees. They arranged themselves: James on his side, head resting on Gabriel's chest, Gabriel with his right arm curled round James's back. Gabriel rested his cheek against the top of James's head.

'Is this all right?' James asked. He was nestled into the warm nook, one hand curved along Gabriel's pyjama-clad thigh.

'It's perfect.'

'You sure this is comfortable? I'm not too heavy?'

'You're not too heavy. Shh. Get your rest.' Gabriel pulled the sheet and duvet over the pair of them. He kissed the top of James's head. 'Good night.'

James sank into his dormant state. As Gabriel had stated, he could hear the world around him, but he didn't listen to it.

He heard the steady beat of Gabriel's heart under his ear. Felt enveloped by the heat of Gabriel's body. Heard his breathing, and felt his even breath as it flowed over his forehead, down the bridge of his nose. The scent of clean cotton, and of Gabriel's breath and his warm skin, permeated his senses. All noted and present, but not noticed, as such. An ambience. Warmth. Safety. Nest. All the parts of his home, present and correct.

After a while, James was distantly aware of something moving in his hair. A careful, even stroke, fingers brushing his hair and scalp. Lovely. Pleasant and comforting. He shifted slightly, then settled, content, not fully realising his face was pressed against Gabriel's throat, where the heartbeat, the warmth, the scent were strongest.

Gabriel continued to pet James's hair, feeling the fine, light brown strands against his fingertips.

James was so still, his body so cool to the touch, it was almost like cradling a dead body. But James did not have that utter heaviness of the truly dead. James wasn't presently breathing, but he had the carriage of a body held in sleep rather than in death.

James could have lain alongside him on the bed and been safe in his dormant state, secure that should something threatening occur, he would wake in an instant. But Gabriel liked this. Knowing he held James safe, as James had held him safe today. So here he was, protecting and being protected; holding and being held.

'James,' he whispered. 'Jamie.'

James's eyelashes fluttered. He could hear, whether or not he actively *listened*. Nobody but Granda had ever called him Jamie. Even in his detached state, the sound of the affectionate diminutive made him feel safe. More than safe. Beloved. *Treasured*.

'Thank you for rescuing me,' whispered Gabriel.

The corner of James's mouth curled slightly in a smile.

Chapter Thirteen

THE DAY BEFORE THE BALL AT KINGS WORTHY, GABRIEL SHOWCASED HIS outfit for the occasion.

'*That*,' said James in deep disapproval, 'is your costume for the Halloween ball?'

Gabriel swooped the opera cape in a dramatic arc and bowed. He straightened and angled sideways to give James another view of the long black trousers, white ruffled shirt and subtly stitched waistcoat underneath the red-silk-lined cape. The spats, James thought, were just insult added to injury.

'It theemed apt,' said Gabriel, then pouted his lips around his awkward dental caps. 'Thethe teeth make it difficult to thpeak properly. How do you manage it?'

James's teeth descended in a mock-predatory grin. 'Practice.'

Gabriel, unfazed, tongued at the points of his dental caps with an air of irritation. 'I thuppothe I'll have to leave them in a while, then.'

'You know, *I* could go as a vampire. Seeing as how *I'm the vampire*.'

'Don't be ridiculouth, Jameth,' said Gabriel with mock-hauteur. 'It'th not a "come ath you are" party. Bethides, I look the part more than you.'

'You're a cheeky bugger.'

Gabriel grinned, fake teeth and all.

James shook his head and retracted his fangs. He knew what Gabriel meant. Creatures of the night, according to the popular culture, weren't shortish, blue-eyed, stern-faced Scottish blokes with mousy hair. Tall, lean Gabriel with his mad artist hair and lanky grace was much more the Hollywood ideal.

'Tho,' said Gabriel, 'What'th your cothtume?'

'Guess.'

'Zthombie Doctor,' declared Gabriel.

'You are an impertinent bastard today.'

'Give uth…us a ki…kiss and I'll behave.'

James ruffled Gabriel's perpetually unruly hair and kissed him on the cheek. 'There you go.'

'Not what I meant.'

'I know.'

'Oh.'

'Here.' James slipped his arms around Gabriel's waist and gave him a chaste kiss on the mouth. 'Better?'

'Getting warmer,' said Gabriel, but he didn't push the issue. He hugged James and stepped back. 'Thith ith… is getting easier.'

'Try keeping the fangs inside your lip. You won't accidentally bite yourself that way.'

Gabriel gave him a keen look. 'Did you accthidentally bite yourself at the start?'

James's mouth pooched out in a clear reluctance to admit the truth, which he overcame. 'Once or twice.'

When he was done snickering at the mental picture, Gabriel fetched the latest volume of vampire case notes from the bookcase. James left him to it. He had a few items yet to prepare for his own costume.

The next night, they donned their outfits ready for their sortie to Kings Worthy.

'*That*,' said Gabriel in a voice of utter delight as James emerged from his room, 'Is your costume for the Blakely ball?'

James swept the tricorner hat from his head and bowed low and deep. The end of his cutlass poked into his long brocade galleon coat, lifting it sufficiently high to reveal his breeches and boots. He straightened and spread his arms wide, showing off the flowing shirt that draped nicely over the scarlet sash at his waist. The flow of the shirt mostly hid his service pistol, tucked into the sash at the opposite side to the cutlass. He hoped not to need either weapon, but he'd rather be unnecessarily armed than defenceless.

'Cap'n Kyd, at your service. *Aaaaarrr.*'

'You look good. Let me know if you need a cabin boy.'

James shook his head affectionately. 'You don't give up, do you? At Gabriel's apologetic grimace, James laid a hand against his chest. 'I don't mind, you know.'

Everything had been so different since James had rescued Gabriel. Those declarations of love may have been made under the influences of protective rage and mind-altering chemicals, but they'd been sincere. James had taken to staying in Gabriel's bed, reading while Gabriel slept, watching over him. He went dormant sometimes, cradled in Gabriel's arms. They kissed as often as they hugged now.

But James had not expressed interest in sex, and Gabriel, while flirting madly, didn't push for it.

'Whatever you want, Jamie,' said Gabriel, pressing his hand over James's. 'As much or as little. I'm pretty sold on you, you know.'

'Aye.' Delivered with a little grin, then, 'My Granda used to call me Jamie.'

'Oh…'

'Granda raised me, along with my mum,' James went on, quietly reflective. 'He was my Dad after mine ran off. He was always there when she had tae work. Nursed me through chicken pox. Taught me to play football and how to fix a car. Helped me with my homework, taught me how to cook so Mum could have dinner when she got home. He taught me how to be brave and to stand up for people less strong than me. I learned how tae be a man from my Granda. Everyone else, from Mum to my mates to the army, called me Jim, but I was always Jamie tae him.'

'If you don't want me to–'

'I do, though. Say it again.'

'Jamie,' said Gabriel softly.

'Aye,' sighed James contentedly. 'That sounds good.'

'Sounds good to me too. Jamie.'

James, smiling, lifted Gabriel's hand to his mouth. 'I hear you've got the hang of the teeth, there.' He kissed Gabriel's knuckles then let his hand go.

'Practice,' Gabriel grinned. He drew himself up to fully present the cape and the foam of white lace that bloomed at his throat. 'I'll do?'

'You will. Gabriel. I like your whole name. Like the archangel.'

'Hardly,' he laughed, though obviously touched by the sentiment.

'Well, it's true he had a flaming fuck-off sword. Are you armed?'

Gabriel held his cape back. The garlic-smeared silver knife was in its sheath at Gabriel's belt.

Satisfied that they were prepared for whatever West might bring, Gabriel and James went to their hired SUV for the drive to the Blakely Estate in Kings Worthy, Hampshire.

The drive west to the M25, then south through Farnborough and Basingstoke towards Winchester took nearly two hours. They filled the time initially by going over their plans and contingency plans until they were both on edge. After that, Gabriel found a classical music station. James hummed along with a few of the pieces, and made Gabriel laugh when he confessed to recognising them from childhood cartoons, and advertisements for laundry detergents and luxury motor vehicles.

James, at the wheel, rested one hand on the seat between them from time to time. When he did, Gabriel placed his palm over James's hand, brushing James's fingers with his own, as natural as if they'd been like this for years.

They turned off Basingstoke Road at a field still redolent to James's senses of the resident dairy herd. The narrow lane led to Lord Blakely's Frankenstein mansion. Only portions of the west wing had stone-and-mortar continuity with the building's Restoration origins. In the intervening 300-odd years, neglect, fires, and the indignities of changing architectural fashion, had given it a "made from leftovers" feel. It had also been altered to be used as accommodation for children evacuated from London during the Blitz and as a hospital for returned soldiers.

Since the 1970s, the Blakely dynasty had invested large chunks of their land-and-portfolio-derived fortune to restoring some continuity to the manor.

'I hated the Halloween parties my father dragged me off to there, when he couldn't be bothered to find a babysitter,' Gabriel had told James during the planning. 'The adults were so boring. I'd slip away to the east wing and study the portraits of Old Blakeley's ancestors. The ghosts were better company than the people. I thought the old man in the wig was funny. The little boy in the soaking wet breeches showed me the bricked up door in the old kitchens. The soldiers who'd died in the war hospital made me sad, though. They were always so bewildered.'

The Blakely manor's long, laurel-hedge-lined driveway was filled already with limousines, spotless four-wheel drives, one or two nondescript black sedans, and the occasional actual horse and carriage. The horses shied as James walked past, instinctively reacting to his otherness.

They stopped in the shadows beside a silver Jaguar and regarded the short stone staircase leading to the front entrance of the wide, whitewashed central section of the building. Without a formal invitation to the party, that wasn't an option – the elegant version of a bouncer was inside the entrance hall, checking arrivals against the guest list.

'You've been here,' said James. 'How do we get in?'

Gabriel indicated the bare grey stones of the west wing. 'Damn. I thought the second floor would be best, but that wall used to be covered in ivy. I assumed we could climb up.'

James followed Gabriel's gaze. 'That part's not the problem. I've just thought – won't they notice we don't belong when we get inside?'

'You've clearly never been to one of these posh country house shindigs. Everyone will assume that since we *are* inside that we *do* belong. If we can sneak in unseen, it'll be fine.'

James peered at the stone wall they were meant to climb. 'And you said the alarms won't be on.'

'They won't be armed because of the party.'

'Good. I can see where we can get up to the second floor.'

Gabriel followed James to a buttress at the corner of the west wing. No windows here. It was as private as they were likely to get.

'You're not afraid of heights, are you?' asked James.

'Not if I don't look down.'

'Don't look down, then. Hang on, tight as you like. It's not as if you can choke me, and you don't weigh much.'

Gabriel clambered onto James's back, wrapping wiry arms across his broad shoulders and chest, long legs around his waist. James jigged up and down to test the security of Gabriel's grip, then bent his knees and jumped straight up.

The leap took him to the angle where the buttress bent inward. His fingers grasped rough corners and edges in the stone. He jammed his feet hard against the wall and, after a moment to again test weight and balance, he began to climb.

Gabriel tucked his head against James's neck, the brim of James's tricorner bumping against his forehead. He saw the ground lurching away from them, then shut his eyes against the vertigo. He concentrated instead on the curious and appealing sensation of James's muscles moving as he climbed, creating very distracting sensations against Gabriel's torso, arms and thighs. More distracting still, Gabriel's abdomen and spread legs were snugged against James's lower back.

'Sorry,' he muttered, because there was no way that James couldn't feel Gabriel's physical response to that proximity.

'Nae problem,' muttered James in reply, accent thicker than usual. Gabriel pressed his pleased grin into James's skin and decided to enjoy the ride before the serious work ahead of them.

They attained the second storey without mishap. James crept sideways until they reached the lip of a marble balustrade attached to an unoccupied balcony. With a little manoeuvring, James held into the base of a marble column with one hand, steadied Gabriel with the other, and helped him climb to the safety of the balcony before following. James didn't even lose his pirate hat.

They had fetched up on a small balcony away from the primary festivities. James waited while Gabriel used a credit card to slip open the hook on the inside of the balcony door (he decided not to ask where Gabriel had learned that trick) and stepped inside a darkened guest room.

'Please, Dr Sharpe,' Gabriel whispered with unnecessary dramatic flair 'Do come in and make yourself at home.'

James stepped over the threshold.

'Excellently done,' said an urbane voice in the shadows, 'But I could have arranged a proper invitation for you both, Gabriel, if you'd asked.'

James inserted himself between Gabriel and the voice, hand moving for the cutlass, fangs descending involuntarily as his eyes adjusted to the feeble light.

'Michael.' Gabriel's tone was filled with shock.

The light clicked on – half blinding James for a second – to reveal Michael Dare at the bedroom door, one hand on the switch.

Despite differences in height and build, Michael was very clearly Gabriel's brother, with those piercing, intelligent green eyes and natural grace. The differences were all too clear as well. Michael was a razor-sharp line next to Gabriel's rough and colourful stripe of paint.

It was as though Gabriel – with his unruly hair, the perennial paint smears on his skin, the barely restrained energy buzzing in his veins and the boyish vulnerability under his shield of aloofness – was a vivid impressionist painting. Michael on the other hand was a complicated diagram. All the pushness that was mostly veneer on Gabriel went all the way through the older brother. He was the antithesis of Gabriel's windswept flair – his hair was elegantly cut and combed; his expensive suit tailored to the perfect fit; his shoes and watch terribly expensive, as was his cologne.

'And Doctor Sharpe, you may sheath your fangs. They are hardly necessary here.'

That jolted James like ice water to a sunburned neck. His stance remained battle-wary. Gabriel's rapidly thumping heart and scent of adrenalin indicated that this was no trap of his – he was genuinely startled by his brother's deadpan observation.

'Truly, Doctor Sharpe,' Michael said, unfazed by the vampire's bared teeth. 'I represent no danger to you and less still to my brother.'

'Forgive me if I don't believe you,' said James coldly. He was counting exits, calculating speeds. He could be out and away in moments, but what about Gabriel? Was he in danger too? Where could they go? Home hardly seemed a safe option.

'I appreciate you are concerned,' Michael responded. 'But I give you my word, as long as you're no threat to Gabriel or to the community, I've no intention to deprive you of your liberty or your... *life.*'

'You think I'm no threat?' He remained between Gabriel and his brother, ready yet to attack or cover Gabriel's retreat as opportunity and cause presented.

'Naturally, I examined your military record and civilian profile when I learned my brother had moved in with you, but we've known about you since your discharge from the army – your medical records were odd, you have to admit. You were clever to be able to alter the results.'

Gabriel, suddenly realising James's potential danger, stepped between James and his brother. 'He's not a *threat*,' he growled. 'He's my *friend*.'

'As you like, Gabriel. I'm satisfied he means the very opposite of harm to you. It's evident he's not even using you as a blood source. We checked with the butcher at Spitalfields, and I'm happy that he's getting enough nourishment. I assume he simply *likes* you. Vampires *are* capable of emotional attachments, rare as they are.'

'And how the hell do you suddenly know and care so much about my life?' Gabriel's shock was turning rapidly to anger, at almost the same time that James asked, 'How do you know so much about vampires?'

Michael addressed his answer to James. 'We know a good deal more about them than you might imagine.'

'Who's this *we* you keep talking about?' demanded Gabriel.

'Can't you guess?' said James darkly. 'He means the government. Or some department within the government.'

'I have alarmed you both. My apologies, I never meant–'

'Of course you meant tae alarm us,' said James. 'Or you'd have spoken tae us before now.'

Michael shrugged elegantly. 'I should say that I had hoped not to alarm you unduly, and at a later date, but here we all are–'

'Who are *you*, then,' Gabriel snapped. 'You're clearly not a parliamentary secretary.'

'I *am* that,' Michael contradicted him, 'but I'm not *only* that.'

'What the fuck does that mean?'

Michael did not dive straight into an answer.

'You were correct that I remember the ghosts in our house,

Gabriel,' he said, in that reasonable, conversational tone. 'I've learned in the years since then that there are stranger and more dangerous things, besides. It transpires that Her Majesty's public service isn't oblivious to the supernatural, either. The public service role I hold is real, but masks most of my main duties, which I carry out in my position as a liaison with the Prime Minister for BUS. Though some wags do insist on calling me Cornelius Fudge behind my back.'

'Bus?'

'The Bureau of Uncanny Sciences. Terrible name, I know. I blame British television of the 1970s, when the Bureau was established. We're stuck with the name now, alas. You need have no fear of the Bureau, Doctor Sharpe. I have no intention of having you brought in. Investigation has shown you're no danger to the community or to Gabriel. Ideally, I should thank you for keeping him out of trouble.'

'I don't need a bloody babysitter.'

'I'm pretty sure I'm just getting into trouble *with* him.'

They spoke over each other, then each caught the other's eye and grinned in spite of the situation.

'Well, that's okay, then,' said Gabriel. 'As long as we're in trouble together.'

'Misery loves company, they say,' said James.

'Hello, Misery.'

'Good evening, Company.' James's smile was pensive.

'Hey, buck up,' said Gabriel. 'I'm not going to let my brother do anything to you.'

Michael sighed. 'If either of you had been listening, you'd know I don't *want* to do anything to him. What I want is for him to continue to be your bodyguard, and for the pair of you to go home. I have the situation in hand.'

'You know why we're here?'

'Of course I know why you're here,' said Michael, irritated.

'You're looking for the vampire coterie that has been committing these murders. As am I.'

'Because you care so much about the fate of the homeless.'

'Why yes, I do happen to give a damn about British citizens, regardless of their circumstances, being murdered by a rogue vampire,' Michael snapped. 'As I happen to give a damn about you.'

'Given that you've just revealed you knew those ghosts were real and then let me in for years of anti-psychosis drugs and shock therapy without saying a bloody word, that's quite the surprise.'

'What was I supposed to do?'

'*Stop him*!'

'I didn't *know how*, Gabriel. I was at university when he sent you away the first time. I didn't even know he'd done it until I came back for the break.'

'And after then?'

'I tried, but he wouldn't *listen* to me. I did what I could. I found Helene for you.'

'*You found Helene?*'

'Do you think that skinflint bastard would have paid for an *au pair* like Helene Dupre? He couldn't even keep a nanny for longer than six months for the first few years, and that was less to do with ghosts than with *him*. Then he packed you off to boarding school, as he'd done with me, and I thought you were safe, until I found out how he put it about that you had a chronic health condition. That he sent you off to quacks and institutions between terms.

'I had no power to stop him, Gabriel, legal or otherwise. None at all. Not at the start.' All the old, impotent anger from that long-past time flashed in Michael's eyes.

'But at last I was able to persuade him to let you be, at least more often than not. It helped that he's a miserly piece of work. He told me he'd let you stay home if I found someone to care for you, and paid their wages myself.

'So I did. I found a job and I paid for her from my own pocket. Over time, he sent you away less often. It was the best I could do. Eventually, I threatened to withdraw Helene if he didn't cease the treatment, and it is our good fortune that he was too lazy and too penny-pinching to let her go. Even *he* could see that you needed someone at home, and he was never going do it. So your so-called therapy ceased, and he put your care entirely in her hands. I protected you as best I could.' Michael held his hands palm-out, beseeching.

Gabriel stared at him, but his shock at the revelation couldn't compete with the rage still inside. It seemed instead to feed it.

'It didn't stop him interfering in other ways, did it? Dictating what I was supposed to do for a living. Making sure I didn't have any options – except I made options for myself anyway, and fuck his money. And then *you* go off and join a literal spook squad and you *don't tell me*? You let me live my life thinking I must be deep-down insane instead of telling me the truth?'

'How was the truth supposed to help you? I've seen strange and terrible things, Gabriel. Why would I want you to see them too?'

'Because it would have been *real*,' Gabriel snarled. His breath hitched and faltered. When James's fingers touched the back of his clenched fist, tentative at first but then firmer, pressing into him – *real, real, real* – he took a deep breath.

Michael's urbane exterior fractured. 'I did what I thought best, within the limitations of my resources and influence. I couldn't help you then. Later, I tried to shield you from…'

Gabriel turned his back on his brother, facing James instead. 'Let's get out there and find this bastard West.'

'I'd rather you went home,' said Michael tensely.

'And I'd rather not have to look at your smug fucking face, but them's the breaks.'

'Gabriel, Cael West is very dangerous.'

'I'd noticed, ta. James and I can take care of ourselves.'

'Don't be stubborn.'

'Don't be a dick. And while we're at it, if you know he's killing people, why haven't you picked him up already?'

'It's not like we knew *all along*. Britain's undead community is very small, and most assimilate without needing much *handling*. This isn't a gothic melodrama. They can't just go around killing people, and there isn't a need. The Bureau monitors them, of course, so when this began we knew it was no-one in our records. We had to start from scratch to discover who was behind it. Eventually we uncovered this Cael West, former army major, supposed to have been killed in action in Afghanistan.'

'I know him,' said James bleakly.

'Then you know how important it is that we remove him from circulation as soon as possible. Our intelligence is that he has allied with someone we've not yet identified, and that they're both coming here this evening.'

'I should hang about then,' James said. 'I expect you'll need all the help you can get. The man's a psychopath.'

'Please take my brother home.'

'Screw you,' asserted Gabriel. 'I mean to make sure you get that bastard off the street. He's murdered friends of mine, and I'm getting the blame for it.'

Michael's gaze raked his brother up and down, taking in his costume. 'This isn't a game. West is deadly.'

'I'm aware, Michael. I've seen the bodies.'

'And you always did find the dark more exciting than frightening, didn't you, Gabriel?'

'Fuck off.'

Michael's disapproving gaze landed on James. 'I'd have thought that you'd know better. Who do you think you've come as? Captain Blood?'

James showed his fangs. 'Aye, I can work with that.'

If he thought Michael would react, he was mistaken. 'Suit

yourselves, but if you see West, do not interfere. Report to me, and allow my team to handle him.' He paused. 'And if you took this unconventional route to the party in order to avoid our father, you should know he isn't here. He believed it more to his social advantage to attend a private affair in the city.'

Gabriel grimaced, and James understood that the lack of formal invitation and the wall-climbing entry had both in fact been ploys to avoid having Dare Senior learn that Gabriel would be here. James was glad the elder Dare wasn't here. He loathed him sight unseen.

Michael turned on an Italian leather heel and disappeared down the unlit corridor.

'Should we go home?' James asked Gabriel after a brief hush. 'He's right. West is bloody dangerous. If he's got people on that bastard, we could leave. Go somewhere safe.'

'Screw safe. I've never *been* safe. I want to make sure Michael and his bloody Bureau get this bastard. If you're up for it.'

'Oh, I'm up for it all right. Let's have a look around.'

They made their way to the central body of the building and into the upper gallery that overlooked the great hall below. A low ashwood balustrade separated the gallery from a vertiginous drop to the oakwood floors of the hall. Sweeping wooden staircases of ash and oak, left and right, led to the ground level. The gallery and stairs were filled with people sipping cocktails, chattering and observing those on the floor below.

The hall was a moving mosaic of serving staff and people in costume. A few hundred were gathered, dressed as cavaliers and ghosts, tigers and zombies, princesses and evil clowns. Three hundred years of Blakely family portraits gazed imperiously from the walls, expressing disapproval in oil paint and patina at the undignified decorative display. The hall was trimmed in a ghost ship motif, with a huge mast rising from the middle of the room. Great canvas sails hung from the beams of it, anchored by thick ropes that extended to the staircases and the gallery itself. *Papier-*

mâché cannon were stationed around the gallery and hall, and fake skeletons dressed in piratical splendour dangled from yardarms and the occasional gangplank. The centrepiece of the room was a huge water fountain in the shape of a treasure chest cascading with glimmering jewels and doubloons. It was all very exuberantly *Pirates of the Caribbean* meets *The Flying Dutchman*.

Gabriel spotted Michael moving across the hall, stiff stride betraying his ongoing internal tumult. Michael had descended one wing of the staircase and was making his way to the foot of the other wing in order to ascend for a complete circuit.

'There's Blakely,' he murmured, and James followed his gaze. Michael had paused near the titled host – a square-jawed, shark-eyed fellow with the build and face of a heavyweight boxer, dressed as a one of his ancestors who'd been in the admiralty. Michael turned as though casually seeking a drinks tray – a waiter appeared with one almost instantly, and Michael helped himself to a glass of champagne – and finished his on-the-spot circle.

James's eyes narrowed as he caught a movement in a darkened doorway on the far side of the hall, from which staff bearing trays of drinks and canapés emerged.

'There he is.'

Gabriel peered but the distance and low light beyond the doorway were impenetrable for his merely human sight.

'He's gone.' James leaned over the short gallery railing, perilously far even with James's low centre of gravity, then stepped impatiently away from the edge. 'Any idea where that corridor goes?'

'Kitchens,' said Gabriel instantly, 'The old servants' hall. That's where the drowned boy showed me around when I was small, the morning after the party. The staff will be using that area tonight. It houses some small dining rooms and back parlours, too. It's a stupidly big house, this. Passages lead to the east and west wings as well as the back of the hall, and there are stairs to the upper floors.'

'Narrow the options, why don't you?' grumbled James.

Michael had also spotted West, but his attention was drawn by someone up on the gallery. James caught a glimpse of a slight, red-haired man with a young-old face, easing back into the shadows. Michael excused himself from Blakely's presence and began the ascent.

'I'll go downstairs, see if I can track West,' said James. 'You have a good overview here. Stay here and keep an eye out.'

Gabriel's gaze didn't waver from the movement in the hall below. 'Be careful.'

James adjusted the cutlass on his hip, grateful for the weight of his gun on the other, and went swiftly down the stairs.

The passage to the kitchen carried a faint scent of West's passing. A second scent, herbal and pungent, accompanied it.

James stepped aside to allow waiters to pass, then followed the trail; past the kitchen, full of busy people who gave him filthy glares for being in the way, to a small parlour where crockery was stored. Two doors led from the room. He prowled around the edges of the parlour twice before he was satisfied. Yes. West had gone one way, the person with the herbal scent another. *Damn.*

With a growl that made a passing waiter flinch, James decided to follow West's trail. It led a merry chase through passages, up and down stairs, in and out of useless rooms.

He knows I'm following, James realised. A second realisation came hot on its heels. *Grimshaw wasn't the trap. He was bait. This is the trap.*

He ran back to the main hall the way he'd come; so fast he knocked people aside and they hardly saw who'd collided with them. Emerging on the main floor, he looked around, up. There. Gabriel at one end of the gallery, glaring straight across the room at second floor height. James whirled and followed Gabriel's line of sight.

There. A second, much smaller gallery leading to the east wing. In its centre, Major Cael West. West's smile was unpleasantly victorious, but he wasn't looking at James, or at Gabriel.

West was looking at Michael, striding across the main western gallery towards the stairs he had first descended, beginning his loop again. His eyes were on West on the eastern gallery. He was furious.

Behind Michael, out of Gabriel's line of sight, in the shadows, small and slight and deadly as a snake, the red-haired man stepped into the light. The man's eyes were black as coals; his smile vulpine.

Michael, nearing the top of the stairs, spoke rapidly into thin air.

He's wired, James thought, ascending the stairs at speed, *his team will be there in a minute.*

Not soon enough.

'*Michael!*' James shouted in warning.

The short man pounced at Michael, but warned by James's cry of alarm, Michael had seized a mostly empty canapé tray from where it rested on a nearby table, bringing it up in his hands in an instinctive shield.

James ran towards them both, but inhumanly fast as he was, he wasn't fast enough.

In his peripheral vision, James saw Gabriel running towards his brother. Michael's assailant, claws out and coal eyes gleaming red, snapped at the tray with his sharp teeth, nails screeching across the metal and catching at Michael's hand.

James could smell the blood drawn by the scratch, the attacker's scent, and something stronger blooming up over that odd herbal smell. Something *unnatural.*

And then in slow motion, James saw Michael stumble backwards, his lower back hitting the top of the balustrade, his shoulders thrown further back still, his feet lifting from the floor as he overbalanced.

Flashes of sight and sound followed. An angry, sharp whine from the throat of the red-haired man; the blur of his departure from the gallery.

Gabriel, lunging, hand outstretched, for Michael, his brother's name a desperate strangled cry.

Michael, tipping, legs flailing as he reached for Gabriel. Fingers missing by fractions of an inch.

Michael. Falling.

James, half way up the stairs, didn't hesitate. He changed his trajectory, leapt onto a banister as he drew the cutlass – the sharp, hardened, absolutely authentically functional curved blade he'd bought from a specialist because he didn't take chances where West was concerned – and pushed off into space.

With speed and momentum and unerring aim, James leapt into the air, galleon coat flaring around him. His trajectory flung him at the body tumbling past the elaborate decoration of sails and ropes. His shoulder drove into Michael's torso, his arm tightened convulsively around Michael's chest. James twisted in the air, trying to right their course, but they were falling fast – too fast; it wasn't exactly good for vampires either, hitting the ground at that speed.

In less time than it took to think it, James's cutlass flashed out and into the stiff canvas of the sail, the lightning speed of the blow enabling the blade to pierce the cloth, slice through it and create drag.

With only one arm wrapped around his charge, James told him to hold on, but he need hardly have bothered. Michael had wound his arms tight around him and held fast as their combined weight pulled them down, while James kept a fierce one-handed grip on the hilt of the sword.

They hit the water fountain and James jerked around to take the brunt of the landing on his back, Michael's weight crushing into his chest.

For a moment they both lay there, Michael breathing heavily against James's neck, James carefully wriggling his toes and making sure his skeleton was intact.

James opened his eyes wide to look up at the gallery.

Gabriel gazed down at them, face pale, his mouth open in shock and showing off his faux fangs; the whole accentuating his Victorian Vampire persona. Relief and outrage vied for the upper hand.

Outrage won.

Gabriel looked across to the eastern gallery again, and whatever he saw made his lips draw back in a snarl. Nearby, people backed away as though the fangs were real. The rage certainly was.

Gabriel broke into a run, darting into a side corridor leading to the east wing.

James sat up abruptly, shoved Michael aside and dragged himself to his feet. His warning 'no!' was too late, as Gabriel disappeared into the building after Cael West.

'I'm fine. Go, after, him,' Michael urged him between heaving breaths.

James sheathed the cutlass and leapt up fifteen straight feet to the nearest rope on the rent sail. He swarmed up it like an old salt, using his body to pull at the rope and build up sway, then swung over to the gallery.

Below and around him, he heard applause. *God. They think it's a floor show.*

He drew the sword again – it was less conspicuous in this context than his gun – and followed West's and Gabriel's scents through the darkened passages, past smashed lamps and light switches pulled from the walls, out into the cold night air on a long balcony.

'I'd hold still if I were you, Doctor Sharpe.'

James held still.

West was on the balcony, teeth extended, expression triumphant. He held Gabriel pinned against his chest, hard nails pressed against the artist's exposed throat. James's hand twitched towards the gun in his sash. The grip on Gabriel's throat tightened. James held his empty hand out from his side, but he didn't drop the cutlass. He and West both knew Gabriel would be dead before James could reach them.

'Looks like I win,' grinned West.

'Hurt him and I'll tear you limb from limb,' James promised him, dark and cold, every bit the hunter. 'You'll think Grimshaw had a picnic, when I'm done with you.'

'Oh, listen to you. Doctor Death. Found your thirst again, have you?' West pressed his face to Gabriel's and licked the pale cheek. Gabriel flinched. 'Tasty, you are. I bet your little doctor hasn't told you about his first time, has he? About the welcome ambush I created just for him, and how I made him the fiend he is today. He woke up so thirsty and wild, our Jim, and there was that poor wounded Tommy in the Taliban compound, screaming for his mummy, when he wasn't screaming for his legs. And there was all that *blood*.'

James's teeth clenched and he couldn't meet Gabriel's eye. Then he could look nowhere else. Gabriel's green, green eyes, wide and on the verge of panic. Staring at him.

James stared back. He wanted to say something. *I'm sorry,* or *I didn't know what I was doing*, or *I didn't kill him, not really*, but he couldn't make a sound.

The story he'd never been brave enough to tell Gabriel stuck in his throat.

Our unit was on patrol, and Major Fucking West joined us out of nowhere for the trip back to base. West did that kind of shit all the time. Nobody ever knew what he was up to, and nobody liked him. The next thing, there's an ambush and we're running for cover in a bombed out village. I got stuck with West in an abandoned hut, and then this, this, this monster, this bastard, this fucking bastard is biting me, and he's too strong and he and he and then he…

I died screaming and I woke up ten minutes later, this undead thing. West was gone and while I was dead, I'd missed Taylor coming in, stepping on the IED West had laid at the door. That lad was screaming and sobbing and blood was pulsing out where his legs shouldae been and I didn't recognise anything or anyone. All I knew was the smell of the blood. I didnae even know mae name. I didnae remember that I was at war, that I was a doctor, or that I used tae be human. I crawled to where the blood pumped out and opened mae mouth tae let it in. I didnae even have tae bite. Instead of helping him, I drank blood like an animal, off the floor.

'I bet he didn't tell you,' West continued, 'about crawling in the dirt and gulping down that fountain of blood like it was champagne, eh Sharpe? The smell of all that blood was *glorious*, wasn't it? And you were so thirsty. You were funny to watch from outside the hut. Like a terrier at a rat, you were, like a pig, on your hands and knees with your snout in the trough.'

James remembered it. He remembered the thirst, and the shame that came after it was temporarily quenched. Newly dead, newly awake, raw with an insatiable need he didn't understand and couldn't control. The beast in his veins roaring so loud it drowned out everything he was. The taste of blood and the thick drench of it on his hands, the sticky, slick wet of it running down his chin and his chest and...

Later, when he realised, he thought, *Corporal Taylor wouldn't have lived anyway*. There was no help for that lad or for any of the patrol, all dead, between Major West's guns and his teeth, and his laughter as he hunted them all down.

James, soaked in blood, tried to flee. He stumbled, dazed, through the carnage and the crossfire towards the trucks. Bullets tore through his arm and the holes healed right up; a piece of shrapnel cut open his face and moments later the wound was gone. He opened his eyes at last to silence; to the stink of blood and West standing there, telling him, 'Cheer up, Sharpe. I'll look after you.'

James was still confused, still so thirsty, and West had taken him away, driving through the shrubs, talking the whole time, about dying and being undead, about what it would mean for him now. West told him about thirst and the will to live and he was James's sire, that West owned him now, and would make sure he had enough to drink.

'I've been wanting a doctor on my team, and you'll fit the bill nicely,' West told him near the end. 'Don't worry, you'll eat again soon. How did you like your first meal?'

Through the thirst, James knew. *Taylor wouldn't have lived anyway.*

But that didn't matter a damn.

'You were stupid at the house, after,' grinned West, now, here on the balcony. 'All those kiddies, dead, because you tried to be *noble*.'

In that house of corpses and wasted blood, James had tried to cry for what he'd done, what he'd become. But he couldn't, because his body didn't make tears any more.

Instead, he swore he belonged to *nobody*; that West had *made* him, but he didn't *own* him. And then he tried to stake West.

West, wounded, fled. James staggered back to his murdered patrol. He waited with the corpses until a new patrol came out to see what had happened to them. James, unable to say, covered in other people's blood, was taken back to the base in a state of shock, it seemed, from which he never recovered. He puzzled his doctors, and frantically faked medical results until they discharged him and sent him home.

'Did you tell your pretty boyfriend all of that, Sharpe? Does Dare let you kiss him with that killer's mouth of yours?'

The look James gave Gabriel was despairing; resigned to loss.

And the look Gabriel gave back to him was defiant, and beseeching, and… *humane.* James didn't know what to make of it, because nobody sane could have heard that story and still loved him.

James adjusted his grip on the cutlass and tried to work through his options. Then a smell struck the back of his nose, a reeking taste in his mouth, harsh and terrible, like ammonia.

'Alreet, pet. What you up to here, then?' The red-haired man sauntered onto the balcony, watching them all with his cold coal eyes.

'Niall,' West grinned, 'Got a present for you.'

Niall with the Geordie accent cast a dismissive look over the tableau. 'Not a present I really want, Cael, ya wazzock. I want t'*other* brother.'

'We'll get him,' West said confidently. 'But I thought–'

'You shouldn't,' said Niall drily. 'You don't do it very well.'

'Now look here, Frazer,' West began to sneer.

'Nee, ya daft fucker.' Niall Frazer's laconic Geordie drawl was suddenly thicker; hard and unyielding. '*You* look. We were here for the older one, and this one's not a bleedin' *gift*. Divvint give us grief. Go wrong with me, West, and you'll know *aaall* about it.'

West cocked his head. 'I meant the other one. The doctor, there. He's a vampire too. I made him for you a while back, only he didn't want to come in with us, then.'

'Well, I divvint want him comin' in with us now. I divvint need a doctor and I definitely divvint need another *vampire*.'

'What about *him?*' West pressed his nails against Gabriel's throat. A trickle of blood dribbled from under West's forefinger. 'If you want, I can fang him up for you.'

'I just said I divvint need another vampire,' Frazer scowled. 'I've got you and *your* lot. Do as ya telt, quit blathering and spit him out.'

'What for? We got the brother here, didn't we?'

Frazer's mouth pursed sourly. 'Dare the Elder opposed my approach more energetically than I supposed he might. Still, a scratch might be enough. I can let him simmer. But I might need that one for later.'

Frazer grinned suddenly at James and James recoiled at the rows of pointed teeth on display below the gleaming coal-black eyes.

'Sorry, forgot myself, pet.' Frazer slipped a hand into his pocket, withdrew it with a piece of gum held delicately between his fingers. He unwrapped it, popped it into his mouth, began to chew.

James could smell the herbal scent of the gum, part of a scent indelibly associated with Frazer now. He inhaled slowly, trying to identify the components.

Frazer grinned again, and his teeth were more normal. More human.

'A pinch of foxglove,' he said, teeth showing as he chewed open-mouthed. 'A little elderberry. Foxglove has digitalis in it, did you know?' He wandered towards James, unconcerned. 'They say fairies used to give it to foxes so we could sneak into chicken coops.' He paused in front of James, and his eyes were almost human again. 'Works a treat for posh parties, too. Lovely, helpful fairies. Probably scared the foxes would bite their wings off.'

He snapped his teeth close enough to James's eyes that James felt the draft against his lashes. 'Genealogy's a hobby for bores, don't you think? Blathering on about roots and forebears and bastard bairns and whose mam married who and shite. But it's not so bad. You never know if they'll find nobility lurking at the roots. Or a fox spirit.'

Chew chew. Grin grin.

'Niall.'

'Leave him, Cael. We've bigger game to *hunt*.' He finished on a hard, teeth-baring T, sharp as the crunch of bone.

'*Niall*,' West whined.

'Goin' now,' interrupted Frazer. 'Don't make me stake you, pet.' He stared hard at West, then grinned. 'Don't I let you have any fun, Cael? Go on then, pet. I can get at Dare another way. Have at the little fucker, and take out the nebby doctor while you're at it.'

West grinned. He snarled and bared his teeth. He pulled tight on Gabriel's throat to expose the pulse of his carotid artery.

'*Gabriel!*' James raised the cutlass in rage, in desperation, as West lunged, bit hard, and blood welled from the wound…

…and Gabriel twisted his arms, not trying to free himself, but angling, one arm down to West's thigh, the other up against his Adam's apple, and his wrists flexed hard.

The snick and crunch of one release mechanism came, then the second, and West's howl of agony rent the air as he stumbled away.

Silver-plated blades, dipped in garlic and holy water, pierced his throat and his leg. Gabriel was half dragged with him while he twisted his wrists again, trying to get the firing mechanism untangled.

West snarled his rage and lunged as James's cutlass whistled down, across, slicing as it was designed to do, through bone and muscle and gristle.

Gabriel heaved in a breath, got the blades to unlock from their harnesses and turned his face away as the cutlass blade whizzed past his neck with an inch to spare. He held that breath as West's body and snarling face froze, crumbled and wafted around Gabriel like ash. The blades clattered to the floor.

James had raised the cutlass for a pass at Frazer next, but his new target had dashed aside. Frazer perched on the balustrade, his wiry frame balanced like an acrobat. He'd spat out the gum and his eyes were glowing, his teeth lengthening again.

'I wasn't finished with my vampire,' he snarled at them. 'I had *plans* for him.'

James dropped the cutlass and snatched for the service pistol tucked into his sash. He fumbled with all the cloth in the way, then got a firm grip.

Frazer grinned, his tongue lolling out the side of his mouth. 'Good luck to you with that, pet.'

As James fired, Frazer's small body folded up, like fleshly origami, and where a man had been, a fox leapt into the night. A moment later, James's keen vision saw a large fox running hell for leather down the drive. He thought he detected a slight limp in its gait. He hoped so.

James flung the gun down beside the blades in the ash. He knelt by Gabriel, who had sagged to the cold stone, ash smeared over his face and clothes and hair.

'Gabriel.'

'Release mechanism,' gasped Gabriel, 'needs work.' His throat was streaked in ash and blood. A tiny fountain of it pulsed rhythmically from the wound. The artery had been nicked. Would tear soon, under the pressure. 'Go on then,' he murmured, 'Fix it.'

James swallowed hard.

'Don't be stupid, Jamie,' Gabriel admonished him. His vampire teeth were incongruous in his pale but very human face. 'West couldn't possibly tell me anything I don't already know about you. Not any of the important stuff.'

The look Gabriel gave him was steady, despite the shock from the attack and his pain. It was grounding; accepting. *I know what you are,* said that gaze, *And you're not a monster. You're my friend, and I love you and I trust you.*

'This may feel weird,' said James. Gabriel tried to laugh at that, then winced.

James lowered his mouth to the wound that West's teeth had made in the pale skin, and he licked. Licked again. He let the saliva pool in his mouth, a natural response to the smell and taste of the blood, then let the spit dribble into the wound. His professional medical instincts rebelled at the technique, but he knew this would work. A vampire bite was the harm and the cure in one.

James waited until the pool of saliva sank into the wound and the blood ceased to bubble and flow. He bent to lick at it again, then drew away to check on the progress.

'Don't waste any,' murmured Gabriel.

'Don't be a prat.'

'I give it freely.'

'You're bleeding all over my rental costume freely, you mean.'

'Better you should drink it, then.'

James bent again to lick and suck the blood away from the now-healed skin of Gabriel's throat. He wiped the back of his hand over his chin, and then licked that blood away too.

The soft sound of someone clearing their throat had James sitting suddenly upright and looking guiltily into the shadows.

Michael limped out of them.

'Don't look like that, Doctor Sharpe, I could see perfectly well you weren't *biting* him. My people saw a fox running from the building. I assume that was West's associate.'

'Aye. His name's Niall Frazer.'

'And West?'

James gestured at the fine ash sprinkled around them.

'A shame. We could have used the information he had.'

'He tried to kill Gabriel.'

'Then you made the right choice.' Michael glanced at his hand, which he'd bandaged in a white handkerchief. Blood spots showed the two lines where Frazer's claws had scratched him. 'I don't suppose you know what kind of creature Frazer is.'

'Foxth thpirit,' said Gabriel as he tried to sit up. He frowned at the return of the lisp and shoved trembling fingers in his mouth to wrench out the fake fangs. James helped to steady him.

'Not a werefox? That is heartening, though obviously, he might be lying. Foxes do.' Michael stuffed the injured hand in his pocket then peered at the empty sheaths he could see under Gabriel's cape. 'That was clever.'

'Yes, we are,' agreed Gabriel.

James helped Gabriel to stand and lean against the balustrade. Gabriel's hands were still shaking, so James unfastened the cloak and used it to gather up Gabriel's poisonous blades before retrieving his cutlass and the gun.

Gabriel squinted at his brother, as though he was having trouble focusing. 'Are you all right?'

'You'd best be off,' said Michael. 'I'll see to things here.'

'I can look at that hand, if you like,' James offered.

Michael reluctantly withdrew the injured hand from his pocket and allowed James to unwrap the bloodied handkerchief. The skin underneath it was unblemished.

'That does not bode well,' said Michael.

'It really doesn't,' agreed James.

'What does it mean?' Gabriel wanted to know.

'Only supernatural wounds heal so quickly,' Michael replied in a tone of studied neutrality. 'Vampire saliva is one thing, and quite useful, but this. I don't know what it means that a scratch from a fox spirit has already healed.' He pushed the offending hand back into his pocket, 'Oh well. I have Bureau resources at my disposal. I'm sure we'll get to the bottom of it soon enough.'

'Do you want them to know about that?' asked James.

Michael's smile was more of a tight grimace. 'I wouldn't like to become a threat to national security.'

'Is that likely?'

'Unfortunately, I'm unable to say at this point.'

The brothers regarded each other, on the brink of speaking, neither knowing what to say.

'I'm glad you're alive,' said Gabriel awkwardly.

'And I'm glad you are too.'

'You're still a dick.' Gabriel tried to make it light, a return to equilibrium, but he looked like he might cry.

'And you're still a juvenile delinquent,' replied Michael with a sad, indulgent smile.

Gabriel huffed a choked laugh.

'You need to get out of here, Gabriel. My team needs to mop up and to be debriefed. Sharpe, please take him home.'

James guided Gabriel towards the doors leading back inside.

'And thank you, Doctor Sharpe, for your most timely intervention.'

James nodded acknowledgement, then took Gabriel inside, down the inner staircase and back outside to the drive, and their car.

Chapter Fourteen

AT THE SUV, JAMES BUNDLED THE CLOAK-WRAPPED BLADES AND HIS cutlass into the back seat and placed his gun in the glove box before getting behind the wheel. When Gabriel hadn't been able to buckle up his seatbelt by the time they reached the main road – the clink and clatter of the metal as Gabriel failed to keep the two halves steady was almost in time with his jittering heartbeat – James fastened the belt for him.

It was ridiculous to ask Gabriel if he was all right when he clearly wasn't, so James opted for resting his hand over Gabriel's, rubbing his thumb across the artist's knuckles, before driving off.

They journeyed in silence, James guiding the vehicle along Basingstoke Road, heading for the M3, which would take them north-east and back to London. He kept one hand on the wheel, the other on Gabriel's clenched fist.

Finally, Gabriel spoke.

'W-what West said. About w-what h-happened in Afg-ghanistan.'

James took his hand away to place it on the wheel. He stared at the road ahead, resolute. *And now it all falls apart.* Gabriel had seemed so accepting of it all and, at the time, James couldn't help thinking that Gabriel mustn't have properly understood what it meant about him.

'It's all true. I'm a killer.'

The lapses had been brief but devastating. He had fought those instincts with everything he had ever since. He had returned to the base after his attempt to kill West, but his behaviour had been so erratic, and his recoiling response to the sight of blood so profound, the army had no trouble deciding to isolate him and send him home. He'd had to do a lot of work to cover up his medical tests, faking pulse and respiratory rates through willpower. To feed, he stole bags of blood that should have been used to save other lives and faked bloodwork results. Staying in a war zone was too dangerous: for him; for everyone. Too easy to succumb, with all that blood spilling so near him, all the time.

After his discharge, James fled to London to hide, where he thought he would go mad from thirst and boredom and despair. Until Gabriel came.

Now Gabriel was going to leave again.

It wasn't a surprise to see, from the corner of his eye, Gabriel glaring at him, but James didn't expect what came out of his mouth.

'I d-don't care what he s-said, Jamie.' Gabriel took a steadying breath. 'I don't hold you responsible for things you d-did then. I've seen what the thirst d-does to you, and back then you'd only j-just… woken up, is that the right expression? West even said so. It was your first time and you woke up undead, thirsty and… and wild. Did you even know what was happening to you?'

James was so startled he took his eyes off the road to stare in disbelief at Gabriel.

Gabriel unclenched his fist and rested it on the back of James's hand on the wheel. 'Better watch the road, James. It'd b-be unbearably stupid to d-drive into a tree at this point.'

James, blinking rapidly in reflex against tears that weren't coming, returned his attention to the road.

'I didnae know what he'd done to me,' James said in a strained voice. 'I didnae know what I was. That doesn't excuse–'

'You didn't k-kill those people on purpose. The s-soldier. West said the blood was already pumping out of him. And the man and his family... He said they d-died because you tried to be noble. He killed them really, didn't h-he?'

'Not the father. That was me. I tried tae stop drinking in time. I... I didnae know when to stop. He was still alive when I did, but he'd lost too much blood. I wouldnae touch the rest of them. So West. He. He killed them. All.'

The words dried in his mouth, and still Gabriel kept his hand over James's, stroking his fingers and knuckles soothingly, as James had so recently done for him.

'I'm sorry. For them and for you. I know you can't have meant to kill anyone like that. That's not who you are. I know who you are. I *see* who you are.'

'Gabriel–'

'You've done nothing but protect people since I've known you, Jamie. You care for your patients at the clinic. You've helped my friends. You've protected *me*. You saved Michael tonight, when he fell, and then you saved *my* life, *again*. You talk about yourself like you're a monster, Jamie, but you're not.'

'I *am*,' said James dully. 'I'm just a very well contained one.'

'No,' countered Gabriel sternly, the jangling stammer of shock gone at last. 'You're a vampire but you're *not* a monster. Maybe you did monstrous things at the start when you weren't yourself, but the responsibility for that is West's. You would never have *chosen* to do those things. *You are not a monster.*'

He continued in a gentler tone, his thumb rubbing softly against James's skin.

'If you think you lost your humanity, you've claimed it back. You've chosen who you want to be. And...' Gabriel's voice began to waver again. 'I've been so alone for so long. Then I met you. You became my friend.' He stumbled over the words now, as tears chased each other down his face. 'I've been a half-mad bastard all these years, likely to end up gibbering on the streets for good, and now I'm... not. Thanks to you. You make me feel *safe*.'

James saw Gabriel looking at him like he was the answer to a forgotten prayer, and a great wave of tenderness swept over him.

'You're that for me too,' he said. He tried to smile but it came out crinkled.

'I love you,' Gabriel blurted. Despite the tears, he lifted his chin in defiance, a challenge in case the declaration should be doubted. And then, slightly alarmed: 'Eyes on the road.'

James took his gaze forward again, but a smile softened his mouth. 'Eyes on the road,' he confirmed. 'See? I'm not going tae drive into a tree.'

'Good.'

'Absurd thing to do at this point, as you say. Now that you've said the L word without being off your tits on ecstasy.'

In his peripheral vision, James saw Gabriel become sheepish, then mulish. 'It didn't make it not true.'

'No.'

'And you said you loved me first, remember?'

'I remember.' James smiled more widely. 'I didnae say it to you though. So here it is. Eyes off the road for a second. Ready?'

He looked straight into Gabriel's eyes. 'I love you, too.'

Gabriel's laugh came out a half-sob, but he grinned. 'Of course you do,' he said, 'I'm lovely. You said so.'

'I did, and I'll say it again.'

'Road, James.'

James, grinning, brought his attention back to the long, dark ribbon of tree-lined road.

All was quiet for a few moments, but in those moments, James's grin began to fade. He could hear Gabriel's breathing grow thicker. Heavier. He could hear Gabriel's heartrate speeding up again.

'Gabriel?'

'I'm... fine. I'm fine.'

'You're not fine.'

'No,' agreed Gabriel, his voice breaking, 'I'm not fine. Some half-Geordie, half-fox psychopath got a brutish thug of a vampire to kill my friends because he wanted to attract *Michael's* attention, for god knows what reason, and Michael nearly died and then *I* nearly died and that fucking vampire exploded into dust all over me and it's not over. *It's not over.* Frazer's *planning* something and...'

He was talking faster and faster, was more and more agitated, not slowing down even as James pulled to the side of the road.

'...and Michael's in *danger* and he was a *fuckwit* when I was growing up and he ignored me mostly except when I thought he was in league with that bastard our father, only it turns out he hired Helene to look after me and I didn't *know* and I treat him like shit and now someone's trying to hurt him and that damned scratch healed right up and god knows what it means...'

James switched off the ignition, undid his seatbelt and twisted towards Gabriel; unclipped his belt in turn.

'...but it's not over, and Frazer said he might try to use me and I can't I don't I can't Jamie, it's not over, and, Christ, poor Alicia and Ben, and that kid Blue, all so Michael would know and pay attention and go looking for Frazer, or so Frazer knew where to find *him*; all those people *dead* and Datta thinks it was me and it was, it *was* me, it was *because* of me, oh fuck, oh fuck, Jamie. It was my fault...'

James wrapped his arms around Gabriel, who was sobbing. Gabriel folded into his embrace, against his chest, and clung, bawling.

'It's nae your fault,' said James softly, holding Gabriel tight. 'What Frazer and West did wasnae down to you. They did it to you, too. Shh, now. Shh. I'll nae let them hurt you, or anyone else if I can help it.'

'We have to stop him,' said Gabriel fiercely. 'You have to help me.'

'All right.' And it was as easy as that.

They sat together, James with his arms wrapped around Gabriel, holding him as closely as possible across the car's console. He dropped kisses on Gabriel's hair and forehead, rubbed his back, murmuring *shh* and *hush* and *there, love, there* until Gabriel's crashing heart and anxious breathing settled.

Gabriel drew slowly back, looking wrecked. 'We won't let them get away with it.'

'We won't,' James promised him. 'But we should work with Michael on this.' He braced himself for the protest. It didn't come.

'Yes. That's… I think that's wise.'

'We should tell him about Sergeant Datta.'

That drew surprise at last.

'Her vision about you and me,' James explained, 'is not what she thinks it is. It could relate to all of this. Spooky shite seems to be Michael's job. Maybe he can make sense of it.'

Gabriel took in a shuddering breath. 'Sorry.' He was embarrassed.

'Don't be. It's been a hell of a night.'

'Are you okay?'

'I'm fine.'

'I mean… with… with killing West.'

'He meant to hurt or kill you, Gabriel. I used to be a soldier, and he was the enemy. That's one death that won't be preying on my conscience.' He traced his fingers over Gabriel's skin, smeared in remnants of ash and blood and tears. 'I'm so sorry he hurt you.'

'He won't hurt anyone ever again. Don't be sorry for that,' Gabriel told him.

'I'm not.'

'Good.'

Gabriel surged forward to kiss James; to bury the fingers of one hand in his hair and fist the other in James's ridiculous pirate costume. James kissed him back, so Gabriel slid his arm around James's waist, under the long coat, and held him.

'Here, ye wee grub,' chided James tenderly, 'Yer a right mess.'

He untied the red sash around his waist and used it to wipe the streaks of ash and blood from Gabriel's face. Gabriel tilted his head up to let James wipe the last of the dried blood from his throat, too. The skin was whole and undamaged, with no sign of the terrible bite that might have killed him.

James's slow heart pulsed in his chest, a spasm of belated fear. He'd come so close to losing Gabriel. The memory of Gabriel trusting him to heal and not harm burned vividly in his mind's eye. His mouth, his veins, his brain, his whole body still tingled with Gabriel's precious blood.

Suddenly desperate to feel the living heat of him, James pulled Gabriel into his lap, pressing their torsos flush together. Through their layers of costume, he could feel the vibrant *thud thud thud* of Gabriel's racing heartbeat, propelled this time by desire rather than fear.

'Mind yer heid,' murmured James, his palm cupping Gabriel's skull, but the SUV's cab was roomy. Soon, James's hands slid over Gabriel's arms and back again; then under the cloak, greedy for the warmth of his body.

Gabriel hummed in deep satisfaction as his lips parted and he tasted the tip of James's tongue, the soft inside of his lip. An answering soft growl was pulled from James.

Gabriel's kiss grew more passionate. He sucked at James's lip and tongue as he crushed his arms around him, hands splayed against his spine to clutch him close.

James responded in kind, exploring the heat of Gabriel's mouth, untucking Gabriel's shirt so he could spread one hand on the small of his back, and dip the fingers of the other past the waistband of his trousers to brush against the rise of Gabriel's backside.

So warm, God, Gabriel's skin was so warm and his body responsive, muscles flexing and moving as he straddled James's thighs and grew hard.

James released Gabriel's mouth and kissed his throat, from the rhythm of his pulse point, down to his clavicle, up again to suck-kiss at the sensitive skin of Gabriel's throat and jaw. Gabriel squirmed wantonly against James's body while James pushed nose, mouth, eyes into the hollow under Gabriel's ear, filling himself with the scent of him, with the heat and rhythm of his strong pulse against his eyelids.

Gabriel fell still, though he held tight to James's shoulders. 'Sorry,' he panted. 'Sorry, I know you said... no sex. You don't like...'

'I like you doing that,' said James. He kissed Gabriel's throat and jaw again, 'I love you doing that. Don't stop.'

Gabriel moaned and tilted his head back. James licked a delicate line with the tip of his tongue, from Gabriel's jaw to the sensitive hollow behind his ear. He sucked on the earlobe, licked delicately at the shell of its curve, lipped and sucked at the tip and edges of it.

'I want to lick you all over,' whispered James. 'I want to touch you everywhere. It doesnae matter that I can't get off. I want you.' And right now he felt as though it might still be possible. All that remembered desire and remembered need filled him with desire and need now.

Gabriel took James's face in his hands and kissed him, softly at first, then harder, then more deeply. 'I don't want to be selfish.'

'I do,' said James. 'I want you to be selfish. I want you to want me. I want you to want this with me. Please, Gabriel. Oh, please.'

They kissed again, hot mouth on cool, hot breath panting against lips and tongue and skin, moaning into the contact. Gabriel's hips jerked involuntarily and James's hands caressed his back and the rise of his backside.

'Gabriel,' James breathed into Gabriel's ear. He licked it and suckled again on the lobe. 'I want you to do that. You are so lovely. Aye.' He lifted a hand to suck wetly on two of his own fingers, then slipped those spit-wet fingers further down the back of Gabriel's pants and ran them into the crease of Gabriel's arse, softly and briefly over the sensitive puckered skin there, then again.

Gabriel's breathy moan became a gasp. He rutted against James's belly. 'Christ. Jamie. God.'

James maintained the gentle but insistent stroke between the cheeks of Gabriel's arse. He finished untucking Gabriel's shirt all the way around. By feel alone, he popped the button of Gabriel's trousers and undid the zip. He kissed Gabriel and suckled softly on his lower lip as he dipped his free hand into the front of Gabriel's trousers and ran his fingers along the length of Gabriel's shaft, so hot to his touch.

'Is this good?' he murmured.

Gabriel shoved his cock against James's fingers. 'Yes,' he panted.

'I'm not too…?'

'God, Jamie, no. You're perfect.'

James pulled Gabriel's erection free. He rubbed his thumb over the sticky-wet crown of him, rubbing over the slit and foreskin, then down the shaft again, up again, down, a firm hold, a steady rhythm. He kneaded Gabriel's backside, hand splayed, then pulled Gabriel closer into his lap and began the soft finger-stroke again, working Gabriel front and back.

Gabriel, chanting imprecations and *Jamie, Jamie*, rolled his hips, chasing friction for his cock and then his arse. The muscles of his thighs tightened as he rocked back and forth between the sensations, clutching James's shoulders.

'That's it, mae lovely,' James said to him, gazing in hungry wonder at the man moving in his lap, 'So beautiful. Yes. God. Keep going. Keep going. That's gorgeous. Fuck. You are so gorgeous. Come for me. Come all over me. Yes…'

Gabriel's back arched as his hips jerked and his cock pulsed once, twice, three times, all over James's hand and shirt. James kept stroking him softly, front and back, slowing down, bringing Gabriel back to shuddering rest before finally moving his hands.

He wiped his sticky fingers on his own costume before wrapping his arms around Gabriel and bringing his head down to his shoulder.

Gabriel wilted willingly against James, pushing his face into the shelter of James's neck. Then he started to giggle.

'Good thing we hired a Land Rover for the night,' he said. 'I'd have brained myself on the ceiling of a hatchback.'

James started to laugh too. 'Or impaled yourself on the gearstick.' He kissed Gabriel's brow, then his cheek. 'God, you're lovely.'

Gabriel wriggled about until he could kiss James's throat. 'You sure you're okay? You don't need...?'

'I'm *fantastic*,' James assured him. 'I loved that.' And he had. He'd felt a buzz, right at the end there as Gabriel was coming in his lap. It had fizzed right through his brain and down his spine.

Gabriel nuzzled into James's hair. James held him and listened to him breathe. Other sounds filtered in to him too. Small animals in the field over the hedge from where they had parked. The hum of cars on the M3 beyond the line of trees separating this road from the highway. The world, going about its business, while inside the frame of this car, their lives had suddenly, irrevocably changed.

For the better, James decided, inhaling the scent of Gabriel and sex, and hearing Gabriel's heartbeat, a lazy, sated *dub-thub* where it thumped through Gabriel's ribs and against his own.

Eventually, Gabriel slid back into his seat and rearranged his clothing.

James tried unsuccessfully to tidy himself up too, dabbing at stickiness with the already soiled red sash. 'We definitely can't send these costumes back to the hire place now,' he said. 'Worth it, though,' he added.

'Totally,' agreed Gabriel. He yawned.

'It's a long drive back,' said James. 'Get some sleep.' He manoeuvred out of his galleon coat and folded it up on his thigh, then guided Gabriel to lie curled on the seat, head pillowed on his leg. James ran his fingers through Gabriel's messy hair. 'I'll keep you safe,' he said.

'I know you will,' said Gabriel sleepy-content. As James started the car and drove north, to where the road intersected with the motorway, Gabriel drifted off to sleep.

When they got home, James helped Gabriel out of the car and up to the flat with one arm, keeping the weapons concealed under the galleon coat he had draped over the other. When Gabriel was too exhausted to undress, James helped him to strip, gave them both a quick flannel wash, and helped Gabriel to get under his own sheets.

'Come to bed,' slurred Gabriel.

Without argument, James stripped and got into bed beside him. Gabriel grunted in satisfaction and wriggled until he had his head pillowed on James's shoulder and an arm slung across his waist.

'I'll always protect you,' said Gabriel sleepily.

James played with a tendril of Gabriel's dark hair. 'That's my line.'

'The concepts aren't mutually exclusive.'

'No. They're not.' He kissed Gabriel's brow. 'Sleep now. We'll talk in the morning.'

Gabriel snuggled in and was soon asleep.

James lay still, Gabriel cradled warm in his arms. He reflected with wonder on the new world in which he now lived. A world where he could be human and vampire, doctor and soldier, protector and hunter, all at the same time; with Gabriel – the one person who knew everything about him, for good or evil, and trusted him anyway. Loved him anyway.

And be all that with the one person *he* trusted and loved with his whole heart, and with his whole soul. Assuming he still had one.

If Niall Frazer threatened Gabriel in any way, shape or form, James Sharpe was going to bring all of his fragmented selves to that fight, and anything and anyone else he thought would keep Gabriel safe.

Chapter Fifteen

IN THE MORNING, GABRIEL STIRRED, MUTTERED IN HIS SLEEP, BURROWED closer to the body at his side then sighed in sleepy satisfaction before kissing the ribs under his cheek.

'M'ning.'

James ran his fingers through Gabriel's messy hair. 'Good morning, yourself.'

Gabriel kissed James's ribs again. He stretched so he could kiss James's chest and collarbone and neck. 'It's nice, you being here.'

'Aye.'

'How are you, after last night?'

'Fair to muddling,' said James, hoping not to talk about the events at the Ball, knowing it couldn't be avoided.

Gabriel sat up in bed. He took James's hand in his.

'We need to talk.'

James froze. 'That's in the top ten worst sentences in the world.'

Gabriel kissed James's fingers. 'I think, after yesterday, you'd better tell me all about what happened to you in Afghanistan. I don't want you worrying what I'm reading between West's lines.'

James told Gabriel the whole story.

He told him about going out on patrol with his unit, for whom he was the medic, and about West's unwelcome presence with the convoy. He explained about the ambush that West later admitted to having organised with his own small band of recruits, two other vampires. About taking shelter with West, who overpowered him, drank his blood, then forced his own vampire blood down James's throat when he was on the brink of death. About tipping over that brink.

He glossed over the dying part and how awful it had been. The greater horror of waking up dead, crazed with thirst and terror, he told sparingly but Gabriel, with his artist's imagination, could picture it too well.

He told of Corporal Taylor at the entrance to the abandoned cottage, bleeding out from the blast that had taken his legs and how James, nothing but a mass of pain and fear and need, had drunk the spilling blood instead of trying to help.

West took him to a village next, where a man begged James to drink only from him, to let his family live. James's mind had been crawling back to the surface, but he was still so thirsty, and he bit. He tried to stop in time and failed.

Sick at heart, he'd tried to save the others, but he didn't know how. West wasted their blood all through the house. A lesson, he'd said. The predator should never spare the prey.

James, in rage and despair and shame, had snatched up a chair, smashed it to make a weapon, and tried to stake West. But he was weak and overwrought, and West was strong and experienced.

After that he'd stumbled back to the ambush site where, to his further humiliation and shame, James had wiped up the drying blood of the dead in his bare hands and licked them clean, while he waited for the base to send help.

'And that's the story.' James held still, staring at his clenched fists in his lap. He watched as Gabriel's long-fingered hands covered both of his.

'Okay,' said Gabriel softly. 'Now I know the worst of it.'

'Aye,' said James, gazing into those green eyes. 'The worst of me.'

Gabriel pressed a soft kiss to James's mouth. 'I don't think we've come anywhere near the worst of me yet,' he said, with half a shrug. 'But if you're willing to give it a try, I'm sure we'll get there.'

'You still…?'

'Of course.'

After the confession: absolution. James didn't know how to fall more in love with Gabriel, and yet he did.

'And you'll help me with this? With Michael and Frazer?' asked Gabriel

'Of course.' James pressed his hand over Gabriel's heart, to feel as well as hear the steady rhythm of it.

Gabriel laid one hand over James's on his chest. 'This is so much better than "just good friends", isn't it?'

James wanted to say, *be my love but don't stop being my friend.* He wanted to say, *you make me unafraid of myself.* He wanted to say, *I don't know how I survived without you.* He wanted to say, *if the capacity to love proves I have a soul, then you planted my new soul in me.* He wanted to say, *I didn't want to belong to anyone but I want to belong to you for as long as you'll have me and even when you don't want me anymore, I'm yours, I'm yours, I'm yours.*

What he said was, 'Aye. Much.'

'Come here, then.'

Gabriel sealed his mouth over James's, kissing and licking, then ghosting his lips sensuously over James's so he could resume waking up in the best way possible. Before long, he had straddled James's hips while the very willing vampire ran his palms down Gabriel's ribs, waist, thighs.

Gabriel trailed kisses down James's throat. He traced his fingertips over James's tattoo; the curve of his shoulders and upper arms. He kissed lines over James's chest again, down his stomach, to the thatch of dark blond curls and James's unaroused cock.

'Is this okay? Do you like it?'

James gazed fondly at him. 'Oh, aye.'

Gabriel brushed the tip of his nose along James's unresponding shaft, kissed the crown, then looked up at James. 'I'd love to have you in my mouth.'

James looked away. 'You don't have to.'

'I want to. I'd love to, if you'd like it.'

'It'd be... nice. But I don't... I dinnae get... I mean, I *can*. I can make it hard,' James glanced at him then hurriedly away again. 'But it isnae *big*. It's not blood flow giving me an erection, it's me choosing tae have one. So. It's not... impressive.' He couldn't look at Gabriel, until Gabriel kissed the inside of his thigh, then the root of his resting cock, then his other thigh.

'I'm not a size queen, you know,' said Gabriel. 'The opposite, if anything. I've... ah...' He nuzzled against James's thigh. 'I've had some bad experiences, I guess. Huge cocks make me literally and figuratively uncomfortable.'

James carded his fingers though Gabriel's hair and Gabriel smiled despite the awkwardness. He bent to kiss the resting length of James's prick. 'Your cock doesn't have to be huge to be fantastic. I like it. A perfect mouthful.' He demonstrated by sucking James into his mouth and swirling his tongue around the crown.

'Oh,' said James again softly, 'I like that.'

Gabriel, eyes sparkling with delight, suckled softly, and as he did, James grew stiff. Hard, his prick was only slightly bigger than when unaroused, but a nice fit, Gabriel thought, a lovely feel in his mouth. Full but not overwhelming. Gabriel hummed and swirled his tongue under the frenulum and glans, sucked again and looked up. He kissed the slit, licked it, then suckled again, raising a querying eyebrow.

James, captivated by the sight, brushed Gabriel's hair back from his forehead so he could better see what Gabriel was doing.

'That's lovely,' he murmured. 'You're so warm. That feels good.'

Gabriel hummed and licked. His enjoyment was so evident that James decided to believe him.

James spread his thighs wider and watched. He found his pleasure at the heat and movement were as bound up in how he felt about Gabriel as in the physical sensations. It was different to how his body used to respond, but there *was* a response. He felt it in the wet warmth and teasing pressure of Gabriel's mouth, lips and tongue. Those sensations intensified in his heart and head.

He wants me. He likes to touch me. Oh, he looks gorgeous doing that to me.

James stroked Gabriel's hair with his fingertips, and flexed his hips. It felt nice when his cock scraped past Gabriel's teeth.

'I'm starting to realise that my early experiments with masturbation are an inadequate baseline to draw on,' he said when he could gather his thoughts. 'It's better when *you* touch me.'

Gabriel took his lazy time over the fellatio, obviously enjoying the texture and weight of James's cock in his mouth, and the soft sounds of pleasure of James's response. Finally, James reached for him, hooked his hands under Gabriel's arms and pulled him up the bed, as though he weighed no more than a feather, to kiss him.

'I might have developed a strength kink right about then,' Gabriel panted when James finally released his kiss-swollen mouth to lick at his neck.

'How do you feel about rimming?' James muttered against his jaw.

'I feel bloody fucking fantastic about it, since you ask.'

'Hmm,' James verbalised his pleasure at Gabriel's response. Again with that easy strength, he laid Gabriel on the bed; kissed and licked and nuzzled at his throat.

'You taste fantastic,' James murmured. He sucked Gabriel's earlobe, licked the delicate skin below it. 'You smell good.' He nuzzled at Gabriel's throat. 'The sound of your heart is the most beautiful sound in the world.'

Gabriel felt the slight scrape of James's fangs against one pebbling nipple, then the other and he arched into James's mouth, encouraging a repeat.

'You're warm as the sun,' James said in tender awe. 'I want to spend my days learning your eyes, green as... as...' He laughed self-deprecatingly. 'I wish I were a poet, to tell you what your eyes are tae me. Who you are tae me. I love you.'

James dotted Gabriel's face with kisses, his eyelids and nose, cheek and jaw, his lips. His tongue flickered against Gabriel's lips, his tongue, before sealing their mouths together again.

On instinct, Gabriel breathed, deep and long, through James's mouth, the air pulled in through his nose, into James's mouth, into his lungs, and out again. Two or three breaths this way, until James moved, slowly breaking away with a series of tongue-tip licks, soft-swift presses of their lips.

'I want tae kiss you everywhere. Taste you everywhere. I want ye tae come in mae mouth, ye braw man.'

'J-j-j-...'

'Ye like it when I talk Scots at ye, I've noticed.'

'I like everything you do.'

'I like everything you do, too. I like your art, I like watching you drink tea. I like your eyes, I like your body. I like your cock.' With a wicked grin, James kissed Gabriel's sternum and down his belly, his abdomen, then mouthed at Gabriel's rosily flushed prick. Sucked. Gabriel wriggled and bucked. James licked his wet slit, suckled again, then moved lower, flicking his tongue down Gabriel's' shaft, then his sac, then between his legs. Gabriel's knees fell open in wanton invitation.

'Let me lift ye?' James asked from between Gabriel's legs, kissing his inner thighs, hands braced below his backside.

'Oh please, yes. Lift me up. Show me how strong you are.'

James grinned, unselfconsciously showing his fangs. He slid his hands under Gabriel's backside and lifted up as he went onto his knees, raising Gabriel's hips up, lifting his jutting erection, his tightening balls, his exposed little pucker, to his mouth. Gabriel, arms flung back on the bed, fists clenched in the sheets, put his feet on James's shoulders so he could hold himself wider.

James responded to the invitation first by swallowing Gabriel's cock and sucking. Gabriel arched and panted, whimpered inarticulate pleasure.

James let Gabriel slide wetly from his mouth and lifted Gabriel's arse higher so that he could kiss-lick further down, and then nuzzled into the cleft.

Gabriel made an undignified squeak, spread his legs as far as they would go, and began a series of shallow thrusts of his arse towards James's mouth and tongue, which was sliding over and over, in, oh-god-*in,* and over, and *Christ*, that tongue, that little tongue-fucking it was giving him, in and out of him, then James licking and kissing the pucker in the centre, filthy-fantastic, cool and wet and *Jeeeeeesus* incredible.

Gabriel wriggled and panted on the cusp of orgasm, but without the friction on his cock it wasn't enough to send him over. But James held him firmly and easily, and licked and tongue-fucked, pausing to kiss the pale, sensitive skin of Gabriel's inner thighs, the crease of his leg, his tightening balls and the base of his shaft, before returning to lavish his entrance with sensuous, wet attention.

Not needing to inhale for a long while yet, he nuzzled into the warmth, pushing his nose into the smooth space under Gabriel's sac, where the scent of sweat and sex was strong. It made his mouth water.

When Gabriel was a moaning, begging, writhing mess in his hands, James swallowed his cock down to the root. He sucked, a soft-hard-soft pull, and then Gabriel was coming in thick spurts right against the back of his throat. James swallowed and sucked some more, as his lover thrashed in his arms in an excess of pleasure.

Finally, Gabriel subsided, sweaty, sated, and limp-limbed, to the mattress. James lowered him to the bed, crawled along his body to kiss him. His thickened cock pressed to Gabriel's sweat-damp belly and James thrust against the yielding warmth.

Gabriel spread his knees to bracket James's hips. His long arms grasped James's backside and encouraged him to rut.

'That's my gorgeous boy, Jamie. Do that. Do that. God, yes.'

Suddenly, James felt a frisson of pleasure, a buzz in his brain that sparkled down his spinal column and all his nerves. Not an orgasm like he had when he was human, but a champagne fizz of wellbeing from cerebral cortex to fingertip. When it ended, he lay in Gabriel's embrace, ear pressed to his lover's chest, listening to his heartbeat.

The most beautiful sound in the world.

Gabriel toyed with his hair, rubbed his fingers lovingly against his skin.

'Jamie?'

'Aye, love?'

'You're poet enough for me.'

James beamed up at him, kissed Gabriel's belly, then crawled up the bed to sit against the headboard. He held out his arms, but when Gabriel began to crawl into them, he wrapped his hands around Gabriel's ribs and pulled him into his lap.

'Definitely got a strength kink,' Gabriel said, laughing, and peppered James's shoulders and neck with kisses.

They showered together, the theoretical efficiency compromised by the extra time allocated to frequent kissing.

Gabriel showed no inclination to talk about the Halloween ball and James wanted to hang on to this happiness a little longer. Time enough to talk later.

'You finish up. I'll get breakfast ready,' said Gabriel, licking rivulets of water from James's neck before stepping onto the bathmat.

James emerged from the shower to find Gabriel, tousle-haired, dressed only in his jeans, placing a mug of warmed pig's blood on the table, beside his own breakfast of toast and tea.

They consumed their respective meals in companionable silence. Gabriel brushed his fingers against James's knee or wrist or shoulder whenever the mood took him. James rubbed his toes against Gabriel's ankles and drank the pig's blood. It didn't fill him with a sense of power the way the merest mouthful of Gabriel's freely offered blood did, but it was enough.

'I need to paint this morning,' Gabriel said when breakfast was done. 'There's a picture in my hands I need to get out.'

'Paint,' said James, rising and reclaiming his hand so he could clear the table. 'I'll call Michael.'

James retrieved Michael's number from Gabriel's phone, after Gabriel threw the mobile to him and refused to allow him back in his bedroom – *I need quiet to work* – but the call didn't last long.

'Michael? It's James.'

'Doctor Sharpe, it's not convenient to talk right now. I'll send someone to you.' Michael hung up, before James could say a word.

Half an hour later, someone knocked at the door. Leaving Gabriel undisturbed, James answered it to find an auburn-haired woman in neat business attire on the threshold. Her eyes opened wide when she saw him.

'Oh, it's *you*,' she said.

James frowned at this woman he'd never seen before. 'Do I know you?'

'I wouldn't think so,' she said, recovering herself and fixing a pleasant smile on her mouth, though not her eyes. 'I work for Michael Dare. He sent me to chat with you about last night's incident at the Blakely Estate, though I suspect he–'

She pressed her lips together. 'It's best not to discuss it in the hall.'

James could detect no sign of the supernatural about her. Her scent was human enough. Despite that moment of surprise at the door, she wasn't alarmed. Did she even know what he was?

'Doctor Sharpe,' she prompted. 'May I come in?'

He stood back and the woman sauntered in, her low heels clicking on the floor. When she reached the kitchen she turned to face him.

'Doctor Sharpe, my name is Anthea Webb. I work with Mr Dare at the Bureau, primarily as his assistant.' Her gaze flicked to the sink and the inverted cups draining on the drying rack. 'To get straight to business, Mr Dare would like to know your intentions towards his brother.'

James's eyebrows arched up in surprise. 'Honourable?' he suggested.

Webb's lips quirked. 'You intend to marry him?'

There's a thought. 'No need to rush things,' said James coolly, 'Though a June wedding is always nice.'

'Mr Dare was under the impression that the two of you were merely very good friends.'

'I was under the impression that Gabriel Dare was a grown man, not an Austen heroine, and that whatever we are is none of your boss's business.'

Two dimples appeared by the corners of Webb's lips. 'I'll tell him you said so.'

'Ta. So besides being an emissary for a nosy git, what brings you here? Or is that it?'

'Oh, that's far from it, Doctor Sharpe. Mr Dare was, I think, initially concerned that your friendship with Young Mr Dare would be solid enough for what he fears may become complicated in the near future. Given the fact that Young Mr Dare knows you're a vampire and that you're wearing his shirt today…'

James's shirt was too long for him, too narrow in the chest to button up properly, and had a splotch of paint on a sleeve.

'…I feel I can reassure him on that point.'

'Reassure away.' James had no idea what to make of this woman.

'As a secondary point,' she continued, 'I think Mr Dare suspected I might recognise you. He was correct.'

'And where do you recognise me from?'

'From a dream, Doctor Sharpe.'

'A dream?'

'Not a very clear one, I'm afraid, but for several years now I've dreamed regularly of a vampire who has an association with Mr Dare's brother and a forthcoming danger.' Again, the dimples as she smiled. 'I'm Mr Dare's assistant at BUS, but I also have some limited precognitive ability.'

'You're the second person to have that dream,' he said.

Webb's eyes opened in surprise again. 'Really? Who else, and in how much detail?'

'Hang on,' said James. 'We need Gabriel for this.'

He tapped on Gabriel's door, which opened a crack. Gabriel peered out, a smudge of green on his nose. 'You can't come in.'

'Your brother has sent someone. She's had a dream, too. We should tell her about Datta.'

Gabriel looked past James's shoulder to the woman standing in the kitchen. 'Not more bullshit.'

Webb's eyes sparkled impishly at them. 'I never bullshit, Mr Dare.' The impish sparkle got sparklier. 'Not even just then.'

'God, you really do work for my brother, don't you?'

'It is my honour and privilege, yes,' she agreed. 'Now tell me all about this Datta and let us work out if such a person might help save your brother's life.'

Part Two

THE RAVEN
&
THE FOX

Chapter Sixteen

JAMES SHARPE WAS LEANING AGAINST THE HOOD OF DI BAKARE'S CAR, arms folded, when Bakare and Sergeant Tavisa Datta stepped out into the street in the early evening. He was better dressed than that night under Chelsea Bridge, but not as smart as the suit he wore to the clinic. His expression was still severe, though an indefinable something in his posture seemed more tranquil.

'Any progress with those homicides?' he asked.

'None yet. There's been another. You knew him, we believe. A patient of yours. We were heading around to get a statement. Young fellow called Peter Lacey, went by the handle of Blue.'

'Blue's a patient of mine. I haven't seen him for a month or so. What happened?'

'Strung up by his feet, with his throat slit like a sacrificial goat,' said Bakare. 'The house was soaked in it.'

Sharpe shuddered at the description.

DI Bakare took pity and backed off. 'We'd like a look at your patient notes for the boy.'

'Don't you want my alibi?' the doctor asked acerbically. 'When did it happen?'

'Last week,' said Tavisa. 'You were scaring the life out of me doing pretend-you're-dead yoga and Dare was at the Spitalfields butcher at the time.'

'You checked me and Gabriel out first, did you?'

'Simply eliminating you from our enquiries,' Bakare said, unfazed. 'But about Lacey…'

Sharpe looked like he was considering telling them both to fuck off, but obviously decided his best strategy was to get Bakare back on-side. 'I'll be back in the office tomorrow. We'll need a warrant for the form of the thing. Send plainclothes, eh? I'd rather avoid spooking the rest of the patients.'

The Detective Inspector sighed. 'I'm only doing my job, Doc. Stay out of it and stop poking around crime scenes and we may be able to leave you out of it.'

'Only too happy to oblige.'

'So why are you here?'

'I want a word with the sergeant,' said Sharpe. 'See how the Donal girl is doing. Find out if she's still having bad dreams.'

Tavisa was aware that the last part didn't pertain to Penny Donal.

'I'll stay for a word with Doctor Sharpe,' she said to her DI. 'See you in the morning, yeah?'

'All right then. And thanks again for your assistance that day, Doctor.'

'Glad to be of help.' The doctor smiled, a not entirely friendly expression. He apparently enjoyed Bakare being uncomfortably aware of what a bastard he'd recently been.

Tavisa turned to Sharpe as Bakare drove off. 'Penny's doing okay. She's living with her aunt. We got the guy who did it – a strong-arm man for big drug interests and you don't care about that do you?'

'Is he locked up?'

'Oh yeah. We got him bang to rights.'

'That's good. But aye, I'm here about the other thing.'

'My dreams.' She pursed her lips sourly.

'Have they changed at all lately?'

She shot him a grim look. 'How do you know?'

'A hunch.'

'The main part's still there. You, dead, and the man that Gabriel Dare killed.'

'Which isn't what you think it is. What are the new things?'

Tavisa folded her arms protectively across her chest. 'Too much. And all these... animals.' *The raven and the fox and the flamingo with all the flowers.*

'The changes are what interest me. There's someone you should meet. He might be able to explain it.'

'Who?'

'Easier if you meet him. There's a lot to explain.'

Tavisa Datta raked a critical eye over James Sharpe. The doctor submitted patiently to the scrutiny.

'I know you don't trust me,' he began.

'It's Dare I don't trust.'

'It's me, too,' he contradicted her. 'If it makes you feel better, Bakare knows we're talking. If anything happened to you, he'd come straight for me. He'd have me... bang to rights.' He smiled.

She scowled back. 'You're not funny, you know.'

'Gabriel thinks I'm a riot. He's all that counts with me.'

'You sound sweet on the little bastard.'

'I *am* sweet on him,' said Sharpe matter-of-factly, 'though that's feeble as descriptions go. Oh, don't look shocked. You're not shocked at all. You think I'm suicidal, which I'm not.'

'He's *dangerous.*'

'He really isn't. But I concede you've seen something peculiar. We'd like to get to the bottom of it. I'm sure you would, too. Come meet this man. See what comes of it. Who knows? You might even save another life.'

Tavisa rolled her eyes. 'Fine. I'll come.'

'Great. You can drive. I don't have a car.'

He followed Tavisa into her small, serviceable sedan. 'Which way?' she asked.

'Satisfied I'm not about to abduct you and eat your spleen with a glass of white wine?'

Tavisa laughed in spite of everything. 'I wouldn't put it past you, but not today. Which way?'

'Left here, then right and head north.'

She drove. 'So who is this man we're meeting? And why do you think he might be able to help?'

'It's not for me to say, yet,' Sharpe replied. 'Those are other people's secrets and now isn't the time. I also don't want to influence your recollection of your dream with new data. When we get there, tell him about the dream. We can interpret it afterwards. Left here, then keep going.'

She followed his directions until they hit a long stretch, when she turned on the radio. They listened to Top 40 hits and drove on without further conversation.

Half an hour later, they pulled up in the car park of a locked-up warehouse. Another car was parked there already, a dark sedan with government number plates. Suspicious, she kept the engine running.

The doors of the government car opened and out stepped Gabriel Dare in his usual scruffy jeans and leather jacket, an older man who bore a passing resemblance to him wearing a dark suit and black gloves, and a woman dressed in conservative but stylish business attire – dark tailored skirt, pinstriped jacket nipped in at the waist, auburn hair held up in a twist with a glossy black hair comb keeping it in place. The driver remained in the car, shielded behind smoked glass.

'If you think I'm getting out of this car, you're crazier than I am,' said Tavisa.

'Wait here,' said Sharpe. He got out of the car and crossed to the others.

Tavisa watched them talk, then decided she was being more paranoid than even *she* could bear. She killed the engine and got out, though she remained poised for trouble.

Gabriel Dare, James Sharpe and the other two stood in a patient line for her to approach.

Tavisa peered at them.

'Is that your brother?' she said to Gabriel.

'Alas, yes,' said the older man wryly. 'My attempts to keep our familial ties a secret have failed utterly.'

Tavisa wondered if he was joking. Gabriel was so sour that it seemed not.

'I'm sorry, Sergeant Datta,' said the man in question. 'Levity was inappropriate. My name is Michael Dare. I work for a government department that has an interest in people with gifts like yours.'

'Like mine?' Tavisa drew away from him.

'Precognitive ability, James and Gabriel have led me to understand.'

'I don't–'

'I apologise. I'm being terribly ham-fisted about all of this. We don't know how much time we have, you see, or where the danger lies. Perhaps it will… I suppose "put you at your ease" is not the way to phrase it. But if you would be patient for a moment. Miss Webb, if you would be so kind as to tell the Sergeant about your dream.'

The auburn-haired woman smiled civilly. 'There's a raven,' she said. 'That falls. And a fox. He's not a *nice* fox.'

Datta gasped. *A fox and a raven.*

'And him,' Miss Webb nodded at James Sharpe, who stood at parade rest, hands clasped behind his back. He still looked dead to Tavisa's eyes. 'Gabriel Dare is nearby. I don't get much else. The smell of disinfectant and the smell of blood.' She tilted her head towards Michael Dare. 'Is that all, sir?'

'Thank you, Miss Webb, that will be all for now.'

The elegant Miss Webb fell silent.

'You can see why I am so interested in your dream, Sergeant Datta.'

'I really can't,' she said stiffly.

'You find nothing unusual in the fact that you and Miss Webb are having very similar dreams?'

'I didn't used to dream about a fox.'

'But you do now?'

Yes, damn it. I do now.

'Miss Webb is the sole precognitive dreamer in our department,' said Michael Dare. 'The talent is rare and her gift is not very strong. From James's description, however, it seems you have much more significant abilities. I cannot stress enough how important this is, Sergeant. That fox has dangerous designs and has already been responsible for several murders – which you have attempted to lay at my brother's feet.'

Tavisa's eyes widened at this. 'Those homeless people?'

'Yes.'

'And that latest one. Peter Lacey?'

'The boy called Blue? Yes. And the person he lived with.'

'We haven't found another body.'

'You'll find it in the roof. All ashes, I'm afraid. Mr Grimshaw was not what you would call entirely human.' Michael pressed his lips together. 'I'm getting ahead of myself. Please, Sergeant. Relate to us your dream and we will review how to proceed from here.'

'You won't like it,' she warned. God knew what she was thinking, taking any of this seriously. But her eyes met those of Miss Webb's and a spark of sympathetic understanding shone in them. That spark promised answers, at long last, for the heart-breaking mystery that had been her life of horrific dreams.

'My liking it or not is immaterial. Describe it. Please.'

So Tavisa Datta described her strange and changing dream.

'I'm walking in a fog,' she said. 'I can't see much. I can sense buildings all around, streets and things. It seems to be London, at any rate. I can just about see my hand in front of my face, but that's all. There's an animal running around. Too fast to see, but I can hear it panting and it's...'

'Go on,' the elder Dare said, when the pause went on.

'It's wicked.'

'Wicked?'

'I know it's an old fashioned word, but it's the one that fits. It's a *wicked* animal.'

Instead of scoffing, Dare was thoughtful. 'What happens next?'

'I step on something soft. It's a flamingo. She's lying on the ground, covered in tiny blue flowers. She has a garland of roses at her throat.'

'She?'

'It's a she. Pink and fragile, a beautiful bird, and she might be asleep. I can't tell.'

'I see. Then?'

'Then out of the fog I can hear the fox laughing. It's definitely a laugh. A... wicked laugh.'

'Can you tell me anything about the animal?'

'I never really see it.'

'Nevertheless. Glimpses, through the fog? Colours? Smells? Sounds?'

'It's red and white and black. Embers and coals. It's all teeth and claws. Sharp all over, even its face. Everything's sharp and wicked.'

'After this, what happens?'

'I'm at a hospital. There's a raven overhead. It's huge. I can see it even through the fog. It's the biggest raven I've ever seen, and it's flying like it owns the sky and then it...'

'What?'

'It falls. Like a stone, like its wings have broken, and it falls right out of the sky, right at my feet. And I know *you're* there.' She glared at Gabriel. 'You were *up* there, doing something to the raven. It's your fault.'

'How do you know I'm there?' Gabriel asked.

'I just *do*,' she gritted out, 'The way you know things in dreams. It's like I can hear your voice.'

'Hmm.' Michael Dare didn't seem especially bothered by this pronouncement. 'And then?'

Tavisa fidgeted. This was always the difficult part. The part that, in her dream, had her shaking and cursing and sometimes crying.

'The raven crashes into the ground, and then it's not a raven anymore.' She spoke rapidly, trying to rush through it. 'It's a man. Covered in blood, his head caved in from the fall, his arms and legs broken. And James Sharpe is kneeling beside the body, and he's dead too. He's like a statue. No pulse. No breath. He's devastated, like the worst thing in the world has happened to him and it killed him stone dead. And it's all your fault.'

Gabriel was unmoved by the description. 'James said you described him as looking *betrayed*.'

She swallowed. 'Yes.'

'Why?'

She tried to capture the sensation of *knowing* that came with the dream. She wished she wasn't telling this to Gabriel Dare and his slightly creepy brother, but damn it, it was good to be telling *someone*.

She glanced at James Sharp, half sorry, half defiant. Perhaps he would listen *now*.

'Because the worst thing is he wasn't *expecting* it. And he was thinking of *you*. It's like there's a-a-a *smear* of you all over him. He expected something of you and you failed him, and now he's dead.'

Michael Dare frowned. 'And the body? The raven that became a man. What does he look like? Have you seen him before?'

'I feel like I know who it is but I can't see his face. He's all in black and red. It's all blood and shadow.'

'What about James?' Gabriel asked, 'Is he clear or obscure, like the other bodies?'

'Clear. He's always been the one clear thing I could see.' Tavisa's hands were trembling. 'I could always see this dead man kneeling beside the body that Gabriel Dare threw off a building, and then he showed up at Chelsea Bridge and I've been waiting for you to murder him ever since.'

'I've told you, I'd never harm Jamie,' Gabriel asserted automatically. 'Although you say I killed the other man. The one that was a raven. And you know *I* did that?'

'Yes. I didn't see it but I know it. So much isn't clear, but those three facts are. You threw someone off a rooftop. It broke James Sharpe's heart. You killed him.'

'Hmm.'

Tavisa glared at Michael Dare. 'Is that all you have to say? I've this minute told you I saw your brother murder a man – *this* man – and all you can say to me is "hmm"?' She didn't know if she wanted to scream, hit him or cry.

'Forgive me,' he said, all urbane contrition, 'I forget that you have less experience of these things.'

'Fuck you. I've been dreaming shit like this since I was six years old.'

'That must have been very difficult for you.'

His unexpected kindness made her want to cry, and that made her angry. 'Hasn't been a picnic. So are you going to tell me what the fuck is going on and who the fuck you are, or are you just going to say "hmm" again?'

Michael Dare ignored the pointed "see what I mean?" glare from his brother and addressed Tavisa.

'It is a singular fact that the world is not as rational as we would like to believe. Or rather, there are levels of reality that conform to different sets of rules, although we can be certain that rules of some kind exist. A world, Sergeant Datta, which is limited and exists in very small pockets beside the more prosaic world of physics and mathematical purity, but is nonetheless very real.'

He smiled in a completely not-reassuring manner. 'A world in which, for example, people may dream of things that are yet to be; things that may become true or may be averted. My assistant, Miss Webb, has this gift to some measure, although I will be honest, her skills as a personal assistant and bodyguard are far superior to those she has as a soothsayer.'

Tavisa scowled at him, trying to cover for the rapid beating of her heart.

'Other things exist, of course. Other creatures that, for want of a better term, may be labelled as supernatural, or paranormal.'

'Such as?' she demanded through teeth gritted against the fearful chattering that threatened.

'Ghosts are as prevalent as one would assume,' he said. 'Though only a fraction of those reported could be truly said to be harmful to the living. On the whole, they are merely echoes of old spirits. There are spirits of other types, however. Animal spirits, as it turns out.'

'Werewolves?' Tavisa asked, attempting to sneer.

'Certainly, though they are more a northern European phenomenon. I'm speaking more of... personifications of archetypes. Bear and fox spirits, for example. The truth is that I have a limited understanding of this field. Very little empirical research has been conducted. Vampires are less prevalent than popular culture would have us believe, but yes, they exist.'

Tavisa's lip curled. 'You're crazy.'

'Not at all,' said Michael Dare mildly. 'Afflicted, perhaps, but I assure you, I'm as sane as you are.'

Tavisa Datta did not find that reassuring.

'A demonstration?' he suggested.

'Oh please, yes,' she said. 'Prove it.'

Michael Dare tugged the glove from his right hand. He held his hand up to show her how perfectly ordinary it was.

And then the nails transformed into dark, hard, pointed claws, and his eyes were black and burning, like embers. His face grew sharper.

'I cannot perform a full transformation,' he said. His voice had changed timbre into something wilder and gruffer and altogether stranger. 'The wound was not severe. But changes enough have been wrought on my DNA. It has been deeply inconvenient, although rest assured I will seek advantage where I may.'

And suddenly his face was his own again, his hand a normal hand, free of claws and that hint of red hair.

'You understand, I show you this in confidence,' said Michael, tugging his glove on again, and his voice was his own measured, cultured, human voice again. 'You are one of a handful of people who are aware of it. As far as we can ascertain, I pose no threat to those who rely on me. My mind is yet my own.'

'I–'

'Miss Webb assures me that I am not the fox from the dream. Is that your impression?'

Tavisa closed her slack jaw. She shook her head. 'No. You're not safe, but you're not–'

'Wicked?' suggested James Sharpe, breaking his silence at last.

She glared at him, suspecting mockery, but he was in deep earnest.

'Not wicked. No.' She swallowed convulsively. 'Crafty, though.'

That seemed to disconcert Michael and to amuse Gabriel.

'There's another thing.' Sharpe said in a terribly serious tone, and she stared at him in dread. 'I won't hurt you,' he continued. 'I want you know that. I'm not a *danger* like that.'

'But dangerous,' she whispered.

'Aye,' he concurred.

'What are you?'

He closed his eyes and she could see his face alter weirdly. He opened his eyes, and his mouth, and she could see his pointed teeth.

'I'm dead, Tavisa. "Undead", in the vernacular.'

'No.'

'James is a vampire,' said Gabriel. 'He's been a vampire the entire time I've known him, although I only learned the truth a few weeks after I moved in. That's why I say that if you see James dead in your dream, I couldn't possibly have killed him. Vampires disintegrate to dust on their second death.'

'I...' Tavisa looked at Gabriel, trapped between hope and despair. 'And you?'

'I see ghosts. I don't know if that's actually been medicated out of me by now, but that's how it was when I was a boy. I only realised when I found out about Jamie that I wasn't completely off my rocker after all.'

'Oh.'

'Quite.'

Tavisa stared at James Sharpe again. 'Can you... turn into... things?'

The doctor's long suffering sigh made Gabriel laugh, which was so startling in the circumstances that she was hardly further surprised when Sharpe rolled his eyes and called Gabriel a numpty with obvious affection.

'No, Sergeant Datta. No clouds of bats or transforming into a wolf for me. I can hold my breath forever.'

'And... blood?'

'I don't kill people for their blood,' he told her. 'What I need I take in the form of pig's blood, which I obtain from the butcher's, as you may recall.'

He cast a quick glance at Gabriel. 'Sometimes I obtain small amounts of human blood from volunteers. I'm not going to bite you, Sergeant.'

'Why are you telling me this? *Why are you all telling me this*?'

'Because,' said Michael Dare, 'your dream is not yet fact.'

'Your dream about the Donal family,' said Sharpe, 'was very precise about everyone but the daughter, Penny.'

'Yes,' said Tavisa, remembering that victory.

'Your visions of her were unclear and surrounded by allegory. Red and eyes and darkness. That's where we found her. In a closed trunk, surrounded by dolls, stuffed animals and a scarlet ball gown. Your vision of her circumstances was unclear. Her fate wasn't sealed.'

'Well, that's a *great* help,' she snapped.

'Annoying, I agree,' said Michael. 'Apparently the rules for the supernatural revolve very much around being as frustratingly vague and egregiously metaphysical as possible.'

'The rules around blood freely given, invitations to enter residences, and all the exceptions to the rule, are positively arcane.' Sharpe was half way between irritated and amused.

'We believe,' said Michael Dare, 'that the fox in this dream is the same one that infected me, though I use the term infected very broadly.

'However, if he is involved in this vision that you and Miss Webb share, and if my brother and Doctor Sharpe are also participants in those events, it cannot be good. Given the link I now have with that...*wicked* creature, I cannot allow your dream to go unchallenged. We must know what it means. If possible, we must prevent it.'

Tavisa Datta's shocked gaze shifted from one Dare brother to the other, and then onto Doctor Sharpe. Then she looked back at Gabriel.

'But you're part of it. I know you are you. If you're right, that the things in clear detail will definitely happen, then *that* happens. You're a killer. You throw someone from a roof.'

'I couldn't imagine a reason for doing such a terrible thing.'

'A big black raven falling off a roof,' interjected James thoughtfully. 'Have you seen what you're like when you're working? Bird's nest hair. When your study objects, you peer at them like you're x-raying them for hairline fractures. You look like a seagull working out how to break into an oyster.'

'My hair is like a bird's nest?'

'A wee bit. It's adorable. Very *painterly* of you. It's how I imagine Turner after a hard day at the easel.'

'Now you're being ridiculous,' Gabriel snorted, hiding his pleasure at the analogy. 'Why would I throw myself off a roof, anyway?'

'I haven't the first idea, love. But I've seen terrible things in my time. As a doctor, as a soldier, and as a vampire. If the Sergeant says I look like a man who's see the worst thing in his life, it must be because of *who* it is, not the mess. I've picked up pieces of people after bomb blasts. You know what I saw in Helmand. What could be worse than that, now? Only if that body is you. If I couldn't stop you. Aye. I'd look as bad as she describes.'

Gabriel took the vampire's hand. 'It won't happen,' he said.

'I willnae let it happen,' Sharpe assured him grimly.

Tavisa was aghast at an interpretation that had never occurred to her. Michael, too, was troubled at this new notion.

'So, Sergeant Datta,' Michael said at last. 'Here we are. And thus we come to the crux of the matter. We are telling you this so that you may know that other interpretations can be placed on your visions.'

Tavisa closed her eyes, because already she knew that the pictures in her head were different. The nuances of her sleeping mind were telling her, yes, James Sharpe was a vampire and his despair wasn't because he was dead, but because he couldn't prevent some other murder. But the identity of the body on the ground beside him was unclear.

'Will you help us learn what your dream means,' said Michael, 'So that we may prevent it? Will you help us hunt that wicked fox?'

Would she seek a way to prevent a murder? Even if it meant helping Gabriel Dare, and a vampire, and a man more unsettling than either of those two put together?

'Hell, yes,' she said. 'What do I do?'

'The question, Sergeant Datta, is what do *we* do,' Miss Webb corrected her. 'And that is something that we need to determine together.'

Chapter Seventeen

Miss Webb's first name, Tavisa Datta learned, was Anthea.

Anthea always had a wry smile hovering about that professionally detached mien and those canny, all-observing eyes. 'I'm the genuine article,' she joked early on. 'Though at heart I'm the definitive article.' She'd used her fingers to space out her name. *An. The. A.*

Tavisa liked Anthea. She appreciated a woman with a sense of humour.

Tavisa wondered if Anthea was Webb's real name, but she didn't mind either way. She wished nobody knew *her* real name. Working for Michael Dare, dreaming precognitive dreams, and being part of this strange hunt for a wicked paranormal fox made her want to shield herself from all the unknown, unknowable threats.

Tavisa had meetings with Michael and Anthea in the days following that first one in the carpark, occasionally in the company of the vampire doctor and the aggravating artist. Michael spent a lot of time trying to unravel Tavisa's dream. Between them, they had a few working hypotheses. No way of knowing which was correct, though. Not until things started to become true in the world, rather than loitering as a hint of the subconscious.

They had theories now about the flamingo; and fears, too.

Anthea collected Tavisa for this latest meeting in a surprisingly sombre mood. Tavisa tried to offer a friendly greeting, but Anthea was not in the laughing vein.

'This meeting is different,' said Anthea.

'Okay.'

'When we get there, stand behind him and don't speak. Just listen. I'll explain afterwards.'

'But what–'

'Trust me.' Anthea was utterly severe for a change. No incipient wry wit there, only grim determination.

Each meeting in the preceding days had been at a different location. Today they went to an empty office building, the upper floors of which were being refurbished. Anthea led Tavisa to a corner office on the tenth floor. A glass window separated the office from the main floor.

Once the two women were in the office, Michael Dare entered the main room. He ignored their presence and stood with his back to them. He was wearing his gloves, and wore sunglasses, even inside this dim-lit building. A faint blue light emanated from the table in front of him, where he had placed a tablet or smartphone screen that Tavisa couldn't see. Anthea hovered by the office door, open a fraction. She didn't say a word to her boss.

Very strange.

Michael tapped a command on the unseen screen.

'Were-creatures,' said Michael Dare as though dictating to a stenographer, 'Are different from spirit animals in a number of respects. It has taken time to separate the fundamental aspects of the two. The infections manifest in similar ways.'

Tavisa raised an eyebrow at Anthea but remained silent, as instructed.

'A bite or scratch from a were-creature,' continued Michael, lecturing the wall, 'alters the victim's DNA. Without further input from what is sometimes referred to as the sire, the were-creature's progeny will undergo change at the cellular level. The curse translates as a disease, if you will, with monthly symptoms that require confinement and management. Outside of those times of physical transformation, however, the victim appears and indeed is human enough; but a carrier, of course, so great care must be taken. Despite the curse – such is the traditional nomenclature, although it is more in the way of a communicable infection – the victim remains essentially independent. Were-creatures are no more beholden to their so-called sire than a person who contracts malaria is beholden to the mosquito; or someone with syphilis owes fealty to the one who passed it on.'

Michael Dare, Tavisa knew, was scratched by a fox spirit, not a were-fox. *There are were-foxes. What a peculiar thought. What a peculiar and unpleasant world.* Given this speech, she would have thought that a good sign, but for the look on Anthea's face. She was indescribably sad; like she was watching someone she loved die.

'Animal spirits, such as the fox that scratched me,' Michael continued, still ignoring their presence, assuming he was aware of it, 'operate on different principles, although at first glance they appear to manifest possession in a manner similar to were-infection. But *possession* is the correct word in this instance. My own wound was but a scratch, superficial to begin with, but where a were-creature may infect against its intention, the spirit animal may only infect as a conscious act. No doubt if it had bitten me, the saliva and greater injury would have hastened the process. That was, no doubt, its intent, but a scratch was all it managed.'

The man lifted his gloved hand, the one that had been injured at the Halloween party, and turned it this way and that.

'*Possession* implies a consciousness rather than a simple viral or bacterial invasion. The blood samples originally examined were misleading, and suggested an alteration to my DNA, but the situation proves more complex, though not without hope. Recent studies indicate that my own DNA is not being altered, but *encased*. The alien casing is very thin on some days, and on others it is thicker, though the parameters for its variation are so far a mystery. My best team cannot identify the casings' substance, though the bolder among them posits a theory that it has psychic as well as psychological and physical elements.'

He shoved the hand violently in to his pocket and steadied his agitated breathing.

'So much work to be done,' he said.

'Although it may be summarised that it appears my body is being possessed. It waxes and wanes with something other than the moon. Proximity, perhaps? The level to which my – sire, progenitor, call him what you will – is focused upon me? I have, until recently, felt secure that I was not compromised beyond an irritating, though fascinating, capacity to display certain fox-like characteristics at will. My mind is yet my own, as I have said, and yet I do not know how much longer this will be the case. Two days ago, ten minutes are missing from my schedule, in which I recall not a blessed thing. Yesterday, fifteen minutes are blank in this fashion. This morning, half an hour of my memory is not accounted for.'

Michael Dare bowed his head, then withdrew his hand from his pocket again. 'I am not sure you can appreciate the terror which accompanies these gaps, let alone the admission that they exist. The gaps, you understand, are accounted for externally. My staff, my bodyguard in particular, know where I was, physically, at those times, and are aware of my actions.

'It is the blank in my own mind which I find so alarming. Examination of the facts, the footage, the witness statements, indicates I have not compromised my duty. It could be that the fox is simply testing the waters. Who knows whether I am shut down at those times, or whether he is using my eyes, my ears, my senses, to spy, like that evil wizard in the children's book that was so popular a number of years ago?'

Michael straightened his spine – a man readying himself for battle.

'And thus, here I am, speaking aloud to a voice recorder as a safeguard against the time that I do not remember myself. Here I stand, ready to declare that if I become a threat to this nation, to my duty, it is the duty of others to neutralise that threat.

'I could perhaps count on my brother to do such a thing, but that is not a burden I would willingly place on his shoulders. I will certainly not take our father into our confidence. He'd never believe me.

'Instead, I will leave instructions for my staff, and trust their knowledge of me, and their own sworn duty to the Crown, to know when they must act, if it becomes necessary. I must put my trust...' His voice thickened. 'Those I trust must save me, if they can. If they cannot, they must save all I have worked for by eliminating me.'

Michael Dare tapped a command onto the screen. He took up a smartphone, then, and placed it in his pocket.

After that, he walked away, along the darkened floor, past building materials and coils of cables.

When he was gone, Anthea gave Tavisa Datta a look that was defiant and sad. Long minutes later, Anthea led Tavisa out to her car.

They didn't speak until the car pulled up outside Tavisa's home.

'This makes everything harder, doesn't it?' said Tavisa. 'You'll have to keep him out of the planning of his own defence, while making it look like he's still in on it, or Frazer will get suspicious.'

'Yes. It's a brinksmanship game now. We'll never know if the fox is listening. Even tonight was tricky. Mr Dare simply suggested he might be there tonight and left the rest to me. He knows he's potentially a tap wire to the adversary.'

'He has to deceive himself to deceive Frazer,' observed Tavisa. 'Shit.'

'If we have to,' said Anthea, her voice dull, 'we'll eliminate Mr Dare. Those are his orders. He'd rather die than be lost to the enemy. He'd rather die than forsake his life's work.'

Anthea's defiant-sad glare collided with Tavisa's one of concern and dread.

'If it comes to it, you'll see to it, won't you? If I can't?' said Anthea. 'We have no way of knowing how much Frazer knows. If Michael's lost, he'll take me out before we have a chance to act. He needs someone he can trust who is out of the internal loop, and he can't ask Gabriel. You can see that he can't ask Gabriel.'

He could ask James Sharpe, Tavisa thought, but no. What James Sharpe knew, Gabriel would know in due course, and Michael Dare was right. That was no burden for a brother.

It was no burden for a copper either. But perhaps it was one for a patriot, or a friend.

'You can count on me,' she said. 'But only in the most extreme of circumstances.'

Relief softened the creases around Anthea's eyes and mouth. 'Of course. Our plan is to take Frazer out first. If the possession is psychic, we postulate there's every chance that Frazer's death will release Mr Dare. Our job is to reach that point before the fox completes the possession.'

Now Michael was Mr Dare again, but Tavisa had no doubt that Anthea – that collection of articles definite and indefinite – was most definitely in love with her boss. Tavisa wondered if the love was reciprocated. She knew that for Anthea it didn't matter. Anthea was resolved to save Michael Dare's soul if she wasn't able to save his body. And she relied on Tavisa Datta to be her back-up.

'We'll beat that bastard,' said Tavisa, 'Trust me.'

'I'll have to.'

Gabriel stood in front of the easel, chewing the end of his paintbrush. It left a dark stain on his lower lip, which joined the general collection of paint smears on other parts of his face and his hands. His thumb, which he'd used to smudge and blend colours in the background, was particularly discoloured with browns and a vibrant red.

For the first time in days, he was calm and centred, his mind cleared of all the endless talk and suppositions and analyses and just plain guesses about what Niall Frazer was planning and how that affected the Dare brothers. Plans were in place. And Plan B. Plans C to F as well – most of those being back-up plans from which Michael had been explicitly excluded, in the event that Frazer's hold on Michael became more profound.

Gabriel and James had taken to making strange excursions of the streets of London in their efforts to ensure these plans were made well away from Michael and his Bureau of Uncanny Sciences. James used his vampire strength and balance to avoid surveillance. They conducted quiet discussions atop high buildings, down disused tunnels, and once in the London Zoo's lion enclosure (the lionesses, Rubi, Heidi and Indi, kept their wary distance from the vampire and the chemical-scented human).

Gabriel led James to the abandoned Tube stations where he'd sometimes slept in his more difficult days. There, they watched the trains fly past: squares of light in the darkness, flashing slides of people reading, daydreaming, picking their noses, texting or gazing at someone three seats down, trying to muster the courage to say hello. Gabriel liked to sit in the dark and sketch them, far from the surveillance of prying eyes and ears.

All the participants of this Byzantine puzzle had their scripts and their prompts and their list of what-ifs. They were waiting for the starter pistol, whatever that would turn out to be, and then they could only hope for the best.

It was a piss-poor solution, but until more data came in, it was all they had.

James and Gabriel slept together every night now – that is, Gabriel slept while James was dormant. Before they slept or after they woke, they kissed and explored one another, James taking tender delight in bringing his lover to orgasm. Sometimes he experienced again that fizz of sensation, brain to fingertips.

They worked, James at the clinic, Gabriel at the paint factory or on his art. They filled notebooks with observations on James's physiology. They discussed and discarded and refined and brainstormed new ideas, new approaches, new ways to tackle the threat of Niall Frazer and the inexorable, inching loss of Gabriel's brother.

After their most recent meeting, Michael had shown disturbing signs of not being quite himself. He was distracted, as though a voice was whispering in his ear. He swore he was fine and uncompromised, but Gabriel had never known Michael in anything but complete command of himself. Michael's distraction frightened him more than anything preceding it; even Cael West.

Today, Gabriel threw it all off. His head was too full of questions without answers and the nerve-scraping anticipation of Frazer's first visible move. He couldn't stand it. He breathed a sigh of relief when James went to the clinic, then hauled out his paints and unfinished canvases.

Separated from all the concern and strategizing of the last few days, Gabriel steeped himself in the *now* of colour and light. He revelled in applying paint with the brush, scraping parts of it off again with a palette knife, brush stem, thumbnail or rag; in taking image, thought, heart and instinct out of his head and hands and trying to make the mere outside world carry meaning for which he didn't have words.

Gabriel had tried to work on other paintings over the last few weeks, but he kept coming back to this one: his portrait of James Sharpe. And every time he came back to it, it changed.

He thought the painting was nearly finished. This blend of dark and light. The background was inky black and midnight blue, but the figure of James glowed. Whether the light was behind him or emanated from him was obscure. James was dressed in the jeans and T-shirt he was wearing when Gabriel first set eyes on him. A hint of James's caduceus tattoo appeared under the sleeve, along with the lines of a tan that Gabriel now understood were forever – James's undead body caught in that snapshot of his last moments as a human being, before Cael West had murdered him.

The clear, sapphire blue eyes in the painting were patient and full of sorrowful knowing; the lift of the chin was strong and defiant. The set of his muscular shoulders and his feet, braced apart, showed him willing for action, but his hands were open, palm up, as though offering help, or asking for it.

His mouth wore an incipient smile, but the tiniest drop of blood red was at the corner, though examination revealed it shaped like a teardrop, and then you could see that the smile was sweet but melancholy too.

Gabriel stepped away from the picture, to where his sketchbook lay open on the bed. That had a more recent picture of James – drawn in soft pencils last night, while James lay dormant in their bed.

In the picture, James was resting on his side, a study in flowing lines. The rise and fall of his shoulder, to the dip of his waist, the rise again of his hip. The light from the window had cast shadows over the sheets draped over his legs and rucked about his waist, and lit James's face softly. He looked younger, resting like this. Less guarded and less troubled, his descended fangs pushing slightly at his lower lip. One arm was bent, with the hand curled under his chin. The other rested on Gabriel's pillow, fingers spread like he was absorbing the heat from where Gabriel's head had rested.

He looked partly like a sleeping boy, and partly like a lion in repose; all that strength under the skin, despite the vulnerability.

Jamie's extraordinary, thought Gabriel, and then he thought, *I will protect him with everything I have.* Considering James was a vampire, it was a strange thought to have.

'Gabriel, Anthea Webb ca- *oh.*'

Gabriel, startled, turned to see James staring at the painting. His first impulse was to throw the cover sheet over it, but that action was aborted when James walked up to the painting. Gabriel was left with the cloth clutched between his fingers.

'It's not finished,' he blurted. 'Why are you back early?'

'I'm not early. You've lost track of time.'

After that, James viewed the painting in silence. He took in every whorl of paint, every smear, every soft painted line and hard-edged drag mark.

Gabriel couldn't tell if James liked it or hated it, but his expression was strange. The edges of his eyes and the corners of his mouth were crinkled.

I want to paint that look.

'Is that what I look like to you?'

'Yes.'

Gabriel finally recognised that expression. If James's eyes had shed tears, he'd have recognised it at once. He dropped the sheet and stepped behind James, winding his arms around his waist so they could view the painting together.

'I look so… human,' said James in a hushed voice.

'Of course you do.' Gabriel pressed a kiss to James's temple.

'Look, this thing with Frazer. You don't have to–'

'Neither do you.'

'We're both in it for the civic duty of it, then?'

'And the moral outrage.'

'And the revenge.' James leaned back into Gabriel's arms. 'That's not it, though. Cael West's already dead.'

Gabriel folded his arms more firmly across James's chest and traced the tip of his nose along the edge of James's ear. 'It's not revenge.'

'No,' agreed James softly. 'It's fear. He's done so much, so fast, so cruelly. Who's going to stop him if we can't?'

Gabriel kissed the side of James's neck.

James turned in the circle of Gabriel's arms and pressed his face up into his throat. It was becoming a frequent gesture.

Gabriel loved it. The sensation of James's cool skin against that vulnerable point; the way James inhaled and sighed softly at the contact.

'Will you do something for me?'

'Anything,' James murmured.

'Drink from me.'

James recoiled. '*No.*'

'You don't have to bite if you don't want to.'

'You're fucking right I don't want to. You're not some handy little blood dispenser.'

'Blood given as a gift is best for you. You're stronger with it, and you need to be at your strongest for this. If you're going to take care of me, it's how I need to take care of you.'

Gabriel cupped James's glowering face and ran his thumb along the lines at the corners of his eyes. 'Use a needle to take it.'

'You hate needles.'

'You hate biting.'

'I–'

'You said it. We need to stop him, and we don't know if Michael can. We don't know what that infection is doing to him. If he can't even be certain of himself, then we can't be certain of his spook team either.

'It may end up down to you, me and Datta. And she still looks at me like I might secretly be Jack the Ripper.'

'She looks at *me* like I'm a ladybug that turned out to be a wasp.'

Gabriel snorted, then laughed outright at James's wounded air.

'Ladybug,' he said impishly.

'Are you saying I couldnae be a ladybug?'

'You can be anything you want. Come here.' He tugged James back into an embrace. 'Think about it, will you?'

'All right, then.'

'You'll do it?'

'It might save your life. Of course I'll do it. But I'll bite.'

'You don't have to.'

'I'm nae sticking unnecessary needles in you, love. Not after what you went through.'

'I trust you.'

'Do you trust me to bite you and stop?'

'You know I do.'

James drew Gabriel close. He nuzzled into Gabriel's throat. He took Gabriel's hand in his, lifted it to his mouth. He kissed the paint-smudged fingers, then his palm. He pushed Gabriel's shirtsleeve out of the way and kissed the muscle of his forearm.

Then he bit and worked the puncture wounds open. Gabriel gasped at the sting, but he stroked James's back soothingly while James sucked at the wound. James swallowed a few mouthfuls of blood and then licked the punctures. They healed shut under his tongue. When they were gone and the last of the blood gathered up by the tip of his tongue, James kissed the spot again.

He straightened – eyes bright, his skin flushed in a healthy glow – and then, with a quirk of a smile, he rubbed his thumb over Gabriel's bottom lip.

'You're covered in paint.'

'Occupational hazard.'

James kissed him, sucking on the stained lower lip. Gabriel held him tight, then loosened his grip and smoothed his palms over James's back and down to his backside. He squeezed and James deepened the kiss.

'I love how you taste,' James murmured. 'Paint and all.'

Gabriel caught James's lower lip between his teeth but he didn't bite. He pulled slowly on the lip, smiling as he did so, and James laughed breathily. Gabriel let go, then sealed his mouth over James's. There was no taste of blood – it had already been absorbed – but he detected a faint, sweet taste, unique and wonderful. It hadn't been there the first time he'd kissed James.

This is what Jamie tastes like, after he's drunk from me.

It should have been appalling, not romantic, but Gabriel couldn't help thinking it fitting.

They drew apart with little soft kisses, ending with James smearing his lips along Gabriel's jaw until he could brush them against his artist's ear.

'I had nothing when I came home, undead, from the war,' he murmured. 'Not even who I used to be. Since you came into my life, I'm more *me* than I hae ever been. I've found myself again. What Tavisa sees in that dream is wrong, Gabriel. You wouldnae hurt me. You're the keeper of my soul. Such as it is. Thank you.'

Gabriel kissed James's hair. 'You've given me back to myself too, you know. I don't know if we have souls, but if we do, you have charge of mine as well. We're good for each other.'

'We are. Thank you for the painting.'

'You're welcome.'

James caressed Gabriel's cheek again, kissed his mouth, then met his gaze. 'I'd like to show you something. I think you'll like it. Tonight?'

'Sure.' Gabriel rubbed his thumb against James's lower lip. 'Here. You've got paint on you.'

The gesture led to kissing, which led to fondling, which led to nakedness and Gabriel sprawled between James's legs, slowly frotting against James's pliant body, his cock sliding in the slipperiness of his own pre-come in the crease of James's thigh as they kissed languorously.

James spread his legs wider and wrapped them around Gabriel's hips, loving the heat of him there, holding him with his whole body. Gabriel moaned against James's lips, a harmony of sigh and whimper and wantonness. His hips rocked more urgently and his aching erection slipped from its course against James's leg, down between his thighs, between the cheeks of his arse. Gabriel's breathing grew hoarser and needier.

James shifted to let Gabriel's heavy cock slide more easily in the crease. A few more thrusts and then Gabriel stopped, forehead pressed to James's shoulder.

'Jamie. Is this okay?'

'Oh, my angel,' whispered James against his skin. 'It's fabulous. Christ, you feel good. Do ye like it, mae love? Do you like your cock there?'

'M-hhn,' Gabriel confirmed, rolling his hips again, but then he clutched James tight again. 'But I don't want to hurt you.'

'You cannae hurt me, mae bonnie lad.' James kissed his brow.

'It fucking *can* hurt if you don't prepare right,' Gabriel said into James's collarbone.

James wrapped his arms around Gabriel's shoulders. 'Did someone hurt you?'

'He didn't mean to,' said Gabriel, but his heart rate tripped up in sudden anxiety.

'Hey, hey, sshh,' James soothed him, stroking his back with steady hands.

'He didn't do it on purpose, exactly,' Gabriel confessed into James's skin. 'But I don't think it mattered to him. He said I owed him for the rent, and that I could pay it off that way.'

Gabriel froze, realising what he'd implied by those words. 'He was my boyfriend. I'm not a–'

'I know. Sshh, sweetheart. I've got you.'

'Eventually I decided I was better off under a bridge than with him, and I left.'

'Look at me.' He tilted Gabriel's face up and kissed his nose. 'You don't ever have to do anything you dinnae want tae do.'

Gabriel pressed his lips to James's. 'I want to be so close to you. Inside you. If you want that.'

'I want that.' James kissed him. His splayed hands moved soothingly down Gabriel's back, over his backside then thighs and up again.

'You cannae hurt me, angel. It's not possible. I'll get the lube and make it so good for you.'

'I want it to be good for you,' Gabriel protested, and so James kissed him some more, and rocked his hips up.

'It will be good for me, Gabriel. The thought of you fucking me is fantastic. I want tae feel you inside me.'

'Please,' muttered Gabriel. 'Please, please, please, yes.'

James retrieved the lube from the bedside cupboard. He returned to kissing until Gabriel was rutting again, his thick cock sliding in the soft space behind his balls, over perineum and more sensitive skin.

'Help me, sweetheart. Here you go.' He squeezed lube generously onto Gabriel's fingers. Gabriel kneeled between James's legs and worked a slicked finger, then two, against and then into the tight pucker. He kissed James's chest over and over, licked his nipples, sucked on the curve of his pecs.

James slid down on the bed and lifted his legs, resting his ankles on Gabriel's shoulders. He spread his knees, and made himself hard. Gabriel bent to suck him, then sat back to watch his fingers moving in James's arse.

'Christ,' Gabriel murmured, 'look at you, Jamie.'

'I can feel your fingers in me,' said James with a wanton grin. 'I can feel everything they're doing. Put another in. I can take it. I can take anything you have for me.'

Gabriel cautiously slid two fingers out, added lube, gently rocked three fingers in.

James jerked his hips to meet the sensation. When he'd been alive, he'd loved this, with boyfriends and girlfriends both. It turned out he still loved it. Gabriel's fingers were hot inside his cooler body, and it felt as brilliant as he'd imagined.

'Come on, angel,' he urged, spreading his legs wider. 'I want to feel your cock in me. I want to feel you fucking me.'

Panting, Gabriel withdrew his fingers, squirted more lube onto them. He rubbed them up and down his own aching shaft. He shuffled forward on his knees, held his cock against James's entrance, relaxed and slick and ready for him, and slowly pushed.

Both men groaned as Gabriel breached James's body. Gabriel kept slowly pushing. James clutched at the sheets and rolled his hips to meet the push, until Gabriel was fully seated inside him.

Gabriel held his quivering thighs still, and bent his head to drop a kiss on James's chest, then on his mouth.

'So hot inside me,' James said. 'Fuck me, Gabriel. Now.'

Gabriel moved slowly at first, then faster. Slowly again. Long, slow slides and short, rapid thrusts. Then hard and fast, a few strokes.

'Give it to me,' James urged him. 'You cannae hurt me. Fuck me hard.'

Gabriel moved again, long and slow, then faster, faster, fast and deep, their bodies meeting with a slap and the slick squish of lube and Gabriel panting and James urging him on with short, deep syllables: *Yes, fuck, yes, fuck me, harder, aye, good, good, fuck, aye, harder, give it to me, give it, more, all of it. Fuck me, baby. Angel. My angel. Fuck me.*

Until, with a sharp, deep cry, Gabriel threw his head back, thrusting with abandon, and came in waves of pleasure so intense there was nothing in the world except his pleasure and James's rough voice saying, *aye, that's it, come mae bonnie, aye.*

He collapsed against James's wonderful, cool body and panted hotly against James's chest. James let Gabriel's cock slip free while keeping Gabriel wrapped up tight in arms and legs.

'That was so good, sweetheart,' he said, nuzzling into Gabriel's hairline.

Gabriel said something almost incoherent.

'I'm good,' James replied, kissing Gabriel's brow. 'That's all I want right now: you, happy. We'll do something for me later.'

Gabriel hummed agreement and they snuggled, too content to stir.

They might have stayed wrapped up together for the whole night after, except Gabriel's phone burst loudly into the triumphal brass-and-strings urgency of *Ride of the Valkyries*.

'Michael?' James asked, smirking.

'Anthea,' Gabriel corrected him. 'Michael's *The Mikado*.' He thumbed to answer the call. 'Anthea, what–'

'There's a problem with your brother, Mr Dare,' said Anthea, brisk and emotionless. 'He's started to lose time.'

'What the hell does that mean?'

'It means he has periods that he can't account for. Mr Dare, your brother has three times returned to his senses, either at his desk or in another part of the building, and he can't account for the preceding period, of up to half an hour. He's no memory of what took place, or how or why he changed location. In short, your brother and I both fear Frazer's influence on his mind is growing.'

Gabriel tried to imagine what it would be like, to lose a half hour of his day. A half hour of his mind. 'Jesus. How's he doing?'

'He is doing remarkably well,' said Anthea. 'But he and I agree it's time to activate the Fortunato protocol.'

'No.'

'We must wall him off, Mr Dare, for our safety as well as his. We don't know what Frazer may learn if he's in command of your brother's mind even for brief periods.'

Two spots of high colour flushed Gabriel's cheekbones. 'You'll look after him?'

'With my life, Mr Dare,' said Anthea matter-of-factly. 'I'll wait to hear from you.'

Gabriel disconnected the call and clutched the phone in his hand, as though he could throttle the bad news out of it. 'You heard all that?'

'Aye.' James closed his hand over Gabriel's. 'It's up to us, now.'

Chapter Eighteen

THEY DISCUSSED THE CONTINGENCY PLANS FOR THEIR CONTINGENCY PLANS. Gabriel pretended, poorly, that he wasn't deeply troubled by his brother's situation.

When they had run out of contingencies, James said, 'Let me show you that thing I was talking about.'

'What thing?'

'That'd spoil the surprise. Put your gloves on. And a scarf. Hat too. Haven't you got a warmer jacket?'

'I'll wear a jumper under my leather one. What about you? That field jacket of yours won't be thick enough, will it?'

'I don't feel the cold.'

Gabriel whipped his dark green scarf around James's neck anyway. 'The colour suits you.'

James dressed more for freedom of movement and the largeness of his field jacket's pockets, which he had filled with Secret Items. He darted away from Gabriel when he tried to find out what they were.

'Be good,' said James, mock-stern, 'or you won't get your treat.'

'This isn't your old plan to poison me and dispose of me in the Thames, is it? Because I'm wise to your wiles, Doctor Sharpe, and I have built up immunity to arsenic through careful small doses.'

'Curses, foiled again. I shall have to tie you to the railway tracks after all.'

'Sounds all right, actually,' murmured Gabriel, pressing his body suggestively to James's thigh and hip.

'All in good time,' James replied, cupping Gabriel's arse and giving it a squeeze.

The walk to Plaistow station took a while. Gabriel fell into another troubled reverie. James kept pace with him in silence, near enough that their arms brushed as they walked. The District Line took them to Tower Hill Station. They emerged into the crisp night and skirted west, around the walls of the Tower of London, through the half empty terrace and towards the Thames.

'You're taking me to the Tower?' asked Gabriel, attempting levity again. 'That's a bit Elizabethan of you, isn't it?'

'Not tonight, but it's a fine idea. We'll break in after dark. You can have your way with me in the White Tower.'

'But not tonight?'

'No. Tonight it's this.' They emerged on the embankment alongside the Thames. Ahead of them, spanning the murky water, was Tower Bridge.

'Tower Bridge is my treat?' Gabriel was puzzled.

James grinned. 'No. Showing you London from the very top of the Bridge, where the flags are, is your treat.'

'But it's closed this time of night.'

'I'm not going through the front door. More like the pigeon loft.'

Gabriel looked up the structure's vast height to the walkway spanning the two towers. The London city flag and Union Jack flew either side of the city's coat of arms in the centre of the walkway.

'Up there, you mean?'

'Aye.'

'How?'

'I thought we'd climb. If you're game.'

Gabriel beamed like a concentrated ray of excited sunshine.

'When?' He stood taller, so eager to be on his way up he was stretching towards the summit already. He bounced on the balls of his feet like an eager sprinter at the starting post.

'We'll wait till it's quieter,' said James, gratified by the enthusiastic response. 'You'll have to do exactly as I say, mind.' He handed over a wad of cloth from his pocket. 'You'll need this, for starters.'

Gabriel shook out the thin tube of black wool. 'A *snood*?'

'Military grade. It's from my own kit. Good for protecting the neck, lightweight, easy to pull over your mouth when there's dust and debris around or it's windy.'

Dubiously, Gabriel pulled the snood over his head and arranged it around his throat. He tested the sensation of it over his mouth and nose, arranged it over his ears. In minutes he'd found four different ways to wear it, making James laugh.

'A bloke I served with used to shin up date palms and use his as a basket for the fruit,' said James, 'I once saw a wee lass wearing one as a skirt.'

Gabriel, recovered from his snood snootiness, was genuinely thrilled with the article. He played with it as they wandered along the embankment in the chilly November air. James talked about his time at medical school. Gabriel told him stories of his university days. They avoided any talk at all about Frazer and what lay ahead in that regard.

By eleven pm, the embankment and the Bridge were sufficiently deserted for James to enact the next part of his scheme.

'Put that on. Do up your coat and for God's sake, hold on. Don't squirm.'

He shook out a few mountaineering straps that had been rolled in his pockets. In a dark corner beside the bridge, he fastened Gabriel into them, and had Gabriel climb onto his back. He fastened the straps securely around his own waist and shoulders.

'Hold tight. Pull the snood up. You'll need it later. Close your eyes if you like.'

Gabriel's gangly weight on James's back hardly made a difference, although he had to be careful with his centre of gravity as he made his way onto the elegant curves of the suspension beams leading to the first abutment of the Bridge.

Gabriel made himself look this time, keeping his eyes wide open to watch London open up beneath him as James ascended, swift and sure, past the first abutment, along the second set of suspension cables and girders, to the roof of the southern abutment. James found footholds and handholds to reach the turrets.

Once on the roof, he scurried sideways in a fashion that Gabriel might have found creepy if he hadn't been so thoroughly fascinated. When they reached the central span, James crawled onto it, found a comfortable place to stop, and manoeuvred until he was sitting, feet over the edge.

Gabriel's legs were locked around his waist, arms around his shoulders, and his breath was hot against James's ear through the cloth over his face. He was hot between his thighs, too, where his arousal pushed against James's lower back.

'My strength kink is showing.' His huff of laughter was muffled and subdued by awe.

'No wriggling. It's distracting. Just relax and enjoy the view.'

Gabriel rubbed his nose affectionately against James's neck, then made himself ignore his erotic response to James's body and abilities. He settled, finding it comfortable and even comforting to be so intimately wrapped around James's body like this. He rested his chin on James's shoulder, cheek against his ear, and looked at his city.

His artist's eye picked out lights, from the muted glows of living rooms and bedrooms to the harsh, bright glares of street lights, vehicles, neon signs and floodlit monuments. He could see the different qualities of darkness in the places between the lights: the greys of office buildings, and a deeper, moving dark of the trees in Green and Hyde Parks to the west.

James, with his keen eyesight, verified what Gabriel saw when asked, but mostly Gabriel clung to him, like a child on the shoulders of an adult. The artist drank in the lofty flood of colours, shapes and sounds sprawled in a panorama in front of him.

He knew this city best from far below, in the dank, dark and dangerous alleys, hollows and walkways of the homeless. He knew the city's grime and pain and sorrow, but here was the majesty of his London, too. The cone of the Gherkin, the sharp line of the Shard, the ring of the London Eye. St Paul's and the Tate. Parliament and the murky ribbon of the Thames. The motorways and the pedestrian malls, the narrow, secret streets and the rooftops: tessellated, sloping, flat or turreted. Glinting lights in the dark, marking the traffic or the tower blocks, flight paths and phone towers. His familiar world shown to him, unfamiliar, in the cold, sparkling night.

'This is one of the best, most beautiful things I've ever seen,' he breathed when he could speak.

James grinned, his vampire teeth unsheathed and unthreatening, totally at home in his skin.

Overwhelmed with emotion, Gabriel tucked his nose behind James's ear and kissed him through the snood. He tightened his arms and legs around James's torso in a spooning hug.

'You're brilliant,' he said. 'I've spent all my life fighting or hiding from things stronger than me. You make me feel like I don't have to hide. I don't have to fight alone. You brought light into me, Jamie. Right inside of me. Whatever happens next with Frazer, however it all turns out, I want you to know that.'

James pressed a hand over Gabriel's, clasped about his chest.

'You know this may end very badly.'

'Yes.'

'I spent years in war zones, patching up the consequences of things ending badly. I was caught in a few bad endings myself. It's frightening how fast things can go pear-shaped.'

Gabriel's arms tightened again around his chest.

'There's something important we need to discuss. I hoped there'd be years to think about it. But we may not have years.'

'It's all right,' said Gabriel.

'It isn't. I've led you into this.'

'You didn't. Frazer had his eye on me and Michael for a long time. He'd been working with West for a long time too. Maybe fate brought us together. I've just finished telling you how glad I am about that, so don't be a twat.'

James's laugh was thick with emotion. 'Well, when you put it like that,' he said, 'I'd best send a thank you card to fate. Only good manners for introducing me to my soulmate.'

'That's better.'

'If fate tries to take you away again, mind you, I'll beat the fucker to death. Which brings us neatly back to the topic at hand. Gabriel. I need to know–'

'Yes.'

'You don't even know what I'm asking.'

'Yes I do. Do you honestly think I haven't been thinking about the possibility of becoming a vampire, since West tried to kill me? I'm a bit flaky, but I'm not an idiot.'

'I'd never try to turn you without your consent.'

'I know that.'

'But we may not be in a position where I can ask, or where you can answer. Best to clarify it now.'

'I didn't take you for a pessimist.'

'Take me for a realist,' said James, 'Which is what I am. I never counted on being turned into a vampire without getting a say-so.

Things are what they are, Gabriel. I need to be prepared, but I won't act without your consent.'

'You'd let me die?'

'I *would* be letting you die if I tried to turn you. That's what it means to become a vampire. You die and then some bastard brings you back.'

James clenched his hands into fists. 'But I don't know that I could let you stay dead. I'd want to try to bring you back. I'm selfish. I can't bear the thought of losing you. I would… struggle to let you go, if you couldn't be saved. But. I promised myself in Afghanistan, once I was back in what approximated to my right mind, I'd never do to another person what was done to me.'

'James–'

'I could never do to *you* what was done to me. Nae without cause. But death's more than a vague possibility here. We're going into battle. And Sergeant Datta dreamed of a body I think is you. It feels inevitable. So. I need to know. If there's no other way to save you, do you want this? Would you want me to let you die human, or do you want me to turn you? There's nae guarantee you'd survive the turning. I'd never attempt it if there were any other chance you'd live. It's your choice.'

'And if I choose to die human, you'll honour that?'

'I'll let you die, if that's what you want,' said James, voice low but firm. 'I swear. I'd let you go rather than turn you against your will.'

'I don't want to leave you if there's an option,' said Gabriel. 'So if the worst happens, you have my consent. I understand the consequences.'

'I'm not sure you do. There's a price to pay for being what I am.'

'And I see you pay it every day.' Gabriel brushed his nose against James's temple. 'Did you really think I hadn't considered this at all?'

'I assumed you had. I was prepared to talk you out of it, but you never asked.'

'I wouldn't become a vampire on a whim, but it was always an option. An inevitability, I should say. Something for my later years, or if I was diagnosed with a terminal illness.'

James frowned.

'My 50th birthday seemed a good time to raise the issue, assuming you can put up with me for that long. I figured becoming a vampire then would compensate for some of the restrictions of age. At least then, you can be my young and pretty toyboy, yeah?'

James snorted an unexpected laugh at that. 'And you can be my sugar daddy.'

'That's the spirit. I thought waiting till my 50s would allow me sufficient human experience to combine nicely with supernatural capacities. By then you'd have a wealth of vampiring experience to be my mentor.'

'You've thought about this a lot more than I'd realised.'

Gabriel's voice grew warm at James's shocked tone. 'Did you imagine I'd allow myself to die of old age and leave you to face virtual immortality alone?'

'I… did.'

'Idiot,' said Gabriel fondly.

James was a picture of confused emotion. Horrified and pleased, warmed and frightened.

'I know you'd never do it without consent, Jamie. I trust you absolutely on that, as with everything else. The answer is yes. If ever there is no hope for my survival, except for you to turn me, then do it. I'm not prepared to risk it now, on the off-chance it'll work. I don't want to die artistically young. When I'm 50, assuming you still want me around, we'll re-evaluate.'

James grinned. 'All right. Is it a bit shite of me to be relieved that you'll consider it when you hit the big 5-0?'

'Don't be daft. Does this mean you think you'll want me around in 20-odd years?'

'I'll want you around in 400.' James shook his head. 'Christ, what a notion. Oh well, if you can stick it, I can.'

'We can make it a competition.'

'Anything you can do, I can do better, eh?'

'Think you can love me for better and for longer than I can love you?'

'I'll lay a tenner on it.'

'You *are* daft. You're on.'

They leaned against each other, watching the wheeling of the night stars and flow of the Thames, and hung on to the hope that they'd both live long enough to laugh about that stupid bet later.

Chapter Nineteen

HELENE DUPRE SAT AT THE TABLE AT IVY GARDENS. SHE RAISED HER GAZE from a new watercolour Gabriel had left by his chair – a view of London by night from an impossibly high angle, the darkness made rich and lively with deep colour and glowing light. A departure for him – he'd always drawn from life before, though this had his characteristic sense of warmth, of hope emerging from the shadows.

Instead, she watched the two men move around each other in the small kitchen. She couldn't put her finger on their mood. An odd tension lay underneath that beautiful, spontaneous choreography borne of familiarity and ease.

Gabriel reached for cups as James fetched tea bags, which he dropped into the cups a moment after they clinked down on the bench. James ducked under Gabriel's arm to get a long serving plate while Gabriel reached over his head to get to the cupboard for biscuits. James patted Gabriel's hip as the taller man arranged chocolate digestives on the rectangular china plate, letting his fingers linger and trail away as he went to the fridge for milk. Gabriel smiled at the affectionate touch, the tightness around his mouth and eyes easing. When James returned with the milk, Gabriel's fingers brushed over James's as he took the squat, half-empty pint bottle from him.

'I see the two of you have graduated from the flirting portion of your programme.'

James looked sheepish, but Gabriel threw a tea towel at her head. Helene snatched it out of the air. 'Cheeky, *coco*,' she admonished him fondly. 'You wouldn't throw things at me if I'd been able to bring myself to give your bottom a smack from time to time when you were naughty. Maybe your doctor can see to that for you now.'

Gabriel promptly choked on his sip of tea.

James regarded her with mock-severity. 'Isn't *coco* French for rooster?'

'Oh, he was quite the little cockerel back then, and I was a regular mother hen about him. Michael used to tell me off for spoiling him.'

'And you didn't listen?' James put her tea and the plate of biscuits on the table. 'Not even to the man paying your wage?'

'Michael never paid my wage,' she replied, puzzled, as the two men took their seats.

'He told us that he did.' Gabriel poked at the biscuits to tidy up the pattern, and Helene snatched one up, gleefully putting the pattern in disarray.

'I suppose he must have, if he says so,' said Helene. She bit thoughtfully into a digestive and had a sip of tea. 'It explains a few things.'

'Such as?' Gabriel broke his morsel in half, put a piece in his mouth upside down and began to suck off the chocolate coating. Helene softened as she watched him, as though he were still a little boy indulging an old habit.

'Such as why I was able to get away with so much cheek towards your father. He threatened to sack me twice a week but never did. I thought he liked me. Oh well.' She waved her hand imperiously. 'I didn't like him liking me, so it's a relief that he didn't. The man is a brute and a bore. It must make him such charming company in that ridiculous House of Lords.'

'They're all pompous asses there,' said Gabriel darkly. 'It's possible the bastard is popular.'

'We can always hope for a hunting accident. He might get mistaken for a weasel, if we're lucky.'

'More likely a Common Snipe,' muttered Gabriel. He noticed James looking at him with a furrowed brow. 'What?'

'Your father is a *Lord*?'

'My father is a twat.'

'He could be a twat *and* a lord. Wouldn't be the first time.'

'He's the Earl of Newstable,' grumbled Gabriel, 'Among other things.'

'Is that a hereditary title? Does that mean I'm dating a viscount?' James grinned.

'Michael's the eldest, he gets to be called viscount. I'm just Gabriel.' He fidgeted uncomfortably in his chair.

'Second sons may be called Lord Whatsit, if all the spare titles have been taken up,' said Helene helpfully.

James hooted merrily. 'I'm shacked up with a Lord. I feel like a Regency romance heroine. I'd better get a bonnet.'

'It's only a courtesy title, and those empire style dresses won't suit you at all, never mind those awful bonnets,' complained Gabriel, but he was laughing. 'There's no need to get all excited. Not like *me*. I'm shagging a Combat Medical Technician, from a regiment and *everything*. That's *proper* Regency sexy, eh, Mr Sharpe, you wally.'

'That's Corporal Doctor Wally, Sir, to you, your lordship.'

'Get yourself one of those sexy red coats and the tight white trousers and the riding boots, and honestly, you can call me whatever you like.'

'Stop it,' said Helene, flicking at them with the tea towel. 'The foreplay is making me envious. All I have to go home to is a box set of murder mysteries.' But she was inordinately pleased with them.

James brushed the tip of his nose against Gabriel's temple, kissed the spot, then made a great show of wrapping both hands around his cup of tea. Gabriel, who could not shut off his delighted grin, rubbed his bare foot against James's calf under the table. They were definitely both more relaxed.

'It's good to see you both so happy,' said Helene. 'And look, more joy for the adoring couple. Income! A cheque for you, Corporal Doctor Sharpe, Sir, and I've transferred a good sum to your bank account, Gabe, my dear, so…'

'Hey, My Vagabond Lord,' James brandished the cheque, 'I have here a metaphorical purse of gold from your personal Medici. We get to keep the roof over our heads another month because the good people of London recognise artistic merit when they see it. As they bloody ought.'

'You're completely bonkers,' Gabriel told him, and kissed him.

Helene took the opportunity to use the tea towel to polish a mark she'd seen on the table. The kiss was short and sweet, but she kept on polishing, distracted.

'You can look up, Helene,' said Gabriel, tapping her on the elbow. 'We're all done with the foreplay for now.'

Helene sniffed at the table and scrubbed at the discolouration. 'I beg you not to tell me why, boys, but you seem to have spilled a combination of crushed garlic, silver nitrate and blood on your table.' Finally satisfied with the clean-up, she flung the tea towel over their heads, where it failed to reach the sink and flopped onto the floor.

'Oh, that was–' Gabriel began.

'I did beg you not to explain, though if I have to include a card on your future pieces to warn that they contain your actual blood, I should point out that Vincent Castiglia already has the paintings-created-in-my-own blood corner of the market. Which reminds me,' she seized her tea before ploughing into the diversionary story. 'A strange man was hanging around the gallery the other day. He wanted to know if your portraits were meant to be vampires.' She rolled her eyes at that. 'I told him that interpretation was a matter of individual perception.'

She looked at the two of them, suddenly so still and tense again, staring at her. 'Yes,' she continued, perplexed, 'I thought it an odd interpretation, too. Vampires are usually much more cold and cruel in imagery. Sensuous as well, aren't they? Still, I suppose, like everyone else, he sees a lot of what he himself brings to it and he brought a lot of "serial killer vibe" with him.'

'He didn't hurt you?' Gabriel lurched towards her, hand outstretched for her wrist.

She flinched from his sudden movement before recovering from the surprise and patting his hand. 'No, no, don't fuss. He was just very strange and off-putting. I didn't trust him. When I asked him if he wanted to buy a piece, he said he didn't collect art, only artists. Then he sniggered like a creep and went away.'

Gabriel grasped her hand. 'If you see him again, get away as fast as you can. Don't be polite, don't let him touch you, and call the police right away. Ask for Tavisa Datta.' He squeezed her hand hard, and she winced. He released her abruptly, muttering apologies.

'Gabriel, I'm fine.' She rubbed at her fingers, alarmed at his distress. 'Who the hell is he?'

Gabriel shook his head, distraught.

'He's a dangerous nutjob,' said James as he rubbed his thumb soothingly over Gabriel's knuckles. 'He's likely involved with the murders the Met's been investigating.'

'Really?' Helene's alarm shot up another few notches.

'If you see him or anyone else suspicious, lock the gallery up, or get away and call for help at once. I'll give you Datta's number.'

'Of course.' Helene bit her lower lip. 'Does Michael know? Is he looking after you?'

'He knows,' said Gabriel.

'Well, that's something.' She put the cup down with a nervous clatter. It hit the side of the biscuit plate, tilting the cup and spilling tea over her sleeve, bodice and lap.

'Oh, for…' She stood up and held a hand out for a tea towel. Gabriel scooped the one up from the floor and unthinking, she dabbed at herself with it, adding smears of silver nitrate, dried blood and the smell of garlic to the damage.

She started to swear then. James fetched a dishcloth but she waved it away. 'No, no, take it away. I'll go home and change. I've done my business here anyway.'

'If you didn't drive, take a taxi. Don't walk,' said Gabriel grimly.

'You seriously think I would get on public transport like this? Don't be ridiculous. The van is outside, I'll go home and–'

'And lock up the gallery and go for a holiday to Calais until we give you the all clear that it's safe.'

'I detest Calais, as you well know, and I have a business to run.'

'Helene, do as he asks.' James was much calmer than Gabriel, his voice deep and crisp and clear, a voice of command neither Gabriel nor Helene had heard before. 'The man you're talking about is dangerous. He's killed people already. You need to be alert and on the lookout for him or people like him.'

'You're frightening me, James.'

'Good. You should be frightened. Gabriel, get her coat. Helene, I'll travel back to the gallery with you–'

'You'll do no such thing,' she snapped. 'If he's dangerous and he's been threatening Gabriel, then you stay here and look after our boy. I can take care of myself.' She pulled an atomiser of perfume out of her handbag. 'It's not mace,' she said by way of explanation. 'But a face full of this was handy some nights walking home when I was at art school. I'll have my keys in the other hand. I can do damage if I need to.' She grin-glared a little savagely at James's surprise. 'Try being a woman walking at night in any city on this

Earth, Doctor Sharpe, and you'll have a grab-bag of self-defence options in your handbag, too.'

He cocked his head in a wry, you-learn-something-every-day fashion. 'Well, take this, too.' From the kitchen, he fetched a slender silver knife, which he held gingerly by the enamel handle. The blade of it was discoloured and smelled of garlic. 'Use it if you have to. I'm not sure how much good it'll do, but a stab to the gut, the thigh or the eyeball will give you a head start.'

'The eyeball.'

'Maybe a bit hard to manage. Just aim for a big target, stab and run.'

'You've already scared me, James.'

'Then be *more* scared. Be more scared and more careful than you've ever been.'

Gabriel returned with her coat. He helped her into it, then the two of them insisted on walking to the van with her. The street was otherwise empty, but Helene couldn't shake the sensation that she was being watched. Damn these two for spooking her so badly. She put her bag on the passenger seat. She decided to leave the atomiser and the knife on the upholstery, in easy reach.

'Get out of the city, at least,' Gabriel said. 'I couldn't bear for you to be hurt, too.'

Helene took Gabriel's face in her hands. She'd known him since he was an unsettled, sad, lonely boy of seven, flinching at shadows, at sudden movements and at his father. Half an hour ago he had been a man happy and so obviously in love. She wanted that happy man back, and for that little boy inside to remember that he wasn't lost and hurt and alone any more.

'I'll change first and go to Cornwall. I'll scout for talent around there, as I've been planning. I'll be careful and I'll text you to let you know I'm safe. And you'll text me back?'

'Of course.'

'Good boy. *Mon coco.*' She stood on her tiptoes and guided him down so she could kiss his forehead. 'Be careful, *cheri*, and let your James take care of you, too.'

'I will. And he does.'

'Good. I'll text you soon. An hour or two at the most. I'll need to pack.'

'Keep the doors locked until you're ready to go.'

'I will, I will.' She hugged him, then James, and got into the car and drove off.

Gabriel didn't dare call Michael. They hardly spoke to Michael at all these days, at his insistence as well as their own, and even then, never in person. They couldn't ever be sure nobody else was listening inside Michael's *head*.

Gabriel called Anthea Webb and told her that Niall Frazer had been hanging around Helene at the gallery. He demanded to know what she meant to do about it.

'What I can, Mr Dare, as always. I'll despatch an agent to keep an eye on her until she's left for, Cornwall, was it?'

'Yes. And for pity's sake, can you tell me why he'd even be at her gallery? She's got nothing to do with any of this.'

'She has everything to do with it, Mr Dare, if your reaction is anything to go by. Frazer is looking for leverage. Your brother is resisting him with the greatest fortitude and courage. He talks about you a lot, you know.'

'He does?'

'I believe he finds it comforting, and it reminds him of his humanity.'

Gabriel tried to be flippant. 'He won't thank you for telling me.'

'He won't, Mr Dare, but at this stage I would welcome him being sufficiently himself to take me to task over it. The truth is, he's struggling to retain his sense of self, these last two days. Talking about you when you were small seems to help him to do that.' She paused, and when she spoke next her voice held the faintest tremor. 'Believe what you will, Mr Dare, but your brother loves you very much, and regrets his inability to express this to you in an acceptable manner.'

James, who could hear every word as clear as a bell, carefully removed the phone from Gabriel's ever-tightening grip.

'We all hope there'll be time for a proper family epiphany, Miss Webb,' he said. 'But we have to live long enough to have one. Frazer's looking for leverage. How might he use Helene? And to what end?'

'That is the question,' replied Miss Webb, returning instantly to her usual brisk efficiency tinged with wry humour. 'While Michael Dare respects her immensely, she's more use as leverage against *Gabriel* Dare. My considered opinion is that Frazer might try to capture rather than kill her as a method of persuading *your* Mr Dare to a particular course of action.'

'What would be the point of that?'

'To force *my* Mr Dare into a course of action.'

'That action being…?' But he realised the answer as he spoke. 'To give himself up to the change. To surrender to the fox.'

'Precisely.'

'Shite. We'd better take good bloody care of Helene Dupre then, hadn't we?'

'An agent is on his way to her as we speak. She lives above the gallery, so we can keep a close eye without alarming her, I'm sure.'

'Good.' He rang off and handed the phone back to Gabriel.

Gabriel shoved it in his pocket without looking at it. 'If he touches her I'm going to fucking kill him.' He shook his head, as though throwing off a vision of stabbing the fox spirit through the heart. 'If we can work out what he wants, we have a better chance of stopping him.'

'Agreed.'

Gabriel began pacing. 'Let's go over what we know.'

'One,' began James, 'Major Cael West, a vampire on a tour of duty in Afghanistan, was recruiting there, we assume, for his coterie, Michael called it. He attacked me because he wanted someone with medical experience in his gruesome squad. For a specific task, I wonder?'

'Frazer didn't seem to care,' Gabriel noted. 'What is it with thugs like West trying to impress some worse bastard. Like they're a demented pit dog taking a dead rat to a new master.' He stared at James with horrified surprise at what had come out of his mouth. 'God. Sorry, Jamie.'

James dismissed the slip. 'I've been called worse, love. So – West is dead and Frazer gave next to no fucks about that, which means he can work around not having West in the plan. We have to assume that West's yahoos, however many there are, are still working for Frazer.'

'Yahoos that, along with West, murdered several of my friends, with a view to involving me.' Gabriel stopped pacing and dropped into a chair, face in his hands. 'Jesus. How did he even know about me?'

'Google? Or Debrett's.'

'It's not fucking funny.'

'I'm not joking. Either he stumbled across you and Michael by accident, or you've both been targeted from the start, which makes more sense. Frazer, West and their crew are supernatural beings. No doubt they know about the Bureau. Assume they've been working from the Bureau outwards, trying to find a weakness. They find out about Michael; look into his family history. Either through online searches or the peerage guide, they discover there's an earl one generation up, and a wayward artist brother further down the bloodline. They could've gone in for random vampire killings to attract the Bureau's attention. That wouldn't necessarily attract

Michael's specific interest. Tying them to *you* meant that Michael took a personal interest. It's why we were both at the Blakely ball. That's the intel we were both fed.'

'Right.' Gabriel scrubbed his hands through his hair, leaving it even messier. 'But that whole thing didn't go exactly to plan, did it? So it's not like they're masterminds of the criminal world. They nearly killed Michael outright when he fell. He ended up scratched instead of bitten, though that's been bad enough.'

'It looks like it's all aimed at recruiting Michael for Frazer's gang.'

'But what for? There's got to be a bigger plan than adding a man with a Saville Row suit for every day of the week to the payroll.'

'Michael must be more important than that, in the scheme of things.'

'Well, until a month ago, I thought he was a civil servant working directly in the House of Commons.'

'An important job?'

'The secretary to the permanent secretary of the Cabinet Office.'

'Important, then. That role has a lot more continuity to government services than actual politicians, doesn't it? Even if it's mostly a cover position, he's obviously the liaison between the Bureau and the Government.'

'Frazer must have long term plans,' decided Gabriel. 'Something that involves not only getting a mole into the Bureau – other agents might have done as well for that – but government. What would a fox spirit want the ear of the government for?'

James shook his head. 'I don't think it's solely about influence. Michael's infected, but can he infect others? If not, can he bring Frazer in to recruit directly? Michael's a foot into the House of Commons. Isn't your father a foot into the House of Lords as well? I know sod-all about fox spirits, but I know a thing or two about vectors for the spread of disease.'

'But what's it all *for*? Say he forces me to do something that'll force Michael to make a choice to surrender himself to Frazer's influence. What does he want with that influence? Why on earth would a fox spirit want to control the British Parliament?'

'Stop thinking about him as a just a fox. He's a *predator*.'

'Fine. What does a *predator* want?'

'Blood,' said James automatically. 'If I needed to hunt, that's what I'd need. On a grander scale? Ways to hunt blood more safely. So. What does a fox want to hunt?

'Chickens,' Gabriel offered. 'Small game. No, we have to think bigger. Foxes are notoriously clever. They're fast, cunning and opportunistic. But this isn't *any* fox. This is the epitome of fox-ness. A fox *spirit*.'

'So he wants…' James tried to picture it. 'The metaphorical chicken coop. The Bureau and the politicians.'

'Not the chicken coop,' said Gabriel. 'That's only a captive feeding ground. Something *bigger*. Does he want the farmer? No. A fox doesn't want a farmer. They're the enemy and they fight back. Foxes hunt *livestock*.' Gabriel's eyes went wide as the thought struck him. 'If Frazer can get command of the coop, though, he'll have access to the whole damned *farm*. Chickens, sheep, piglets, the lot.'

'It's a grand analogy, but what's the farm, here? London? Surely that's just a particularly large chicken coop.'

'Try *all* of the United Kingdom.'

'Jesus,' breathed James, horrified. 'That's a farm worth murdering for. Fuck, the scope of this is way out of our league.'

'Only if he succeeds,' said Gabriel. 'But he makes mistakes. He slipped up with Michael at the ball, and we've bought extra time. Neither of them knew you'd be part of the equation, which meant West failed in his attempts to turn me as well. Fuck this. Fuck him. I survived my father and years of psychiatric treatment and living on the streets. And you've been a brilliant badass since day one. We're *not* in his league. We *outclass* the son of a bitch.'

He jerked his chin up at the end of this speech, daring James to contradict him, but James was grinning.

'Fuck, aye, we do.'

Gabriel's phone buzzed. He plucked the device from his pocket to check the message. He went chalk white.

James snatched the phone out of Gabriel's hand before he dropped it. There on the screen was a text message and a photograph of Helene Dupre. Helene had changed into a new dress – a dress of pale salmon pink, with little blue forget-me-nots scattered all over the skirt and sleeves.

A flamingo covered in tiny blue flowers.

Her wrists were bound in a pale pink scarf and she was gagged with a length of stocking. Her brow was smeared in blood. She did not appear to be conscious.

Below the image was a text message:

> Meet me with your brother in two
> hours. If he comes you can have
> your French hinny back. Don't tell
> him it's me. Daft fucker'll put
> up a fight. Want her back in one
> piece don't you?

Gabriel called Miss Webb and began by hurling abuse until James confiscated the phone.

'Our agent's dead,' she told him grimly. 'Frazer sent three of them for her. I'll give her this, she fought them. I'm loading up the CCTV footage now. She stuck one in the face with her keys and sprayed another in the eyes with her Estee Lauder atomiser.'

Gabriel passed from furious to frantic to stone cold. He reached across James to tap the speaker on.

'We have to plan this out,' he said. 'We have to get a step ahead.'

The three of them argued about the plan, particularly when Webb suggested London Bridge Hospital as the rendezvous point.

'We have someone who does discreet bloodwork for us there,' she argued. 'They can get us in, and Mr Dare would plausibly go there for results.'

'Does he need a plausible reason to be anywhere?'

'We want Frazer to think your brother is walking into a trap unawares.'

'He *is* walking into a trap,' James pointed out.

'But not *unawares*.' Webb's exasperation was beginning to show.

'Has it escaped your memory that you have visions of probably Gabriel falling to his death from a height. London Bridge Hospital, it may surprise you to learn, *has a roof.*'

'Everywhere has a roof, Doctor Sharpe.'

'Not Hyde Park. Not the Serpentine.'

'What possible reason could I have for sending Mr Dare to a garden?'

'Fuck plausibility.'

'We need a place where our people can get in unobserved. A park is too open. The hospital building gives us access, cover and medical back-up if it's needed.'

'I can provide back-up.'

'You have your own set of instructions,' Miss Webb rejoined waspishly. 'If you want your Ms Dupre to survive.'

James turned to Gabriel. 'Don't tell me you're doing this. You *know* what Datta saw.'

'I know what she *thinks* she saw,' said Gabriel, 'But Anthea's right. We have to make it look like we're leading Michael into a trap, but we have to be able to set the trap for Frazer. The hospital gives us scope that none of the parks offer, and everywhere else has a roof anyway. It might not be me. Datta says I'm responsible for the raven falling. I'm hardly going to fling myself off a building on purpose. Maybe it's Frazer she's seeing. I'd throw him in front of a bus for tuppence.'

'I'm coming with you,' asserted James. 'And I'm staying with you.' James's fangs had descended in his anger.

'You're doing no such bloody thing. I don't need a fucking babysitter.' Instead of recoiling from those sharp teeth as a sensible human should, Gabriel grabbed James by the collar and dragged him up until they were nose to nose.

'You have to go after Helene,' Gabriel growled. 'I need you to do this. I can't have anything happen to her. I trust you, Jamie. You can get her back. Anthea and I know what we're doing.'

'You haven't a bloody clue what you're doing. We're *all* making this up as we go along. It could go tits up in a dozen ways. I can't have anything happen to *you*.'

'It's dangerous for everyone,' Miss Webb snapped out over the speaker. 'If you want to be a step ahead, this is how we do it.'

James and Gabriel grasped each other's hands.

'Fine,' James agreed through gritted teeth. 'I'll call Datta. You get onto Michael.'

'I'll handle Mr Dare,' said Miss Webb coolly. 'Tavisa already has her head around our other contingency plans. She'll debrief you, Doctor Sharpe.'

She rang off to make her calls. James called Sergeant Datta and they arranged to meet at the gallery. Gabriel received Miss Webb's text with confirmation of the rendezvous at London Bridge Hospital.

James put on his field jacket and headed for the door. He went back to Gabriel. He tried and failed to speak.

'You can do this,' said Gabriel quietly, leaning into him, brow to brow. 'We can do this. I trust you. With my life. With *Helene's* life. And Michael's.'

With a gulp, almost a sob, James wrapped a hand around Gabriel's neck and drew him down for a hard kiss. 'I'll come back to you, soon as I can.'

'Of course you will.' Gabriel mustered an affectionate smile.

'Stay off the roof.'

'I hope to.'

They kissed hard again, too frantic to be gentle. Finally, James tore himself away. He broke into an inhumanly fast run towards the Dupre Gallery.

Gabriel took a breath and held it until his fingers stopped shaking. Then he sent a text to Niall Frazer.

London Bridge Hospital. 4pm.

He thinks it's for a blood test.

Chapter Twenty

THE HELICOPTER WAS SMALL, LIGHT AND, STRICTLY SPEAKING, DID NOT have clearance to land on the rooftop of London Bridge Hospital, by the Thames. The hospital roof had barely enough space for the landing – its area being made up of flat, square planes that corralled a curved, clear skylight running along the centre.

The small chopper touched down and the passenger alighted, ducking under the rotors. Then the machine lifted off again, swooping like a dragonfly.

Michael Dare straightened his spine; smoothed down his suit; ran the palms of both hands over his hair. Once more impeccable, he tilted his head, listening.

'Gabriel.'

'Michael.' Gabriel stepped out from the shadow of the stairwell door at a corner of the rooftop.

Not a blood test. A trap. Michael closed his eyes. *What I cannot see, I cannot betray*, he thought. He could sense that the fox was listening. An alien part of him was joyful at the knowledge. Something foreign that wanted to wag its tail, roll on its back, show its belly.

Michael shuddered and grit his teeth. He deliberately bit the inside of his lip, drawing blood. He had command of himself yet, but not for much longer. As he listened for a creature who was listening through his blood, he also calculated steps to the edge of the roof; the time it would take to fall. How many seconds of fear would he need to endure before the end came?

He shouldn't have left Anthea behind. Or he should have contacted Sergeant Datta. They had made promises, and it appeared that soon, those promises would have to be fulfilled.

Perhaps it was the fox in him that made him leave Anthea and forgo the call to Datta.

Michael berated himself for the untruth. He was not accustomed to lying to himself. He'd known it would come to this, and had walked willingly into this trap, because the fox in his blood had told him to.

The thought made him ill with terror. Michael had never been afraid in his life, before now. He didn't much like the feeling.

'Blood tests?' he said. 'Really, Gabriel?'

'It sounded plausible.'

'I suppose it does.'

'You came anyway.'

'There's little point in delaying the inevitable,' said Michael. 'What did he offer you for this betrayal? I hope you don't mind my asking. It is simply that I can't imagine what constitutes 30 pieces of silver for you. I thought you cultivated a lofty disdain for monetary reward. Oh. Of course. Not silver. A life for a life. Who has he threatened?'

'Helene Dupre went missing three hours ago.'

'Not James Sharpe?'

'It's difficult to threaten James.'

'And killing him outright would not serve Frazer's purpose,' Michael noted.

'He needs me cooperative.' Gabriel's voice shook on the last word.

'Of course. Doctor Sharpe is searching for Helene, I imagine.'

'Well, of course he is, man,' said a lilting voice, with its drawn out Geordie vowels and the soft roll of the r's.

The brothers turned to see a small, sleek fox – the actual red and white animal – pad into the sunlight on the rooftop. It was *smiling*.

Gabriel blanched. Frazer wasn't supposed to be here. There were meant to be agents at all the entrances. They were meant to have checked all the rooms and wards. He'd only come onto the roof to meet Michael's helicopter. Frazer wasn't supposed to *corner* them up here.

The fox's mouth stretched into strange, wrong shapes as it spoke.

'It's funny, watching you trying to work it out. Your brow does that wrinkling thing.' The fox drew its own brows together, mimicking Gabriel's furrow of distress.

'A vampire brought him up here,' murmured Michael. 'The moment you made the rendezvous point. Isn't that right, Mr Frazer?'

'You've got lovely manners for a bureaucrat,' said Frazer approvingly. 'Yes, that's right. I had one of West's boys drop me off and then he went back on Nanny Watch for Dupre, before your men-in-black got here to take up their positions. We'll do something about their inefficiency, when you're running the Bureau for me.' And the fox *winked* at him.

Michael flinched.

The fox rose on its hind legs, fur receding, long nose shrinking, paws spreading. Then Niall Frazer stood naked on the rooftop, grinning, his ember eyes fever-bright.

The fox within Michael swelled, and the red fur grew on the back of his hands. On his face. He whimpered and grit his teeth, and then glared, and the change halted.

'Oh, hark at you,' said Frazer, like a proud parent, 'still trying. Bless. What do you think is keeping you human now, hmm? It's not like you have much to hold onto in a human life. No wife. No bairns. You only speak to your Da on business. There's no-one who actually *matters*. Except *him*.'

Gabriel stepped between Frazer and his brother. 'We're here. Where's Helene?'

'Safe.' Frazer's nudity did not in the slightest diminish the threat of him. Rather than vulnerable, Frazer was at ease and in command. 'I'm not finished with her, yet. Nor you.'

Gabriel's gaze darted to Michael.

'I've had Michael from the start, you idiot,' Frazer's grin was unpleasant. 'It's not like I needed you to get him here. In another week I could whistle for him, and he'd come running.'

Gabriel didn't dare look at his brother any more. He could hear the change in Michael, though. The sharp, shallow breaths, schooled back to evenness.

'It will make it so much easier, mind, if he doesn't have any conflicts of interest, at least when it comes to choosing between you and me. Once his loyalty to you is knocked on the head, all the other conflicts go away.'

'Such as?' Michael asked, tone conversational.

Frazer cocked his head at Michael. 'You haven't asked *why me?* yet. Aren't you curious?'

'Fine,' said Michael tersely. 'Why me?'

'Because, pet, you're the fulcrum. You hold a senior position in the Bureau of Uncanny Sciences – shit name, by the way, we're going to do something about that when I'm running the joint. And I *am* going to run the joint. You're going to make sure I get in, and then we'll have no more of this hunting creatures and keeping the world safe for prey. I mean humans. No, I really do mean prey. All the pretty chickens will belong to us.'

'The Bureau isn't that powerful.'

'No, and that's a crying shame. What you need is a proper budget. And who controls the budget? Why, the elected government. And there you are again, in the spotlight, waltzing into the halls of power and working with all those grubby politicians. The wonderful thing about being what I am, and making little foxes of my own with just a bite or a scratch, is that I only need one or two kits before the whole thing increases exponentially.'

'Wouldn't extending your control like that be exhausting?'

'Oooh, I appreciate your concern for daddy. It might at that, so you'll be helping me select candidates for turning. Vampires and werewolves are only the start of it, as you well know. The useless ones will be prey, of course.'

'You'll never–'

'*You'll never succeed in your villainous schemes*!' Frazer declared in a cartoon-hero voice. Then he sneered. '*Of course* I'll succeed. Do you think the unwashed masses give a toss about Whitehall? And I haven't mentioned the other part of my classic pincer manoeuvre, have I? Because through your posh daddy, we have an in to the House of Lords – and there we are, the government all sewn up. And with it the civil service. And with both of them, access to all the richest and the most influential people in this country.

'Didn't I say you were the fulcrum? Not that it'll stop there. Once I've got us bedded down here, we can expand the empire. That'll be nice. England misses having an empire. I will be the lovely King to give it all back. We'll have a land fit for monsters! Lloyd George would be so proud.'

Michael had gone pale. 'You're mad.'

'Oh don't be like that. My mam used to say that I was an ambitious lad, and finally I've found the right medium to be ambitious *in*. She was a treasure, my mam. Shame I had to eat her.'

Michael wished he thought Frazer was joking, but the razor-toothed smile indicated otherwise.

'What do you want from *me*?' Gabriel asked through gritted teeth.

'Well, there are two options for you,' Frazer grinned again. 'The way I see it is you're either with me, or you're dead.'

'What?'

Frazer adopted a charming coquettish pose. 'You can paint my portrait, when I'm not using you to keep your big brother in line.'

'I don't–' started Gabriel.

'You *do*,' said Frazer. 'You *will*, because if your Michael tries to make things difficult for me, I'll do awful things to *you*. That way you'll both have a stake in your good behaviour. You can paint without thumbs, can't you? Or I could train you to paint with your feet.'

Michael lurched towards Frazer. 'Don't you touch him.'

'Oh, I'm only playing with you. I have all sorts of plans for our wee Rembrandt here. Sending him off to the homes of the wealthy and influential, a fox among the chickens, is a grand idea, don't you think? A scratch here, a nip there, you'll be a very influential painter. And don't think your precious James is going to be of any help to you. He is definitely not included in any of my plans. Except as grit for my driveway in winter. He's off trying to save the nanny, is he?'

'No.'

'You're a terrible liar, Rembrandt, and your tame vampire is tediously earnest. I have no idea what Cael West was thinking, trying to bring him over to Team Niall. What possible use is a vampire with a conscience to me? Going around *saving* people instead of *eating* them. What an utter waste of fangs and food. A complete wazzock, as my mam used to say.' He heaved an exaggerated sigh of disappointment. 'Ah well, he won't be a problem much longer. If my boys don't get him, he'll drop you like a hot potato when he finds out you've signed on *my* dotted line.'

'And why would I do that?'

'Because if you don't, I'm going to have your French hinny's throat cut. Or turn her into a werewolf, though she might make a vicious little vampire given half a chance. She's so charming with the visitors at the gallery, but not, you know, *obsequious*. She's *sassy*. Give her fangs and a blood lust and who knows what she might achieve?'

Gabriel finally found the courage to look at his brother. Michael stared back in blank despair.

'Time is of the essence, Gabriel, lad,' said Frazer in a harder voice. 'So come on over here and let me give you a nip.'

Gabriel's head whirled with panic and confusion. 'And if I let you,' – Michael made a horrified, strangled whimper – 'how will your thugs know to let her go? You haven't a phone, unless you're keeping it up your arse. You can't signal them.'

'You think your brother is the only leashed fox in my pack? You're not very bright, are you? Too much inhaling turps, I expect. Pet, what I know, Jack Cray knows, if I choose it.'

Michael struggled to speak. 'Let him go, Frazer. I won't r-resist if you leave him alone.'

'It's sweet how you imagine I give a fuck what you think,' said Frazer. 'You don't get a say. This is between me and Gabriel. He joins up and plays his part, and Helene lives, or he refuses my reasonable offer and I'll kill him and Helene and his vamp-on-a-leash to boot, if that's not already taken care of.'

'I see. I'm lost either way.'

'I like to think of you as found,' Frazer contradicted. 'Like a little lost dog.'

'I am so very sorry, Gabriel,' said Michael, hands steady, and he meant it. But he was painfully aware that there were worse things, more dangerous things, than death.

'It's not your fault,' said Gabriel, misunderstanding.

In that moment, Frazer read the fox inside Michael, and he understood perfectly well, just as Michael raised the snub, small calibre gun he'd worn concealed under his smartly tailored coat, and pressed it under his own jaw.

'*Michael!*' Gabriel lunged, panicking, towards his brother.

Frazer emitted a chittering scream of outrage as he reached out to the fox inside Michael and *pushed*.

Michael's hand jerked as he pulled the trigger. Thus, instead of taking out his own throat and brain, he sent the bullet lower, into the side of his neck, above the clavicle. The collarbone shattered and blood sprayed out – over his hands and his face, over Gabriel's as his brother reached him.

Michael folded, sinking first to his knees, then to his back, legs sprawling. He panted through the pain. *I've failed. I have failed. I failed. Oh god.*

He tried to find a way to ask his brother to finish this for him, but words wouldn't come. Gabriel's face and chest were spattered with blood; he looked like the one bleeding to death.

Michael could not even comfort himself with the knowledge that this wasn't true, because Frazer's cruel game wasn't over yet.

'I'm…' *sorry* he tried to say again, but it hurt. He could feel the blood leaving his body. Although he hadn't died instantly, surely the blood loss would be sufficient. Surely he would die soon.

'Not quite yet, Michael, pet,' snarled Frazer. 'I don't appreciate you trying to cheat me, after all the work I've put in.'

Frazer's hand extended towards Michael's chest. 'Give me a minute and you'll be… well, *fine* is putting it a bit grandly. But my spirit in you will keep you alive long enough to work a little animal magic, I think. This is far from over.'

Frazer grinned that manic grin again. 'You're a sneaky bastard, Michael Dare. I knew you'd be a fine recruit. Comes naturally to you. We just have to tidy up that one last detail of having an inconvenient baby brother to *care* about. You won't be needing that anchor to humanity anymore.'

His head whipped suddenly to one side, the force of his gaze halting Gabriel in his tracks as he reached for the dropped gun. 'I wouldn't,' he said darkly. 'I really wouldn't.'

Gabriel curled his hands into fists, and didn't.

'See, I've got all the cards. I can save your brother. I can save your French nursemaid. All you have to do is let me give you a nibble. Let me into your veins. Or die. I can take care of that part for you as well.'

Michael panted with the effort of trying to die when the alien in his body wouldn't let him go.

Gabriel couldn't make himself look at his brother.

And then he had to.

Their eyes met, and all they found was despair. Michael shut his eyes. Gabriel turned away.

Frazer's became sullen. 'Rembrandt, I have things to do and I don't need you making your brother all mopey and noble and shite. Make your choice.'

'If I choose… death. How?' asked Gabriel, thinking of Datta's vision. Fear made his voice tremulous. 'There's the gun.'

'And have you think you can shoot me, or finish Michael off like an honourable little twat? Fuck, no. If you say no to me, then I'll kill you, and I'll make sure Michael lives and your Ms Dupre goes home.'

'I need. I need. A minute. To think.' Gabriel crept away from the fox, his skin crawling with horror, and found himself too near the edge of the hospital roof. He couldn't stop thinking about Datta's dream. At least now he had a reason to jump.

He looked nervously to the river. The narrow walkway between the hospital and the Thames had a few pedestrians on it, people cutting between the pier a short distance to the east and London Bridge itself, to the west. River traffic chugged each way along the waterway. On the far side of the river, he could see the Tower of London and, further west, Tower Bridge, where James – gorgeous, sensitive, funny, perfect James – had shown him his city with new eyes.

Gabriel didn't want to lose himself to this vicious fox and his pack. He didn't want to die, or to lose Michael or Helene, or James, oh god, *James*. Gabriel could only stall for so long, before a choice was forced on him.

It surprised him that he knew already what the choice would be.

'If I jump, will you leave James be?'

'You know, I've changed my mind. You'd be such a waste as a gory splat on the footpath when you could be helping me make little foxy bairns all over the country. You can't have a choice after all, Rembrandt. I want you on the team.'

'No.'

'Did you miss the part where I said you can't have a choice?'

Gabriel edged away from Frazer, heart racing. When he got near the lip of the building, he craned his neck to look down. *Such a long way to fall.*

He thought three things as he stood there.

He didn't want to die, but he would not be a slave to this wicked fox spirit.

Where the hell were Datta and Webb?

And where the *fucking* hell was James?

Chapter Twenty One

TAVISA DATTA WISHED MORE THAN ANYTHING THAT ANTHEA WAS BY HER side right now. Michael Dare's bodyguard-cum-assistant was smart, cool-headed and funny. A crack shot, too. Tavisa wasn't a bad shot herself, considering, but even in her line of work, she wasn't much called on to discharge a firearm. This was *London*, not New York.

Actually, what Tavisa Datta wished more than anything was that none of this was happening. Not the vampires and fox spirits, not the precognitive dreams, definitely not the kidnapping. But all the wishing in the world couldn't make it not true – well, she assumed it couldn't. Maybe in this bizarre world she'd come to inhabit, it was possible to wish all of this away, and she might live a semi-normal life.

She was a realist, though. A lifetime of precognitive dreaming had taught her she had to be a pragmatist or go mad. Wishing Anthea was here to have her back, and go over the changes in their dreams was a waste of time.

Tavisa knew perfectly well how her and Anthea's dreams had both changed. Anthea's precog powers were a fraction of Tavisa's, but she still saw the raven that Gabriel threw from the rooftop; the bird that fell and broke and turned into the body that dead James Sharpe mourned.

They both dreamed something new. A second raven, the black feathers of it gilded with an auburn sheen; bathing in a pool of blood. Anthea had smiled ruefully as she'd described it. 'Like the Tower Ravens,' she said, 'Once they're gone, England will fall.'

There was no doubting who those ravens represented, just as there was no doubting the identity of the flamingo.

James had called her with the news that Helene Dupre was taken, and she in turn had alerted Anthea through their new, secret phones, used solely to contact each other. If Michael had discovered this ploy to keep him out of the loop, he hadn't said anything. It was all about his protection, anyway, and the protection of the Crown if the former failed.

Tavisa was sorry the flamingo with the blue flowers and the blood red roses around her throat turned out to be Dupre. She seemed a nice woman.

Tavisa had another new dream that Anthea did not share.

The new thing was a blazing figure wielding a sword. An angel, in the Christian parlance – otherwise a *deva* or *apsara* or *malachim* or *malaikah* or whatever terrifying, celestial forces were called in other cultures. It shone too fiercely bright to make out a face or limbs or anything but the towering, righteous rage. Tavisa couldn't tell if the angel was blazing like a beacon on the ground or in the air or over water. She couldn't see its face. She didn't know what kind of omen it was, only that it was an almighty creature of awe and flame, and unstoppable.

Tavisa had met James Sharpe by the gallery within fifteen minutes of Helene's kidnapping. The doctor had easily picked up the scent of the perfume bottle Helene had used defensively. The bottle had broken, splashing the tyres of the kidnapper's vehicle with strong scent – strong enough for a vampire to follow. Helene had managed to use her keys, if not the silver knife, drawing supernatural blood too. It all helped.

Anthea's team sent the first CCTV image to their phones. The kidnappers were on their way towards Shadwell.

James Sharpe set off on foot, following the scents. Tavisa followed the technological leads from her car as the team sent her CCTV updates and she traded observations in quick phone calls with Sharpe. Tavisa was unnerved at how swiftly he was covering ground on foot.

Their joint intel led them past Shadwell. The kidnappers were taking their hostage into Wapping. She followed from a distance, sometimes driving down alleys, taking shortcuts, one right over a newly paved public area between renovated rows of cottage housing.

With confirmation that the van had stopped at a block of old apartments, likewise under renovation, Tavisa pulled over and continued the pursuit on foot.

She emerged on a tiny cross-street. The offender's truck was backed up to an old shopfront. The faded gold lettering on the cracked and partly boarded window on the ground floor showed that it had once been a florist. *Rose In Bloom. Wreaths and Wedding Garlands a Specialty.*

Rose garlands. Tavisa couldn't erase the dream image of a blood red garland of flowers around Helene Dupre's throat, wet and glistening like paint; like actual blood.

The van driver had flung open the vehicle's back doors, two other men emerged from the van to assist, and another man surfaced from the florist to help them with their cargo – a lumpy roll of carpet.

Tavisa sent three rapid texts.

The carpet roll wriggled. One of the men shoved at the middle of the roll and it was still.

A snarl at her ear made her jump, though she managed to swallow the tiny shriek.

'Sorry.' James Sharpe, not at all contrite.

'Do you have to be so fucking stealthy?' she hissed at him.

He grinned at her, vampire teeth glinting ferally in the light. She couldn't suppress a shudder and suddenly there was the contrition, as he closed his mouth over the fangs.

James led the way to the back of the building, his demeanour as much cold fury as concern. Tavisa edged along the brickwork of the alley behind him and tried to measure the doctor's state of mind. Anthea had briefed her on working with vampires, but it was way outside her field of experience. One piece of advice came immediately to mind, though.

'Are you all...' Tavisa gestured vaguely, reluctant to put it into words, 'Fired up?'

James's brow creased then cleared. 'Yes, I've eaten,' he said. 'If that's what you mean. Gabriel gave–'

'Don't.' She took a breath. 'Let's get Helene out of there. Where can we get in?'

Tavisa wasn't terribly fond of the next part, where she clung to James Sharpe's back and he climbed, fly-like, up the outside wall to the sloped rooftop of the second storey. She climbed quietly down to the slate tiles and drew the gun Anthea had given her, loaded with very much non-standard ammunition, infused with silver, wolfsbane and god knew what else. A broad spectrum firearm, Anthea had called it.

James reached into his jacket and withdrew a wooden stake.

'Oh,' whispered Tavisa. 'Vampires.' She lifted the gun. 'Is this even any use?'

'Aim for the heart or the head. That's very effective on pretty much everything.'

With infinite care, he crept to a skylight and undid the screws with his fingernails. He regularly paused to listen but no-one disturbed them. He removed a pane of dirty, stippled glass and put it aside. He tucked the stake back into his belt and gestured. She holstered her gun and let him take her hands.

He lowered her easily into the attic, then followed her down, hanging by his fingertips first, then landing light as ash beside her.

They drew their weapons again, and he opened the access hatch a fraction. James listened. Sniffed deeply. Noiselessly lowered the hatch.

James held up four fingers and a thumb. *Five of them.* He hooked two fingers in front of his mouth and held up three fingers. *Three vampires.* Identified by their scent, she supposed. He held up one finger and made a ridiculous growly monster face. She arched an eyebrow. He shrugged, then mimed howling at the moon. *Okay. So. Werewolf. One thereof.*

She held up her hand indicating "five" and gave him a questioning look. He mouthed "fox" at her.

Right. All supernatural then. Not exactly *carte blanche* for a shoot-out, but this was definitely going to be a fight for her life. Worse, she would be handicapped by having to avoid being scratched or bitten by the fox or the werewolf.

James eased the hatch aside and peered into the dimly lit interior.

Suddenly, so fast she hardly saw him move – though she felt the breeze of his lightning motion on her cheeks – James struck downward, pulled upward, his right hand wrapped around the throat of a fang-faced man who was trying to snarl and couldn't make a sound because of the hand crushing his larynx.

James's left hand slammed the stake into the vampire's chest and then all was dust, dust, dust, sprinkling to the floor.

James Sharpe adjusted his grip on the stake. He looked into her startled face and pointedly held up four fingers.

Right. This was war, after all. This was saving the Tower Ravens. This was saving not only the Dare brothers: it was, very possibly, saving all of Great Britain.

James checked again, then took Tavisa's hands, lowered her to the floor below and then followed. They tip-toed to the stairs.

'Marek?' someone shouted up the stairwell, 'Get the fuck back down here. That bitch is getting twitchy again. You said you wanted a bite when she woke up.'

When no reply came, the voice said: 'If you don't want a go, I will. I want to take a photo of her little face when she sees the teeth. That's always hilarious, when they see the teeth.'

James thumped his hand against the wall once, then twice, and then he did a really creepy thing. In the low light, he jumped up to take hold of the light fitting and pushed his feet high against the wall. He seemed suspended on the ceiling, though Tavisa could see how he used the ugly lightshade, a nearby door frame and the wall that met this one at right-angles as braces to hold the position. James's body was mostly concealed in the dark, although he would be visible to anyone who reached the top of the landing.

A sandy-haired man came warily up the stairs. He wrinkled his nose. 'You got someone up there with you, Marek?'

James nodded at Tavisa. At her confusion, he pulled strange emphatic faces.

'Marek, have you been bringing snacks home?' The blond took another step. 'Because I've fucking told you about not sharing, you dick.'

James kicked a heel against the wall this time and glared at her. Tavisa took a guess and shrieked in fright. Tell the truth, she didn't have to fake it all that much.

'Bloody knew it,' grumped the blond. 'Leave some for me, you little shit.'

Tavisa cut-off another cry mid-scream, which she thought was a nice dramatic touch. It certainly brought the blond into view. He hardly had time to register her, standing there with her gun drawn, when a compact body swung across, using the light fitting as a fulcrum, and wrapped legs tight around his neck before twisting and throwing the blond man onto the carpet.

James sat on top of the vampire, knees pushed into his throat, but he was in no position to stake the vampire's heart from there. Instead, James plunged the stake through the vampire's right eye before, almost too fast to see, he half rose while yanking the stake out again and then plunged it into the vampire's chest.

More dust, settling quietly.

James stood up, brushed down his jacket and gave her a challenging look.

He's ex-army. Afghanistan veteran. Front line combat medical technician. He's not solely a doctor; he's a soldier.

Tavisa held up three fingers and nodded.

Movement in the foyer at the bottom of the stairs made them pause. James sniffed then did that ridiculous growly face again. So this must be the werewolf. Tavisa peered at the figure.

He was a muscular man, at this time of the month looking like nothing more than a scarred costermonger. He took one look at the dust-grimed vampire on the stairs and the woman next to him pointing a gun at his chest, and he swallowed. He pointed towards the kitchen and held up two fingers. Then he put prayerful hands together as he edged towards the front door.

Tavisa aimed the gun at his head, and he stopped.

James, not interfering with her sightline, sidled up to the kitchen door. He glared at the werewolf. 'Call her,' he mouthed.

The werewolf shook his head.

Tavisa levelled the gun between his eyes.

'Spaulding!' yipped the werewolf, 'What do you think is taking Marek and Gav so long up there?'

'Don't know, don't care,' said the concealed Spaulding, 'And what's that I smell out there? Do I smell gun oil, you idiot? The boss told you no guns. And that's... those morons. No guns, no girls. Don't you idiots ever listen?'

Then she was there, a petite thing with dark hair, darker eyes and a vicious grin, coming out low and fast and flying at James Sharpe with deadly intent.

James leapt, twisted, grunted with the pain as something aimed at his chest slammed instead into his leg. He landed badly, clutching at the silver blade – the one they had given to Helene – protruding from his thigh.

Spaulding fell on him with fanged mouth open, biting as she grasped for the hilt of the knife. James punched up into her chest, over her heart. That made the vampire pause ever so briefly, wondering if he'd staked her after all, but he was bluffing. He'd dropped the wooden spike in the opening skirmish.

Spaulding jabbed at his throat with her fingernails, splitting the skin as he struggled to get away.

Gunfire – a single shot – a door slamming – Tavisa shouting *stop*! – Spaulding's head turned to snarl at her, giving James space to shove a little distance between them and then….

Dust. Raining down. And Tavisa Datta, chest heaving, holding the stake and staring at James through the ash haze in the weirdest combination of horror and triumph.

'Werewolf did a runner,' she said.

'You hurt?' James wrapped a hand around the silver knife in his leg and tugged it out with a hiss. He rose unsteadily and threw the knife away, shaking his fingers to cool the burn. The deep scores in his skin from the vampire's fingernails were already healing, 'He didnae scratch or bite you?'

'Nope. He just bolted.'

She returned the stake to him and together they entered the kitchen.

Helene was sitting, blindfolded and gagged, at the table. Dried blood was smeared on her forehead and in her hair. Next to her was a man with dark red hair and a very pointed nose and face. His eyes were ember dark, and glowing.

'You're earlier than we expected,' he said. 'But you're still too late.'

Tavisa raised the gun.

'Jack Cray. At your service.' The man grinned with his pointed, foxy face.

'Too late for what? What have you done to her?' Tavisa demanded.

'Nothing. A sleeping draught. She wasn't the point. You can have her.' He spread his hands wide. 'You've rescued her, but how will your artsy fartsy flatmate know that? He hasn't long now, before he has to sign up or die.'

'What happens,' snarled James, limping up to the man and pressing the stake to Cray's throat, 'if I kill you?'

Cray the fox-man tilted his head to one side, listening to something in his own head. 'He says… *que sera sera. But Gabriel won't* know *she's safe. Then there's brother Michael to consider. Gotcha.*'

Cray shook his head, no longer hearing his master's voice.

'Niall Frazer is happy to let you die,' said Tavisa.

In the distance, the sirens of the DI and the back-up team she'd texted from outside were wailing, getting louder.

'I surrender,' he said. 'It's not going to make a difference to Dare now, is it? Like the boss says. He won't find out she's safe in time to save himself.'

James grabbed Cray by the throat and threw him across the room. Cray crashed into the wall with a yelp but then lay on the floor panting and sniggering.

James checked Helene, dropping a gentle kiss on her forehead as she stirred. Tavisa, gun trained on Cray, watched as James dribbled a generous amount of spit into his palm and smoothed it against the French woman's head wound. Helene moaned but her breathing became less laboured and colour came back to her skin.

After inspecting the blood on his palm – Tavisa had the awful notion he was about to lick it up – James limped to the sink instead to wash his hand. He then tore a larger hole in his jeans, to rinse the swollen knife wound. It had improved but was puffy and discoloured when he left off the task and took out his phone.

'I have tae go,' he said. 'Gabriel needs me.' He was texting rapidly.

'Go,' said Tavisa. 'I'll be there as soon as I can.'

James stepped out the front door as the blaring sirens announced the arrival of back-up at last. Despite the limp, he was gone before the arriving police could see him.

Tavisa picked Cray up by the collar and pushed him out the door. Her colleagues raised weapons, then lowered them again as they saw her.

'Just this one,' she said to Bakare as he strode up to her. 'He's alone. Dare's friend, Dupre, is in the kitchen. Call an ambulance.' She shoved Cray into a constable's hands. 'Cuff him.'

Several minutes were spent on untying the hostage and getting a rapid debrief, from which Tavisa had to omit very nearly everything. She'd seen the van pull up, she said, and saw the carpet removed. It made her suspicious, but when she came in, this is what she found. No, she didn't know where the other people had gone. Yes, it was a lucky break.

Yes, this was a hellaciously dusty house.

Cray didn't contradict a word, only grinned at her.

Five minutes after James had left, Tavisa couldn't stand it anymore. 'I have to go, sir,' she said to Bakare. 'Family emergency.'

Well, she didn't have to say *whose* family, did she?

Bakare started an irate protest, but she was already gone. She ran to her car two alleys away, flicked the siren on and drove hell-for-leather to London Bridge Hospital. She didn't know what she was going to do there. She was afraid of what she was going to see.

The *deva* angel, perhaps, if that's what it was. *Blinding light. Flaming sword.* Vengeance or justice or some other bizarre monster rising up from the guts of London to screw up her life. Whatever it was, she had to know. And whoever that falling raven was, she had to know that for certain, too.

Gabriel won't find out she's safe in time to save himself.

James was right, she thought, *the falling bird is Gabriel.*
It made her sick to know it.

James's leg hurt, but that meant less than nothing right now. If things had gone to plan, Gabriel would know Helene was safe, but the reference to Michael was unexpected.

Everything had gone tits up. He could feel it. He wished he'd had time to clean his wound better – vestiges of silver and garlic made the gash burn with pain and prevented it from healing quickly. The effort of running so fast – across Wapping and St Katherine's, along the foreshore between the Tower of London and the Thames, towards London Bridge and the hospital on the other side – didn't help at all. Incrementally it hurt less than the first blow, but he hadn't the time to stop, he hadn't the time to waste. The seconds he'd stopped to spare a smear of saliva for Helene's cracked skull and flush the worst of the poison from his own wound might cost him everything else that mattered.

James Sharpe had not prayed in a very long time. But he prayed now, as he ran through London, leaping across traffic, between buildings, nothing but a blur, an eddy of solid matter, towards the hospital.

Please. Please. Please. Don't let me be too late.

Chapter Twenty Two

ANTHEA PRESSED AGAINST THE WINDOW ON THE TOP FLOOR OF LONDON Bridge Hospital and tried to see if the message had been received and the protocol implemented. Tavisa's text – hostage located; getting her out now – followed by James's confirmation had been welcome, but this was far from over.

It had gone badly pear-shaped from the start, when Gabriel had failed to arrive at the rendezvous point on this floor with Michael in tow. The chopper had come and gone as she was making her way up, but no Dare brothers were waiting when she got there. They had to still be up on the roof.

Not knowing what might be on the rooftop, Anthea had been forced to take things slowly. No use bursting out and getting everyone shot before she knew what was going on.

In the stairwell leading to the roof, she found another of the Bureau's agents, dead and bloodless, with ragged bite marks in his throat. Well, that answered *that* question, she supposed. A vampire had brought Frazer up here ahead of time.

There'd be a goddamned review of procedures if they all lived through this debacle, and a hotly worded demand for better funding.

She might personally introduce the Chancellor of the Exchequer to the prisoners held under silver and iron at Bletchley to see how he felt about his bloody austerity measures then.

She had withdrawn to make her calls, to reorganise the troops in the face of new facts and suspicions. It ate at her to wait, but storming in with no plan was worse than waiting here while she patched up the plans they'd previously stitched together.

Then she'd heard a gunshot from above. Small calibre, but distinctive. It sounded like the boss's own compact Sig Sauer P938, with the blackwood grip and the custom-made, silver-coated bullets. That was not good.

She'd had to keep so much from him, and he knew she was doing that for his safety as well as the nation's. He'd all but begged her to do that, ordering an auto-update of all his most vital codes and then, instead of opening the list of encrypted alpha-numeric strings, "dropping" the envelope at her desk. She wasn't supposed to have those codes, but better her than the fox.

Whatever that gunshot meant, the plan was obviously well and truly FUBAR. Was she going to have to kill Mr Dare after all? Shoot her Michael through the head to spare him something worse? After she'd worked so hard to save him?

If she must, then she would. She'd promised him, and she'd keep her word, if she could do nothing else. She'd save his soul if she couldn't save his life.

Anthea smirked at herself. She wasn't a romantic at heart, and yet here she was, choosing to save souls. Even supposing Michael Dare *had* one, or a heart even, for anyone other than Gabriel. But a life, certainly, he had that, and it was precious to her.

She pressed her forehead to the first floor window once more. She gazed down onto the path running along the river, separated from the water by a low wall lined with railings and decorative black lampposts.

And there, yes. Dare Minor's friend from the streets, Switchblade Roy, who had received James's message too. He had tied a bunch of yellow helium-filled balloons to the railings, the frivolous things bobbing below the line of lightbulbs strung between the lampposts.

Anthea sent a text to the BUS crew waiting below.

Hostage released. Send up the team.

If he stood near enough to the edge of the roof, Gabriel would see Roy's balloons – the signal they'd devised in the morning's pow-wow to show that the rescue had succeeded, on the expectation that texting or calling might give away their advantage to Frazer. They'd had to work quickly to build a scenario that gave them time to find Helene Dupre and then circumvent the fox's plans for the Dare brothers.

(Anthea tried not to think about that indistinct image of the broken raven, and her own beloved bird, from the dream. Dwelling on it wouldn't help.)

If only Anthea knew what the gunshot meant.

Gun drawn, Anthea made her way up the stairs towards the roof.

Gabriel looked over his shoulder at Frazer. The fox spirit was sullen; petulant; impatient.

Michael lay panting at Frazer's feet. The fingers of his right hand were straining towards the dropped pistol; he was still trying desperately to reach the sole salvation available to him.

Blood had stopped welling out of the wound in his neck, but that was only because Frazer stood over him, a hand extended in his direction, willing Michael's body to obey the commands of the invading spirit.

Frazer's wicked grin returned. 'You divvint want to die, Rembrandt, and you divvint want him to die, which he will if I get too far away. So be a pet and get yersel' over here.'

Gabriel, shaking, looked into the square one last time.

And… There. Below.

The signal at long last. Switchblade Roy's bunch of yellow Get Well balloons tied to the fence railings. Gabriel nearly laughed in relief. *Yes, Roy, you'll get your nice biscuits and all the tea you can bloody drink.* Helene was safe.

James would be on his way to him, now that Helene was out of danger. Assuming James hadn't been…

No. He wouldn't think that way. Instead, he concentrated on the knowledge that Anthea Webb, on the floor below, was free to set the next phase in motion. She'd be here soon.

To do what? Idiot Michael had messed up so much careful work by trying to be *noble.* That task – the killing of Michael Dare if no other avenue was left – had rightly been allocated to Anthea; and Michael had ruined it all.

Gabriel needed time. Time for Anthea to arrive with her back-up; for James to reach him from wherever they'd held Helene. He needed Michael to hold on a little longer. Maybe if he teased this out with Frazer.

'Will it hurt?'

'Becoming mine? No, hin. Not like dying which, I won't lie, stings like a bastard,' said Frazer.

Oh, but there, at last, there, movement on London Bridge, crossing from the Monument side of the river, the uneven blur of James arriving at last – *uneven? But he's not hurt. He's here.*

'No more wasting time,' snarled Frazer, 'Come to papa, or I'll come to you.'

Frazer had a link with Cray. He must know he's defeated there, Gabriel thought. *He doesn't know I know. But Michael–*

'And don't think yer precious James will save you,' Frazer continued to sneer. 'Even if he's found yer Helene, he won't get here on time.'

Michael cried out in agony as Frazer worked fingers into his gory throat wound purely to cause pain; to get Gabriel's attention. In his other hand, Frazer held Michael's compact gun.

'Get over here, you little fucker.'

'Please don't hurt him.' Gabriel knew that James had seen him, up precariously high. He could imagine Jamie's horror, and how mad he'd be, after he'd made Gabriel promise to stay away from the roof.

Jamie will save me, one way or another. He'll save me and together we'll save Michael, because we have Anthea. We're not out of options yet.

'Oh, I'm sick to death of waitin' fer ye, pet.' Frazer rose, fast and smooth, and lunged for Gabriel.

Gabriel took his leap of faith, flinging himself over the precipice, narrowly avoiding the fox's claws swiping through the space where his body had been.

And he fell and he fell and he fell and he fell, wind whipping the cry from his throat, the terror and the hope both conspiring to blank his mind as the ground rushed towards him and all he could think was *Jamie,* a voiceless sob, before suddenly, and much too soon, the air was slammed out of his lungs.

James, so near the Southwark side of the bridge, saw Gabriel either fall or fling himself off the hospital roof and found reserves of speed he had no idea existed, even in this strangely strong dead body of his.

He was so fast that everything around him seemed immobile.

Gabriel falling into nothing.

Run.

A blur on the bridge, leaping over and across the moving cars, pushing off a bonnet to add to his momentum, onto the footpath, up onto the metal-capped wall beside it, and on, on, on.

Gabriel, arms flailing, black jacket flapping like useless wings, dark hair wind-wrecked in the fall.

The stairwell ahead would rob him of impetus, and in any case the shortest distance between two points was a straight line, not the sharp angle of street-to-twisting-stairs-to-embankment.

Run.

Measure distance, run, push hand to the edge of the bridge, shove feet at the ledge. Leap into the space, ten metres across the river to the brown marble walls, to the path on the bank; cutting corners, saving vital seconds.

The broken raven, falling.

He crashed – shoulder, arm, back – into the smooth stone of the walls, and he used the energy to pivot as he slid down. His feet hit the path, he leapt down the steps without touching them. Land on his feet, push off, and run. Run. *Run.*

Gabriel, falling with a faint, breathless cry of fear.

A second of Gabriel out of his sight, his passage a blur through the underpass, and then light, and *Gabriel, God, no, Gabriel.*

Another leap, one foot on the edge of the wall to push, push, up, arms stretched out wide to catch him. To save the one important thing. The only thing. To keep safe the breath his body no longer breathed; the heart for whom his own slow heart beat; his very soul.

James's body crashed into Gabriel's, his shoulder driving into Gabriel's stomach at this awkward angle, his arms clutching wildly to Gabriel's torso.

He grasped, twisted, trying to put his own body between Gabriel's and the unforgiving ground. The motion took them over the river wall, over the top of the lampposts and the string of lights and the yellow balloons bobbing in the air, down to the muddy shore exposed by the low tide.

James's back slammed into the wet bed of mud and chunks of stone and river detritus, his spine, arms, legs braced to absorb the violence of the landing, to hold Gabriel up, away, up, *safe safe safe oh please safe. Please.*

Carefully, James tilted to deposit Gabriel gently on the uneven ground. Unthinking, he shoved and kicked huge chunks of black stone away to clear the ground. '*Gabriel!*'

Gabriel stared up at him, green eyes wide with shock, blood smeared over his face.

Not breathing.

Not breathing.

Chapter Twenty-Three

TAVISA SAW WHAT WAS HAPPENING FROM HER CAR AS SHE CROSSED LONDON Bridge with her siren wailing; the blur that could only be James Sharpe leaping from the bridge to the opposite bank. A grey smear of motion pushing off from the river wall, into the air, up towards that plummeting black bird.

Not a bird.

Gabriel.

Tavisa realised it would take longer in this afternoon traffic to find the exit to Tooley Street and down the roads to the hospital, than to follow James's lead.

She pulled over on the bridge, right next to the stairs, and flung herself from the vehicle. Anthea's gun in her pocket, she ran for her life (*not hers, for others, for everyone else's lives*) down the stairs to the path towards her nightmare made real.

James rolled Gabriel over carefully, cradling Gabriel's head to lay him on the ground. He assessed his own damage as negligible, feeling the ache as he moved. All of his attention was for Gabriel's needs.

Gabriel. Face covered in blood. Not breathing.

James bit back the keening that rose in his throat, instead falling into old army habits. Triage.

No major head injury. The blood wasn't Gabriel's. It smelled of fox.

Gabriel's eyes were darting, searching James's face. He was distressed but focused. His pulse was strong; James could hear that without needing to take it, so the problem was–

Ah. The catch had been awkward, James's body slamming into Gabriel's diaphragm. James pushed Gabriel's leather jacket wide, tore open the T-shirt beneath it. The red blotch on Gabriel's body would bruise spectacularly but, running his hand over the mark, James could detect no swelling or heat. Nothing to indicate a serious internal injury.

Winded then. The diaphragm was spasming.

James pressed gently into the muscle and leaned over Gabriel.

'You need air,' he said calmly to Gabriel's panic, before closing his mouth over Gabriel's and puffing a lungful of oxygen directly into him.

Gabriel coughed, then heaved in a laboured breath. Then another, sucking in the air with a desperate hiss. A third, and then he started laughing.

'Gabriel?'

'Knew you'd do it,' said Gabriel, wheezily but perfectly audible. Perfectly fine.

Then he woofed air out again as James pulled him up into his arms and hugged him. And hugged him. And hugged him. And hugged him. And hugged him.

Gabriel wrapped his arms around James, curled one arm up to run fingers through James's hair. He didn't say anything, simply held and stroked James's back, his head.

'You did it,' he whispered.

'Havenae ever run so fast,' the tears he couldn't cry were in James's voice. 'Never. I didnae know I could.'

'Sorry about the roof,' Gabriel managed with a choking breath.

'He was waiting there when I went to meet Michael. Sorry. Sorry.'

'Shh, now, mae bonnie, mae angel, shh.' James pressed kiss after kiss to Gabriel's cheeks and forehead, heedless of the dried blood and the fear-sour sweat. 'I've got ye, love. It's all right.'

'It's not.' Gabriel struggled up, 'Michael's badly hurt and Frazer's still got him.'

James pulled Gabriel to his wobbly feet.

'We have to hurry,' said Gabriel. Ignoring the gathering crowd of puzzled bystanders, he led the way, staggering towards the underpass to take them to the other side of the building, towards the hospital entrance.

James leant him against the spiked fence that separated the car park undercroft of the hospital's nearest neighbour. He boosted Gabriel over the fence, following so swiftly after that he was able to steady Gabriel's descent as well. Then they were off again, darting between stationary cars and to the entrance.

Tavisa saw Gabriel falling like a broken bird. But she'd never seen James like this in her dream, all speed and grace – well, until he'd crashed into the wall, but then he twisted in the air, landing perfectly and instantly running once more. Something of a dark angel, in his way: concentrated power and speed and intent.

Then the two of them were over the river wall and crashing into the low tide mud and rocks. Tavisa stumbled to a stop on the path, grasping the rails as she leaned over to see (*terrified to see*) the man in black, covered in blood, and *oh god,* James's face – the devastation in it. Gabriel had thrown the raven from the roof, and Gabriel was dead, and it was Gabriel's doing and James Sharpe, a man already dead, looked like he had seen the worst thing, *the very worst thing*, this terrible world had to offer.

But no. No, because then the doctor was tearing open Gabriel's

T-shirt and kissing… no, not kissing. *Mouth to mouth.* Gabriel coughed and breathed and then the two of them clung to each other, as though each man was the other's greatest gift from the world. Not nightmare and perdition after all, but life, and joy.

It was almost more painful to see than the loss, but it was a better pain.

But this wasn't over yet. Tavisa checked the text she had received from Anthea.

Michael compromised. Need your backup.

Tavisa left Gabriel and James to their miracle, turning to the narrow alley leading to Tooley Street, which would take her to the hospital entrance.

She ran as fast as she could, wheeling left on the larger road, then finding the shortest route to the hospital entrance. In to the lifts to get to the highest floor. She squeezed out as the doors were opening and ran along the corridor to the stairs that led to the roof.

She drew the gun Anthea had given her, and began the ascent.

'Well, that was a waste, wasn't it?' Frazer said to Michael Dare. 'Did you hear the thump? I heard the thump. It was less wet than I imagined it would be.'

The bleeding slowed again. Michael groaned, less in pain than in despair.

'You're going to be such a lovely kit,' said Frazer. 'They've taken Jack Cray, but I don't need him anymore. Not now I have you. But here, stop fighting us. Give in and I'll fix that hole in you, lickety split.'

Michael gave him a look of pure, cold poison.

Frazer crouched and brushed his fingers over the wound. 'I can keep you alive, ye knaw. Give you more of the fox. Ye'll heal up in naw time.'

Michael tried to move away; he managed to shove his feet against the concrete and put an extra half inch between them. It cost him in pain and blood.

'Oh, Mikey, stop fighting me. I appreciate yer strength. I do. I've never had anyone fight me so hard with just their brain before. All that willpower. It's delicious. But give it up, would ye? And don't feel bad about Gabriel. Ye should be proud. What he did was kind of noble. Stupid, but noble.'

Frazer raised his head suddenly, surprised by a noise. Then he grinned again.

'Ah. Yer bodyguard is here. She smells lovely, doesn't she? Positively *edible*. And she's still trying to guard your body. How about I make me final push, then. I can let the fox loose in you, and you can go eat yer little chicken.'

Michael Dare shut his eyes. When the fox pushed against his brain, he pushed back, and hoped to God it would give him an aneurism.

Tavisa waited at the entrance to the roof, gun drawn, watching. Anthea had crept out onto the rooftop and was crouched behind a cooling tower, her gun trained on Michael Dare. Anthea's gun hand was trembling.

Frazer halted in his awful speech to cock his head. Tavisa heard that terrible, wicked voice tell Michael that it was over. Michael was about to become utterly possessed by the fox, and then he'd be made to kill Anthea.

Michael was losing the fight. He was almost as pale as James Sharpe from the loss of blood, but his waxy skin was covered in a sheen of perspiration. His lips were going blue.

He wasn't long for the world, one way or another. Dead soon, or alive as a puppet of the fox.

I'd rather be dead too, Tavisa thought. *That was our job. To let him die human, not be used.*

She noticed Anthea had adjusted her grip on her gun, her hand steady as she took a bead on Michael. *And she shouldn't have to do that. She shouldn't have to kill the man she loves.*

Lying in the spreading pool of his own blood, Michael began to change. His hair turned a deeper auburn, the fur thickened on his hands. His eyes began to turn ember dark.

And suddenly, the roof wasn't there. Frazer, Michael, Anthea, all gone, replaced by a dizzying swirl of images.

A fox, with Michael Dare's eyes, lapping, slurping, at a rose garland around the Queen's throat.

Anthea's face twisting, growing teeth and madness at the sight of a pendulous pearl in the black velvet sky, bones popping and skin splitting and the ragged tail wagging as the wolf that used to be a woman crunched fragile, newborn bones, and sang to the moon.

Helene's red mouth all teeth and thirst, feeding on a little girl.

A cloud of fine snow, the finest, falling, falling, and she knew, she *knew*, that it was the dust of James Sharpe, settling like grief on the carpet of the flat at Ivy Gardens.

Behind the cloud of dust, holding the sharp-ended tree branch, was a black-and-silver fox, with ember eyes. DI Bakare's body only, his mind and heart belonging to the fox now.

Gabriel Dare, hand to his chest that was blooming flowers – red roses, red carnations, red poppies, red, red, red – and the Michael-fox howling a shrill cry before launching himself at his brother's throat.

I'm dreaming, Tavisa realised. *This is the future.*

And as suddenly, the vision was gone, leaving Anthea, squeezing the trigger; Michael, still fighting, teeth clenched, his voice a rising whine as he succumbed.

No. No. No no no. This stops. This ends now.

Gun raised, Tavisa stepped onto the roof; she stepped into this crucial point, this fulcrum of the future, between Anthea and Michael.

Let Michael die human, but on his own. No-one should have to kill the one they love.

'Leave him be.' Stupid to alert Frazer, but she couldn't shoot him in the back. A failing, probably. James Sharpe might think so, given his stealth earlier, despatching the vampires, the deadliest of their obstacles, with such ruthless efficiency. So, yes, it was stupid to give this monster warning, but Tavisa Datta was who she was, and she couldn't do it another way.

Frazer darted a look of annoyance at her, then his brow cleared. The pressure on Michael eased, and his eyes were filled with pain and despair, but they were his own human eyes, at least.

'Well, well, you're the other dreamer my kit thinks about. Look at you, hinny, running around trying to make sense of all yer funny dreams.' His nose wrinkled with distaste.

Tavisa's aim didn't waver. She took a step towards him.

Frazer spread his arms wide in mocking invitation.

'You won't,' he said confidently. 'Ye're one of the good guys. You should have wings and a fucking halo.'

Sergeant Tavisa Datta pulled the trigger and Frazer staggered back a single step, his surprise almost comical. He looked down at the bloom of red in the centre of his diaphragm.

Tavisa scowled in aggravation. She'd missed.

Aim for the heart and the head, James Sharpe had said. *That's very effective for pretty much everything.*

Tavisa strode towards Frazer as he began to change.

Tavisa adjusted her aim. 'Have you seen pictures of the Christian angels in churches? Big fuck-off swords, they've got. You should pay attention.'

His face grew long and sharp, his hands shrank and become clawed as he scrabbled away from her. His foxy face twisted wrongly as he spoke.

'I can shift,' he whined. 'I can *heal*.' He was at the edge of the roof, bleeding onto the concrete yet bizarrely confident that he was going to get away.

And another flash in Tavisa's head, another kaleidoscope of

images. Dust and red blooms and the crunching of bones. Different images, perhaps, but the wicked fox remained in the centre of them. Healed and warped as ever.

The fox whined again and began to rise, to transforming human feet, a human hand pressed to its bloodstained, white-furred belly that had stopped bleeding.

Tavisa Datta's second bullet caught him between those burning eyes and he pitched back, his body poised between fox and man, between sky and earth, between surprise and oblivion.

Then gravity wound around his corpse and pulled it down, hard and fast. Tavisa kneeled, put her hand on the ledge and leaned over to see.

On the path, a fox. What was left of a fox. Blood. Fur. Pieces and parts. It was disgusting. Horrific. *Over.*

The bile rose up and Tavisa turned her head to be sick on the rooftop, heaving until she was empty.

Once she regained her breath, she peeped over the edge again. Michael Dare's people were there already, herding pedestrians away from the path, from the bridge where they were gawking. Other agents wearing blue latex gloves gathered up the pieces of the fox, placing them in separate bags, sluicing down the pavement with buckets of bleach-stinking water. Making it all go away.

Her uneasiness made way for relief.

In her mind's eye, that future of blood and blooms, of dust and death, blew away. Something else was there. She couldn't see it yet, and it wasn't devoid of darkness, but mostly it was green and growing. Mostly it was good.

She heard a soft cry. Anthea was sitting with Michael's head cradled in her lap, heedless of the blood soaking her clothes as she stroked his hair.

Chapter Twenty-Four

GABRIEL'S HEART WAS HAMMERING SO HARD, JAMES THOUGHT HE'D BE able to hear it from space. On reaching the hospital entrance, the artist had dragged James towards the nearest lift. His breathing had become erratic again.

'Sod this,' muttered James. He seized Gabriel by the hand and took him to the stairwell, away from prying eyes. His leg hurt but the lift was too slow and would stop on all the bloody floors. This was the more viable option.

'Hop up, then. Hang on tight,' he commanded.

'No. You're hurt.'

'It's nothing.'

Gabriel brushed his fingers over the rent in James's jeans, through which the swollen, unhealed knife wound was still visible. 'It's not nothing.'

'I got stabbed with silver and didnae hae time tae clean it properly. I ran here on it; I can make it up the stairs. Michael doesnae hae time for this blether. Now, hop up or I'll leave ye here.'

Gabriel leapt up onto James's back. James gripped Gabriel's thighs to keep him hitched up. Gabriel hissed at the pressure on his bruised torso. 'Let's *go*.'

They went. James's gait was uneven, but they were fast, whipping past the occasional other stairwell occupant without interruption.

Near the very top, they encountered a team of BUS agents ascending the stairs at a run. James assumed that's who they were, given the compact firearms and that one of them had a tail.

James had to slow down to pass or risk a collision. The team leader blocked their path, and James was forced to stop.

The team regarded the sturdy vampire giving the lanky man a piggy back with the studiously neutral expressions that could only be maintained by a complete professional in the face of the utterly bizarre.

James let Gabriel to the ground.

'Mr Dare's bodyguard is on the scene,' reported the team leader quietly. 'She indicates she does not have a clear shot at Frazer.' The man was staring at Gabriel with consternation.

'What?' snarled Gabriel. He touched his face, encountering the sticky blood he hadn't yet had a chance to remove. 'This isn't mine,' he said, raising a flap of his torn T-shirt to scrub at his forehead. 'It's Michael's.' Gabriel faded to grieving silence.

'Congratulations on surviving Frazer's attack, Mr Dare,' the team leader said crisply into the charged pause. 'I've sent the message to Miss Webb.'

'Party hats later,' snapped James. 'What about Michael?'

'He's in control,' declared the team leader. 'Or he was. It keeps slipping, and he's been shot. Webb says any move will definitely lead to his death. She's delegated to make the call on our next action.'

From the rooftop, two floors away, came a short, sharp report.

Gabriel lurched to the next step, stumbled, righted himself and began to run.

A second shot rang out. In Gabriel's peripheral vision, a shape hurtled past the window. Behind him, three of the Bureau men began the rapid descent. The one with the tail barked instructions into a two-way.

James scooped Gabriel around the waist mid-step and resumed the ascent, carrying Gabriel up the final flights of stairs.

They burst onto the rooftop to see Anthea sitting with Michael's head in her lap, stroking his hair. She sat in a pool of his blood, soaked in it, uncaring.

Tavisa Datta was standing grimly next to Anthea. She still held her gun. There was no rush after all. There seemed nothing left to do, now.

Gabriel stood at his brother's feet, hands clenching and unclenching, while James knelt by the dying man. He pulled Michael's suit and shirt aside to inspect the terrible mess the bullet had made of his neck and collarbone.

James flinched at the smell of so much blood, then bent over the wound, allowing the saliva triggered by the scent of it to pool in his mouth. He let it flow into the ragged hole. Carefully, he spread the spit with the tip of a finger, and the skin, bone and muscle began to mend. The bleeding slowed and finally stopped.

But the healing properties of vampire saliva could only achieve so much. Stop the flow and repair damaged tissue, yes. Replace the blood lost? No. That, the body did, but it took the body's own time. The saliva accelerated the process to a degree, but not with sufficient speed. Not with the amount of blood Michael had lost.

Michael gazed mutely up at Anthea, labouring for breath as she stroked his hair. His hand clutched hers. James scented the fading remnants of the fox in Michael's spilled blood, but nothing of the fox was left in his body now. Michael's mind was at last his own again.

He got to die human, at least. And he would die soon.

Gabriel's expression was twisted with anger and distress. 'You idiot, Michael.' His voice broke even as he berated his brother. 'We had it under control. You were supposed to *wait*. You'd *delegated* your suicide to people who knew more than you did. You should have *trusted* them. Trusted *us*. Trusted *me*.'

Michael, in wonder and an agonised happiness, gazed upon Gabriel. 'You're alive.'

Gabriel dropped to his knees, reaching for Michael's free hand. 'Don't. Don't die. I forbid it.'

Michael looked at James. 'Thank you.'

'I'll nae let anything happen to him,' James said softly. 'I promised.'

Michael's eyelids fluttered shut for a second. When he opened them again, his old steel was back.

'Can you…?' he started; he took another sharp, shallow inhalation before he could continue, '…turn me?'

'Turn you what?'

'Make me. A vampire. Is it. Too late?'

'Michael, do you know what you're asking?' It was one thing to have agreed this ahead of time with Gabriel. This was the request of a dying man, desperate to live.

Michael glared haughtily. It almost made James laugh – such a typical superior expression. Michael definitely *thought* he knew what he was asking.

'So much. To do. So much. Still. I'm. Not ready. To die.' Michael squeezed Anthea's hand feebly, and she stroked his cheek.

'You have tae die anyway, Michael,' said James grimly. 'That's how this works.'

'Please.' Michael's voice was a ghost.

'James. Jamie. Please.' Gabriel's imploring, impatient hope was painful to hear.

'He knows the risks, Doctor Sharpe, it's his *job*,' said Anthea fiercely. 'Save him.'

'*Saving*'s not the word,' James said, and he looked to Tavisa Datta, as though hers was the deciding opinion.

'Don't look at me,' she said. 'I just shot a naked, homicidal fox spirit in the head and watched it fall off a building. I'm not sure I'm a good judge of *rational* anymore.'

'That makes you the perfect judge,' said James. 'I want to do it. I can. I dinnae know if it's *wise*.'

'Is he as important as he thinks he is?'

'To the government? I'm certain he is.' James's gaze alternated between Gabriel and Anthea. *To these two, definitely.*

Tavisa's chin jerked up in decision. 'Well, you're not so bad for a vampire. Maybe they don't all have to be arseholes. Turn him, Doctor Sharpe, and if he goes rogue, you and I will know what to do about it.'

Decided, James pressed fingers to Michael's cheek. 'You cannae come back without dying first. Some people dinnae come back at all. And it'll be hard, after. You've nae idea how hard.'

'I have,' rasped Michael, 'some idea. Miss Webb. You will. Keep your. Promise. If you. Must.'

'I have your back, sir. If you lose yourself to the thirst, I'll keep my promise. I will, sir.' She stroked his hair again. 'I will never let you down again, Michael.'

'You. Have. Never. Failed. Me. Anthea.'

Anthea pushed angrily at a tear with the back of her wrist. Instead of replying she glared at James Sharpe. 'He knows the risks. He's *studied* them. Turn him, Doctor Sharpe. *Try*.'

James took Michael's jaw in his hands and held his head so they were eye to eye.

'Tell me again. Is this what you want?'

'Yes,' breathed Michael. 'Do it.'

James sat astride Michael's body, pinning his legs and arms with his strong hands.

'Stand aside, the lot of you.'

Nobody moved.

'If I'm doing this,' he snarled, 'you do what I say, or it turns to shite, very fast. Stand aside. *Do not touch him* unless I give you the all-clear. If he wakes from this, he'll wake *thirsty*. *Stand the fuck back*. That includes you, Gabriel. *Especially* you.'

As Gabriel began to complain, James snapped, 'And bloody *watch*. You may change your mind about our contingency plan once you've seen this.'

Reluctantly, Anthea rose. Tavisa drew her away. Gabriel stood with them, *watching.*

'Michael.' Michael didn't respond to James's voice. He spoke again, more sharply, commanding attention. 'Michael Dare!'

Michael's eyes opened.

'In a moment, you'll drink my blood. Then I'll hold you down,' said James. 'When you wake, remember who I am. Remember who *you* are. Try not tae fight me.'

Michael smiled wanly. 'I shall do better than try, Doctor Sharpe.'

James pressed the nail of his left thumb to his right wrist, opening a shallow wound in the flesh. Dark vampire blood welled.

'Open wide.'

Michael opened his mouth. Blood beaded in James's wound; began to drip.

'This'll taste disgusting,' James warned.

Michael's eyes crinkled in an actual smile as the first drop hit his tongue. Then he flinched. He scrunched his face up. The next drip landed on his closed lips and he tried not to let the fluid in.

'It's not nearly enough,' said James. 'You need a higher ratio of vampire blood to your own that's left for this to work. Do I go on?'

In answer, Michael opened his mouth again, green eyes full of resolve, and only a little fear.

'You dinnae have tae do this.'

Michael glared and opened his mouth wider.

James dug his thumbnail into the wound, and his blood flowed more freely. A few more drops fell onto Michael's tongue. James pressed the gash directly against Michael's mouth.

Automatically, Michael – with strength that had, until a moment ago, abandoned him – seized James's arm and held it firmly as he sucked on the wound. Greedily. Noisily. James grit his teeth on a cry and then, as Michael actually bit at the bleeding cut, James hissed a string of swear words – but he didn't pull away.

Michael gagged and went rigid, his back arching in seizure upon seizure. James pulled his arm free and instead grasped Michael's upper arms, holding him down as he thrashed and cried out.

It was horrible. This urbane, polished, disciplined man, flailing on the ground like a rabid animal, in a pool of his own blood, his lips and teeth stained dark with the substance inhabiting his body, harrying it towards death. His eyes contained no intelligence. Only fear and pain and desperation, and a burning will to live.

Gabriel and Anthea both stirred to assist. James, fangs extended, hissed at them. '*Stay away!*'

Soon, the convulsions ceased. Michael sagged limply against the roof surface.

Dead.

James looked little better, his always pale skin ashen, his movements lethargic. His fangs were descended and his eyes glazed.

'Jamie.'

'I didnae know... it was so hard... to be the initiator. Fuck. I feel rubbish.'

'How long?' Gabriel asked.

'Took me... a few minutes, I think.' James shook his head. 'Didnae exactly have a timer. I didnae know what West was doing till after.' His whole body shuddered.

'I didnae know what I was when I woke. Where I was. *Who* I was. Not for hours.' He straightened his spine. 'Don't come near. If I cannae hold him, run. He may not know you, and he'll be raging thirsty.'

James knelt more firmly on the dead man's legs and pinned his limp arms above Michael's head, braced against being bucked off in a wild fury.

And they waited.

The seconds ticked by in terrible silence. *Tick. Tick. Tick.* Like a bomb.

Gabriel breathed short and sharp through his nose. He began to move away, only to be brought up short by James's ferocious glare.

'Stay,' growled James, his gaze wild; untamed and bleak. 'You need tae see this. You need tae understand what it is.'

'He'll need blood,' Gabriel said, forcing himself to be calm.

'You. *Stay.*'

'I'll…' began Anthea.

'You're covered in blood,' Gabriel pointed out, and the two of them stared at each other. She was covered in *Michael's* blood. Michael's blood was still crusted on Gabriel's face; in his hair, too.

Tavisa looked from one haunted face to another. 'Stay with him. I'll go.'

Her departure was stymied at the door to the stairs when she encountered the BUS team leader. The rest of his team was on the street below, clearing bits of dead fox from the footpath.

'Do you have a situation report?' he asked. 'Miss Webb signalled I should wait. Do you have further instructions?' His professional aloofness faltered. 'Is Mr Dare alive?'

Tavisa looked over her shoulder, then back at the agent. 'We need bags of blood from the hospital. I don't know how many. Three or four, at least. Is that something you can do without having to answer any questions?'

His gaze flicked over her shoulder, full of questions himself, but he nodded. 'We have a contact here.'

That was a huge relief, because Tavisa had no idea how she was supposed to convince the nursing staff to give her bags of blood without explaining why she needed it. And she was absolutely not going to tell them why she needed it.

'Fast as you can, then,' said Tavisa in as firm a command voice as she could muster. 'I'll wait here for you.'

The agent took off, speaking swiftly and quietly into his two-way, reassured to have new purpose. Tavisa stared after him, then decided that she *had* seen a tail, and that it wasn't the most peculiar thing she'd seen today.

Tavisa returned to the rooftop tableau. Those four people. Still as stone. Still as death.

She closed her eyes, but there were no more visions. She hoped it meant that this was not a crucial moment. Not the fulcrum of the future she'd interrupted when she walked between Anthea and Michael. She hoped the darkness she'd sensed in the future was only the usual kind, the run-of-the-mill human badness of murder, extortion and assault.

She tried not to think about the blazing angel from her dreams, and how she *was* that righteous creature. She was *not* an avenging angel or *deva* or whatever. She was an ordinary copper, in way over her head. That was all.

Tavisa opened her eyes again. Gabriel had lifted his gaze from Michael's slack face to regard James, poised over Michael's body.

'Jamie?' Gabriel said soothingly, like you would to a snarling dog. 'Are you all right.'

'Of course I'm not all right,' replied James tensely, but not angrily. 'I know what this is like from his side.'

The sun moved incrementally across the sky. The traffic hummed below. An ambulance came, another left. There were cars and helicopters and pigeons and ships' horns in the distance – London being London; although part of her lay dead on this rooftop.

That dead part of London – its defender, Michael – suddenly moved; a twitch of his pinkie finger.

Tavisa approached, determined to bear witness; to understand.

The finger twitched twice more. A foot jerked.

James Sharpe crouched over the body, straddling its thighs, holding its hands down, ready.

Ready for what?

Then a pair of green eyes snapped open.

They were blank.

And then they were filled with terror.

Michael's body arched up and he was choking, suffocating, trying to take a breath but unable to remember how.

Then the terrible dragging gasp of it filled the air: that first lungful of oxygen his body didn't need, of his body reacting instinctively with horror and panic at the realisation, trying to breathe anyway.

The exhale was a bellow of agony and rage, devolving into a shriek of abject terror. Michael's body spasmed in a way that must have been painful, collapsed, arched again, as he gasped for air, wailed, gasped again, and began to flail about, trying to rise.

He screamed.

The convulsions as he died and the vampire blood inhabited his body were nothing compared to this wild, frantic, terror-fueled thrashing.

From the start, James had him pinioned by legs and arms. Michael Dare – a man of elegance, of poise, of the utmost self-containment and grace and cool charm – sobbed and struggled to escape not from James but from the invisible, unknown monster in his veins.

James wrestled him down, viciously almost, except that he was saying: 'Sshh, hush now. You're not alone. Sshh. I'm here. I'm here. You're not alone, Michael. It'll be all right. Come on, now. Hush. Don't be scared. I've got you. I've got you.'

Michael's face contorted and he bared his fangs in an animal rage.

Without warning, James responded in kind. He pushed Michael down and roared in his face, fangs bared, blue eyes blazing. Michael thrashed, sobbing.

'What's your name?' James yelled, pulling back. 'Tell me. Remember who you are.'

Michael snapped his teeth, trying to bite. He looked ruined. Lost and alone.

The other witnesses to this atrocity – Tavisa, Gabriel, Anthea – looked much the same.

Michael fought to rise. James slammed him back to the ground.

'Stay down. Stay *still*. Remember your name. You can. Come on. Tell me. Tell me your name. *Tell me who you are.*'

Finally, exhaling cries and then gulping desperately for air again, Michael subsided.

'I'm... I'm...'

'That's it. You can do this. Tell me your name.'

'I can't.' The despairing wail rose up again.

'You can. You promised me you could. Tell me.'

'Mmm-m-mei...'

'Come on, now,' James's voice was gentler again. 'You can do this. Come back to us. It'll nae be so hard if you remember who you are. Please.'

'Maaaah... Mmm....Mii...'

'That's it. You know who you are. You know.'

'Mi-mi-mi–' and he shuddered. 'Michael.'

'Good man. Michael. Good.' James slumped over him, forehead pressed to forehead. 'Good man. Michael. Do you know me?'

'J-j-j-James.'

'Aye. I'm James. Good.'

James eased up. Michael bucked, trying to throw him off again. James was forced to hold him down once more.

'No. Be still. *Be still.*'

'I can smell...I can...I can smell blood.' Michael twisted, teeth bared, and looked wildly around. His gaze alighted on Tavisa first and she took an involuntary step back at the ravenous, unthinking hunger in it.

'Michael. *Michael!*' James banged Michael's head on the concrete to make him listen. 'I know you're thirsty. I'll get you all the blood you need. Soon. Right now you have to look at me.'

The vampire who used to be Michael Dare glared at him.

'Breathe. It helps.'

Michael began to moan.

'I know,' said James, his voice almost breaking with what he knew. 'But you're not going to die again. It feels like it, but you can wait. I promise you can. Tell me your name. Your full name.'

'M-Michael B-b-Balmoral D-d-Dare.'

'And what are you?'

A keening followed by a growl. 'I don't know.'

'Yes you do. Tell me.'

'A-a-a-a…'

'Concentrate.'

'I'm a… civil servant.'

James grinned at him, without letting him go. 'Aye, you are. The most civil civil servant on the planet, except when you're being an enormous prick. Aren't you?'

Michael panted a despairing laugh. 'Yes, I am.'

'You're a disciplined man. So start being disciplined. Inhale.'

Michael took a breath. He gave James a look of distress and doubt.

'Exhale now. Slowly,' said James. 'Now in. Good. Concentrate on that.'

Michael concentrated. Breathed in. Out. In. Out. Physically unnecessary but psychologically calming. James kept Michael pinned with one hand and reached out to the pool of blood under them with the other. He swiped his hand through the congealing mess and wiped it against Michael's mouth. Michael whined.

'Lick it up. It'll help.'

Michael licked and whined again, more softly.

'There you go.' James scraped more of the blood up, stuck his fingers in Michael's mouth. 'Good, good. Calm down, now. I cannae feed you till you calm down. Shh, now. Shh.'

Michael suckled his own blood from James's fingers and quieted.

'Where the hell is that blood,' James scowled.

'I'll check,' Tavisa said, backing away from his feral growl.

James flinched. He checked on the others.

Anthea's eyes were fixed on Michael. They were filled not with horror, which would have been the sensible reaction, but hope.

Gabriel, though, was looking at James with understanding and... and *anger*. James flinched again.

'I'm not angry at *you*,' snapped Gabriel impatiently. 'I want to kill that bastard Cael West all over again. He did *this* to you. He left you to wake up like *that*. Alone and terrified, and *starving*. No wonder you–' He snapped his jaw shut on the sentence. 'It wasn't your fault, Jamie.'

James swayed slightly.

Michael bucked again, teeth snapping, and James battled to keep him still.

'I cannae get him down to the blood stores, like I hoped,' said James. 'I'm not strong enough. I can barely keep him under control here. You two, off the roof. If I lose him, he'll go straight for you.'

But Anthea knelt beside him. She held out her arm. 'He needs blood. Give him mine.'

Michael surged towards her; James slammed him down again.

'Dinnae be stupid,' snarled James. 'If he gets his teeth into you, he'll nae know how to stop. He's *thirsty*. He's *starving*. He doesnae truly remember who he is yet. He could kill you, and when he finally comes to himself again...'

Anthea rolled her eyes at James. She drew a small, sharp knife from an ankle sheath and held it to her forearm. 'I never said he should *bite* me. Come on, sir,' she said to Michael, who was staring at her avidly. 'You don't want to waste any.'

He opened his mouth wide. Anthea drew the blade along the skin, deeper than comfortable, but not dangerously so. Blood welled and dripped. She held it over his mouth and he gulped at it. Licked the drips from his lips and opened his mouth for more. Like a baby bird.

She didn't seem to notice that James stared at the blood just as avidly.

After a short time – too short if Michael's enraged growl was anything to go by – she withdrew, wrapping her hand over the wound.

'Blood given freely is best,' observed Gabriel quietly. 'Is it enough?'

James shook his head. 'He woke up with nothing much in him but vampire blood. It's nae enough. I cannae describe it, the *thirst*.'

He flinched again as Gabriel's hand pressed against his scalp.

'In case you havenae realised,' said James shakily, 'I dinnae know what I'm doing. I havenae done it from the outside. I can only make educated guesses. I dinnae think it's enough. Look at him.'

Michael looked tortured, and debauched, and terrifying.

Gabriel held out his arm. 'We'll give him some of mine, then.'

James used his thumbnail to score a wound in Gabriel's arm. Michael opened up again to swallow the drips greedily. A few minutes later, Gabriel held his arm up for James.

'You can close the wound. And you need the blood, too.'

'I cannae. I dinnae know if I can stop. Best back away now, love.'

Gabriel did as he was told.

Finally, Tavisa and the agent returned, bearing bags of blood. The team leader froze, even this hardened field agent shocked at the carnage in front of him. Tavisa thrust a bag of blood at James. 'I'm assuming blood type doesn't matter.'

James grabbed the bag, tore a hole in it and pushed it into Michael's mouth. Michael sucked greedily on it.

James put his hand out for another and had it ready when Michael had drained the first.

On the third bag, James carefully released Michael's hands and let him hold the bag, squeezing it for every drop of blood it contained.

'Jamie,' Gabriel tried to push a pouch of blood at James. 'You need this.'

But James was shaking his head, and his hands were shaking too, and he was whimpering without realising it. 'He needs it, he *needs* it. He'll be so thirsty. I remember… the raging thirst. I… the things I *did*, Gabriel. I was so thirsty. I cannae let him do… I cannae. I cannae let…'

He was shoving the blood that Gabriel had tried to give him into Michael's mouth. 'If this is nae enough, he'll kill you. He'll kill all of you. I cannae let him. God. This was a terrible idea.'

Gabriel stroked James's hair soothingly, softly. Tears welled and fell. 'You're doing fine, baby.'

Michael was blinking in a daze, less savage now, but more lost.

'James?' said Michael in a bewildered voice.

James turned instantly to his patient. 'Here, Michael.'

'Has it… have I… did it work?'

'Aye, but you need to stay there right now. All right?'

Michael frowned and looked around. He saw Gabriel first, and his frown deepened.

Then he saw Anthea, her clothes stiff with drying blood. She was wrapping a length of cloth she'd torn from her shirt around her arm. 'Anthea?'

'The genuine article, sir,' she said, as calm and cool as ever, while looking like a murder scene.

Michael snapped suddenly back into focus. Fully aware. Of everything. Every single thing from the last fifteen minutes.

He'd looked lost before. Now he looked damned.

He buried his face in his hands, as much to not see them as to hide himself. 'Dear god. Dear god, what am I? This is not. This is…' He swallowed convulsively.

'You havenae killed anyone,' said James gently. 'We can help you through this.'

Michael felt a gentle hand on his cheek and dared to open his eyes. Anthea was stroking his cheek with the back of her fingers. 'You're not alone, sir,' she said, with that Mona Lisa smile of hers. 'We've got you. Like I promised.'

She stroked his cheek, and Michael leaned into her touch.

'I'm so sorry, my dear. I always meant for there to be time, but the time was never right.'

'Don't fret, sir.'

'You've botched the timing wretchedly today,' said Gabriel suddenly, the attempt at waspishness not covering the tremor in his voice.

Michael, more like the man of old, guarded and in control, looked on his brother. 'I realise that I made a mess of your plans. It was difficult to do otherwise, with *him* increasingly invading my thoughts. It was necessary to *not* consider what you might be planning. By the end, what I knew, he was starting to know. At that moment, when I began to realise what you were planning, I had to act to keep the knowledge from him.'

'So you tried to shoot yourself in the head?'

'It was effective,' said Michael, his own voice quivering. 'The pain did keep my mind off your schemes. It seems to have paid off.'

His urbanity was in sharp contrast to his state of bloodied dishevelment and the exhausted vampire sitting on his legs.

'Doctor Sharpe, I think you can get up now,' said Michael, trying for acerbity and failing. When James didn't respond, Michael repeated, more firmly. 'Doctor Sharpe.'

James raised his head slowly. Stared at Michael. Blinked. Showed his fangs and hissed.

When Gabriel knelt beside him, James snarled wordlessly at him.

'Blood,' snapped Gabriel, holding out his hand. He wiggled his fingers impatiently. 'Come on, Datta, *blood.*'

'We only brought the four bags.'

Gabriel glared at her.

'I didn't realise. There's not exactly a study unit on this at the police academy!'

'Well, *get more.*'

Tavisa and the agent obeyed.

Gabriel slid his arm around James's shoulders. James hissed at him.

'Shh, Jamie,' said Gabriel as soothingly as he could. 'You'll get blood soon.'

James lunged for Gabriel's throat, fisting his hands in Gabriel's jacket, pushing his face into that warm hollow, and the tips of his teeth were pressed to that delicate, fragile skin.

Gabriel held perfectly still.

James whimpered, pushing his nose into the scent of him. He hung onto the leather; he pressed into the stripe of warm, bare skin where the T-shirt had been sundered. He whined and shivered.

'Gabriel,' he said hoarsely. 'Help. Me.'

Chapter Twenty Five

GABRIEL ROCKED JAMES IN HIS ARMS, TRYING TO SOOTHE HIM. JAMES whimpered again, inhaling deeply of the scent. Blood, yes. But wool. Paint. Gabriel. Nest. Safety. Home. Gabriel. Not food. *Home home home*. James clung to that, desperately.

Gabriel tried shoving his bleeding arm into James's mouth, but James recoiled, terrified that once he started he wouldn't be able to stop. Gabriel gave it up and resumed rocking him instead.

'Tavisa's getting blood for you,' he said. 'Michael, are you okay?'

'I'm fi– Oh. You mean, am I *safe*? I... believe I am quite restored.'

Gabriel returned his attention to the man in his arms.

Michael, sitting in a pool of his own dried blood, peered at them. 'What's wrong with his leg?'

James curled his body into a smaller space, getting closer to Gabriel, an injured creature seeking shelter in its burrow – but his leg wouldn't obey. His wounded thigh was swollen horribly, and black blood crusted the skin and torn cloth.

'He was stabbed with silver while he was rescuing Helene,' said Gabriel. 'I need to flush it clean. Any taps up here?'

Anthea found an outlet by the side of the staircase, where some enterprising hospital worker was growing a pot of personal-use marijuana. Beside the planter was a green enamel watering can. She filled it and brought it over to them.

'I need to see to your leg,' Gabriel murmured to James, who didn't reply, but shivered and huddled against him. Awkwardly, Gabriel reached around, but couldn't get in the right position. Anthea crouched and cut away the cloth around the wound with her little knife.

The injury was worse once revealed. Dark purple lines radiated from the shallow stab wound, and congealed black blood oozed from it. Anthea passed the steel knife to Gabriel. Using the tip, Gabriel pressed. A gout of congealed blood pulsed out and James hissed in pain. Gabriel prodded with the hilt of the knife and more gunk came out. Anthea then poured water over it, washing the foul matter away.

'This'll hurt,' Gabriel warned him.

'Hurts now,' James said.

'It'll hurt more.'

James managed a laugh and released his grip enough to allow Gabriel to manoeuvre. With his hands, Gabriel spread the cut wide, and Anthea poured water over it. Gabriel dug a finger into the wound, clearing out congealed blood until James's dark, sluggish vampire blood was all he could see in the flesh. The veins began to clear, James's vampire skin to return to its normal pallor. The flesh and skin began to knit together again, and James relaxed marginally.

'You should have seen to that,' Gabriel admonished him gently.

'If I'd taken the time,' mumbled James, 'you'd have died.'

Gabriel rested his cheek on James's hair. 'Do you think you can drink from me now?'

'I dinnae know. I'm afraid to try.'

'Can you hold on, then?' Gabriel raised his head, listening. 'They must be on their way back.'

James nodded. Gabriel kissed the top of his head, then rubbed his cheek against James's hair, tender amidst the carnage. He was so glad he could hold him like this, so he could breathe in Gabriel's scent and feel safe.

The click of the opening door was loud in the stressed silence. Tavisa and the Bureau man, carrying bags of blood, emerged onto the rooftop with a young man who carried two more.

'Oh!' said the young fellow, 'Mr Merriweather was right.' Smiling, he strode up to them. 'This is for you, Mr Dare. God, you've been in the wars, haven't you?' He handed a bag to his seated boss, unfazed by all the drying blood.

Michael stared at the bag as though offended, but Anthea pursed her lips impatiently, so he tore it and drank from it, though more daintily than before.

'And one for you,' said the young man, crouching beside Gabriel and James. James stared dumbly at the offered bag.

'Come along then,' the fellow repeated in a jolly-you-along tone, jogging the bag at him. 'Mmm, yummy blood. Just what the vampire ordered, eh?'

'You're disturbingly chirpy today, Jay,' observed Anthea.

'I'm disturbingly chirpy every day, Miss Webb,' he countered with a grin, then flinched as James snatched the bag from his fingers. 'Ah, that's the idea. Get that in ya.'

James tore the bag clumsily open, spilling blood over his hands. With a desperate whine, he sucked at the opening, slurping the blood down ravenously. He threw the bag away and licked at his hands, sucked at his shirt where the blood soaked in, until Jay pushed another into his hands.

James bit it this time – bit and sucked and whimpered, and reached out for a third even before he'd finished the one in his mouth. It was animal and wretched, the way he drank.

Instead of recoiling, Gabriel rubbed James's back and tried to shield him, as much as possible, from those on the rooftop who had never seen him like this. Gabriel glared at Tavisa Datta, who gave James a look of bewildered compassion and turned away.

Michael was staring, though. Horrified. Gabriel's lip curled at his brother. 'Don't you presume to judge him, Michael.'

'No. No you're right. I'm sorry.'

While James drank, cradled in Gabriel's arms, Gabriel contemplated their saviour with puzzlement. 'What did you mean about Mr Merriweather being right?'

Jay's eyebrows rose in surprise. 'You don't know about Mr Merriweather? I thought everyone in the Bureau knew about Mr Merriweather.'

'I'm not in the Bureau,' said Gabriel through gritted teeth.

'But I thought Fudge here… Oh, sorry, Mr Dare. I thought your brother was getting you in and, um, I'll shut the fuck up now, sir, yes I will, look at me, disciplined as all fuck, sir, not a word.' He pressed his lips together.

'My brother, Mr Ren, has a different calling,' Michael said severely, though the effect was ruined by the fact his legs were trembling too hard to allow him to rise without stumbling.

'Probably just as well. It's a whackadoodle life, isn't it, Miss Webb?

Anthea refused to be a participant of this ludicrous conversation. 'You were explaining Mr Merriweather to young Mr Dare,' she said pointedly.

'That's right. Mr Merriweather's our ghost, Young Mr Dare. He works in the hospital mortuary. Worked, rather, back in the 1950s. I suppose he still works there, in a way. He likes to give me advice.' Jay's nose wrinkled, as though that advice was not always welcome.

'Anyway, he told me to wrangle a few pints of blood to bring up here, 'cos *shit was going dooooooown on high.*'

At Michael's glare, Jay settled again.

'Not that Mr Merriweather talks like that. He is very much a genteel man. So, ah, here I am, and everything is hunky dory, yeah?'

Gabriel looked at him, looked around the rooftop at the people caked in blood, the vampires drinking from bags of blood, at all the torn clothing and the aftermath of terror, near death and actual death. He wanted to cry.

'Never dorier,' said Anthea. 'Thank you for the blood, Jay. Back to work you go. Shoo.'

Jay, thankfully, shooed, after shoving the last of the blood bags into Gabriel's hands.

Anthea shrugged apologetically. 'Mr Merriweather has a wealth of knowledge but for some reason he'll only talk to Jay, so we're stuck with him, I'm afraid. He waffles on like a toddler on speed, but he's very useful.'

Beside her, Michael finally started to rise. 'Anthea, if you would…'

She took his hand to steady him and he made it to his feet with the slightest wobble, though his suit had to grotesquely unpeel from the coagulating blood on the ground. Despite the gore and ruination of his suit, despite his wax-pale skin and mussed hair, he had gathered around himself an air of self-possession and command that would have been eerie, if it hadn't been exactly how he operated when he was human.

Michael also had to literally peel off his coat, which stuck to his skin. His collarbone was mended and the hole in his neck was healed shut. He turned to his team leader, standing at attention.

'Mr Travers, organise the helicopters so that we may leave this roof. I'm not allowing anyone to catch the Tube like *that*. Arrange for changes of clothes for Anthea and myself to be ready on arrival. Gabriel and Doctor Sharpe will also need fresh clothing. I shall debrief you fully once we return to the office.'

Travers shuffled uncomfortably.

'Debrief, Mr Travers, not *eat*. I'm fully sated, and I certainly will not be in such a perilous state of hunger again.'

'We'll have a routine delivery of pig's blood established from tomorrow,' said Anthea crisply. 'Supplemented by volunteers. Freely given, sir, as per the manual.'

'Yes sir. Ma'am.' Travers disappeared to make the arrangements.

Tavisa wished she could make things happen so effortlessly. She looked at her mostly stain-free clothes and wondered how she'd managed to be the one who'd killed someone but ended up without a bloodstain on her.

James had stopped feeding. He'd been licking his fingers, his lips, smearing a hand over his chin to catch every last drop of blood, but now he was still as stone, eyes wide with distress. The thirst had passed, and Gabriel (indeed, everyone) could see that James was disgusted with himself. That he felt exposed. Filled with shame.

'James Sharpe,' Gabriel growled at him, 'don't you dare be ashamed of yourself.'

James gave him that haunted look again, the one Gabriel hated.

'Don't you *dare*. That's what West did to you, without even giving you a choice?' His tone was thick with outrage and compassion. 'The fact that you remained sane at all, that you did as little harm as you possibly could, that you resisted and survived without becoming a brute, is astonishing. My God. You did that *on your own*, Jamie. You controlled the vampire in you *on your own*, without *anyone*'s help.'

'Gabriel, I'm–'

'*Stop it.* Jamie, you saved my life today, even wounded by silver. You keep saving my life. You've saved Michael twice now. You saved that Donal girl. You do nothing but *save* people. Don't you *dare* be ashamed of who you are or of what you need.'

'Even if what I need is six litres of warm blood straight from the source?' James said bitterly.

'Even then. Not that you ever will. I keep *telling* you. You're the most amazing person I know. You have nothing to be ashamed of. I *trust* you. And I will *always* take care of you.'

'Because vampires as a whole need so much protection,' said James, moved to quiet laughter in the face of Gabriel's impassioned declaration.

'Some of them, yes.' Gabriel tugged on his arms and James eased against the comfort of his chest. He caught Tavisa's abstracted gaze, though, and the tension began to rise again, until she shrugged.

'I've met court clerks with meaner streaks and grosser personal habits for a lot less reason than you've got for yours, Doctor Sharpe. Gabriel's right. You've no cause for embarrassment. You saved lives today. I'd say you're well ahead of the game.'

James and Gabriel were two lost men, found; Tavisa could see that now.

She remembered that flash of the future that wouldn't now happen. James falling to dust. Gabriel murdered by his fox-possessed brother.

It occurred to Tavisa that by stepping out onto the roof, keeping Anthea from attempting to shoot Michael, and by shooting Frazer off the rooftop herself, she had saved them all. Anthea and Michael. James and Gabriel. Victor and Helene. She had saved every one of them, and there was nobody to tell her she was amazing for doing it. Nobody to tell her she didn't have to be ashamed of murdering that wicked man and watching him fall.

But it didn't matter. She didn't feel amazing. She wasn't ashamed either. She'd done what had to be done, and she didn't want them to know how close they came to the end of the world.

'I'll get some water,' she said, taking up the watering can.

'I'll help,' said Anthea.

At the tap, Anthea scooped water up and over her face, throat, hands. She bathed her wounded arm and peeled out of the trousers that stuck to her skin.

She smiled at Tavisa.

'I saw the vision,' she said kindly. 'Fragments. I'm not very strong, but it was a powerful vision. My hands were shaking. My shot to Michael's head would have missed. The vision made that very clear.

'So, Sergeant Tavisa Datta, thank you for saving us all from Niall Frazer.'

Tavisa regarded her solemnly, then grinned. 'You're very welcome, An. The. A.'

Chapter Twenty Six

MICHAEL'S TEAM AIRLIFTED EVERYONE AWAY FROM THE HOSPITAL AND TO a modest Georgian hotel-that-wasn't-a-hotel near Battersea Park – actually BUS's base of operations. Besides meeting rooms, an ops centre and a few neat, functional crash spaces, it had a small number of handy iron- and silver-reinforced holding cells in the former wine cellar.

Each of them – in various states of dishevelment and blood spatter – parted to clean up. Gabriel and James leaned against each other, blood crusted in their hairlines and under fingernails. James could still not meet Tavisa Datta's gaze and Gabriel's arm remained protectively around the vampire.

'I'm glad I was wrong about you,' Tavisa said to Gabriel. 'What I mean is, I'm sorry.'

'Having visions must be a bitch to live with,' said Gabriel. 'Ghosts are easier. They mostly float around looking grotesque and put out.'

'Yeah. Well. Things will change.' She tugged fractiously at her hair, looking at the strands of it instead of at Gabriel. 'I'll clean up and head home. Look after him.' Then she winced, because of course Gabriel was going to look after James. 'See you around, maybe.'

Before he could reply, she strode off in Anthea's wake towards a room where she could wash up before heading home.

Michael, shadowed by an armed guard, showed his brother and his vampire to another of the rooms in the not-hotel. The apartment was equipped with bed, desk, refrigerator, kettle and, in the bathroom, towels, shampoo, soap, and an array of bathroom items sealed in plastic hygiene-guaranteed bags.

'Stay as long as you need,' he said. 'One of my staff will see you home when you're ready. I may not be able to see you again tonight, but I'll come by your flat in the next few days.'

Gabriel reached out for Michael's wrist. 'Are you going to be okay?'

Michael smiled self-deprecatingly, unaware of the traces of blood between his teeth. 'I'm fine. All right, perhaps not entirely *fine*, but I will be in time. I have your Doctor Sharpe's example to show me the way.'

James, who had sat on the edge of the bed, lifted his head wearily at the mention of his name.

'I'll have the staff send more blood up,' said Michael. 'And soup.' He patted his brother's fingers on his wrist. 'All will be well. We've done extraordinary work today, Gabriel. For the nation and... and for each other. Your doctor is someone particularly special, as man or vampire. Take care of him.'

'I will.'

Michael and his guard left. Gabriel sat beside James.

'Why does everyone keep telling you to look after me?' James asked. 'I don't need looking after. I'm a vampire.'

'You are. You're badass as all fuck.'

'That's me. Doctor Badass.'

'Doctor *Hot*ass,' Gabriel corrected him teasingly as he slipped an arm around James's waist to draw him near.

'You finally found out my army nickname, huh? When they weren't calling me Jim-Jam, any road.'

'Come on then, Doctor Hottie. Let's clean up.'

In the bathroom, Gabriel stripped James and then himself, though it was awkward going. An ugly black and purple bruise spread from his diaphragm to his chest, where James's shoulder had knocked the wind from him. It hurt like the devil, but it wouldn't kill him. He'd deal with it later.

For now, he took James with him into the shower cubicle. He made the water as hot as he could stand it.

He soaped James from shoulders to toes, massaging a nearly scentless shower gel into foam, chasing the bubbles away with a facecloth. He unsealed a packaged nailbrush and scrubbed under James's fingernails. He washed James's hair. Conditioner next. He used a second facecloth to gently wash James's face, ears and neck. James submitted, practically in his dormant state, and Gabriel's eyes prickled with emotion at the trust it showed.

Gabriel patted James's ribs in a gentle hushing motion. 'Stay right there,' he murmured, as though James would go anywhere else. Then he soaped himself up, and his hair, sluicing rust coloured rivulets down the drain until the water at last ran clear. He couldn't help gasping in pain as he moved.

He suddenly felt James's hands on his waist. James was inspecting the bruise.

'You're hurt,' James said. 'I hurt you.'

'You *caught* me,' Gabriel corrected him.

James tried to spit on his fingers, but the water washed the very little saliva he was able to produce away before it could do any good.

'Don't worry about it now,' said Gabriel gently. 'We'll see to it after the shower.'

James nodded, but slowly, so tired he could hardly move. He wouldn't meet Gabriel's eyes.

'James. Look at me, Jamie.'

Reluctantly, James did so. 'I'm fine.'

'You're not.'

'I'm… I don't know if tired's the word. Weak. I need more blood. Then I'll fix that bruise.'

'Michael's sending some up.'

'Mm.'

Gabriel pressed a kiss to James's brow as warm water cascaded over his back and shoulders, splashing onto James's torso.

'You think what happened today is going to change how I feel about you, don't you?'

'No,' said James in a tone suspiciously like "maybe".

'You're daft,' replied Gabriel affectionately. 'Here's what we're going to do. When we've had our shower, you're going to drink, and then I'm taking you home so you can rest properly in a safe place. Tomorrow, we're spending the day in bed, sleeping or fooling around or shagging or blowing raspberries on each other or watching something stupid on TV or whatever the fuck we want to do. Then we're going to keep on doing whatever the fuck we want to do together for the rest of our lives.'

'Raspberries sound fun,' said James, eyes brightening. 'You've got a terrific arse for it.'

'So finally you're going to kiss my arse?'

'Kiss, blow. Lick. Whatever.'

'*Whatever* sounds promising.'

'Doesn't it, though?'

'Good.'

They finished bathing. On the bathmat, they dried off and then freed two clean toothbrushes from their plastic seals and brushed the taste of blood and fear from their tongues.

When they re-entered the bedroom, they found a couple of plain, dark tracksuits laid out on the bed, their stained, torn clothes having been taken away.

'Your brother's crew have nicked my pants,' grumbled James.

'We'll have to go commando, then.' Gabriel patted James's backside in approval.

They pulled on the sweatpants, but when James went to the thermos on the table, which was filled with warmed pig's blood, Gabriel put a hand on the container.

'No,' he said.

'I need more than I can take from you.'

'Then you can have it after.' He took the thermos to the bed and sat against the pillows. 'See? I'm not being an idiot. It's here for you for after. But you'll drink from me first.'

'I can't just take from you, Gabriel.'

'I'm offering it.'

'Just because you're offering, it doesn't mean I should accept. It's uneven. What do you get from me in return?'

'I know what I get. So do you, when you're thinking properly.'

James squinted at the nasty bruise on Gabriel's body. 'You get... No. You don't mean the magic vampire spit.'

'No, I don't.'

'You get all of me,' James said at last, looking into green eyes, smiling as he made the offer. 'Everything I have. Everything I am. Everything I can ever do for you, to keep you safe, keep you happy and healthy. It's all for you: this sluggish heart, my soul if it exists, and my body, magic spit and all.'

'And you get all of me, too. Heart, blood, brains, art, soul. The bits that are crazy and the bits that make macabre jokes. Probably huge swathes of me you haven't any use for.'

James crawled over the covers on hands and knees until he could stop Gabriel's mouth with his own. He kissed, kissed again, kissed once more; soft insistent pushes until Gabriel stopped speaking and instead parted his lips. He sucked gently at Gabriel's lower lip, then licked a line along it before brushing the tip of Gabriel's tongue with his own. Gabriel pushed his fingers into James's damp hair, his kisses growing deeper and more impassioned.

When finally they parted, Gabriel brushed his nose against the tip of James's. 'Your heart isn't sluggish, you know. It's slow but it's strong.'

'There isn't a part of you I don't love,' said James. 'I'm especially fond of the bits that make macabre jokes, as it happens.'

'That's lucky,' said Gabriel, 'Because that's a big bit. Here. Cuddle up. I don't want to be clinical about this. I want to hold you.' He opened his arms in invitation and parted his knees to make room. James inched into the warm crook of his body, arranged himself carefully so that he didn't press on the bruise, and rested his head on Gabriel's shoulder.

'That's it,' murmured Gabriel approvingly. One arm was tucked around James's back, a hand resting on his hip. He brushed his thumb along James's jaw, and over his lip. Then he bent to kiss him.

James took his time, first running his fingers down Gabriel's free arm, shoulder to elbow, elbow to wrist. Then he raised Gabriel's hand to his mouth and kissed it, knuckles and palm, then the wrist, then a line of kisses towards the crook of his elbow. At the softest, plumpest part of Gabriel's arm, he pressed three reverent kisses, and then bit down, piercing the skin, before sealing his mouth over the wound.

Gabriel hardly felt a thing except the sensuous pull of James's mouth sucking at his arm. A few seconds passed and then James was licking the wound, lapping up blood and encouraging the small holes made by his teeth to heal. Gabriel ran his fingers through James's hair as he did so.

He'd never seen James drink while semi-naked before, and he could see now how his pallid skin grew faintly warmer in hue. Gabriel traced his fingers down James's spine, then up again. He repeated the gesture, a gentle, reassuring stroke against his skin.

'Sit back,' James encouraged him, moving to his hands and knees between Gabriel's legs. Gabriel reclined on the pillows. James nuzzled at Gabriel's chest, then softly licked at the edge of the bruising. He pressed his curled tongue to Gabriel's sternum, allowing saliva to pool there before licking a long wet stripe up towards Gabriel's neck.

James huffed self-deprecatingly. 'It'd be more efficient to do this with my fingers.'

'Sod efficient,' breathed Gabriel. 'That's brilliant.'

James hummed and kissed Gabriel's chest. He allowed the saliva to pool on his tongue again, then licked Gabriel wetly from belly to sternum.

Gabriel feathered his fingers over James's cheek and jaw as James repaid the gift of lifeblood with a gift of healing.

When he was done, James lay wearily curled in the shelter of Gabriel's arms. Gabriel opened the thermos and held it to James's mouth.

'Sip. Don't give me that look. I keep telling you; I don't mind. And even if we've just promised each other everything, I don't think I can persuade you to drink from me again. No, I didn't think so. So have this until you're stronger, and then we'll go home.'

James drank the flask dry. As he licked the last of it from his lips, Gabriel kissed the top of his head.

'The answer is still yes, by the way,' said Gabriel.

'What was the question again?' James asked warily, though he knew the answer.

'The contingency plan. If there's no other way, the answer is still yes. I've seen what happens, like you wanted me to, and the plan holds.'

James nodded.

'You're not going to ask me if I'm sure?'

'No. You couldn't see *that*, and tell me it's still the plan, if you weren't sure.'

'No doubts of your own?'

James smiled crookedly. 'Plenty. If we have to do it without planning and we're not near a convenient blood supply, it'll be spectacularly awful. But for about three seconds today, I thought you were dead. You weren't breathing. I couldn't stand it. When I realised your heart was still beating, it was...'

He trailed off, unable to find words to adequately express the relief. 'So. The plan holds.'

'Good. Because James Sharpe, I aim to keep you. Forever, if possible.'

James shook his head, but he was smiling. 'You're stealing my lines again.'

'It's still not mutually exclusive.'

'I guess it's not, at that.'

While Dare Minor and his vampire paramour tended to each other's post-fox-hunt needs, Anthea Webb, after a quick stop to freshen up and change into clean clothes, directed her attention to numerous other mop-up tasks.

She arranged for a thermos of warm blood and a simple change of clothes to be sent to their room, and sent blood to Dare Major's private chamber, where he stayed on those frequent nights he worked late and already had spare suits in the wardrobe.

While Sergeant Tavisa Datta tidied up, Anthea also prepared reports regarding the apprehension of a suspect in the recent spate of murders; a crime with national security implications. Further documents referred to the related kidnapping of Helene Dupre and the sergeant's subsequent disappearance on that urgent family matter. Support activities included departmental clearance, a phone number on Michael's desk so that he could notify Datta's superiors that she had been briefly seconded on a classified matter of national security, and advice to Datta that her arse was effectively covered with a Teflon shield.

It was harder to know what to do for the people Frazer and West had murdered; for their grieving families and friends who had no rational explanation for their loss. The conspirators were both dead, which was justice of a sort, but the fact remained that their deaths had been cavalier. A ploy to manipulate their real targets, the Dare brothers.

Anthea would be making recommendations, but none of it would be adequate. None of it would make up for the dead being treated as nothing but pawns without meaning or value of their own.

Datta was greeted with the arse-covering information when she emerged showered and refreshed. She also received from Mr Dare, via Miss Webb, an offer of a role within the Bureau – most especially since there were, as the result of Niall Frazer, several vacancies.

Tavisa reacted as though she'd been offered a shot of acid to the eye.

Anthea, unoffended, gave Tavisa her card. 'It's a whackadoodle life, as Jay Ren so colourfully puts it, but it's another way to serve, Sergeant Datta. We know very little about interpretation of precognitive dreams, but the little we know is more than everyone else's nothing at all. We may be able to help each other. Keep us in mind. There's no rush.'

Tavisa took the card.

That night, Tavisa dreamed.

She dreamed of going to the theatre in her pyjamas, and being annoyed because she didn't like the theatre. Suddenly she was selling ice cream at interval, a job she'd had during the holidays as a kid and liked because she got free ice cream out of it, except in the dream, the ice cream was liquorice and bacon flavoured, which was disgusting, but she liked it anyway, because *ice cream*, and then the foyer turned into a beach and she swam and could breathe under the water and a lobster told her in sign language about the ice cream kiosk on the moon and she flew up high, with the lobster. It was all pretty much the kind of dream she always had after too much cheese.

But at the very end of her sleep cycle, Tavisa dreamed she held a bright and flaming sword, which made her frightened and proud all at once.

Then she simply slept, without dreams, and it was the most peaceful, refreshing sleep she'd had in her entire life.

Much later that night, after all the sudden guests had departed for their homes, Anthea made a few necessary adjustments to both Mr Dare's security and her own arsenal. She'd promised him she would stop him if he ever went rogue, so it was best he didn't know all of her secrets.

She was good at keeping secrets. She didn't expect to ever *need* them, but she lived by her professionalism, by her promises to Mr Dare, and she didn't aim to get sloppy now.

Even with the bunch of white carnations and blue violets that had appeared on her desk – the first time a bouquet of any sort had ever appeared there. This bouquet had a stalk of garlic stuck in the middle of the symbols of loyalty and trust.

He had a sense of humour, her Michael.

Chapter Twenty-Seven

A BLACK GOVERNMENT SEDAN TOOK JAMES AND GABRIEL BACK TO IVY Gardens.

Almost everything they'd worn yesterday was ruined beyond saving, including James's favourite jacket. Only Gabriel's leather jacket had been saved, and he wore it over his shoulders. Otherwise, they were both dressed in the Bureau's dark tracksuits and brand new running shoes that reminded James of the army and Gabriel of the school he'd so despised as a child. James agreed that burning was a deserved fate for the awful things, but that Switchblade Roy or his mates might make better use of them.

James leant up against the car door and Gabriel, in the spirit of never respecting the tedious pomposity of the Establishment, had sprawled out on the broad seat, his head in James's lap. James rested a hand on Gabriel's chest, inside his track top, so he could feel the steady rhythm of Gabriel's beating heart against his fingertips.

Gabriel was talking to Helene on speakerphone.

'But you're all right?'

'I'm fine, darling. My head aches and I don't remember much, but the doctor gave me the all clear and I'm home with a glass of Cointreau on the rocks, a tub of espresso gelato and a BBC costume drama full of beautiful gowns and pretty men.'

For all her chirpiness, they could hear how shaken she was.

'They got the man who was behind all of this,' Gabriel told her, his concern evident. 'You don't have to worry about him anymore.'

'Don't I?'

'No. I promise. He's gone. He can't hurt anyone anymore.'

The silence from Helene's end went on too long. Finally, she said, 'Is this something to do with where Michael works?'

'Michael works for parliament.' He wasn't even convincing to himself.

'He does something else as well,' said Helene warily. 'I don't know what it is, but he's worked for whatever that department is for a long time. Since before he was your age.'

Gabriel looked troubled. James rubbed his thumb over his cheek.

'His job... has something to do with it, yes.'

'And you say it's over?'

'Yes.'

'And... and nobody else will be coming for you. Or for me. Or anyone else.'

'Nobody,' said Gabriel gently.

Helene's sigh was shaky but also full of relief. 'Good, *coco*. I'll talk to you tomorrow, hmm?'

'James and I will come around. I'll bring chocolate.'

'Yes,' she agreed. 'But not early. Come late in the day. I'm sure you and James will want a long lie-in.'

'Cheeky.'

'But observant,' she said, giggling earthily.

Gabriel rung off and shoved his phone in his pocket. 'I know I said we'd spend tomorrow in bed...'

'We'll see Helene,' said James.

'But not early.' Gabriel waggled his eyebrows lasciviously, making James laugh.

Finally back home, James set about his usual routine of making a soothing cup of tea. He'd placed the teabags in the cups when

Gabriel came up behind him and wrapped his arms around James's waist.

'I don't want a cup of tea,' he said. He kissed the back of James's neck. Still kissing, he smoothed his hands across James's stomach, then up over his chest.

James leaned back into Gabriel's warmth. Gabriel rolled his hips forward, his crotch pressing warmly against James's behind.

James abandoned the tea making and turned in Gabriel's arms to kiss him. 'I'll make you come so hard,' he murmured against Gabriel's mouth.

'You too,' Gabriel murmured back.

James pulled away, puzzled.

Gabriel's eyes crinkled in affectionate amusement. 'You have orgasms, Jamie. I've seen your O face when you have them.'

'But my body doesn't…' But even as he spoke, the penny dropped, 'Oh. Oh, of course.'

'You don't ejaculate,' Gabriel said matter-of-factly, sliding his hands down to James's arse. 'But you're definitely coming.'

James thought about those sensations that began in his brain and fizzed along all his nerve endings. 'I really am, aren't I? God.'

'Hmm.' Gabriel busied himself with kissing the corner of James's eyes, his cheek, down along his jaw, then added, 'Usually it's after you've drunk from me. It's gorgeous. You always look so surprised.'

'It *was* surprising. I didn't have them when I tried it on my own. I didn't think I could anymore.'

Gabriel finally left off trying to seduce his boyfriend. 'What did you think was happening?'

'That I was imagining it. That my memory was tricking me into feeling what I wanted to feel.'

'I read once that orgasms and ejaculation aren't necessarily the same thing.'

'No,' agreed James. 'Orgasms aren't solely a genital function.

They happen in the brain as well. After I've drunk from you, you say? Makes sense. Lifeblood. Symbolic, I suppose.'

Gabriel kissed him again, then nuzzled at James's neck. 'Blood, sure. And at least once after you gave me a terrific blow job. Essence of life and all that.'

James was mortified. 'God, really?' He thought back over the last few weeks. 'Jesus. Really. I remember that.'

'Seriously, Jamie. You knew you were having orgasms but you didn't *think* you were having orgasms?'

'In my defence, they're not like the ones I used to have. God. And me a doctor. What a plonker.'

'Yep. Especially since you keep *talking* about it instead of getting on with having another one.'

James laughed and bared his throat for Gabriel to kiss and lick, to suck on. It wouldn't leave a bruise, and James was sorry about that, but it felt good.

Gabriel bit his earlobe too, and cupped James's crotch in his palm. 'Stop talking,' he said in a low voice, 'Come to bed with me. We can *experiment* with what makes you feel good. But first, and I really, really mean this, Jamie, I want you to fuck me. I want your gorgeous cock in me, and for us to go at it until I'm passed out from coming so hard, and then I want you to keep going until you have your braingasm and then after we've had a kip I want to do it all again. Maybe with me fucking you. We'll see how we feel when I have my strength back. How about it?'

'Are you sure, love?'

'Yes, I'm sure. You'll make it good. I love your cock. I want it in me. I want to feel you fuck me with your perfect, perfectly sized dick.' He smeared kisses along James's jaw. 'I want you.'

'What an excellent idea.' James scooped his hands under Gabriel's backside and lifted him. Gabriel instantly wrapped his long legs around James's waist and clung to his shoulders, tilting his head down to kiss James's upturned face.

James walked them to Gabriel's room, and Gabriel was so turned on by James's show of easy strength that he was already flexing his hips, rutting against James's stomach.

James walked-and-kissed Gabriel until he reached the bed, and then lowered him slowly to the mattress. Gabriel, grinning, eyes dark with desire and mouth red and plump from impassioned kisses, refused to unhook his legs from James's waist. He spread his arms wide on the bed, gripping the blankets for any leverage he could get, and rutted his arse against James's covered crotch some more.

James placed a hand under Gabriel's back to support him. 'Go on then,' he urged, 'show me how much you want it.'

Gabriel rolled his hips luxuriantly, pressing the firmness of his backside against the bulge James was presenting in his clothes. James palmed Gabriel's erection through his track pants. Gabriel moaned, shuddered, and tried to both grind down against James's cock and up against his hand.

'Keep going,' James urged him and while Gabriel breathlessly obeyed, James removed his hand from Gabriel's crotch to tug down the track pants. Gabriel's flushed cock stood out from his body. James wrapped his hand around it and pulled along the shaft, slowly and firmly, dragging sensitive skin up and making Gabriel even harder.

James rubbed his thumb over the crown of Gabriel's cock, gathering moisture from the beading slit.

'Look at me,' he said.

Gabriel looked. James licked the moisture from his thumb. Gabriel moaned and ground down, moving his hips in a little circle against James's erection.

'You're gorgeous,' James breathed.

'I need fucking.'

'So you do.' James firmly unwrapped Gabriel's legs from his waist and pushed Gabriel's feet to rest on the mattress. 'Wait.'

Gabriel looked at James through the space between his bent knees and licked his lower lip before biting it.

James gave Gabriel's cock another gentle pull – Gabriel moaned and his hips jerked up – before stripping. He placed his hands against Gabriel's hips, above the waistband of his partly pulled-down track pants.

'Legs up.'

Gabriel, grinning wantonly, raised both legs straight into the air.

'That's mae lovely boy,' said James, the fronts of his thighs against the back of Gabriel's legs. 'That's beautiful.'

He tucked his fingers into the waistband of the track bottoms and in a single movement, lifted Gabriel's backside off the bed and slid the garment over Gabriel's bare rump, past his thighs and knees and calves, over his feet and off. He flung them aside and caught hold of Gabriel's ankles before he could place them back on the bed, holding them up and wide. He nudged his crotch against Gabriel's exposed backside. His hard cock prodded right between Gabriel's arsecheeks and dragged against the hot, sensitive skin.

Gabriel bent his knees, trying to spread them, which brought his whole body closer to James. 'Fuck, yes, Jamie. Fuck me.'

Grinning, James slid his hands down Gabriel's legs again, hands cupping calves and thighs to encourage Gabriel to keep them in the air. Then he dropped to his knees and nosed into the crease to lick at Gabriel's entrance. Gabriel keened.

James pushed his mouth right into the fold and let saliva pool from his tongue onto Gabriel's skin. He pushed his tongue rhythmically into the centre of the wrinkled indentation. Gabriel spread his raised legs wider and when the strain of it got too much, he dropped his feet to James's shoulders.

'Christ. You not having to come up to breathe for ages,' he paused to make a sweet sound of pleasure, 'gives you an unfair advantage.'

For a reply, James nuzzled into the intimate warmth and wriggled his tongue right in the centre of the pucker, nearly reducing Gabriel to whimpering tears, which turned into an almost broken-hearted groan when James withdrew to kiss each side of his inner thighs instead.

'Lube.'

Gabriel scrabbled with one hand for the tube on the side table. He flung it haphazardly in James's direction. James caught it neatly and smothered his fingers in gel.

'This'll be cold,' he warned, then rubbed his slick fingers in slow circles against Gabriel's entrance. He repeated the action two or three times, each time pushing a finger carefully and more deeply into Gabriel's body. Gabriel was whimpering again, and again gave that small cry as James took his hands away.

'Soon, love.' He smoothed his hands between Gabriel's body and the mattress, one hand between the artist's shoulder blades, the other under his rump. He lifted and moved Gabriel's whole body up the mattress. He grinned at the way it made Gabriel's cock twitch and leak.

'You like that.'

'Brand new strength kink,' gasped Gabriel, laughing and panting. 'Just for you.'

James kneeled between Gabriel's spread legs. 'Well then,' he said, 'I think you might like this.'

He smeared more generous amounts of lube over his fingers, over Gabriel's arse and carefully inside. Gabriel continued with the undignified noises and tried to thrust himself onto James's fingers. His cock was slick with the pre-come beading and slipping from his slit. From time to time, James wrapped a free hand around his shaft and gave him a couple of gentle, maddening pulls. Gabriel moved his hips, chasing sensation in each direction.

'Patience, you lovely thing,' James said, and kept right on with the slow slide of his fingers, adding lube as he went, until he was satisfied that Gabriel was ready. He bent his head to lick Gabriel's sticky-wet crown and grinned at the noise Gabriel made.

'I love the taste of you,' said James, 'The smell of you. You're so warm, mae braw lad. My love. My heart. *Mo ghràdh; mo chridhe*. That's almost all the true Scottish I know. I'll learn more, if you want, to woo you by. *M'eudail*. My darling. You're beautiful.'

'So are you. I'll paint you every day, so you can see how beautiful you are to me.' He wriggled. 'Fuck me.'

James wrapped one arm behind Gabriel's back and the other behind his hips, then lifted Gabriel up and into his lap. Gabriel moaned with giddy arousal at the show of strength before seizing James's mouth with his, kissing deep, his body quivering. He mouthed a line from lips to cheek to temple, then down to bite at James's ear. 'Love you, love you, love you.'

'And I love you, aye, I do. Keep your legs wide for me.' Gabriel eagerly obeyed as James's sure hands adjusted Gabriel's angle in his lap. James rose to his knees and bumped the head of his cock against Gabriel's entrance. 'Hold onto my shoulders.'

Gabriel gripped James's shoulders while James ran his hands over Gabriel's ribs and around his back, down to his hips, holding firmly.

'You ready, angel?'

'Christ, Jamie, *yes*.'

James pushed up against Gabriel's entrance, then pulled Gabriel slowly down to meet him, using his strength to bring their bodies together.

As James breeched him, Gabriel curled his hips to meet the welcome intrusion. He moved again, trying to take James deeper, but before he could do what he so clearly wanted to do, James grinned at him. 'Hold still. I'm doing all the work for this one.'

Gabriel gripped James's shoulders more tightly. James settled Gabriel's impaled weight in his lap, dipped his hands slightly under Gabriel's buttocks for stability then began to lift him. Then he tugged Gabriel back down firmly. He kept his own hips still, too. Lift; pull. Lift; pull. Faster and faster, strong and untiring.

'There, my lovely, there. Is that good? You like that?'

Gabriel's "yes" was huffed out breathlessly and he spread his legs yet wider, feet splayed. He arched so his cock rubbed against James's stomach, he curled his arms closer around his shoulders and pressed his mouth to James's temple. James altered the angle of Gabriel's' body to increase the friction and Gabriel's pleasure.

'Look at you,' murmured James. 'Christ, look at you. Beautiful. I like this, Gabriel. I… god… love this. Love you. Being inside you. So much. So warm. Is it… all right? Are you…?'

Gabriel tilted his pelvis and tried to bear down more firmly. 'Fuck, yes, Jamie. Christ. I can feel you. Inside. All the way. Feels good, so good.'

He tried to change the angle again, so James rose higher on his knees and pulled Gabriel's body closer, so that the head and shaft of Gabriel's cock were sliding in longer strokes against James's stomach, while he thrust his own prick into the irresistible heat of Gabriel's willing body.

Gabriel's toes began to curl and stretch, his fingers too, and his feet to flex, his hips to roll spasmodically as he frotted against James's skin in one direction, wriggled down to feel James filling him in the other.

'Oh, oh, oh Jamie. Ja-Ja-aaaamie. I want I want I want…' He arched his back, presenting his chest, his nipples peaked. James licked one then the other. Sucked them in turn. Gabriel keened, wriggling to encourage James to suck harder on each circle of pebbled skin for longer. James scraped his front teeth ever so slightly over the nubs, his fangs pressing against the pecs but not breaking skin. Gabriel's keening got louder and even less coherent.

'Come, *m'eudail*.' James jerked his own hips, pumping up into

Gabriel at the same time as tugging him down onto his cock, licking at Gabriel's nipples, feeling Gabriel's prick leaking warmly all over their stomachs. 'You lovely thing, my angel boy. Come for me.'

Gabriel threw his head back, exposing the long line of his throat. James licked and sucked at it but didn't bite as he held Gabriel through his orgasm, continuing to fuck shallowly upwards, and to hold Gabriel close as he pushed his hips and cock against James's belly, smearing them both with come.

'Don't stop,' Gabriel gasped, clinging to James's shoulders. 'Keep going, Jamie. Keep doing that. Fuck me. Fuck me till you come. Inside me. Yes. That's it.'

James wrapped one arm right across Gabriel's lower back, the other across his shoulder blades, holding him against his chest as his hips moved in tireless pleasure, the heat of it infusing his cool body with joy that still surprised him with its humanness.

He nuzzled right into the hollow under Gabriel's jaw. He could hear/feel the pounding rhythm of Gabriel's heart and the blood through his veins; the warm scent of him – sweat and sex; shampoo and soap; a hint of tea and of home, god, yes, home and humanity and this was his now, this life he thought had been taken from him. All those hungers, for home, for love, for purpose, for touch, for someone he could love and who loved him, and *wanted* to, all here in Gabriel.

He felt the pressure built up in his brain. The little bundle of cells that signalled a pinnacle of pleasure, soon to starburst along the trail of nerves to every extremity. Gabriel was panting filthy encouragement in his ear, but more enticing still was the hard heat prodding him once more in the belly; Gabriel, hard again so quickly, writhing with lusty delight in his lap; his Gabriel, so much more than unafraid – jubilantly embracing everything about him.

Gabriel sealed his lips over James's, sucking and biting and licking at his mouth, and James arched into the taste of him. The bloom of energy spiralled outward from his brain, down his spine, through every limb.

James, clinging to Gabriel, slowly subsided to awareness. Gabriel was nip-sucking rough kisses against his shoulders and wriggling in his lap, seeking friction. His fresh erection bumped against James's abdomen.

James captured Gabriel's mouth with his again, and kissed him breathless. Then he laid Gabriel back on the bed, his soft cock slipping free.

'Look at you,' Gabriel murmured appreciatively.

James wriggled down between Gabriel's thighs and slid his open mouth over Gabriel's stiff prick, glistening with the residue of his recent orgasm. Gabriel gasped as James's fangs pressed briefly to the over-sensitive flesh. James willed his fangs to retract, surprised to realise they had been unsheathed all this time. He swirled his tongue all around Gabriel's shaft, mending any minor injury, then pushed down further, until he could feel the head of Gabriel's cock brushing the back of his throat.

He swallowed, flexing his throat around the tip of Gabriel's prick. Then he sucked, long and hard and deep, until Gabriel was bucking up into his mouth, swearing and sobbing and crying out his name; until he came again, three hot spurts against the back of his throat, which he swallowed.

Slowly, James pulled off, soft-sucking at Gabriel's spent cock while Gabriel shuddered and finally laughed as he tried to wriggle away from the hypersensitivity of it.

James stopped teasing and instead laid his head on Gabriel's stomach. He kissed the warm skin under his lips, then nuzzled into the faint arrow of dark hair.

He started to laugh.

'What?' Gabriel asked in sated good humour.

'Essence of life,' said James, shaking his head, 'I don't know if it's brilliant or the most ridiculous thing I've ever heard.'

'Brilliant,' declared Gabriel. 'Especially if it means there'll be a lot more spectacular blow jobs in our future.'

'Oh, you can depend on it, aye.' James planted a final, smacking kiss on the base of Gabriel's shaft, then crawled up the bed to lay his head on Gabriel's chest, to listen to his heartbeat.

'You're not sore?' he asked.

'Nope,' said Gabriel, 'I mean, a bit, but in a good way. I like how it feels.'

James licked his finger wet and slipped it between Gabriel's legs. Briefly, he rubbed his spit-slick finger against Gabriel's entrance. 'That should help.'

Gabriel snorted, then started to giggle. '*That* part might be ridiculous.' Then he hugged James ferociously tight and nuzzled his hair. 'You're brilliant. Seriously. How did hundreds of years of folklore get it all so bloody wrong?'

'Wrong?' James kissed Gabriel's chest and listened to how it made Gabriel's heart beat faster.

'Vampires aren't parasites,' said Gabriel. 'They're symbiotes.'

James was glad that he couldn't cry anymore, because he would have made a complete ninny of himself. He did kiss Gabriel's chest, though, again and again and again, until Gabriel took James's face in this hands and guided him up for a long, long kiss that only ended because one of them did, in fact, have to breathe.

'Gabriel,' said James, wanting to communicate the absolute truth of his love through voice alone.

'I love you,' said Gabriel, eyes glistening, having no impediments to shedding overwhelmed tears.

'Of course you do,' replied James with a smile so full of happiness it could have produced light. 'I'm lovely.'

Gabriel went right back to kissing him, settling at last against James's chest. When James brought up his arm to lazily caress Gabriel's hand over his slow but steady heart, Gabriel in turn traced the outlines of the caduceus tattoo with loving fingertips.

'You call me angel,' said Gabriel. 'But that's not me. That's you. My guardian angel.'

'Nae, love. It's definitely you.'

'You only say that because of my name.'

'No.' James dropped a kiss to the top of his head. 'I say it because you saved me.'

Gabriel bumped his nose against James's chest. 'So it's mutual. But you've got the wings.' He traced over the caduceus wings again, then the staff and snakes and the poppies, so bright against James's skin. 'You can be my Regency hero, though, if you like.'

'Or heroine. I'd like a bonnet.'

Gabriel snorted with sudden laughter, and then they were both a mess of merry cackling, ending when Gabriel nipped at James's skin and James blew a raspberry on Gabriel's bum.

James didn't slip into dormancy. He stayed perfectly awake and very still, with Gabriel snuggled up in his arms. He listened to Gabriel's soft, even breathing and to the steady bump of his heartbeat. When James smoothed his hand from the nape of Gabriel's neck, down his spine to the rise of his backside, he listened to Gabriel sigh in contentment and settle again in his arms.

Eventually, he also heard the odd, uneven tap-rattle of someone throwing stones at Gabriel's window. Slowly, trying not to wake his sweetheart, James extricated himself and padded over to look into the garden.

Hannah waved up at him. Grinning, he waved back, and then realised he was naked and it was entirely possible Hannah was getting an eyeful. It was dark inside; so maybe not. The streetlight wouldn't–

'Are you giving the neighbours a free show, Jamie? Because I think I might have discovered a jealous streak I didn't know I had.'

James turned, aware he was also showing off his arse to the neighbourhood, and reached for his pants. 'Hannah's here.'

Gabriel grinned and scrambled out of bed, searching for his own clothes.

Ten minutes later they were both outside, dressed for warmth. Gabriel had brought a beer out with him. James had slapped together a few cheese sandwiches. He offered to make tea, but Hannah, with a mouthful of sandwich, shook her head, then took a swig of beer.

''M all right,' Hannah told them. 'Switchblade got word through to my girl it was okay to come back. Bout time too. Bloody cold in Bournemouth.'

'You have somewhere to stay tonight?' Gabriel asked.

'All set, Gabe, don't you worry.'

'Come see me at the clinic on Wednesday if you need anything,' said James. 'Or here. You're welcome any time.'

Hannah jammed the other half of the cheese sandwich in her mouth. She washed it down with another swig of beer and said, 'I'll 'ave that tea now and another twenny pounds, yar?'

Gabriel went upstairs to get both tea and cash. James suffered the intense scrutiny to which Hannah subjected him in equable silence.

'You making our Gabriel happy?' she asked at last.

'I aim to,' he said.

'Good.' She nodded. 'He makes you happy.'

'He does.'

'Nice he got a feller with a good body,' she added sagely.

James thought it was good he didn't blush any more either.

Hannah grinned impishly at his mortification and winked bawdily. 'Nice arse.'

'Ah, thank you?'

Gabriel returned with a thermos of tea and biscuits, grinning. He leaned over to Hannah as he poured tea for her. 'He does have a nice arse,' he said. The two of them giggled together as he handed over the instalment of her sitter's fee.

James considered letting his embarrassment become annoyance

for about half a second, but Gabriel's happy, proprietorial smile in his direction elicited an answering, though sheepish, delight.

Gabriel fished two more plastic mugs from his pockets and they drank tea together while Hannah finished her sandwiches. When she was done, she said, 'Too-rah,' and was away.

Gabriel slung his arms around James's waist and kissed him. 'Didn't mean to embarrass you. But you do have a very nice arse.'

James squeezed a handful of Gabriel's own bum. 'We make a nice matching set.'

Gabriel turned in his arms and looked towards the roof. 'I'm not tired yet. How do you feel about taking us up for the view?'

'Put this on, then.' He wrapped his dressing gown around Gabriel for added warmth; and then Gabriel wrapped himself around James and held on tight while James climbed up to the tiled roof.

He found a stable place to sit and kept a firm hold around Gabriel's torso as they gazed over the suburb and up at the night sky. It was mostly cloud, but the brighter stars were visible in the gaps. The gibbous moon hung low.

'I'd like you meet a friend of mine,' said James suddenly. "Sunil Juhekar. I served with him.'

'I'd like that.'

James kissed the back of Gabriel's neck. Nearby, a burst of birdsong rose into the night.

Gabriel listened to the sweet, high trilling, full of complexity and confidence. 'That's a robin,' he said. 'They sing at night sometimes.'

James held Gabriel more firmly his arms. 'Oh, aye, I can see it now. See, above the streetlight? There it goes.'

'What else do you see?'

James described to Gabriel the things he could detect with his uncanny senses. The fragrance of nearby night-blooming evening primrose and more distant honeysuckle. A couple dancing on a balcony to the faintest music, swaying and smiling together. A cat sitting on a rubbish bin, washing its ears with dainty swipes. Several streets away, an urban fox crossed a road – just a fox, nothing sinister about it.

Gabriel rested his head on James's chest, smiling at the world James was painting for him. His fingers in their turn painted whorls and dancing patterns on James's thighs, a rehearsal for the new canvases he would create tomorrow, full of the night: its danger and beauty, and the promise it held.